Timeless Women
are never forgotten

Ellen Sheedy
'03

Land in the Sky

Coming Soon by Ellen Sheedy

River of Fortunes

Winds of Change

Wild Ducks

Land in the Sky

ELLEN SHEEDY

HERSTORY PUBLISHING INCORPORATED

Herstory Publishing Incorporated

LAND IN THE SKY , Copyright © 2003 by Ellen Sheedy. All rights reserved.
Printed in the United States of America. No part of this book may be used or
reproduced in any manner whatsoever without written permission except in the case
of brief quotations embodied in critical articles and reviews. For information address
Herstory Publishing Inc., PO Box 506, Hopewell Junction, NY 12533.

Herstory Publishing Inc. books may be purchased for educational, business or sales
promotional use. For complete information on Ellen Sheedy's books, please visit her
website at www.ellensheedy.com.

FIRST EDITION

Printed on acid-free paper

Library of Congress Cataloging-in-Publication Data
Sheedy, Ellen
Land in the sky / Ellen Sheedy – 1st ed.
ISBN 0-9741606-0-1
LCCN 2003107377

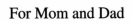

For Mom and Dad

Land in the Sky

One

Spring 1674
Manhattan, English Province of New York

Death never comes at a convenient time. Catharyna van Broeck looked at her father Cornelius in denial, unable to accept that the vital man who had led every day and adventure with purpose, was now gone.

Like a fallen leaf, she crumpled to the floor at the side of the bed, blindly reaching out for comfort from his cold hand. A familiar, painful emptiness began to rise, but it was promptly squashed under years of training to survive in their homeland.

Cornelius had personally handled her education, which was a brutal and relentless task. There were many lessons, and each hinged on one sacred rule: Failure is forbidden.

On her tenth birthday, he had promised, "You've battled your fears until there are none, Ryna. Now, I will train you to be the best trader on Manhattan. The adventurers and fortune hunters that roam our province will try to devour you, but it shall be your fearlessness which will control them."

He had wanted his two surviving children, Catharyna and son Dirck, to inherit his Patroonship of Broeckwyck, as was Dutch custom. But, Dirck had left them for adventure on the seas, and had not been seen or heard from in five years. Catharyna had been trained to be a world class trader in the seaport town which boasted eighteen different languages. Now, that would be second to the family Patroonship.

The Dutch government had offered large land grants with feudal authority to wealthy investors, patroons, willing to transport, at their own expense, fifty adult settlers to New Netherlands. Settlement was slow for many patroons, but it came quickly for Cornelius who became the most successful and powerful patroon in the province. English rule came in 1664, but did little to touch his tight rein on the most lucrative Indian relationships in the region. The English made treaties with the Iroquois, but decades of successful trading between the Dutch and Iroquois proved a difficult feat for the English to copy. Cornelius made certain of it.

The grip on her father's hand was released in order to focus on an unopened message delivered days ago, the morning of his death. Seconds ticked away to the rising tempo of her heart.

Catharyna announced to her dead father, "We've received news that our war with England has indeed concluded *amicably*. Peace negotiations awarded our mother country full possession of the sugar trade in Surinam in exchange for our surrender of New Netherlands. Broeckwyck resides *once again* in the *English* province of *New York*!"

She began to pace the tight confines of the bedchamber like a caged lioness. "I knew this would happen! We reclaimed the province a year ago, but suspected they'd weasel their greedy noses back in again." Her hands tightened in frustration. "All we've known is war with England, and on your death, our mother country abandons us to peace negotiations with the braggarts!"

The ramification of the news, what it meant for her and the Patroonship of Broeckwyck, soon disintegrated all emotion from her mind that focused now on facts. The small seaport colony was so diverse that the Dutch barely held the majority. Not one of the eight thousand people settled there raised a sword in battle for it ten years ago when five English vessels entered their harbor and claimed it, nor would they today.

The lack of spirit to fight was shared by young, old, woman or man, who learned from the brutality of loss, to live by one binding, unspoken, law - self survival. It wasn't religious freedom that lured them across the treacherous Atlantic Ocean. Instead, their colony was established to make *money*. As long as English rule made money for the hard and fast fortune hunters, adventurers and merchants, there would be no effort to fight them off.

Such greed didn't blind the instinct inside Catharyna, which warned against trusting the English. Greed she understood, but their's knew no bounds. Their antiquated law which forbid married women property rights proved it. Englishmen took possession of everything the wife brought into marriage, leaving her no rights in their future management. This was in direct contrast to Dutch law and custom, which groomed Catharyna to be an independent businesswoman, single or married.

A knock on the thick oak door did nothing to distract Catharyna's concentration, but her eyes shifted when a petite woman with warm brown eyes and delicate facial features entered the room.

Maria van Hoesen drew closer before whispering, "Ryna, my father wishes to speak privately with you."

"I cannot leave my father."

Maria squeezed her cousin's hand. "Please, let him handle matters with Broeckwyck. You needn't be strong now, cry and release your pain."

"Such weakness is a choice I cannot risk," Catharyna whispered, and deliberately avoided the sympathetic gaze of Maria. "I stand alone in protecting all my parents built and perished for."

"Don't give up on your brother, Dirck will return to us!" A lone tear slid down Maria's cheek, the only sign of personal agony over her betrothed's continued absence. "But, he isn't here now. You must share the running of Broeckwyck with a husband. When my own father died, my mother wed your uncle, who has been a valuable partner to our patroonship, and now a dear father to me and my brother. You are healthy and young enough for a choice in suitors."

A dry laugh erupted from Catharyna, who stopped pacing and stared into her father's face for guidance. Her heart tightened at the shell of a great man. Denial, anger, and sadness merged, but her stubbornness snuffed them out. The years by his side would not be forgotten. She turned back to Maria, no longer alone.

"I was raised a Dutchwoman to think, act and speak as I choose, free to conduct my own business. If I marry, English law will take that from me and give everything my father built to my husband. I'll have to hide behind him in order to operate Broeckwyck, or fear his mismanagement of it."

"Ryna, how do you expect to run Broeckwyck alone?" Maria asked in amazement. "I urge you to listen to my father. We both know it serves his interests to have you happy."

Catharyna warned, "I understand what you think I must do, but it is an impossibility."

"Oh, hodge podge!" Merriment filled Maria's voice and face. "All you do is boast that nothing is impossible for you, and then your stubbornness proves it. Make marriage such a challenge and you shall indeed conquer it."

Catharyna saw sincerity in the eyes that pleaded to listen. Her cousin was now the only person alive she trusted. Desperate to connect with someone living, she felt compelled to confide a promise made long ago. In a voice deep with emotion, she whispered, "The evening my mother died I had a nightmare."

"Ryna, you were only five. Your mother's death was..."

Catharyna cut off the comforting words with a hand. "A burgeoning river forced me along into dark, murky water, its force so great it kept me powerless under its strength. It returned each evening until I could bear it no longer."

Their eyes met, Maria's with fear.

"I fled to my father to seek peace from it. He dried my tears and ordered me never to be frightened again, that I must be fearless to survive in our new homeland. Then, he explained my dream."

Maria took hold of her cousin's cold hands in comfort. Both women gazed at Cornelius, seeking the strength that was always assured in his presence.

"He said I must never fear the river, but welcome it, that I must open my mind to its uncertain destination and leap into the darkness with excitement, eager to know where it will take me. I was ordered back to bed to dream of the river that had once haunted me, and swear I would never divert from it again."

Their eyes locked and Catharyna swore, "While there is breath within me, I will follow it."

"I don't understand?" Maria whispered in awe of the determination found in her cousin's eyes.

"I must have the courage to follow my own unchartered life. You offer marriage as my only choice, yet it will surely dam the path I have come to love, and drown me."

Maria tightened with frustration over her uncle's arrogance in raising a child to believe they were invincible. Life is unpredictable, but in an uncivilized land, it is suicidal to believe anyone could do it alone.

The task before her was great, so Maria straightened in preparation to battle Catharyna's stubbornness. "Very well then, let's consider the facts about you." Her eyes narrowed and hands were placed on hips when Maria began to inspect Catharyna, like a horse to be purchased. "You possess several positive physical traits."

Catharyna beamed proudly, and rose straight and tall.

"You are uncommonly tall for a woman, taller than most of the men at Broeckwyck. This is good, it demands their attention. Your voice is strong and firm. No trace of weakness or hesitation is found when you issue an order. There isn't much flesh on your bones. The absence of womanly curves won't entice men. You possess neither grace or meekness, and no frills or laces mark your dresses. But, there is a strength in your features, more handsome than soft, much like your father. The only feminine features you can't disguise are your lips, which

13

are too red, and your long black hair. Nonetheless, keeping it tucked tightly into that detestable hat works well," Maria observed, glaring up into her cousin's cold stare. "You may find a measure of success, but never the satisfaction of working beside a strong husband."

"What's wrong with my hat?" Catharyna questioned, yet quickly countered, "Besides, you know I've no patience to stumble around a man in running Broeckwyck. Truthfully, if our mother country listened to me, we'd never have lost New Netherlands to the English in the first place."

A low groan was heard from Maria in anticipation for the coming tirade. It was an old argument, and she knew, once released, her cousin wouldn't stop until finished.

"How many times did I warn our fathers we were being squeezed on both sides from the English? New England and Virginia surround us and their settlers outnumber us four to one! Why couldn't they see that Amsterdam merchants, like the Verbrugge's and De Wolff's, had no interest in *our* colony? The West India Company cared about one thing, how to deepen the pockets of their merchants who sat in their townhouses and filled their coffers in *Amsterdam*. We had to move quickly to build a viable colony with money that stayed *here*. A babe could understand the perilous position we were in, yet," her hands rose in the air and bewilderment traced her next words, "our fathers chuckled, arrogantly believing the English were no threat to us!"

Catharyna's voice lowered to mimic her father's deep baritone voice, "Ryna, we rule the seas and economy. The English are mere nuisances, gnats to be squashed by our invincible fleet."

Maria countered, "And he was right. There was no battle, simply an amicable treaty exchanging our province for their sugar trade. Our mother country prized that more than us. We all accept that, Ryna, you must too."

Catharyna looked at her father and asked brokenly, "Ha, but now who suffers for choosing sugar over Her colonists here?" She turned and her eyes pierced Maria. "We

Dutchwomen who lost our property rights! Do not be deceived, for such English greed will soon squeeze all the Dutch settlers out too."

"The English law is no threat to us," Maria reasoned. "Dutch fathers will continue giving their daughters their share of property, and, by marrying within our tight community, it shall stay protected from greedy English fingers."

Amazement spread across Catharyna's face. "The English have no morals, Maria! They won't hesitate to steal our trade, the North River, *Broeckwyck*!"

The two stubborn women faced each other with no trace of weakening in their argument. "I disagree. Their need is greater than our own. They need Dutchmen to make their colony succeed here and to open trade with the Indians."

A loud 'humph' escaped Catharyna's throat.

Maria quickly amended, "Or Dutch*women*!"

Maria's face sparkled with pride. There were several successful Dutchwomen who were traders, even some who traveled ships in the triangle trade - New York, the West Indies and London. However, her cousin's relationship with the Mohicans had made Catharyna one of the most successful Manhattan traders.

Finally, Catharyna relaxed and a smile emerged. This was the Maria she knew. One step closed the distance between them with a hug. "Your talk of marriage made me believe I had lost you, too. I see now your father sent you to weaken my resolve, but it hasn't changed my mind nor love for you."

All fight was gone from Maria, who now decided to beg. "Please speak with my father, Ryna! I promise, all will go well."

Catharyna finally relented and was led into the large kitchen crowded with Broeckwyck's tenant farmers, who were waiting to pay their final respect to Cornelius. Wives and daughters held platters of food. Men held animal skins filled with wine. All their gifts were placed on the large table. The smell of samp, an Indian treat of corn porridge, drifted across Catharyna's nostrils, and a smile lifted her stiff cheeks. It had been her father's favorite treat.

She accepted each person's embrace as they silently entered the darkened room to bid good-bye to Cornelius before the burial that afternoon. When Uncle Peter approached, Catharyna kissed him in welcome.

"Let us speak outside, Ryna."

Maria watched the two people she loved walk out of view, and prayed the outcome would be just.

They walked some distance and stopped at Turtle Bay where a wind mill was perched atop a cliff overlooking the East River. Catharyna surveyed the view that always brought intense pride. Broeckwyck's manor sat nestled in a valley, perfectly set among the rolling fields behind it and the river before it. The manor was built in the style of northern European elegance distinguished by parapet gables rising about its steeply pitched roof. The exterior had decorative iron wall anchors that secured heavy interior framing to the brick in which the bond formed an attractive pattern.

Its tenant farmers, grist mills and vast fields of wheat were north of Hell's Gate with a ferry service they operated. Catharyna stayed in Manhattan to manage the trade, and Cornelius had an overseer on site at the mills and ferry.

Catharyna's eyes were sad when she confided, "Each morning I would meet my father here to discuss the day's activities."

Peter did not possess his brother's height or charisma, but he was an equally shrewd businessman. He handled the family's business relationships in Amsterdam, traveling for long lengths of time, which permitted little time or opportunity to know Catharyna's life and activities in Manhattan. "I recall the day your father stood here with Governor Stuyvesant and set the terms to pay for all the land his eyes could see north of Turtle Bay." His eyes sparkled when he added, "No one could believe his audacity, yet Stuyvesant was eager for a strong patroon like your father to bring new settlers in."

He took a deep breath while surveying the beauty of rolling fields, sandy beaches and view of the harbor. "No one disputed the choice in location." Peter's hand reached out to turn Catharyna to face him. "Times are uncertain now that we are back under English rule. Even though we have several months to prepare before the formal surrender, we must take steps to protect it now."

Catharyna appeared ignorant. It was the first rule Cornelius had taught her. "What worries you?"

Peter grinned at the common ploy largely due to losing out to it too many times by his older brother. The neat penmanship of Catharyna was recalled in the trade ledgers he reviewed that morning. "Your father trained you to manage his Ten Broeck trade business, not patroon for Broeckwyck." When she began to protest, a hand was raised to silence her. "No one in the family challenges your abilities to manage Broeckwyck, but you stand alone now in protecting it from the unsavory fortune hunters who roam our province. You are my brother's blood, which means you are determined to protect Broeckwyck at any cost."

"Yes," Catharyna swore.

"Yes," he repeated, "and we shall protect it!" An arm wrapped around her shoulder. "I have arranged an excellent marriage for you with Johannes Bleecker. His patroonship of 80,000 acres is fertile. Johannes is a good man. He thinks as your father. You will operate Broeckwyck and work beside him at Furwyck to bring it the same success. This is an excellent match for Broeckwyck, our family and you."

The reasons were clear. Words spoken realistic, except something inside Catharyna set off warning bells. Desperate for clarity, she turned away and gazed at Broeckwyck's manor, sitting so securely in the distance. She tried to recall her mother's face but the memory had long since faded. It was Cornelius who filled her vision, thoughts and soul. With it came a certainty there was no choice to be considered.

She met her uncle's eyes and responded, "What Bleecker has is a patroonship that begs for tenant farmers to cultivate it. Marriage to me would benefit him greatly, but Broeckwyck?" A soft laugh floated across the valley. "I think not."

Peter could not meet his niece's piercing stare. "I never said marriage would guarantee Broeckwyck, it is one of several steps that must be taken."

She smiled at the frustration in his voice. "Women are no concern to the English. I am simply a pawn to be used or discarded by them. I agree to this."

Peter's eyes sparkled with hope.

"However," she added, "you are my father's brother, which now makes you the most influential Dutch patroon in the province. If the English wish to prosper here, they need to form close ties with you. Knowing that, they would not dare any such attempts at Broeckwyck."

Her ability to go straight to the matter at hand impressed Peter, but not enough to end the argument. "We've no knowledge if your brother is dead or alive. You equipped him with a ship to smuggle your trade out to Amsterdam, yet for years now Dirck has been silent to us. Maria is the only person who believes he still lives."

"And I," she whispered.

"You cannot be certain of Dirck, nor when death will claim even yourself, Ryna. If you die, Broeckwyck would indeed go to me, but your father's blood would be gone forever. Is that your wish?"

Catharyna stood in silence.

Emotion, nor any recognition in his words, was not found in the statue standing before him. Peter knew it was greed that was prompting the marriage to Johannes. He wanted Broeckwyck at the lowlands and Furwyck in the highlands. It was an immensely valuable location for his own patroonship that was near Albany.

Sensing victory, he added, "Gaining Furwyck would protect and benefit our *entire* family."

18

Catharyna stared blankly at her uncle, who had just placed the life line of her father and welfare of over 150 relatives in her decision. She had underestimated him. The thought of Dirck and her death had never occurred, blocked out by youthful arrogance.

"My father's death clouds my mind. I need time to consider this."

"Of course, my dear, your father's death has been a terrible loss for us all. I will await your answer tomorrow morning."

They stared at each other, yet neither gave their true thoughts away. Catharyna agreed with a silent nod, and turned away. She grumbled inwardly with each step back to the manor. One day had been given to make the most important decision of her life. There was only one thought on her mind. Time was truly her enemy.

Peter van Broeck smiled at the departing form of his niece. There was no doubt she would wed Johannes. The mere thought of ending Cornelius' bloodline would never be permitted.

A whistle caught his attention and eyes turned toward its direction to the East River to see William Hawkins, the Albany Indian Commissioner, departing from a sloop with his friend Fairfax following a step behind.

Peter raised an arm in greeting and waited as they approached. Several years ago, he had employed Hawk as secretary for his own patroonship, even though he was one of the hated English, and shunned by the Dutch town of Albany. Hawk had many assets that immediately impressed Peter and the town. He was born in England, educated in the Netherlands, astute on the intricacies of business and trade, and fluent in English, Dutch, Spanish and a few Iroquois dialects. While in Albany, the thrifty Dutch used all of Hawk's talents, yet still kept him an outsider to the tight knit family community, which refused to give their acceptance or friendship to any Englishman. Hawk's ambitions quickly moved him out of Peter's job to gain valuable alliances. His current position made him the most influential Englishman in the province.

Peter looked warily at the odd pair. Hawk had auburn hair that was tied tightly behind the neck and a beard that concealed most of his facial features. Somber gray eyes were the only feature visible. Their affect prompted the easily intimidated souls to take a few steps back from their coldness.

Fairfax was a gracious and handsome man with an open face and mind. Everyone knew each thought was placed there by Hawk.

Peter's smile was measured as the men shook hands, though he only spoke to one of them. "Hawk, what news do you bring for me?" The man towered above Peter's head, which now rose to search for a sign of emotion. His eyes met a bleak stare.

"I come on behalf of Chief Konkapot. He has made a claim to the commission that you never made payment to him for a 10,000 acre parcel that you legally claimed at the mouth of the Roeloff Jansen Kill."

"Nonsense, we settled that over five years ago."

A brow rose in warning. "He claims otherwise and demands payment now, or threatens retaliation on your holdings."

Peter tried to swallow the large lump that suddenly filled a tight throat. He wasn't like his brother Cornelius, who had formed relationships with the powerful Mohawk and Mohican tribes. He couldn't speak their language and their savage faces intimidated him. It was impossible to meet with the Chief. Suddenly, a smile spread; seeing a way out. "You were my secretary at that time, you handled these arrangements for me."

Hawk's eyes grew colder. "You never permitted me to negotiate any deal with the Mohicans *on your behalf*. Your brother handled this with the Chief."

Peter's smile didn't falter when his voice lowered in

privacy, for Hawk alone to hear. "Must I remind you these agreements are seldom in writing."

"Is that your intention?" The tone in Hawk's voice spoke loudly the silent implication of Peter's words. He had no intention of paying for the property. It was a common ploy of white settlers to use duplicity with the Mohicans who dealt fairly with them in trade. They were a peaceful tribe until situations of dishonest land purchases arose that would cause a threat or actual massacre. Now that the English and Dutch traded guns and ammunition for furs with the Indians, retaliation for payment of land threatened a bloody battle.

Peter straightened at the anger now looking down at him from Hawk's eyes. "I *spoke* no intentions."

The two men stared at each other in silence for several minutes, each waiting for the other to speak. Eventually, Peter relented, knowing Hawk would never budge. "I won't pay him twice for the land."

Hawk motioned to Fairfax, and they both began to turn toward the East River.

"What is *your* intention?" Peter demanded at their departing backs.

Hawk paused and turned around. "I am here to inform you that the Chief has given this matter to his son to handle. Minichque will *not* deal with you, but with a relative of yours, here at Broeckwyck, whom he trusts to deal fairly on the matter."

Peter mumbled, "My brother Cornelius died a few days ago."

"It isn't your brother that Minichque spoke of."

Peter grew suspicious of a ploy, knowing Hawk was powerful enough to find a way into Broeckwyck. Rumors of his past before coming to the colony had circulated from being a pirate, a knight of the court, to a bastard son of the Duke of York himself. Regardless if any were true, Peter treaded prudently. "His son Dirck is at sea. We await his return."

"It isn't Dirck."

Peter was relieved. There was no other person left,

except, "Catharyna?" he whispered in disbelief.

Hawk nodded. "They are friends and trade for precious goods. She is known as Ten Broeck to Minichque."

Peter disguised the shock of learning Ten Broeck was his niece's trade name. For years, he had assumed it was one of Cornelius' many ventures that surrounded him like air. It should have occurred to him long ago that his unruly brother would train one of his children to be such a trader.

An adventurer through and through, it was Cornelius who led the family to the wild and uncivilized province. They had been modest merchants, all thriving in the Golden Days of the Netherlands' wealth and good fortune. Yet, somehow, he had tantalized them with stories of grandeur that had fifty relatives take a dangerous, transatlantic crossing to New Netherlands. Cornelius had invested heavily to become a patroon to a large tract of land, and had full control of the government and courts on it. He offered passage and provisions to settlers obliged to work the land for ten years, grind the corn, wheat or rye at his mill. After a certain time, they became tenant farmers who paid him, as their patroon, a small annual rent.

Peter married a wealthy widow in order to obtain a patroonship, whereas Cornelius had built one. Everyone who followed Cornelius had flourished in their new homeland.

Peter's pride struggled with the realization that his niece had received better training than himself. It was only a brief lapse of envy. Years of following his brother had taught Peter that there was no greater instructor, or man, than Cornelius.

Slowly Peter met the impatient stare of Hawk, whose next words were spoken for a babe to understand, "Your niece is your chance to deal peacefully with the Mohicans. There are five outstanding payments owed to them from white settlers and numerous squatters. They will seek retribution for this; your holdings will be their first attack."

Peter began pacing again, his face dark with inner thoughts. The bloody Indian massacres had sent many settlers back to the Netherlands during the Peach War, so great and horrible the deaths. His wife had survived one attack as an eye witness of what the Indians had done to the men, women and children on Hoesenwyck's lands, with little or no regard to their pleas for mercy. The threat was too real to ignore.

"My wife will never permit Ryna to meet them."

Hawk dismissed the words. "Fairfax and I will take her."

Peter looked at the giant man, but found no comfort. His eyes latched on his son Rolfe, who was leaving the wind mill, and an automatic hand rose in greeting. At that moment, an idea took root. Seconds ticked by until it was no longer unthinkable to send his brother's only child into the wilderness with two Englishmen for protection. Fear and greed for his 10,000 acres, prompted the unimaginable. "I agree under the terms my son Rolfe accompanies her on the trip," Peter gushed and added absentmindedly, "and Ryna confirms Minichque is her friend."

The men exchanged a silent glance before Hawk smiled for the first time at Peter. "Agreed. Let's speak with your niece," he ordered, and proceeded to walk briskly to the manor.

Peter ran to catch up with the determined pair, and beat them to the front door. The top half of the Dutch door was open and he barked into the crowded kitchen, "Ryna, a word outside. *Now!*"

Never accustomed to being ordered, Catharyna did not rush. She kissed a baby cousin's forehead and handed the child to her Aunt Anna before answering. "Yes."

His eyes glanced nervously at his wife, Anna. There was no intention to allow her to hear any of the discussion about to transpire. Peter mumbled, "Come, let us speak farther from the manor."

In Peter's haste to leave, Rolfe's entrance into the kitchen, and heated discussion with Anna, was missed.

Peter led the private group back to the wind mill. "Gentlemen, my niece, Miss Catharyna van Broeck, Patrooness of Broeckwyck. Ryna, this is Mr. Hawkins and...," he stumbled trying to recall if Fairfax was his first or last name.

The blonde-haired man quickly took over the introduction. With a gallant flourish, he bowed low before her skirts. "Fairfax."

Catharyna's face softened under Fairfax's handsome features. "Welcome to Broeckwyck, gentlemen."

Peter took a step back in silent signal to Hawk to proceed with the discussion. Hawk bowed a bit too swiftly, but a sincere voice made up for it. "Miss van Broeck, please accept our condolences over the loss of your father. I was honored to have met him once. He was a man of great courage and character."

"Yes, he was," she stated with eyes trained to intimidate.

Hawk's own glance narrowed, but a smile spread under his thick beard that concealed it. "I am the Albany Indian Commissioner. Your uncle has a personal matter open with Chief Konkapot. The Chief asked his son, Minichque, to settle this with you. With your agreement, we will leave at dawn to escort you to the village of Shekomeko."

Her eyes slowly took in Hawk's features. There was a confidence in his presence that charged the air. He was a leader, accustomed to having his way. And, although he was very good at hiding himself from people, his ambition was naked to her knowing eye. Such ambition would not go unchecked. Every instinct told her the man was too dangerous. She would never permit such a powerful Englishman to speak to Minichque without her present.

A quick glance at Fairfax satisfied her initial opinion. He would do whatever Hawk commanded. Therefore, he was manageable to her as well.

Cornelius' death made her pause. This was the normal time for grieving, yet there was no intention to remain idle to mourn a physical end when his spirit directed her to live life. In this, she would not fail him.

Catharyna faced Hawk, the decision was made. "Yes, I agree."

Hawk's eyes narrowed on her exactly as a hawk's which had just caught its prey. Catharyna sensed it was deliberate, so refused to pay any heed to the sudden flutters in her stomach. Instead, she turned expectantly to Uncle Peter, who was grinning broadly. "There is much to do by dawn. What plans have you for the expected gifts?"

Peter began to stutter. "Gifts, argh, of course, some corn or flour is easily attainable."

Catharyna's face tightened over his stingy nature. She began to mentally count her supply of wampum, and any other possible offerings for Minichque. The soft pink and white sea shells, known by everyone as wampum, were more valuable than money to the Indians. Aunt Anna's sudden interruption made her lose count.

Anna's bosom was heaving, and her face was flushed from the walk up the hill, when she interrupted their group. "Good day, gentlemen. Would you please excuse us? I need a moment of privacy with my husband and niece."

The two men smiled warmly at the gracious woman. "Of course, Mrs. van Broeck, our visit is concluded." One man bowed swiftly, the other gallantly, to both women. "Please accept our condolences over your family's loss."

Hawk spoke a parting reminder to Catharyna. "We leave at dawn."

The moment the men were on the deck of the one mast sloop, Anna erupted. "What *lunacy* is this about our niece going to meet with savages?"

Peter began backing up several paces until his back was against the wind mill.

Anna's eyes trapped him. "Don't deny it," she warned. "Rolfe heard every word of your discussion with Hawk and told me."

Everyone knew Anna ruled equally in all business decisions in Peter's household and holdings, especially since two thirds of their property was brought by her in their marriage. Anna's first marriage had been to the wealthy Patroon Jan van Hoesen and it bore two children, son Gerrit, her only daughter Maria, and the Patroonship of Hoesenwyck.

"They aren't savages. Ryna is going to meet with a gentleman named Minichque, who is a good friend of hers." Peter's smile was weak and trembled at the sides.

"A *gentleman* Indian? I've never heard of such nonsense in my life!" Anna's dark eyes pinned Peter to the wind mill with the question, "*Why?*"

Peter turned hopeful eyes to Catharyna, who had no intention of jeopardizing the opportunity. She smiled reassuringly and said, "Aunt Anna, Minichque and I have been friends since the age of ten. I taught him Dutch and he taught me Algonquin and the bow and arrow. The antlers above our doorway are from the first buck I pierced with Minichque's arrows."

Anna's eyes saw her niece's determined face and fears mounted. "My child, we live in an uncivilized world, this you know far too well. It is incomprehensible to allow you to knowingly meet with Indians. I simply cannot permit this."

Catharyna's eyes saw her uncle's guilty gaze, and persisted. "I am no child, Aunt Anna, but older than your eldest son, Gerrit. You know of my trading business as Ten Broeck."

Anna began to weaken. "Yes, but with the Indians, Ryna?"

"There is no other way to be a successful trader. My trade with Minichque has meant survival for his tribe, and he has made me much wealth. Such a relationship ensures my safety in meeting with him."

Anna challenged, "Then why have I heard none of this until now? I cannot believe your father would condone such when your mother..."

"It is what it is," Catharyna answered with a shrug.

Worry was etched deep on Anna's face. She turned to Peter and found acceptance on his face. In defeat, she took Catharyna's hands. "Very well, Ryna," she added weakly, "I do trust you. Never have you failed your father, nor will you me. I shall pray God will speed your journey and return you safely to us, my dear."

Tears were wiped away, and then Anna faced her husband. "And I shall pray God forgives you for knowingly placing Cornelius' *only* child into such danger." With those parting words, Anna returned to the manor.

Catharyna looked at Peter, who appeared even shorter than a few moments ago, and went straight to business. "What am I to settle for you with Minichque?"

Peter's weary eyes watched Anna's departing figure; each step away erased all guilt until his confidence was rising once again to the surface. "His father claims I failed to pay for a parcel of 10,000 acres. He's threatening to attack my holdings. Your father handled this for me," his hands rose in the air, "and I'll not pay twice for the land! You must persuade Minichque to acknowledge my right."

"And if I succeed?"

Peter looked confused. "No blood will be spilt."

Catharyna drew closer, never once letting go of his eyes. "And for me?"

Peter paused by the familiar look on his niece's face, having witnessed it only in Cornelius' presence. The trade ledgers examined that morning rose again before Peter's eyes, all listed under the Ten Broeck trade name. Abundant shipments of furs, grain, wine, brandies, tobacco, horses, lumber, rum, molasses, and Hawk's words of Catharyna's relationship with the Indians, all merged. Never did he imagine Catharyna had achieved such success under her own ability, and yet, now Peter was convinced his niece, not Cornelius, was Ten Broeck, the most successful Manhattan trader.

All misconceptions were cleared away. Peter faced her in the same manner he dealt with Cornelius and his wife. "What do you want?"

There was no hesitation. "My freedom."

Peter's eyes narrowed, considering the request. The reason Cornelius had allowed his only daughter to remain unwed at such an old age, was now answered. She had inherited the same independent spirit that had led Cornelius across the Atlantic Ocean. There was no person who loved freedom more than his brother.

Pride filled his voice. "You know that's too high a price, Ryna."

Catharyna remained focused. Enduring one day with

Johannes Bleecker would tax her sanity. Marriage was out of the question. "If I am successful with Minichque, I want the freedom to choose my own husband."

Peter smiled, knowing a compromise could be achieved. "*If* you are successful, I agree to six months to select your husband. After that, the choice will be mine."

"Five years."

"One."

"Four and a half."

"One and a half."

"Four years."

They faced each other. Peter's voice invited no further negotiation. "You are ready to risk leaving Broeckwyck with no direct descendants of your father?"

Her heart raced, knowing there was no choice but to take the risk, and pray life would oblige it. "My children will come when I select their father, no sooner."

Peter nodded. "Very well, if you wish to risk such, and if you are successful, you will have two years to select your husband. Any longer will make you too old to wed. If you fail, you will marry Bleecher upon your return. And, I'll need written proof by Hawk of your success. I'll not have the Chief do such again to me."

Catharyna was not pleased, but took the offer. "Of course," she replied, and extended a hand to seal their agreement. A second later she was headed back toward the manor with a mind occupied on wampum and other possible gift offerings. What remained clear was that the first battle had been won. Time had been gained.

Two

The howl of wind, sails and groans were heard in the crisp spring air when dawn arrived. Instantly, the water came alive under the one mast sloop that carried the party of four up the Hudson River.

Catharyna sat beside her cousin Rolfe, who fought valiantly to control the nausea building within his frail body. The battle was soon over when he raced to the side of the boat and emptied the contents of a queasy stomach into the river.

Fairfax waved a hand in front of his nose. "Rolfe, be a bloke and hit Hawk's side next time."

Rolfe raised an ashen face to the laughing man for a moment, and quickly turned back when another spasm racked his body.

Catharyna patted his back in an effort to help soothe him. "Fairfax, where are we landing?"

He looked at Hawk and received a negative shake. "Up river," he mumbled.

Catharyna blinked in surprise at the answer given. "A babe would surmise that, I asked *where*." In disbelief she watched Fairfax's eyes swing to Hawk who shook his head no again. A shrug of Fairfax's shoulders was the only answer given this time. Hands tightened with the realization it was wasted energy to ask Hawk's shadow any questions.

Determined to deal with the cold Englishman directly, she approached Hawk with a warm smile. "Perhaps you will answer my question."

"You'll know soon enough."

She warned, "Rolfe can't travel further, we need to anchor now and travel by horse."

A smile spread under the thick beard. "As you wish."

"Thank you."

Another silent exchange occurred between Hawk and Fairfax, and within moments the sloop was heading toward the east shore. Rolfe was escorted by Fairfax from the sloop while Hawk threw his leather satchel ashore. Then Fairfax pushed the nimble sloop back into the water which propelled Catharyna against Hawk whose arms immediately imprisoned her.

Rolfe rose unsteadily from the ground and groaned, "Wait, I say! Don't leave me stranded in the woods!"

Hawk's reply was a laugh that echoed against the rising mountains, that reached high into a deep blue sky.

Catharyna was furious. "Go back and get Rolfe immediately!"

Silence answered. Frantically, she dug nails into Hawk's arms, but still received no response, even when blood trickled from the wounds. With no other recourse, she threatened, "I swear I won't meet Minichque unless Rolfe is beside me."

Hawk released her and their eyes clashed. "Our business is urgent and Rolfe will delay us. We move forward without him."

Catharyna demanded, "What is so urgent about settling a land dispute? Minichque won't attack until he speaks to me." Hawk's eyes remained steady on her but a certainty grew that all was not as it appeared. She persisted, "What demands such urgency, Mr. Hawkins?"

Anger soon shined down on her and he growled, "You must trust me."

Soft laughter now echoed through the narrow passage of the Tappan Zee. "You abandoned my cousin in the wilderness and then ask for my trust?" Within seconds a thin knife was pointed at his throat. Her eyes warned Fairfax away and she whispered, "Do you believe me a fool to trust an *Englishman*? I've no faith in any of you!"

"No, but you will trust me," he swore and cursed when

30

the blade began to cut into his neck.

"Why?" she whispered.

Like a flea, she was picked off his body and captured underneath his hands. Hawk's eyes blazed down at her. "Take the necklace around my neck as proof."

Hesitantly, she reached out and pulled at the leather string to find a tarnished and battered silver piece of jewelry. Her fingers trembled at the sight of her mother's locket. "Where did you get this?"

Hawk's voice for the first time was human with emotion. "You must trust me."

Catharyna stared in bewilderment, not understanding how a trip for a land dispute had any correlation with her mother who had been dead almost twenty years.

She whispered, "You ask too much."

Suddenly, emotions destroyed her focus when her thoughts returned to September of 1655. A Dutch farmer on Manhattan named Van Dyck had shot and killed a Wappinger Indian woman when he caught her "borrowing" a peach from a tree in his garden. This prompted more than 200 Wappinger warriors to canoe down the Hudson River to Manhattan intent to kill Van Dyke, but their arrow only managed to wound him before the Dutch militia fought them off. Fleeing, but still intent for revenge, the warriors crossed the river and began burning Dutch farms at Pavonia, Hoboken, and Staten Island. At least 50 Dutch were killed in the fighting, including Catharyna's mother and two baby brothers, who were visiting relatives on Staten Island.

Their deaths had a tragic effect on Cornelius who had sworn to end the Indian raids that terrorized the colonists. Only, the fighting continued between the tribes until, finally, the powerful Mohawk were called in to end it.

Cornelius had been instrumental in achieving a Iroquois peace treaty with the help of their Dutch Governor Peter Stuyvesant in May of 1664. Catharyna was present and scribed the parties agreement and terms. In September, the British fleet captured Fort Amsterdam and claimed the province for

England. Though, neither Dutch nor English treaty were able to stop the fighting within the Iroquois tribes. The Munsee, a close tribe to the Mohicans, continued to resist ending their warfare.

Catharyna was lost in thought, which provided Hawk the opportunity to take the knife from her hand. The far away look in her eyes disappeared at the sight of her knife sailing into the river.

Hawk ordered, "We are no longer your enemy. You must remember that." And then, he left her to maneuver the sloop with Fairfax.

Catharyna's distrustful eyes followed him, struggling to determine whether it was safe to trust the man. Everything warned her not too, yet how did he come across the locket? And did it really serve any purpose in their meeting with Minichque? Nothing made sense as the distance grew wider between her and Rolfe.

Guilt burned inside as she remained idle in allowing Rolfe to be in the wilderness by himself. And then a gradual acceptance grew with the knowledge that he was fast footed and would get to White Plains by night fall. Left with no other choice, the thought relieved a guilty conscience. This time there was no luxury to distrust the Englishman whether she wanted too or not. He just dangled potential information on her mother's death, which was impossible to ignore.

With that decided, there were no more delays. At Wappingers they docked the sloop and found three horses and a pack mule waiting for them. Hawk's confidence in her agreement to journey with them to make such arrangements in advance, was left unspoken. They mounted their steeds in silence and began the journey to the village of Shekomeko over muddy dirt paths that held the last remnants of winter's snow patches melting away.

Hours passed and the sheer dreariness of being in the company of two Englishmen who possessed no communication skills began to simmer inside Catharyna. Hawk continued to withhold information and made it clear none would be forthcoming any time soon. It was a rare position to be in, one that didn't sit well with her. A crinkle across his forehead would have thrilled her at this point, and the puppet Fairfax was worse. It became all too clear her escorts were less entertaining than a bucket of dirt.

A rustle in the forest caught their attention and soon a herd of deer erupted out of it. No warning was given when Fairfax scooped her from the saddle to be held protectively in front of him. Her horse and the pack mule remained beside Fairfax's horse, obedient to a series of soft whistle commands.

"Quiet," he whispered and exchanged silent signals with Hawk.

Catharyna's eyes scanned their position and exposure in the middle of an open field with the forest, and the unknown that lurked within it, surrounding them. Fairfax shot off in the direction of the woods and, simultaneously, Hawk raced in the opposite direction. Before long she was dumped on the ground in front of fallen trees for protection, and Fairfax landed on top of her.

"Quiet," he repeated as she fought for air.

With all her strength, Catharyna obeyed when she wanted to tear him off of her body. Her impatience spread to the sound of geese flying overhead, returning for the spring season, and the wind that twirled the leaves covering the ground.

At the sound of human voices, she rose stubbornly, pushing Fairfax away. Crouched behind fallen trees, her eyes darted across the field to where Hawk stood, now surrounded by five Mohawks who were shaking fists at him.

She whispered, "What do they want?"

"Quiet."

Her jaw locked tight and not another word was said until the Indians left. At Hawk's signal, they came out of hiding and a whistle brought forward the horses. The men mounted without offering Catharyna a hand, just a nod for her to do the same. With what little patience was left, she obeyed and was soon staring at the broad back of Hawk, who didn't offer a word of explanation.

Catharyna asked, "What did they want?"

"You'll know soon enough."

She mumbled a string of curses and was rewarded when he ordered the horses into a canter. Nothing could stop her horse from following. Everything the man did had the horses, and herself, follow in complete obedience. Her curses grew louder but both men ignored them.

At dusk Hawk chose to make camp for the evening. The men unpacked the mule, set up a tent and had a fire soon blazing. Catharyna walked passed them in need of privacy and headed toward the creek. Out of the air sailed a small copper pail that fell in front of her feet.

"Bring back water."

It was another order. Nerves grew taunt, but she picked up the pail and plunged it defiantly into the cold creek. A loud growl gained her attention, a reminder that they hadn't stopped all day to eat. The food Aunt Anna had packed for the journey brought a warm smile to her face. Never had she been more grateful not to depend on the Englishmen. There was no doubt their food would be something cold, raw and tasteless.

Fairfax shouted, "We can use that water now."

Catharyna bestowed a bright smile at him, but remained beside the creek. Leisurely, she unpinned her hat, brushed out her hair and washed her face and hands.

Hawk ordered, "Now!"

It was one order too many. Frustrated hands grabbed the pail. She approached with angry strides and threw the bucket of water at Hawk. Her eyes challenged him but there was no rise to the bait. Wordlessly, she grabbed the leather satchel that contained her food and stomped into the only tent. Tense moments passed with no retaliation from either man, and, finally, Catharyna felt peace return.

"Come out by the fire, Ten Broeck." It was Hawk's cold and uninviting voice.

"I eat alone on this trip."

It was the only attempt the men made, which was fine with Catharyna, who used the remaining strength to eat a chunk of bread and cheese before falling into a deep sleep.

The next morning she rose with a renewed attitude to be civil to her escorts. After all, the men had honorable intentions. They were doing this to prevent the bloodshed of settlers. Any discomfort that came from traveling with the two callous Englishmen would be endured. In the light of a new day, she knew the desertion of Rolfe was as much her fault as their own. She could have fought harder to make them go back and fetch him. All traces of frustration and rudeness from the day before, melted away. Nothing would deter her from being courteous to the men today.

The tent was departed with a determined smile. She stretched cramped limbs to their full height, and fingers plowed through long wayward curls, trying to place them in order when Hawk approached with a hot cup of tea. There was a noticeable difference in his appearance. Half his beard was gone.

"Morning, Ten Broeck."

"Thank you," she replied and accepted the cup of tea. Her eyes roamed over Hawk's face, that had improved greatly from the day before. There was no softness in the rugged and sharp lines of his face, but it suited the man. While he was still well concealed by a beard, now she could see his lips, which smiled down at her. "You clean up nicely, Mr. Hawkins." A warm smile spread on her own face while sipping the hot tea. Hope grew that this day would end better than the previous one.

Hawk reached out a hand to brush away a long tendril of hair that fell across her face. "No hat today?"

"I left it at the creek," she mumbled and turned to retrieve it when she saw Hawk's horse eating what was left of the hat. Her eyes shifted in disbelief to Hawk, and found his eyes twinkling with silent laughter.

She bolted toward the horse and began a struggle to claim the remnants of the straw hat. With all her body's strength, she clung to the hat, dangling below the stallion's mouth, yet the horse refused to relinquish it. To add to her frustration, a soft whistle sailed passed her ears, causing the horse to drop the hat, and herself, on the marshy ground. The victory in holding the tattered remains of her straw hat disintegrated under her growing anger.

All good intentions vanished as she fought to rise from the muddy ground. Her fingers plowed into her hair, now thrown in wild abandonment, to pull it away from her overheated face. In three quick strides, Catharyna stood face to face with Hawk and slapped the pieces of straw on his one hand. "You owe me a hat."

There was no attempt to hide his laughter which rang loudly throughout the forest. "Any bird's nest would be nicer than that *thing*."

Catharyna stood in amazement at the rude assessment of the hat, which drew more laughter from both men. There would be no more time or energy wasted to be friendly to either man. She brushed past the pair and angrily packed her horse, intent to get out of camp immediately. Not another word would be spoken until they reached Minichque's village.

They arrived the following morning with the sun rising steadily in a violet blue sky. Children rushed to greet them, with their mothers a few paces away. All were eager to see what treats Ten Broeck had brought for them.

Minichque's wife, Susquehanna, moved ahead of the crowd. She greeted Catharyna warmly as they bowed respectfully to each other. "Welcome, Ten Broeck, Minichque and men hunting. We gather in long house to wait their return."

Catharyna walked a pace behind Susquehanna with no care to introduce Hawk and Fairfax. They were deliberately left out of the discussion. "Where is your son?"

"He joined Minichque, eager to show off hunting skills with new knife with ivory handle."

Catharyna laughed freely. "Ha, Minichque gave him the knife he caught his first meal with..." and both women said in unison, "a hickory nut."

The Englishmen exchanged a glance but remained silent. Hours later Minichque and the hunting party returned with horses loaded with deer and turkeys. Everyone gathered outside to welcome them and help carry the animals into a long house in preparation for dinner.

Minichque stood the same height as Catharyna. His body and head was shaved, numerous tattoos were found on his arms and chest, and on his head, he wore a headdress made from deer hair.

They bowed to each other in greeting. "Welcome Ten Broeck. Your hair long and free. I approve."

He then looked suspiciously at Hawk and Fairfax. Minichque would never acknowledge them unless she declared them friends. The power was in her hands to introduce them for entrance inside the tribe.

Hawk's eyes pierced Catharyna in the timeless moment it took to answer Minichque's silent question. Seconds passed until she fulfilled her promise. "These men are friends who come to speak with you on an important matter."

Minichque nodded and then wrapped an arm around his wife, which motioned all to follow them inside the long house. Before taking a seat, he said softly to Catharyna, "You lost a father, Ten Broeck. Spirits kind, he at peace with your mother." He and his wife placed a hand on her shoulder, and all three nodded their heads.

Everyone sat at Minichque's command. Hawk opened the discussion. "I am William Hawkins. My friend Fairfax and I are honored to be welcomed into your tribe."

"Honor Ten Broeck, honor me," he ordered and smiled at Catharyna. He touched the colorful wampum belt wrapped around his waist, a gift from Catharyna, that held a hunting scene and his initials. In a proud voice he added, "She is my white sister."

Murmurs from the tribe confirmed it.

Hawk nodded. "We honor Ten Broeck."

No business could be discussed until gifts were presented. Catharyna rose and unpacked a large bundle that contained six varieties of corn - white, blue, red, yellow, orange and multicolor. The bags were grabbed by two women, who were eager to make samp from it. Then she presented a gift to Minichque's wife. "Susquehanna, this is a tool called a chisel which makes designs in the copper jewelry you make." She reached inside the leather bag and withdrew a piece of copper and a small hammer. Then she demonstrated how to use the chisel. Everyone watched Susquehanna imitate her. When she succeeded, all the women and men cheered.

Minichque smiled brightly to his wife, but noticed some members of the tribe continued to watch the two white men suspiciously. He looked at Hawk and said, "Your people have great interest in our jewelry. Susquehanna barters tools and tobacco for it. Our women will use them well."

The few doubters were now seen murmuring an agreement which brought a proud smile to his face. His voice was absolute when it stated, "Ten Broeck's gifts are treasures for our tribe."

The women's excitement testified to his words as each of them examined the tools. Minichque's face relaxed and he raised a hand to Hawk. "Speak your business."

There was no hesitation. "We passed Mohawk warriors in the low lands. You are at war with them again."

Catharyna froze at Hawk's statement. If she had known it wasn't a peaceful time to visit Minichque, she would never have agreed to come.

Minichque looked at his wife and nodded, "Yes, the Munsee have convinced my father to their side. Now, we fight the Mohawk."

"I join Ten Broeck to urge you to make peace and sign treaties of trade and friendship with the Mohawks. Your tribe has already fallen to half your original number. You cannot afford to wage the Munsee's war with the Mohawks any longer."

Minichque nodded slowly and then turned to Catharyna. "I understand your visit, Ten Broeck. Your mother's spirit seeks peace as do our people from this fighting." Susquehanna's eyes grew damp with unshed tears. Minichque drew a deep breath and released it loudly. "But, my father refused negotiations, so now we battle."

Hawk countered, "Ten Broeck and I are here to offer your father three barrels of cider and three quarts of rum to begin peace negotiations."

Minichque gazed down at his wife, contemplating the white people's request. Never before had he questioned his father's decisions for the tribe. Once a Chief decided war for the tribe, victory or defeat would end it, nothing else. "I am uncertain."

Catharyna leaned forward and added, "If we gain your brother Sokoki's agreement, together you can open this discussion with your father. He will listen to you both."

Their eyes met and Minichque smiled. There were too many years of successful trading with his white sister to discount her words. The plagues that rolled through the valley had taken many Mohicans, yet she had provided needed supplies and knowledge in how to fight it, which saved many from death.

Tradition would be second to listening to her. "I am open to discuss in morning. Tonight, we feast on venison and my son's first turkey!"

Hawk and Fairfax stared silently at each other, and nodded in agreement.

The Englishmen remained aloof throughout the evening festivities, but watched Catharyna's dealings with the tribe. When Fairfax was demonstrating his bow and arrow skills to a warrior, Catharyna finally slipped away into the darkness of night for some solitude. A deep breath of fresh spring air revitalized a weary spirit. It had been a long day to be on display to Minichque's tribe who still held distrust of white people.

"Tired?"

The word was spoken from above Catharyna's head in a deep resonant voice. Her eyes shut tight knowing the few moments of peace were over. Hawk was behind her.

There was no energy to deal with the Englishman, or to be on guard to his potential tricks. Unfortunately, she needed to. With no alternative, she took a cleansing breath before facing him.

"A bit," she replied.

"I came to thank you for today and apologize for keeping you ignorant of our plans. You can see now why we needed your connection to Minichque to gain access to him."

Catharyna's eyes narrowed when they met his own. "A thank you and apology all in one sentence?"

Hawk smiled boyishly down at her. "I'm not a complete oaf."

Finally, he acknowledged hearing her words along the journey to Minichque's village, and that his silence had been deliberate. "Ha, you heard that."

"And other words."

His confession and rare smile brought Catharyna's attention to his facial features. Suddenly he was a breathing human, but, somehow, still completely hidden from view. She countered, "Were they deserved?"

"Some."

His continued arrogance released her pent up frustration. "Some?" she repeated in disbelief. "You tricked my uncle in order to use my connection to Minichque, abandoned Rolfe in the wilderness, dangled my mother's locket while keeping me in ignorance and silence for days, and now I'm supposed to forgive all of that?"

The darkness of night hid the clouds that entered Hawk's eyes. "Yes."

Catharyna's hands rose in frustration, uncertain how to deal with the man. Instead, she began pacing around him. The cool night air calmed riled nerves and brought clarity to what could be lost without his support. It was difficult to admit Hawk was needed to gain her own freedom. Thoughts raced for the best way to handle this correctly. The fact that he was indebted to her now rose above all else.

She faced him and replied, "I'm a reasonable woman,

Hawk. You brought me here under fraudulent circumstances. However, I will forgive all of that when you write my uncle that I negotiated an amicable agreement over his 10,000 acre parcel."

"Why?"

A look of bewilderment was briefly revealed. It was the one word she least expected to hear from him. "That is not your business."

Hawk shrugged and turned to leave.

Catharyna's hand reached out and spun him back around. "I'll make certain you and Fairfax get kicked out of here by Minichque if you don't agree to my terms."

They stared at each other for an ageless moment, but neither budged.

Hawk remained stiff and aloof, but inside thoughts were raging. Never had he known a woman so masterful at manipulation, nor so open about it. Many had warned him about the Dutchwoman's skills, but never did he anticipate demands would be made to him. Yet, there she stood, staring defiantly at him with the determination to remain through morning.

"You would allow the Mohawks and Mohicans to wage battle with innocent settlers in the middle of their fighting?"

Catharyna's eyes blinked under the impact of his words.

He drew closer and whispered, "Was not your mother's death and that of your brothers enough to end such Indian feuds for you?"

Her body and mind tightened when her eyes rose to his, expecting to find the usual cold arrogance, but, instead, found sympathy. Catharyna moved away to widen the distance separating them. There was no intention to expose herself to his probing eye. "How did you get my mother's locket?"

"Your father gave it to me when learning I slit the throat of the Wappinger warrior who wore it around his neck."

Their eyes clashed and emotions thickened her throat. "I don't believe you."

Hawk drew closer. "I assure you, the warrior was very

41

proud to display it."

"No," she said in confusion, "if my father had known, he would have told me of such and about you."

"It was his idea that sent me to you to gain entrance to Minichque, not mine."

"Why didn't he tell me?" she whispered.

"He was dying. Telling you this would have forced him to share that before he was willing to."

The idea that Cornelius had held anything from her left a deep ache in a grieving heart. She stepped farther into the darkness for distance from Hawk, but now the man, who had avoided her for days, refused to leave. Her voice was that of a child when it whispered, "He knew he was dying?"

A silent battle began to control emotions that demanded release. There was no knowledge of when Hawk's arms cradled her in comfort. There was only pain as time passed by in a blur. "I wish I had known," she confided.

Hawk looked down at the woman who had fearlessly pulled a knife on him and now clung to him through a crumb of trust. "Such knowledge can be a double edge sword."

Their eyes met and she slowly nodded. "Yes, in facing his death, my father would have protected me. I am sorry for doubting you."

"And for being irritable?"

A smile peeked through. "I'll not deny you've no gilded tongue, a curse shared by most Englishmen."

"Ha, I hear Catharyna returning."

She chuckled aloud, and then swallowed it quickly. His arms relaxed, and she stepped away feeling free and alone at the same time. "I shall support your work with Minichque," she stated and added, "but you must write my uncle that I negotiated an amicable agreement over his 10,000 acre parcel."

"Why?"

Once again his question startled her. Catharyna looked at the giant man as though he were a simpleton. "Why I need it is no business of yours. It is the law of trade."

"And that is?"

Her hands clenched at the sound of laughter in his tone. "Give equal, receive equal."

"I shall forgive such selfishness due to your mind being clouded in grief."

"Selfishness?" she squeaked and quickly whispered, "And what might you receive if peace is gained for the Iroquois League? I hold no belief that noble intentions brought you here."

Hawk's eyes blazed, but his voice held no emotion. "If you expected something from me, you should have set your terms before introducing me to Minichque. In this you failed."

She stood in amazement for several tense seconds until whispering, "Fine! You can forgive or condemn anything you bloody like, but I'll have that letter!"

"There is no question of my indebtedness to you, so, I agree to return the same whenever you are ready to explain the why to me."

They stared at each other until Catharyna nodded her head slightly. Hawk watched her kick the dirt in frustration, all the way back to the long house, and a boyish smile spread, erasing the sharp lines of his face.

The steady pounding of heavy rain the next day awakened Catharyna. A soft grumble was stifled so that the young women in the long house didn't hear the displeasure. Now it would take them twice as long to travel home.

She rose quickly, and went outside in search of Minichque for a private discussion before he met with Hawk and Fairfax, only to find the three men together already.

Minichque summoned her inside the long house. "Come, Ten Broeck. I have agreed to bring this discussion to my father." They smiled at each other. "It has been many seasons since his Sky Eyes white daughter has visited. Your presence will please him greatly."

"And me as well," she replied, deliberately ignoring the two Englishmen beside her.

Before there was time to think over the situation, she was again on horseback riding to the Mohican ancient capital at Shodac. This journey was far different. Now there was lively conversation with Minichque, whose gift of story telling made the hours on horseback fade away. She spoke freely, and all but forgot she was surrounded by Mohican warriors who were at war with the Mohawks.

They made their way slowly through the mud that was getting thicker and more difficult to travel in. At dusk they entered Sokoki's village of Schaghticoke. His face was similar to Minichque's, except it held a fierceness that was absent in the younger brother. Sokoki dealt with the fur traders for the tribe and bore several wampum belts that proved his success in the trade. He welcomed their party and led them inside the long house.

"Ten Broeck, what brings you away from Broeckwyck? We concluded much during Beaver Moon."

"Sokoki, I come with friends, William Hawkins and Fairfax, to meet with you."

Minichque nodded.

Sokoki acknowledged both white men with a nod.

Minichque stated, "We journey to Shodac for a war council to arrange peace between the Mohawk and Mohican."

Sokoki's eyes narrowed and turned to Hawk. "What do you offer?"

"Ten Broeck and I offer your father three barrels of cider and three quarts of rum to begin discussions. To you, I promise open trade if peace negotiations are successful."

Sokoki smiled and turned to Catharyna, who handed him a wampum belt that was purple in color. "Your daughter marries soon."

His eyes brightened over the gift, reading the shells sewn intricately into a wide belt. "This once belonged to a chief's daughter who sacrificed herself to protect the tribe. She was a protector to all, instead of mother to few." A bright smile spread. "You honor me and my daughter with such a wedding gift, Ten Broeck."

She bowed.

He then turned to Hawk. "I will join you tomorrow."

Hawk nodded and accepted the apple cider Sokoki's wife extended to him. Another important Indian friend was made in a matter of days, thanks to the Dutchwoman. His eyes sparkled when he looked across the long house at Catharyna. His plan was coming together far easier than anticipated.

Weeks passed until Catharyna was finally ready to return to Albany. Nightfall would have her reach Uncle Peter's house, but she was no closer to receiving an agreement from Hawk then when she had left Broeckwyck weeks ago. It felt selfish, largely due to Hawk, who made sure of it, to negotiate terms for herself when he was trying to organize peace treaties between the two tribes. And there was nothing she wanted more than that peace treaty, other than her freedom.

It was impossible to find Hawk alone after they left the village of Schaghticoke. And there was no doubt he made certain of it. Minichque and Sokoki took an immediate liking to him, which made her work feverishly to be included in most of their conversations. It was all the more difficult to accept that Hawk was speaking freely and hurriedly with them in their native tongue, and in apparent delight. His success with her Indian friends did not sit well.

While preparing to leave the Mohican ancient capital that morning, Minichque paid her tribute with twenty beaver skins. "Susquehanna will name our next child Brook, after you, our white sister who led the water of life to our tribe."

Catharyna bowed. "Peace for your people is peace for mine. You honor me by having your daughter named such."

Sokoki laughed. "Let us hope she does not have Ten Broeck's tongue."

Hawk added, "Or taste in hats."

All the men joined in the laughter, and Catharyna smiled tightly, while bundling the beaver skins on her horse's saddle pack.

Hawk left the men to join her. "Fairfax will take you to Albany. I am joining Chief Konkapot to proceed with peace negotiations. I shall return to you when my work is done here."

"Don't come unless it is with my letter."

Confidence sapped the air around her when their eyes met, and she was gathered into his arms. "Trust me and I shall give you much more," he whispered against her lips, before teasing them lightly in a kiss.

"All I want is my letter," she replied numbly, with a body in a state of confusion over the feelings Hawk just aroused with a brush of his lips.

For the first time in her life, she backed away like a coward, and refused to meet the challenge in his eyes. Hawk's arms fell away, and she mounted the stallion. With a final wave to the tribe, she galloped out of the village, and Fairfax followed a step behind.

No matter all the arguments and battle of words, at the end of weeks in the man's company, she was returning to Uncle Peter with no written agreement from Hawk. And yet, the failure which should be blazing before her eyes, was now a distant memory, covered over by a weak kiss.

Fury at herself began a personal battle. She was no innocent maid, easily wooed by a man's attention. There had been too many men in her past that had attempted that path and failed. Each lacked one thing or another that made any future impossible. Even her father had stopped discussing marriage. It was the reason she refused to believe Dirck was dead. Broeckwyck would go to his heirs. There would be no future heirs coming from her womb.

She had known from the moment of meeting Hawk that he was more dangerous than the others. Somehow, he had managed to best her, and that was now sending her empty handed to Uncle Peter. It was impossible to accept the failure. The foreign taste was bitter and humiliating to swallow.

"We should be in Albany by nightfall," Fairfax said, finally speaking to her.

"*Beverwyck*," Catharyna snapped. It was too late to be friendly with him. The past few weeks of his cold presence, no matter the circumstances, made her unreceptive to be civil with him.

Weeks of enduring her rudeness wore on the exhausted Fairfax. "Beverwyck is under English rule, Ten Broeck, and is now called Albany. So is your North River, which is now the Hudson. The Indians call them such, why can't the Dutch accept them too?"

"The only reason the Indians do so is because of all the barrels of rum you give to them," she snapped.

Disbelief filled Fairfax's face. "I thought the Mohicans were your friends?"

"Some are, others are like a leaf tossed by an *English* breeze." Fairfax stopped his horse, which made Catharyna's horse stop, which only served to increase her irritation.

The charming Englishmen snapped, "Why do you hate us so? We've allowed you to continue trading with the Indians, and most of our business continues to be conducted in Dutch. There hasn't been any significant changes for you since we took over."

The first taste of failure overruled Catharyna's tongue to speak the truth. "We Dutch dislike anyone who is narrow-minded, arrogant, aloof and cold. By definition, that is an Englishman."

Fairfax's jaw tightened. "And the Dutch disagree for the sake of disagreeing, yet that doesn't make me hate you."

"I don't disagree, nor do I hate you."

Fairfax's face resumed a cold and distant look.

"I don't!"

Fairfax's determination to succeed in his new country tried to breach through her stubbornness. "Your mother country chose their sugar trade over the colonists here, the English agreed to the terms. Now all we hear are disgruntled Dutchwomen leering at us as though we're the bloody devil

47

himself."

Catharyna's laughter ricocheted across the valley. "That's nonsense, an Englishman doesn't care what a woman says or thinks. You have laws to make sure of it!"

Fairfax's hand raked through loose wavy hair and replaced his hat. Weary eyes looked at the striking woman, who was glaring at him with hatred deep within, but now he knew its cause. "What has changed for *you* since we occupied New York?"

Catharyna glared at him while considering the question. It was difficult to answer. In her mind, everything had changed. In reality, nothing had changed, yet. It was the power the English law held over her, dangling, threatening, suffocating, as if she were a caged animal. "You took away my freedom."

Fairfax threw back his head and laughter erupted.

Catharyna snapped, "This is *not* funny, Fairfax."

"No, it is not," Fairfax replied seriously, with eyes that now sparkled. "The Duke of York has opened trade here, unlike your Dutch West India Company, who forbid anyone outside of the company to touch it or anything else of value to their coffers in Amsterdam. You are a trader, Ten Broeck, and benefit most by English rule."

She looked at Fairfax with new eyes. This man was not at all the man originally seen. He just hit a bull's eye into her hatred of the English. Refusing to allow it to crumble so easily, stubbornness made her reply, "That isn't the point."

He pounced, "That's *exactly* the point. The English have made you a wealthy trader." His eyes held respect when they locked on her face, and his hand reached out to capture a long curl of hair bouncing in the wind, to tug on it lightly. "It is why Hawk came to you to open discussions with the Mohicans. Your reputation is the Dutchwoman who opens all doors. What Englishman would be fool enough to entangle himself in your wrath when he gains more from your friendship?" A wink and dazzling smile followed and then a whistle commanded his horse to canter.

Catharyna's horse immediately followed, but, this time,

there was no resentment over the order. Instead, her mind was focused on what his words implied. Their affect on her brain felt as though rusted wheels began to turn for the first time, ever so slowly, only to gain speed until they were spinning with new thoughts and ideas. She knew the value of her trade, friendship with the Indians and the strength of her strong family ties in the province. Yet, until that moment, never did she think of *herself* as valuable. It was an awakening experience. All at once, her father's words took on a richer shape. The seed was there, but faith in herself was needed to allow it to grow.

This new inner belief saw opportunity before her to learn about the man who held her freedom in his hands. A warm smile spread when she approached Fairfax again. "How did you meet Hawk?"

Fairfax smiled in turn, delighted she now viewed him as friend instead of foe. It had been Hawk's order to remain silent to the Dutchwoman until he gained commitment from the Chief. That was accomplished, so there was nothing barring it now. "Ten years ago aboard a ship headed to the West Indies. I was a ship hand, Hawk, an officer."

"What brought you here?"

A bright red blush bloomed on Fairfax's face. He whistled to his horse to canter, only Catharyna wouldn't be ignored this time and placed her horse in front of his own. "Fairfax, if you want to be my friend, you should never ignore me again."

Without meeting her gaze, he mumbled, "I was caught with a Captain's wife."

Catharyna held no censure or surprise. Just looking at Fairfax's handsome features made it believable and knowing his open mind made it inevitable. She nodded in understanding while eyes ordered him to continue.

"Hawk paid for my life with his career. He promised we would never board another ship heading to the West Indies. The Captain was waiting for an excuse to oust Hawk, so he was eager to take it. We came here."

"You owe Hawk much."

"Everything."

Catharyna nodded, and they proceeded the rest of the journey to Albany in silence. The last thing she wanted to hear was something that would make Hawk human to her, yet it was the best way to find his weakness. Now, she knew several. Whenever the opening presented itself, she would get her freedom from Hawk, regardless of who got in the way.

Nothing would allow her to fail again.

Three

Indian summer was at its peak when Hawk entered the unpaved street of Manhattan's Broad Way. After six intensive months of negotiations with the Iroquois League, it was time to bring his plan into a living, breathing, reality.

An arrogant smile tightened his facial features, but pride warmed his eyes surveying the view. The morning sun's rays on the Hudson River sparkled like a sea of fine cut diamonds and its bordering mountains towered in superiority kissing the sky. Sweet air filled his lungs, renewing a weary spirit that had roamed everywhere in the province the past seven years to get to this moment. An eagle's cry in the distance confirmed he had arrived home.

He turned off at Pearl Street to stop at the Blue Dove, the most popular tavern in town. The room was crowded with traders and frontiersmen from the four corners of the world. All were adventurers, a rough, tough, quarrelsome crew consisting mainly of Dutch, Irishmen, Swedes, Germans, Danes, and Englishmen who all shared one common code of conduct - every man for himself. Most were illiterate, few unintelligent, all hard, shrewd, lawless, brave and cruel.

Hawk surveyed the room, finding one person he called friend. Captain David DeVries was in the middle of the room placing a bet on the tavern's favorite game, "Clubbing the Cat." The players soon took their positions at a given distance away from the cat, who was imprisoned in a cask hung from the ceiling in the middle of the room. Minutes later, the winner was a tall Swede who broke the cask and let the cat loose.

Hawk slapped DeVries on the back. "Another loss?"

"Who'd have suspected that skinny Swede could best the German?"

Hawk laughed and motioned to the barmaid with a wave of a hand. A young buxom red haired girl approached with a fearful face. "Sir, whatcha be needin'?"

Hawk's features tightened under a thick beard over the maid's fear of him. "A pint of your best rum."

DeVries echoed, "Make that two Kill Devils for us, Sally."

The barmaid smiled warmly at DeVries and hurried away to fetch the drinks. DeVries leaned closer to his friend and whispered, "If you'd shave that hair off your face you wouldn't frighten all the beauties away."

Hawk's reply was a hand stroking the beard.

DeVries chuckled and asked, "What's kept you away this time?"

"Governor's orders."

David DeVries' eyes sparkled with merriment when Sally returned with their drinks and a private invitation in her eyes for him. "You tell me what they were, and I'll pay for Sally to give you a bath that will change your life."

"After I meet with the Governor," he said and drained the pewter mug dry.

Hawk rose from the chair, but DeVries halted his departure with a shout heard across the room. "Sally, my friend is meeting our Governor - *prepare him!*"

The crowd cheered. Bellows of laughter and jeers followed when Hawk was besieged by the three loveliest barmaids the Blue Dove offered, which meant they bathed, weekly. There was no resistance when they led him upstairs.

Two hours later, a clean shaven and relaxed Hawk emerged. His face felt naked; too many years had passed since he had seen it. The eager hands and warm smiles from the barmaids had him conclude his beardless face was more favorable.

Minutes later he was striding up the stairs of the

Governor's mansion, the largest building on the island. It was a hundred feet in length and fifty feet wide with three full stories and architecture equaled to London's. The door was ajar to the Governor's office, so Hawk entered silently. He nodded to Lovelace, who was reviewing maps that were spread across a wide mahogany desk. A silent order to be seated on the sofa was obeyed.

Lovelace was a short man with graceful, long fingers that began pointing to all the roads that were in his plan, but were not on the map. "Wagon Way isn't on the map, Rudolph. This road must be in the plan for pavement to connect the town to Harlem. Who did you hire to publish this map? A fool can see they've never stepped foot on the island!" In a flourish, he ripped up the maps and threw them at his secretary. "Don't waste my time until you have an accurate map of the town."

Rudolph scurried from the room in embarrassment. Lovelace turned around to face Hawk, his face full of frustration. "Leave now if you bring me bad news, Hawk."

Hawk's deep arrogant laughter bounced around the office walls. He rose from the sofa and took the chair opposite the desk.

A brilliant smile spread across Lovelace's face. In amazement he whispered, "Damnation, you did it!"

"Yes."

Lovelace reached into the desk for a bottle of Jamaican rum and poured each of them a drink. He saluted Hawk. "To peace in the Iroquois League and our province!"

The two men drained the glasses quickly and smiled at each other. There was no friendship, just two ambitious men seeing opportunity. "You fulfilled your promise to the Duke of York, which makes you a rich man. What are you going to do with 200,000 acres?"

Hawk reached into a coat pocket and pulled out his own accurate survey map of the province of New York, and handed it to the Governor. "10 miles of land along the east and west bank of the Hudson River is what the Duke promised to me. I have paid Chief Konkapot for the parcel, and now need a confirmatory manor grant of this agreement from you."

"It's always business with you, Hawk." Lovelace's face tightened. "Of course you'll get your bloody grant, but not from me. Yours will be reviewed with the other ten men seeking it. If you wish to be the first Lord of the Manor in this province, I suggest you take the next ship to England and claim it personally from the Duke himself."

Hawk's eyes narrowed. Anger raged within that even now, all his efforts were still not enough to secure the honor, but none of it was visible to Lovelace. "I will."

Lovelace grinned. "Excellent, I have a few matters you can handle for me while you're in London."

"Of course," Hawk replied tightly. "With free passage for Fairfax and myself."

Shrewd eyes met the hawk stare. "Of course, Hawk. Now, we celebrate!" Lovelace refilled their glasses and leaned back in the chair. "This is exactly what we needed to prove God's blessing is and always has been with England to rule this province. Paving the roads won't bring settlers here, but the news of the Iroquois Peace treaty will!" His arm sliced through the air when he added, "The Dutch cleaned out the fur from here to Ohio, such was their boundless greed! Whereas we're making it a thriving colony."

"The Dutch left us an orderly town to build upon thanks to their Governor Stuyvesant," Hawk stated. He gave men their due no matter who they were, but there was little room in his personality for socializing. With business complete, he was eager to leave. "There is no dispute that the Dutch landowners hold little, if any, loyalty to their mother country now; however, they still distrust, and some hate, our English rule."

Lovelace looked appalled. "They would be nincompoops to think that way."

Catharyna van Broeck's face appeared in Hawk's mind. "There are still those we must turn into friends."

The Governor leaned forward. His eyes pinned the man who was the most respected Englishman in the province. "Who are my enemies here, Hawk?"

"You have been faithful to Governor Nicoll's promise that they can retain their property and worship as they choose. You are viewed as a just and merciful governor to the Dutchmen in the province."

The Governor's eyes sparkled over the words. Hawk was a man he didn't like to have dinner with, but whose honesty he greatly respected. No matter how ugly or beautiful it was, Hawk spoke truthfully. His words were a great comfort to the Governor who was ruling an untamed land with no guidance from the crown, other than to protect it. He had already failed last year with the Dutch surprise attack when he was away, and they reclaimed their colony. England had to forfeit their sugar holdings in South America in order to reclaim it once and for all, to gain control of the entire east coastline. It was clear he was on thin ice with the Duke of York, another mistake would not be permitted.

"If the Dutchmen are pleased with me, and the Indians are at peace, who isn't?"

Hawk rose from the chair and walked toward the window to view the East River. In the distance was Turtle Bay, the beginning of Broeckwyck's lands. He turned back to Lovelace and answered, "Dutchwomen."

Bewilderment, amazement and then laughter filled the Governor's face. Lovelace slapped his hand loudly on top of the desk. "By jolly, you do have a sense of humor, Hawk! You almost had me believing you."

Hawk approached the Governor's chair and stood silent until the laughter stopped and bewilderment was restored on Lovelace's face. Hawk's eyes twinkled in merriment and a smile appeared. "I was wrong."

Lovelace chuckled, "Bloody right!"

He continued laughing until Hawk elaborated, "Not Dutch*women*, but a Dutch*woman*."

The Governor stopped laughing.

Hawk sat back down in a chair. "Catharyna Helena Maria van Broeck, or known by the traders as Ten Broeck."

Lovelace's eyes widened. "Ten Broeck is a *woman?*

But..."

"Yes."

Ever since arriving in New York, the one name Lovelace heard over and over again, a name that rose above all other traders in Manhattan, was Ten Broeck. "That cannot be possible. Ten Broeck is the best trader in this port!"

Hawk continued, unmoved by the Governor's words. "Yet, it is true. Without Ten Broeck's support, I would never have been admitted into the Iroquois League for peace negotiations. She has the respect of the Indians and her Dutch family is the oldest and most powerful from the mouth of the Hudson River up to Albany. She is influential and equally intelligent and fearless. But more than anything else, she hates our English hide."

The implications of Hawk's words penetrated into the Governor, who began to accept Ten Broeck was a woman. "How did *she* get so powerful?"

"She's the daughter of Cornelius van Broeck, Patroon of Broeckwyck and now his sole heir. Many claim it's a fortune, I can only verify Broeckwyck's holdings. He trained her as a world class trader. Rumor has it, she speaks over ten languages." The doubt on the Governor's face prompted Hawk to add, "How much of that is true, I cannot say, but I know she speaks five fluently."

Bewilderment remained on Lovelace's face. "It isn't possible for one woman to be so powerful in a province populated with ruthless fortune hunters."

Hawk's silence spoke loudly.

Lovelace leaned back in the chair and closed his eyes. A groan was followed by, "How do you suggest I deal with this paragon of a woman?"

Hawk's eyes narrowed and lips curved into a smile. "We play cat and mouse."

Lovelace's eyes instantly opened, and he straightened in the chair. Excitement filled his voice. "Tell me how we begin this game."

The harvest moon cast a bright silver glow upon
Broeckwyck Manor as the crowd celebrated the harvest. It was
a festival held since the dawn of man to thank God for food that
would grant them life during the cold harsh winter months
ahead. Candles burned in their sconces making the night appear
day for the dancers and frolics to continue well past midnight.

Hawk made his way through the crowd, picked up a
turkey leg from a table laden with sweet cakes and meats, and
munched on it while surveying the surroundings.

In the middle of the crowd appeared Catharyna, dancing
with children, her long hair free and bouncing to the rhythm of
fiddles and pipes. Even from a distance, Hawk felt the familiar
pull to her. There had been many women in his life, but no faces
were recalled. This woman had remained etched in his thoughts
the past six months, and he was eager to be rid of her. It was
the challenge that aroused him, and like all others met, the
interest would eventually wane.

The moment the dance was over, Hawk tossed aside the
turkey leg and approached his prey with measured steps.

Catharyna's soft laughter ended when she turned about
and confronted a ruggedly handsome man smiling down at her.
Unprepared for such a meeting, a hand unconsciously rose to a
wayward curl to shove quickly behind an ear, and she smiled
expectantly up at the stranger. Her cousin Rolfe and servant
Alice stood at each side of her, both becoming part of the
conversation.

"Good evening, Ten Broeck. I come with good news."

Bewilderment touched Catharyna's face, trying to place
the man's name. He knew her trading name, yet there was no
memory in doing any business with him. "Come," was all that
was spoken as she led him from the crowd toward the wind mill
for privacy. Rolfe and Alice followed a pace behind. It was
always a treat when Broeckwyck received visitors with news.
There was excitement in Catharyna's own voice when she
asked, "What news do you bring us?"

Hawk answered, "The Mohican's have made peace with the Iroquois League."

Rolfe whistled in the air. "I say, you're forgiven for bailing me out of the sloop!" And he slapped Hawk's back in comradeship.

Catharyna had no such reaction, but simply stared at the tall Englishman, finally recognizing Hawk.

Alice leaned against the wind mill for support as amazement consumed the aged face. She began to weep and whispered brokenly, "How is this possible?"

Alice had lost both a husband and two sons during Indian raids when they arrived in the colony twenty years ago. She and her daughter had indentured themselves as servants at a patroonship north that had also been attacked. They had lived in continuous fear of the Indians until coming to Broeckwyck.

Catharyna went to comfort her cook, only to be nudged aside by Hawk, who took the widow's trembling hands in his own. "On behalf of Governor Lovelace, I arranged the peace between the Mohawk and Mohican tribes. It was finalized with the Iroquois League a fortnight ago. Several of the low tribes will be dispersing to Delaware and northeastern Pennsylvania. There is now peace in our Valley."

Alice's face rose to Hawk, no longer hiding the tears that flowed freely down her cheeks. She hugged him tightly and kissed his cheek. "God bless you," she whispered and then stepped aside.

He now stood in front of Catharyna. "This wouldn't have been possible without your support. I've come on behalf of the Governor to thank you."

Catharyna had never been so torn with different emotions. There was overwhelming gratitude with the success of the peace treaty, mixed with resentment of Hawk's role in it, and cynical suspicions with his praise of her contributions. Those and many other darker thoughts twirled inside her mind, the darkest being the attraction to the beardless Hawk. Every instinct urged her to bolt, but she refused. The cowardliness of backing away from him months ago had plagued her. Finally, the man was once again in her presence, on her land, and in her control. This was what she had waited for, and nothing less than taking full advantage of it would be permitted.

Catharyna's face and voice softened. "I never doubted your success."

Hawk beamed. "It was challenging."

"What reward has our Governor given you for such a feat?" The words were sarcastic but they were spoken in an alluring tone that hid all of it.

Hawk gazed into the ice blue eyes that held a warmth that finally invited him closer. "Ten miles of land along the east and west banks of the Hudson River."

Her eyes sparkled. "Ha, you have become a land baron."

"Farmer."

Her laughter was soft and enticing. "Never so simple a trade for you, Hawk. Would you honor us by sharing this news with our people?" A hand was extended to him in invitation, and Hawk immediately took it. Their eyes met and she smiled while leading them back into the center of the festival.

Rolfe whistled loudly to draw everyone's attention. "We've exciting news, draw forward!" Farmers, blacksmiths, tanners, bakers, and other tradespeople soon encircled them.

Catharyna shouted, "Welcome a friend of Broeckwyck's, Mr. William Hawkins."

Cheers and applause filled the evening air. Hawk viewed the crowd quickly, but eyes remained fixed on Catharyna, who was backing away to give him the honor to share the news. The gracious gesture would not be forgotten.

Catharyna's eyes narrowed watching the crowd listen to Hawk. Understanding the male mind had made her the best trader in the province. Hawk was like any other man. Even now she felt his pleasure and a smile of anticipation blossomed.

The roar of cheers from the crowd had their eyes meet. Her smile spread, seeing Hawk busy weaving through the throng of people, who now clung to him with questions, tears and sharing horrible losses along the way back to her. Music, dancing, drinking and boasts of peace penetrated the air as the festival resumed in fever pitch.

Hawk's hand reached out through the madness and captured Catharyna. "Come," he ordered, and lead her back to the wind mill. The sounds of the festival were now distant and allowed his mind to clear. "That was smothering," he admitted.

She sensed his guard was down, and excitement grew. "Let me show you my father's favorite spot." They entered the wind mill and took the stairs to the widow's walk that overlooked Broeckwyck and the harbor. A blanket of stars littered the midnight sky and the crystal clear East River was its bed. The height of the widow's walk allowed the eye to view the east and west coastlines of the narrow island, its rolling meadows, ponds and fields in all their beauty.

Hawk took in the scene of nature surrounding them and smiled. "I see why he missed your mother."

Catharyna stammered, "Excuse me?"

"This you must share."

It was happening again. Control was quickly slipping away from her grasp and there was no warning or clue how to gain it back. Uncertainty now laced her voice. "There had been many widows who approached my father to wed and many fathers who offered their daughters to him. All had been rejected. He didn't wish to share it."

Confidence surrounded Hawk's words. "Perhaps God gives us only one to share it with."

Catharyna laughed, "That's ridiculous."

"Perhaps."

"No matter," Catharyna shrugged, "we live our lives by the sun, few are awake to see the stars." Then her eyes sparkled when they clashed with his. "Though I find it astounding a man as yourself believes such."

He drew closer. "I said perhaps."

The look in his eyes prompted her to whisper, "Then what do you want?"

Hawk swore softly at the transformation a simple smile could create. Eyes, the color of the Caribbean Sea that had bewitched his youth, now stared up at him under the full moon's rays. The familiar pull toward her tightened. He broke free of her piercing stare to view the seductive smile that looked convincing, but had never played the game. "You're not ready for what I want."

A slap to her face would have been preferred. Catharyna laughed to cover the impact of his words. "Foolish men make assumptions." Her taunt brought a sensual smile on the face of the man who changed by the minute in her presence. The challenge was becoming irresistible and drew her closer. Something deep inside and unrecognizable prompted her to whisper, "Tell me what you want."

"If I reveal myself to you, would you do likewise?"

She felt like they were fencing and it drove her closer into the danger. "Perhaps," she whispered.

They stood a breath apart from each other, but neither spanned the distance to touch.

"I leave for London and want you to join me."

Again, he surprised her with the unexpected and it made her laugh softly. "Why would I do that?"

Adventure sparkled in his eyes. "To introduce you to the most powerful merchants London offers."

"Why would you do that?"

"I've land that needs settlers and you seek ways to increase your trade. Together we'll find more success when both follow us back to New York. And if you desire it," Catharyna's heart pounded until he said, "I'll introduce you to the Duke of York himself."

Again, he startled her. And again, it was well received. There was no more powerful rule than to know your enemies. Englishmen swarmed over her homeland. Time was overdue to step on their own soil. She confided, "This I would consider."

Hawk's eyes narrowed, but the pleasure in them could not be disguised. He was learning it was give and take with this woman. His voice held desires that had been dormant since a young man who knew no deceit or corruption. "Tell me what you want from me to make it so."

There was no hesitation. "Agree to my terms which we

discussed this spring."

Hawk's face remained unreadable even though his mind raced to recall what she was talking about. There had been many negotiations conducted since they were last together, everything blurred. The original purpose that brought him to Broeckwyck rose to the surface. She had been the foundation that built the peace treaty. This Dutchwoman had unknowingly secured his future, and for that he was indebted to her. Whatever terms she requested couldn't be important or of significance. He decided to be generous. "This I agree too."

Catharyna took a step back and eyes remained locked on his face. "Swear it."

"I swear it."

For the first time she looked openly at his clean shaven face and enjoyed its chiseled features. A breathtaking smile spread and she extended a hand to seal their agreement. His large hand consumed hers and she chuckled over the observation. She confessed, "I believed you came here tonight wishing something from me, but instead, you granted me two years of freedom. I shall not forget such generosity."

He brushed aside a loose tendril that was being tousled by a soft sea breeze, and fought the sense of foreboding that grew inside. "How have I done that?"

"By your agreement that I met the terms set by my uncle in reclaiming his 10,000 acre parcel. He granted me freedom to choose my own husband."

Hawk grew excited, but none of it showed. "Are you not betrothed to Johannes Bleecher?"

Suspicion sparked in Catharyna's eyes, it had never been publicly announced. All thoughts remained hidden. Instead, she replied smoothly, "You delayed my return when we visited Chief Konkapot. Time demanded the alliance be made, so my uncle exchanged me for my cousin Maria. She has been wed to Johannes these past months and carries his child."

Gaining two years of freedom made her impatient to make it reality. She pulled his hand. "Come, we must return to the manor! You have to write a letter to my uncle straight away confirming this, so I may break the contract to wed Jochem Wessel in a fortnight."

Hawk stood rooted to the ground. He had been told many times, and by many men, that he was lucky, but for the first time it was felt. All of it was hidden when he mumbled, "Why are you rejecting Wessel?"

Catharyna turned back from leaving the widow's walk, and approached him. "Ha! I see you've never shared a meal with him." A hand sliced through the air in anger. "It is beyond my ability to sit idle and watch my husband behave like a pig at my table."

"I understand," Hawk whispered, and he finally did. The future was within his grasp. He was now the largest landowner in the province of New York, but that meant little to the close knit Dutch that kept business, and most of the province's money, tightly within their circle of family and friends. The day he stepped foot on Manhattan he had been an outsider to them. It didn't matter what manor privileges or title he was given by the crown, the Dutch would reject him all the same unless he had a prominent *Dutch* wife.

And there were none more influential, adventurous or independent than Catharyna to consider marriage to an Englishman. A transatlantic voyage was all the time needed to convince her he was that man.

Knowing all that, Hawk knew her relatives would prevent it. There was only one way to guarantee her journeying to London with him. "It was my belief your marriage was settled. Now that this is not the case, my pledge to Minichque to honor you, makes me share this." Their eyes met. "There are a few prominent Englishmen in England who have petitioned the Duke for Broeckwyck."

Catharyna's female machinations dissolved as fury was unleashed. "The blood sucking, no good, scandalous, devil loving thieves! They've no right to claim my property!"

Hawk pushed onward. "Broeckwyck is vulnerable without your father and no husband beside you to protect it."

"Do not the English obey any laws? I hold legal title as a

single woman under your law. This I know!" she said, while fighting the disbelief that all her fears were now descending down to reality. The feeling of suffocation began to slowly unfurl inside, but determination to find a way out halted its progress. "They'll not force me to wed in fear. I swear the first man who touches Broeckwyck will feel my wrath!"

She began to pace, but Hawk's hand halted her. "Marry Wessel and be done with it," he reasoned with no faith in the words.

Their eyes met and she confessed, "I've yet to decide whether I will marry at all under your antiquated law." Bewilderment traced her question, "Why must I give my husband Broeckwyck to control and manage as *he* desires, leaving me no legal rights in any of his decisions?" And then, her voice trembled with anger when she swore, "This I'll *never* permit."

Hawk was stunned by the new development, but hid all of it. This was why he didn't believe in luck. He cursed the lapse of judgment, and remained true to his beliefs. Nothing ever came easily, everything came with a plan.

Catharyna's next words only confirmed it. "I may return to Holland and marry there, under *Dutch law* which will guarantee Broeckwyck will remain in my control. And, my trade will be far more profitable." She growled up at him, "I've choices! Your law won't control me."

There was amazement in his voice when he asked, "You will leave the land your parents loved and perished to build, due to a law?"

She blinked, and then automatically scanned the view of the harbor her father and she loved more than any of their material possessions. Catharyna whispered, "No... but if there is no way out from it, I must."

A grin spread across Hawk's face. The obstacles before him were now understood. "Join me in London, and together, we shall speak to the Duke's barrister to discuss ways this can be avoided." The man who survived many battles added, "I have learned all laws can be navigated according to one's wishes."

Catharyna was overwhelmed at the offer. Suspicions in his interests to aid her were strong, but the offer to find a crack in the law that strangled her future was far to potent to resist. "You would do this for me?"

His face relaxed by a genuine smile and the truth of the words. "I owe you a great debt by introducing me to Minichque."

Catharyna's hand reached out to touch Hawk's face that was finally naked to her eyes. Adventure looked back and it beckoned her to rise and meet it. "Yes, but can I trust you?"

There was hope in her tone and his smile grew. "Perhaps," he whispered and watched the window of her mind open to him at last.

"I shall journey with you to London," she said and warned, "but it will be always or never in my trust of you. There is no other way I live." And with that, she left the widow's peek.

Hawk's shrewd eyes roamed over the midnight view of rolling hills, rivers and beaches that hugged the narrow strip of Manhattan. The sense of opportunity surrounded him. A deep breath of crisp October air filled him with confidence. It was released by a whispered, "Perhaps."

Four

The world had turned upside down. Dawn was yet to break across the horizon when the front lawns of Broeckwyck began filling with men of all ages, languages, races, and means. All were eager to meet its Patrooness.

An unusual noise vibrating from the window pane awoke Catharyna. Rising to find its source, bleary eyes roamed the crowd finding familiar faces she had traded with over the past few years. Within minutes she was dressed, believing a ship was in port that required her speaking skills.

Thoughts wandered over what type of cargo it contained that would cause such a crowd at her stoop before sun rise, and excitement grew. Mentally, she listed Broeckwyck's needs, some rare spices and oranges would be a treat. It was the last thought before opening the door.

The throng of men rushed into the manor, speaking nonsense. Words of love, devotion, and a few marital contracts fluttered in the air. She pushed them away, only to move deeper into the room as they shoved harder until her back was against the fireplace with no where else to turn. A whistle opened a path and Hawk moved forward to stand in the middle of the room.

"Move out, *now!*"

There were grumbles, and many more curses, but eventually the crowd returned outside. They remained on the front lawn, waiting for their suit to be heard.

Catharyna locked the door and leaned against it trying to think, but the men were now chanting her name, demanding she come out and choose a husband. Her heart began to pound and frantic eyes turned to Hawk in bewilderment.

"What caused this lunacy?"

A smile filled every crevice on Hawk's face, clearly enjoying this new development. "You sent Rolfe off last night with my letter and his haste to reach Albany undoubtedly spread the news of your freedom to marry as you choose. So, you did."

"Nincompoop!" Catharyna shouted at the room in general, knowing it was not Rolfe's fault, but her own. There was no possible way to have anticipated such a response. Her brain was empty of ideas as desperation filled it to be rid of the threatening crowd. Trapped eyes scanned the room, searching for support. They locked on Alice, who timidly entered the room to start breakfast with shaky limbs. Across the room stood the servant boy Jacob, who was no more than eight years old, busy stroking the embers. The child was humming, completely alone in a world of daydreams.

A breath of defeat rushed out of Catharyna's lips. There would be no help from the servants. With no alternative, she turned to the only capable person in the room.

"Hawk, order them to leave."

In one evening he had come far in gaining her trust. After their agreement to journey to England together, she had enjoyed the festival with him and Broeckwyck's tenants as a special guest. And as such, he was provided the best bedchamber in the manor. It was as much a surprise to Hawk to be awakened at dawn to a crowd of men chanting Ten Broeck's name, as it was to her. It was also another opportunity to gain her trust.

Hawk nodded and stepped outside to face the crowd. He bellowed, "G'day!"

A rumble of voices echoed across the lawn until a few strong men stood out among the crowd, their leader being Captain David DeVries. Hawk recognized him as such by speaking only his name. "DeVries."

DeVries stood furious in front of the men. While he was drinking and frolicking with barmaids at the Blue Dove, Rolfe's news circulated around the tavern that Ten Broeck was free to choose a husband and that "The Hawk" was slumbering in Broeckwyck's guest chamber, ready to strike. DeVries believed he ruled the port of New York, not some Indian Commissioner from Albany. The town knew he brought Ten Broeck the best traders, ensured they respected and treated her as equal. DeVries did it because it was the only way to win a woman like Catharyna.

"I'm not here to speak with *you*, I've come to speak to Ryna."

Hawk saw competition. It was clear the handsome Dutch sea captain shared a close relationship with Catharyna, since only family called her Ryna, a trust he had yet to establish. His eyes narrowed into slits.

"She wants you and your crowd off the premises immediately."

"*I* will see her *now*!"

Hawk approached DeVries until they were separated by a blade of grass. He looked down at the stubborn man and reasoned, "You're drunk. Clean up and come back later."

"I leave when you leave."

A shot fired into the air and the two men spun about to find Catharyna standing on the stoop. "So, you all seek my hand?"

Shouts rang out across the lawn. "Aye!"

"Very well," she stated and approached with a bow and a quiver full of arrows. She pointed the bow to a wooden post over a hundred feet away. An arrow then stretched the string and was released into the air to land in precision one inch from the top of the beam.

All eyes turned back to her and she explained, "The first man to splice my arrow in two will be given an opportunity to bring his offer to me. For those who wish to be heard, take your chance. All others should leave now."

The men raced to get in line. Arrows flew in the air, hitting grass mostly, with only a few nicking the beam. One by one the men began moving behind DeVries as they lost their opportunity for Catharyna. An hour passed and they came full circle with DeVries and Hawk standing side by side.

Hawk bowed to DeVries and confessed, "I've no skill with the bow."

A brilliant smile spread across DeVries' face. The men behind him all cheered when he pulled back effortlessly on the bow and the arrow sailed in the air and landed beside Catharyna's arrow.

DeVries approached Catharyna and said, "I preferred kissing your arrow than splicing it."

Her throat tightened at the handsome man's openness. It had always been so, suggestive comments and innuendoes were a part of their work relationship. All knew there was no Dutchman more persuasive or attractive than DeVries, but those qualities weren't high on Catharyna's list. The advantages to marry him were already in her control. He smuggled her trade out of port since her brother's absence, and sent the best traders who anchored in the harbor to her.

And yet, her eyes sparkled with a warm invitation to him. "I'll have no crowd behind us when we talk. Take your men back to the Blue Dove and return later."

He bowed and kissed her hand. "Very well," he said, and tapped Hawk on the shoulder. "You follow too."

Hawk ignored him and took a step forward. A knife flicked out of his hand and sailed threw the air splicing Catharyna's arrow in two. A hush fell over the crowd of men who took a step back when Hawk approached DeVries. "I follow no one," he warned, and then took the bow and arrow and aimed it at a bird in flight overhead. Seconds later it landed at DeVries' feet pierced by an arrow in its heart. The crowd of men rushed backward, several falling on top of each other, when Hawk faced them.

Catharyna grinned openly at him.

Hawk's shoulders shrugged and he confessed, "Minichque said I had no talent."

DeVries growled, "What do you seek to gain by this show?"

Hawk simply laughed and began to walk toward the manor. A wide path opened and Catharyna followed.

DeVries shouted at her back, "I return later for our meeting."

Catharyna raised a hand in agreement before closing the door on him and the crowd.

DeVries arrived later that afternoon, rested, clean, sober, and determined that this time Catharyna would listen to him. A mahogany box containing blue silk from the Orient was in his arms, a gift to present his suit. He found her inside the wind mill, watching the grinding of wheat, and reviewing the flour shipment that was being readied for the West Indies.

He interrupted by shouting, "When does she sail?"

Catharyna's eyes smiled as he drew near, and a rush of excitement was felt. This visit was different. It was not business that brought him here, but personal. He wanted to marry her.

For the first time she admitted to the infatuation with the handsome Dutch sea captain. No woman could avoid it. Unconsciously, she reached for a curl and tucked it into the straw hat. "Good day, Captain."

DeVries leaned closer and spoke softly into her ear, *"David."*

A blush tinted her cheeks, and eyes lowered. It suddenly became a sweet and torturous experience being in his presence. Her woman's heart soared only to plummet hard with the naked awareness of her physical shortcomings. No other man made her think such vain thoughts, yet DeVries' handsome face made her wish for the womanly charms he found at the Blue Dove.

She repeated, "David."

If possible, his face grew more handsome at the pleasure of hearing her speak his name. Catharyna's heart tightened with joy, and so many other emotions, that she blocked them out.

He took her elbow. "Come, let's enjoy the sunset together." There was no resistance as they walked to the cliff overlooking Turtle Bay.

DeVries confessed, "This is the first site I look for when I arrive in port knowing you are here." Then he gathered her in a warm embrace and took her lips in a kiss.

Their eyes clashed. Hers, protective and wary, and his, full of serious intentions. He whispered, "Don't pull away, Ryna."

But she did.

Mindlessly, Catharyna walked to the edge of the cliff, focusing on the sea gulls flying overhead. He approached from behind and whispered, "Your father is gone, there is nothing to separate us now."

The words penetrated the deep recesses of her heart.

He swore softly and added, "All these years, I have stood by, patiently waiting for this moment. Let's marry, Ryna." When her hands began to shake, DeVries tightened his hold on them. "Trust me."

Thoughts returned of the myriad of times she had heard those same words from her father and brother. She had trusted them and each had left her. There was no doubt DeVries would hurt her, just looking at him made her heart tighten. She wouldn't permit herself to love him, only to deal with his death, disappearance at sea or unfaithfulness at the Blue Dove. Each would be unbearable.

It was then she knew there would never be a time for her to be weak, to be a woman in love. She left his embrace and wrapped her arms protectively about herself. "I cannot think of marriage until Dirck is found, dead or alive."

DeVries snapped, "And I cannot wait for your selfish brother to return at his whim! I want to build our family now, our sons and daughters will fill Broeckwyck. This is what your father would want for us." His hands captured her face and kissed it again so that there was no doubt inside Catharyna with the truth of the words. Water gathered in her eyes. A lone tear slid down her cheek and erupted the dam of tears held since a child. The thought of children's laughter filling the silent rooms of the manor once again pierced her heart at its core. Tears spilled over her mother, father, brothers and every other loss.

DeVries cradled her. "Let me care for you, Ryna."

And just as instantly as the tears were shed, they dried up. Her mind crystallized. Whatever feelings DeVries brought from inside her were weak. Uncertainty, doubt and insecurities were intolerable emotions that guaranteed failure. No matter how much she craved him or children, this she would have no part in.

She faced him with the decision made. "I will not marry you."

The cold words spoken were so absolute that DeVries was ill prepared when she bolted in the direction of the manor. His shouts from across the field only hastened her steps.

Catharyna was determined never to speak of such things again.

Five

Winds blew fierce across the frigid waters of the Atlantic and merchant ship that carried thirty people and Ten Broeck's trading goods of furs, precious lumber, tobacco and flour in the direction of London.

The moist sea air hit Catharyna's face when she entered the deck for the first time in weeks. Her legs wobbled and eyes narrowed, trying to find land in the horizon. Instead, she saw Hawk, Fairfax and her cousin Maria's eldest brother, Gerrit van Hoesen, her companion and guard on the trip. Gerrit was two years younger than Catharyna, but was tall, strong, blonde and fearless. He was also ready for his first trip to Europe.

Thus far, the voyage had been calm, uneventful and mundane for the men. In Catharyna's view, it was a torture chamber. She lived her life on the island of Manhattan, traveled its bordering rivers daily, but she hadn't been on an ocean voyage since the age of two. Never did she anticipate the feelings it wrought from inside that refused to be silent.

Sleep was impossible. The fact that she was a speck in a vast body of water with no land within swimming distance, made her control-oriented mind snap. Every effort was made to appear unaffected and hide it from the men who smoked tobacco, shared survivor stories, and played cards and chess from morning till night. Their ability to shut out both mind and body to the forces of nature, kept her tongue silent.

She approached them with a weak smile.

"Evening, Ryna," Gerrit said, and drew deeply on an outrageously long smoking pipe.

There seemed to be no difference to morning or night since stepping foot on the ship. She croaked back, "How can you tell?"

"The pace of my smoking."

The men laughed and Catharyna simply nodded. It had been days since she entered the fresh air. Their laughter was greatly needed. From the deepest shadows within, she was tired of being lonely.

"Are you feeling well, Ten Broeck?" Fairfax asked.

"I'm fine," she grumbled.

"You look green," Hawk observed.

Her shoulders shrugged. "The sea brings out my beauty."

Hawk advised, "Just get rid of the hats, that should do it."

The men laughed in unison and she smirked. "At least I don't look ridiculous smoking a long pipe."

Gerrit looked insulted. "That's because women don't smoke."

She reached out and grabbed the long pipe that curled at its bottom and took several puffs. Each were blown into her cousin's face. "*Some* don't. I've smoked several pipes with Minichque, though his aren't ridiculous like yours."

Gerrit wouldn't let it go. "What is so ridiculous with it?" And he held it out for inspection. "I'm eager to visit the smoking houses in London to see what pipes they are using."

"Roll the damn tobacco and smoke it; why must you men create these five foot long pipes? To savor the experience? Ha, but that's not enough, you've gone and built bloody houses to smoke them in!" Tormented eyes gazed out at the ocean that surrounded her, and suffocation began to heat her face. "Such stupidity leaves me speechless."

Gerrit growled, "Ha! If we could only keep you speechless for a minute, I'd be an agreeable man!" Then, he said, much like a child debating their side, "And it is not five feet long!"

She shrugged. "The length is absurd no matter the

number."

He glared at her, but ignored the bait this time. "Tell me about Portobelo, Hawk. Did Morgan really put priests in...?"

Hawk interrupted, "Later. Fairfax, tell the captain the wind is changing."

Fairfax nodded and grabbed Gerrit's arm to follow.

Catharyna's face turned a greenish hue. "If our Captain doesn't know when the wind changes we're in bloody trouble."

"You curse too much."

"What are you, a Puritan?" she snapped and stomped away to the other end of the ship. It mattered little in which direction since water surrounded everything. There had never been a time when her mind was on the verge of shattering. Her hands clung to the rail and she wondered if it would keep her afloat.

"Don't try to control it."

She felt Hawk's presence directly behind her back, and took a deep breath. There was no intention to admit to the weakness to anyone, especially him.

"You've grown thin. Share dinner with me."

Eager to change the subject, she faced him and smiled. "I am hungry."

He led her below deck and grabbed a loaf of bread and a chunk of cheese. An arm reached inside a dark hole and withdrew a bottle of Madrid. "Fairfax's stash," he confided, and led them inside her cabin and kicked the door shut with a boot.

She stood at the door. "We can't eat in here."

The tiny room barely contained a narrow bed, desk and chair. There were only two cabins on the ship and the captain held the other one. Hawk slept in one large room with the rest of the men. "Unless you wish to share our wine, we stay here."

"You said it was Fairfax's."

"Sit."

This time she obeyed and sat on the edge of the bed. The desk was used as a table. He handed a chuck of bread to Catharyna, and she chewed into the hard thick crust. Cheese followed and two glasses of wine. Warmth began to spread in her body.

Hawk sprawled his long body out by leaning the chair against the wall and putting his feet on the bed. "I was fifteen on my first voyage across the ocean. To men I say it was adventure at its best."

"And to me?"

"I nearly went mad."

Catharyna swallowed more wine and relaxed. "How so?"

"Youth deceives us into believing we control our destiny. I actually thought I could swim to land with a piece of the ship wreckage if we met up with disaster."

A blush spread across her face. "And now?"

"I enjoy the ride."

Their eyes locked and she confessed, "I've faced many situations that most fear, but this...," failure was found in her voice, "this I cannot control, and makes me...desperate."

Hawk refilled her glass. "You need rest. I promise these thoughts will fade."

"Aye, the closer we reach London!" she chuckled and drained the glass that shook in her hand.

He drew forward and held her hands. "No, because you must let go to ever trust."

Catharyna looked away but mumbled, "I don't think I can."

His laugh contained confidence that reached out to her. "There is too much life in you to live it half measure." A finger stroked her cheek. "You and I squeeze life tightly, but there are moments we must let go and let it guide us by its will."

"And what do we receive for this mental torment?" she asked.

"To watch your life unfold in ways you never imagined."

The words reached deep inside her soul and a smile appeared. "If such is true, I would welcome it."

"If you seek adventure, there is no other way."

A yawn escaped and eyes grew heavy under the wine and Hawk's soothing words. Weeks of little sleep caught up. "I shall rest and think of this later."

Hawk ordered, "Just rest." And remained until it was obeyed.

Catharyna rose early, refreshed for the first time in weeks. There was no suffocation or feeling of being consumed by the powerful and unrelenting ocean. Instead, she joined the men for breakfast. "Good morning," she announced and sat down beside Gerrit. The platter of wheat cakes was taken, and half the pile was pushed on her plate.

Hawk grinned, but the rest of the men stared as though she were a ghost. Seeing their faces, she questioned the Captain, "Women are allowed to dine at this table?"

Unanimously, the men stumbled upon words of assurance that she was most welcome. A bright smile spread across thin cheeks while accepting a basket of hot scones from the Captain. "Thank you."

She took a large scoop of butter that became a thick layer on top of the scone, and ate it in an unladylike manner. Recognizing the poor manners, only due to the men's eyes still on her, she ordered, "Carry on, men. I've weeks of catching up to do."

The men nodded and began to speak freely, once again ignoring her.

Hawk stared at Catharyna's dress that hung on a much thinner frame, and handed her a cup of tea. "Join me in a game of chess."

Catharyna nodded in agreement, chewing on a wheat cake. It was time to get thinking again. Hawk guaranteed a worthy opponent to sharpen the mind.

Thus began a daily ritual between them and the chess board. Most games lasted until evening, one for three days. It was during the lulls in the game that they gathered information on each other.

Hawk questioned, "How did you get the trade name Ten

Broeck?"

"I found Minichque stuck in a trap, his foot badly mangled by the spikes. I was ten years old at the time. He was asking for my name and I misunderstood the word for age." She leaned closer and confided, "My language skills weren't so good at that time." Laughter followed. "Somehow my age and name were combined to Ten Broeck. My father allowed me to care for him at Broeckwyck. We taught each other our languages, and, when he healed, his father presented me with a bow and arrow. I was given the high privilege of accompanying his hunters one morning and pierced my first arrow into a buck."

Hawk's eyes held respect. "You cared for Minichque after Indians had killed your mother and baby brothers?"

"He was an injured boy." A shrug was followed by, "I gained a friend, a trade name, a new language and knowledge of the bow and arrow." Her eyes blazed at him when she added sarcastically, "Some men know the rules of trade, even as children."

"You think I'm frugal."

Her eyes looked up at the ceiling and an unladylike grunt answered.

A sensual smile spread on Hawk's face. "Perhaps I am waiting to surprise you?"

A groan was heard. "Why do you...?" she stopped in frustration and then resumed, "I find it impossible to keep to my subject when you shift it in all different directions."

Hawk's face appeared ignorant when he looked back at her.

She pushed on undeterred. "Trade is trade. Shall I educate you on its law again?" A lone brow rose on his forehead, and she added, "You never should have asked why I needed a letter from you. You should have been happy and eager to supply so *simple* a trade."

Hawk countered, "What if someone gives you something that there is no possible trade for?"

Her laughter answered back. "Impossible!"

"When I am presented with my son, what can I offer my wife for that?"

Catharyna's smile brightened. "You gave her your seed and she presents you the child. That's an even trade."

Hawk was speechless.

She mistook it for surrender and laughed. "Ha! You finally see I am right."

"No, I simply give up trying to change your mind," he replied, and rose to leave the game.

Catharyna followed him and barked, "Now wait here, Hawk. There is nothing wrong with my thinking!" A blast of cold air greeted her when stepping outside on deck. The icy wind went right through her bones. Stubbornly, she continued to follow Hawk who was found rolling tobacco intent to light it.

"You won't change my mind. Go below, it's too cold," he ordered.

"But it's fine for you to try to change mine?" she countered while turning her face away from the smoke that was intentionally blown into its path. "Well, I can be just as determined as you in my views. That doesn't make me wrong."

"No, that's who you are."

Catharyna's eyes narrowed and her teeth chattered, "That sounded insulting."

Hawk shrugged.

She was furious. "I am the best trader in our port for the very mind you now insult!"

Hawk threw the tobacco in the ocean and wrapped his arms around Catharyna. "What shall I trade you for a kiss?"

The taunting words unleashed a host of foreign emotions and thoughts. And they all told her she had failed once again under the mind of Hawk. Only this time the anger evaporated and a different woman emerged than the one who existed a moment ago. "Must you always win?"

He laughed and held out hands in defense. "You're changing the subject this..."

She silenced him with a kiss and soon was enfolded inside his long coat. The warmth of his body took the cold from her own. The rising beat of her heart blocked out all sound as it vibrated loudly in her ears. This time there was no thought to step away from him.

The kiss ended and another began. It seemed impossible to get close enough to the man. The cycle continued until Catharyna could stand no more. Questions filled her eyes when she drew away and met his. "I don't trade my affections," she whispered, "the kiss was given because I wished too." A hand rose in warning when she added, "And don't ask why."

Hawk leaned against the side of the rail and brought her against him. There was no protest when his arms tightened around her body. "So, now you prefer my silence?"

"Yes," she whispered, before kissing him again.

Weeks passed and, one morning, Catharyna awoke to find Gerrit sitting in the corner of her cabin. A sneeze erupted and was repeated again and again. In between, she said, "Morning."

"Your late night walks on deck developed a cold."

She shrugged and sat up in the bed. "What's wrong? Did you lose to Fairfax at cards again?"

Gerrit's long legs kicked the bed. "Wake up, Ryna! The whole ship is laughing at you."

"Laughing?"

"You're all over Hawk whose sniffing after Broeckwyck. For weeks I've been waiting to see where you were leading him with all the strolls on deck, but now I fear you've been taken in by him."

Fingers rummaged through a tangle of curls. She laughed, "I know what I'm doing."

Gerrit's eyes said otherwise.

"Hawk will never lay a finger on Broeckwyck. This I guarantee."

He visibly relaxed. "You know I trust you, Ryna."

"Yes," she replied, with eyes that pinned his.

"Very well, so I exaggerated about the men's laughter," he confessed, but then glared, "but Hawk wants you, that I know!"

"Me or Broeckwyck?"

Gerrit paused. "Ryna, you're no beauty, nor do you desire to be with such cheap gowns and hats. Even if you did improve such, your sharp tongue would never be tamed."

"This is true."

"But then again there isn't a man in Albany who hasn't asked my father for your hand while believing Dirck is returning for Broeckwyck. I suspect it's the adventure of taming you. It's difficult to say what Hawk wants."

"Interesting."

"Don't play games with me, Ryna! Tell me what you seek from Hawk so that I don't fumble it up for you."

"And how would you do that?"

"By keeping you under lock and key until we land in London."

She laughed.

"There's a key to this door and I'm here to protect you, however I see fit. Those were my father's orders."

"Relax, Gerrit," she replied and rose from the bed. "You enjoyed Joanna last summer, there is no difference in my enjoying Hawk now."

Gerrit rose hastily from the chair and it crashed to the floor. "Holy thunder! You play such a game as that with Hawk?"

"Chess is interesting for so long."

"Ryna! So help me, if you tease me like this for naught I shall..."

Her laughter halted his words.

He whispered dubiously, "You are teasing, are you not?"

Catharyna's hands held his face. "I am my father's daughter and will not fail him."

Gerrit hugged her tightly. "Then stay away from Hawk."

She pulled away. "Why should I?"

"Why? Even I like him! That man has a gilded tongue to bring you across the Atlantic to London. Have you not wondered what he seeks from your being here?"

"What does any man seek from a rich woman?"

Gerrit grew tense again. "There's no chance of marriage between you."

She thought of the past weeks in Hawk's arms and was no longer certain. "We shall see the true Hawk in London. There is where I shall find your answer."

"Answer? You mean it is possible?"

Catharyna smiled. "Anything is possible, Gerrit." And with that revelation, she opened the door. "I must dress now."

Gerrit's bewildered eyes clung to her until the door shut them out.

That afternoon she strolled the deck with Hawk and Gerrit's fears deep in her mind. Her cousin's every word had already been thought by herself. Even so, they prompted an overdue question yet to be answered.

Catharyna smiled warmly and asked in a voice of innocence, "Why did you leave your career as a seaman?"

Hawk wasn't fooled by either. Now he knew the full extent of her calculating mind, which was a worthy and crafty chess opponent. "My grandfather was a seaman, it was expected I would be too. I grew up and decided I prefer land."

Catharyna only saw the closed expression on his face. He was holding back information. "Was it difficult to walk away from?"

"Failure is always difficult to accept."

"You should never accept it," she swore passionately.

The statement made Hawk laugh and gather her against him for a kiss. The crew, Fairfax and Gerrit surrounded them. All the men ignored the couple's behavior that was now common place.

"Are you mocking me again?" she whispered.

Hawk's eyes roamed over her face, still unsure why time was increasing his appetite for it. "Let's just say I've found it's impossible to stick to one plan. If I am to charter my own life, I will obtain my goals any way possible."

She questioned, "Am I such a goal?"

The mask was lifted and a boyish smile appeared. "Definitely."

The air locked inside her chest at the impact of his smile. It was becoming clear that his past would not be shared, yet the future was open to her. The man knew exactly how to arouse her interest, and it was irresistible to ignore.

"What do you want from me?"

His eyes and words challenged her. "Everything you're capable of being."

The words startled her, breathing grew raspy. "Why should that matter to you?"

Hawk was honest. "I spliced your arrow. You know my intentions."

Catharyna's mind twirled over the clever change in conversation to marriage. Once again, Hawk had easily shifted the topic away from his past and placed her effectively into a corner to expose more of herself. An electric eel was easier to hold than a conversation with Hawk.

"I am uncertain if marriage is my intention," she replied. Wary eyes met his, unsure of what they would find. Her body tightened when a sensual smile spread across Hawk's rugged facial features. The impulse to reach out and kiss it overwhelmed the tight control on her normally obedient body.

And Hawk saw all of it. Catharyna's physical desires were learning their place each day, due to his expertise in guiding them there. "You've never given it any attention. Once you do, there will be no doubt, for then you will desire what our marriage will offer you."

Heat rolled over her skin, and blood rushed through her body, as images flashed quickly into an overly curious mind, now aroused by his words.

Their eyes held each other's in a timeless dance between man and woman until Catharyna nodded. It was all she could manage while inwardly fighting the clever web he was spinning around her instincts, trying to choke them out.

Every effort was made to focus on the fact that once again he had effectively avoided the topic of his past. There was no more information about the man than a few moments ago. Battered instincts warned it would be her greatest test in trusting him. And there was no doubt he was preparing her for it.

Catharyna's desires were tucked away by the knowledge that everything up to this point was in preparation for the game that would begin in London.

Six

The first sight of London was exhilarating. Land had been in sight for days yet it was the pulse of energy that reached out to Catharyna from the frenzied activity in port that brought waves of excitement again and again.

Never had she seen a port of such size. The smell of rotten fish, the sounds of men singing and cursing, and the sight of incoming goods from ports all over the world, piled up in mounds on the docks, left an imprint in her fast absorbing mind.

All too soon a carriage appeared and she was being escorted into it by Hawk, without being part of any of the action. The first minutes on London soil passed in a blur.

"Why do we rush? To be whisked away without so much as a word to the docking crew wasn't..."

Her cousin interrupted her with an odd look. "They're anxious to return home."

The coach dropped down suddenly into a large hole in the road and pitched Catharyna against the wall of the carriage. Hawk's arm reached out and gathered her tight against him. "We'll be there soon."

Now she saw the look of home sickness on Hawk's face and Fairfax's. "Where is home?" she asked, in complete ignorance of his life.

A smile beamed brightly in his eyes. "The outskirts of London."

Fairfax added, "Your mother will believe you a ghost for how long you've been away."

"That I bring back company from New York will soothe

her," Hawk said, with eyes fixed on Catharyna.

Fairfax's hands rubbed together. "It's been three years since I've held Emily."

"You're married?" Catharyna asked.

"Not yet," Fairfax grinned and added, "join me, Gerrit. You'll have more fun with the Fieldings than Hawk's family."

Hawk's face darkened but he remained silent.

Gerrit's eyes locked on his unruly cousin. "No, I must remain with Ryna."

Catharyna's eyes rolled and decided to switch the conversation on Hawk. "Tell us about your mother. Do you favor her in appearance or personality?"

Gerrit feigned horror. "Pray neither!"

Hawk's face turned into a scowl. "She's not like me at all."

Gerrit mumbled, "God is good."

"She's much more," Hawk whispered. It drew Catharyna's eyes to his face, which held a rare softness.

Fairfax groaned. "I'll have no part in your first visit home in ten years!" A hand wrapped loudly on the door to order the carriage to stop. "I'll be at the Fieldings if you need me." Fairfax appeared indecisive before departing, and softly asked Catharyna, "Am I presentable?"

She smiled at the man who rolled out of a bed of leaves in the wilderness looking handsome. "You'll do."

Fairfax still looked uncertain, but jumped out of the carriage. Hawk threw a bag at him. "Gerrit, last offer to join me."

Gerrit looked torn. "How old is her sister?"

"Old enough."

Gerrit left the carriage with satchel in hand. "I'll be with Fairfax for a few days and will catch up with you later."

Catharyna appeared crushed. "I shan't survive your absence, cousin."

"Watch your tongue around Hawk's mother! I'll just be a few days."

"She's fine with me," Hawk said, and slammed the door.

Gerrit went to reach for the carriage door, but was cut off by Fairfax. "Leave them be. Neither you nor I will ever control those two. Come on."

Gerrit knew full well the truth of Fairfax's words. Even so, he watched the carriage until it grew faint in the distance.

The carriage lurched back and then across, but this time Catharyna reached out for Hawk and didn't get tossed against the wall. Safe in his arms, they remained quiet the rest of the journey.

Hawk released her the moment the carriage entered a long driveway. An elegant mansion was found at the end and appeared two times larger than their Governor's mansion. The front door was immediately opened by a tall man in a red uniform with gold buttons that sparkled so brightly that Catharyna saw her face in each of them. She wondered what vain Englishman devised the idea.

The aged butler bowed respectfully to Hawk. "Sir Hawkins, welcome home!" Dampness was seen in his eyes when he rose. "We've missed you, Sir."

"It's good to be home, Thomas," Hawk replied, and hugged the family butler. He led Catharyna forward. "This is Miss van Broeck from our province of New York."

Thomas bowed. "Welcome to Twining Oaks."

She curtsied, "Thank you, Thomas." There was no anger or tightening in her body over the reference of New York being their province. What did startle Catharyna was an awakening sense that it may be possible to live in peace with the English rule. Hawk's word "our" made all different connotations race through her mind, and each were favorable, some exciting.

The butler opened the massive thick door and Catharyna whispered to Hawk, "*Sir* Hawkins?"

The question was ignored as expected.

Hawk escorted her inside to a silver blue room that was thirty feet in length and twenty-four feet high. Five sets of double doors were on the outside wall facing a spectacular view of London in the distance.

A petite woman sat on a long sofa holding out hands to Hawk. Meredith Hawkins began to rise, only to be scooped up into her youngest son's arms, and held tightly for several long minutes.

Catharyna strained to hear their whispered words to each other. She looked away when Hawk wiped tears from his mother's cheeks and hugged her again. Crossing the ocean together had not shown her this man.

"I've brought a friend from New York. This is Catharyna van Broeck whom I wrote you about."

Meredith's eyes roamed intently on Catharyna's every feature and stopped at the sight of the straw hat. She exchanged a look with Hawk, and a smile appeared. "Welcome to Twining Oaks, my dear. I am honored to have you as a guest." Then she bellowed, "Thomas!"

Instantly, the man in uniform reappeared.

"Please escort Miss van Broeck to her room. Ensure she is comfortable while I get reacquainted with my prodigal son," Meredith ordered with hands clasped tightly around Hawk's arm.

Neither gave Catharyna a second thought, which was just as well. She was practically propelled out of the room and led upstairs to a bedchamber by the butler. Amazement kept her feet and tongue frozen at the threshold of the doorway.

Thomas assumed it was exhaustion. "A bath and tea tray will be sent up shortly, Miss van Broeck. We dine at eight o'clock." He bowed and left her in a room that was larger than the kitchen at Broeckwyck.

"Eight o'clock!" was whispered in horror. That was bed time back home. Disbelieving eyes surveyed the room, trying to figure out what else they used it for other than to sleep. All different ideas took form, trying to come to terms with the wasted space. After several minutes of finding only items that belonged in a bedchamber, she gave up trying to understand why anyone would waste so much space just to sleep. Most of the colonists had a two room cottage. Broeckwyck was one of the largest manors in the colony and it had ten rooms.

No sooner had the butler left than a bath was being readied for her. Distractions ended in preparation for the first hot bath in months. Three chamber maids assisted her out of layers of woolen clothes and into the hot water. One washed her hair, the other her feet. Her eyes closed, no longer aware of what the third was doing. It was one English luxury she found complete agreement in. Clean and revived, her skin was pink all over when rising from the water. Wrapped in warm linens, the maids led her to a chaise in front of the fireplace. There was no argument when they reached out to deal with the tangled web of curls, beginning on her head and falling in a wave down her spine.

"Miss, which dress would you like to wear for dinner?"

Catharyna's eyes remained shut while mentally reviewing the contents of the travel trunk. There were two dresses and a nightgown in it. Everything else were goods to be traded.

"You decide," was mumbled. A wardrobe was never a high priority, especially when she was enjoying the warm fire and head massage. A mental note was made to hire Alice's daughter as personal maid. The English were completely forgiven for wasting space.

"We'll dress you in this."

A shrug of the shoulders was the only response, her focus was placed on getting toes closer to the flames of the fire. The ship had been cold and damp, it felt wonderful to feel warmth in her bones again.

When a hand commanded her to rise from the chaise, she obeyed, raising hands to allow the dress over head. Catharyna knew instantly something was wrong.

"This is not my dress."

"Lady Hawkins instructed us to dress you in one of these dresses." The plump maid stepped forward and continued with the dressing, roughly tying the laces until Catharyna's breath was temporarily taken from a cinched chest. The silence was taken for acceptance. Within moments the dress was fastened and her hair was piled on top.

Catharyna's tongue was held, since the maids were following instructions, although it was clear to all the women the dress was far too short. Her ankles were visible, and the plump maid grew frantic. All three maids began chattering to each other while Catharyna tried to keep pace with their foreign tongue and odd dialect. Hawk didn't speak like these women so concentration was needed to keep up with their speech.

The few words recognized were, "bony, boyish, and giant," and worry increased on their faces. Finally, she could take no more. With a hand in the air, she ordered them to be silent.

"This is *not* my gown. It is in the trunk over there." A hand pointed to the corner where the trunk was located. When none of the maids went to fetch a dress from it, she went herself. The truck contained no clothes, just her trading goods and hats. "Where are my clothes?"

The plump maid began to shake, but no words were spoken. Then a shaky hand pointed to the fireplace. Catharyna's eyes followed its direction, but saw nothing. Clearly, it was a communication problem. A confident smile appeared, knowing there was no better expert in dealing with them than herself.

She approached the women, pointed to the dress on her body, and repeated, "Where are *my* clothes?"

The plump woman stepped a few paces away and pointed again at the fireplace. This time Catharyna grew worried and looked at all three women's faces. "*My* clothes are in the *fireplace*?"

They all nodded in agreement. Catharyna wondered why would they burn her dresses, was it one of their customs, and if so, why hadn't Hawk warned her of it? It was clear no answers would be received from the fearful maids, and they had just given her a wonderful bath. The decision was made. "This dress will do."

They smiled brightly and curtsied several times before leaving the room. Catharyna looked down at her naked ankles, and frugal eyes closed shut. Now she would have to spend money on clothes in London. Such an expenditure had not been allotted for in the travel budget. The new contract with the English merchant Farnsworth was going to reap a much larger profit than her father's previous one. The money was there, which soothed her thrifty nature, a bit.

A knock at the door and a voice requested admission. Catharyna opened it, and the sight was breathtaking. A tray of hot tea with sweet cakes stood at the entrance; and, it appeared to be all for her. As if in a dream, she sat down on the chaise beside the roaring fire and enjoyed each sweet morsel and sip of the hot brew. The burned dresses were forgotten as another English custom captured her full attention. Another mental note was made.

Hours passed until another knock was heard on the door. Catharyna's long body stretched to awaken the lethargic limbs back to life. The forgotten book of Greek mythology landed on her toes. A yawn escaped as she hurried to the door, eager to find what the next treat would be.

This time it was a clean shaven Hawk. There was something new about him as well. Practical cotton clothes were replaced with silk and jacquard. The richness of the materials instantly caught her merchant's eye. Seconds later his warm stare was felt on her visible ankles.

"This won't do, Ten Broeck."

She looked up at him like a simpleton. "They're covered with stockings."

"What happened to your dresses?"

She shrugged, "A communication problem with the maids."

He looked at her oddly. "What?"

"They burned them."

Hawk's eyes narrowed on the travel trunk. Seconds later, hands were searching its contents. "Unbelievable!" he growled, and her supply of straw hats were held up for inspection.

Within a blink of an eye, Catharyna watched them being tossed into the flames of the fire. A shriek followed, and then she grabbed an iron poker to retrieve them, but only charred remnants remained. Her eyes rose with the fire poker in fury at Hawk. "What sort of fetish do you English have on burning personal property?"

"I ordered the hats burned not the dresses."

"You *what*?"

"I gave you more than enough warnings. The hats were hideous." He pushed aside the fire poker and began to survey the room. "There must be something we can use to cover your ankles up." He opened an armoire and began shifting through its contents. A linen sheet was inspected that contained an embroidered hem. It was soon held against her length, and then handed to her. "Here."

Catharyna stared blankly at him. "What am I to do with a sheet?"

He began to loosen the back ties of her gown. "Lift up your dress above your waist and wrap this around it. Then I'll fasten your dress to keep it in place." She didn't budge. "*Now*, Ten Broeck."

She turned around and followed his order. "You can fasten me now."

He whispered into her ear, "Hold your breath." And instantly her waist was pulled in several inches. When the pent up air was released, her waist remained tightly cinched. He turned her about with lingering hands, and eyes glowed with approval over her face and fashionable coiffure. "You look beautiful."

Memories of horse eaten and burned hats were forgotten. "Ha, but you don't like my ankles."

"I like them too much," he confessed, with eyes that said much more.

A steady strong rhythm took hold of her heart that pounded loudly up to her ears. "I'll not fault you for it."

He grinned. "Did you enjoy your tea?"

"It was," she paused searching for the right word, "heaven."

"Careful, it's an English custom."

A slim brow rose and a crooked smile appeared. "I see much wastefulness here, but some of your customs have merit."

Large warm hands encircled her waist. Hawk's lips hovered above her own when he replied, "There are other more pleasurable ones." The kiss was expected, but more irresistible than the one shared just that morning. "Welcome to England," Hawk whispered.

"It's not as cold as I imagined," she confessed against his lips.

"There are more customs we share. I shall warm you to each of them, Ten Broeck."

The words caused a familiar surge of adrenaline to race over her body. On the ship, she had convinced herself that he had served as an enjoyable distraction. A growing acceptance was building that no excitement equaled the impact of having Hawk in her presence and challenging her mind.

"Don't call me Ten Broeck."

The order said much more to him. His lips teased her own and whispered, "Ryna."

"Yes," she confirmed.

A knock on the door disentangled them from each other. Thomas whispered inside a narrow crack in the door, "Your relatives and friends are waiting below."

"We're coming," Hawk said, and closed the door. Their eyes met, Catharyna's in excitement, and Hawk's uncertainty. Thus far he had controlled all of their encounters. The moment he stepped out of the room they would be part of an unchartered ocean.

Even so, he opened the door, ready to face the uncertainty. They walked together down the staircase into the foyer just as a man was entering. He was tall and looked like Hawk, but a sophisticated, older version.

"Welcome home, brother."

"Charles," Hawk replied, and they embraced. "I was sorry to learn of Jane's death."

Charles stared blankly upon hearing his dead wife's name. Meredith Hawkins entered the room and kissed her eldest son. "Good evening, Charles. William, come, let's introduce your friends to Catharyna."

Charles turned toward Catharyna, finally seeing her, and bowed gallantly. "Welcome to London, Miss van Broeck. I am eager to see if the rumors of your courage are true or exaggeration."

Catharyna curtsied in turn and raised sparkling eyes at him. "Sir, I am a Dutchwoman in England, need there be any more proof of my fearlessness?"

Charles smiled, but his eyes narrowed while offering an arm in escort to her. She looked undecided at Hawk before accepting the invitation, and entered the silver blue room that had grown in size.

The room beside it was now open, allowing the fifty or more people inside of it to roam about. It became clear why Hawk hid her ankles. She was on display and scrutinized by everyone in the room. They were all interested in stories about the savage Indians that killed white colonists for sport. At each introduction, she found herself repeating the same words, "The Mohicans are friendly people now and live in peace with us."

Charles had taken over Hawk's role seamlessly. He introduced her to family while whispering important facts about them in her ear.

"This portly family is from my mother's side of the *Seldom Satisfied* branch, Uncle Francis in the corner is *The Savings Bank* for his stingy nature, cousin Paul is *Early Spoiled* and my Aunt Gertrude is *The Vulture*."

His eyes sparkled with merriment. "There, now you know all our family secrets."

Catharyna laughed softly. "What is *your* secret, Lord Hawkins?"

He drew closer and raised a brow. "'Tis obvious, you know my brother and now me. We are from the branch of *Bad Manners*."

Catharyna lifted a hand to cover the laughter that threatened to erupt. After a valiant fight, she whispered, "You've a gilded tongue, my lord."

His eyes lowered to her lips causing her to lick them. "Only with a beautiful woman."

There was something about Charles that made Catharyna believe he meant every word. That his eyes reflected it made their impact that much stronger.

Lady Hawkins signaled dinner was ready, and they joined the crowd inside. Hawk was seated beside his mother, but his eyes remained on his brother and Catharyna all evening, who were only interested in conversing with each other. He began to rethink the decision that burned her hats and brought her to London.

Seven

Frivolous activities soon became of utmost importance. London's pageantry lured Catharyna, but nothing more than the theater. She was anxious to attend her first play. Meredith had provided her all of Shakespeare's works to read, accompanied with the invitation to take her to see them performed at the King's Theater.

Now there was no ignoring the dressmaker. Endless fittings were essential with no appropriate wardrobe to go out in public. The chore was quickly detested by the amount of time it took to stand still for hours, all for dresses that would be of no use at Broeckwyck.

Gerrit sat idle in the corner, being fawned by pretty and voluptuous seamstresses. After a fortnight of fittings had passed, Catharyna began to suspect the delay in her wardrobe may be due to the seamstresses' infatuation with her tall, handsome cousin. Huffs, grumbles and unladylike grunts would rise from her mouth, yet none were recognized by the women.

Gerrit tried his best to soothe her irritable outbursts. "Ryna, such things must be endured if you wish to be seen in public."

Their eyes clashed. "'It's clear the dresses are required, but not so much of the *fittings*."

The seamstresses all began to flutter around her in anxiety. Gerrit countered, "It's your mammoth height that

96

demands greater work. The ladies are doing a splendid job."

Two more circled around him. Catharyna's eyes closed shut. She growled to the room in general, "Will one be ready this evening? I am going to the King's Theater with Lady Hawkins to see *Hamlet.*"

"Yes, my lady, we'll have the sapphire gown sent to Twining Oaks before tea time."

The words calmed Catharyna, who now stood patiently until they were done. No sounds rose from her throat, even when giggles were heard from Gerrit's private corner.

Hours later, she entered the King's Theater with Meredith and Hawk, who was immediately swallowed up by a group of friends that led him away. Catharyna's eyes narrowed, being deserted once again by him. Ever since their arrival, she had been stranded at Twining Oaks with Meredith, waiting for dresses that required endless fittings, with little results. London thus far had proved to be a suffocating experience of cabin fever. Blizzards in the New York winters had never been so isolating.

Meredith met the familiar, frustrated stare of Catharyna, and ignored it. She said brightly, "'It's wonderful having William home, so many have missed him."

Catharyna surveyed the crowd, only seeing a dark haired woman clutching Hawk's arm. The exchanged looks and body language between the woman and Hawk assured Catharyna they were close friends. A sharp pain slivered through her chest, but it was ignored as she followed Meredith meekly to their seats. Impatience began to rise as she waited for Hawk to join them, except it was Charles who took the empty seat beside her.

"Good evening, ladies." He whispered into Catharyna's ear, "You look beautiful this evening."

She mumbled something proper while jealous eyes scanned the theater. Hawk was found seated beside the same dark beauty. The candles flickered, signaling the play was beginning. When the trumpet blasted, Catharyna's face and hands tightened. Her first play would not be ruined by Hawk's desertion. Interest in the couple waned under Shakespeare's words and Hamlet's dilemma.

The play soon took on a cold and chilling reality. Catharyna understood Hamlet, a man suffering over the death of a great man and father, and grappling with the difficulty in knowing the truth about other people in his life.

She became transfixed on the characters, determined to see their guilt or innocence, their motivations, their feelings, which were cleverly hidden from Hamlet. She was certain, if she tried hard enough, the truth would be exposed. She had been trained to know people's motives and anticipate their next move. This had made her a successful trader.

And yet, Hamlet challenged all she knew, demanding she consider a startling concept. The world is one of appearances not the truth behind them. Being raised in an untamed province did not prepare her for this. In New York, every man and woman knew the code of the land was self survival. But, here in civilized London, a chill went up her spine when she realized deceit, manipulation, and court drama barely scratched the surface of the evils behind the smooth and polite faces that graced the theater.

Suddenly, she felt the fool.

The play ended far too quickly for Catharyna, who now had to face the drama of life. Unknown emotions left her overwhelmed, and they refused to be reined in. Hamlet's quest for answers had released a tidal wave inside herself, and it began to crash around the mysterious and elusive William Hawkins.

There was little time to rise from her chair before Charles began discussing his reactions to the play. And no matter how hard she tried, her eyes wavered across the expanse of the theater to find Hawk standing, once again, in the middle of a crowd of men and women that now grew in size.

An ache tugged at her heart, which she promptly ignored, thanks to Charles, who began introducing a crowd of men who were impatient to meet her. They spoke respectfully, yet all continued to push closer to get a better look at her.

Catharyna began to feel like a freak of nature that Englishmen enjoyed gawking at behind a piece of glass.

Many of them whispered, "She's the one Hawk brought back."

When the crowd dissipated, she questioned Charles, "Is the men's interest in me solely because I arrived with Hawk?"

Charles replied, "My brother is a living legend. There's always a crowd interested in his activities."

Finally, someone was sharing something about Hawk without him present. Catharyna drew closer to ask, "Living legend? How so?"

Charles' eyes grew guarded. "Will hasn't shared his past with you?"

"He mentioned a sea career."

Charles smiled, but envy was in his eyes. "He would make light of it," he mumbled and then straightened. "You must ask Will to share it with you. I'll not steal his thunder."

Catharyna probed deeper. "It sounds exciting."

He laughed, and then explained, "There is no other way for my brother to live."

They were interrupted by Meredith before Catharyna could gain more information. "Come, Catharyna, it's time we return home."

"Hawk mentioned introducing me to a few gentlemen," Catharyna countered, in a smooth lie. This was the first evening out since the maids burned her dresses. There was no intention of returning to Twining Oaks. Merchants were here with their wives and she planned to be introduced to them.

Meredith's slender fingers tightened on Catharyna's arm. "Will is going to a late dinner with friends. You shall meet these gentlemen another day."

After weeks in the charming woman's presence, it was becoming clear to Catharyna that Hawk's mother had another woman in mind for her son. A woman who lived in England. The pleasure in attending her first play had disintegrated into a dismal nightmare.

Charles, on the other hand, beamed while he bowed

gallantly. "It was my pleasure to share your first play. I look forward to many more such evenings."

She mumbled, "Thank you, Charles." And quickly took off in frustration toward the coach, with Meredith a step behind. It was incomprehensible to Catharyna that Hawk had ignored her the entire evening. Thoughts returned to the hairy beast who kept her in silence and refused to trade with her many months ago. That Hawk hadn't caused a whirlwind of emotions to rage. That Hawk she could ignore. In London, Hawk, Meredith, Charles, and the ever growing crowd, shut her out.

The obstacle before her was that there were few moments of seeing the real Hawk, if those were to be believed at all. She thought about it while waiting in the cold winter night, with Meredith silent beside her. As the coach approached, the thought emerged that just perhaps Hawk wasn't sure who the real William Hawkins was himself.

The arrival of the man was felt before she saw him. Meredith blocked her son from entering the coach. "You are attending Lady Wellington's dinner this evening."

Hawk grumbled, "I've done my share of parties to last another ten years."

Meredith nodded regrettably and extended a hand to be escorted into the coach, and Catharyna followed. He sat beside his mother, but his eyes bore down on Catharyna, who deliberately turned away to stare into the dark shadows.

"How was your first play?" Hawk asked.

There was nothing good to say about it. With Meredith in the carriage, there was also no other alternative but to rein in her tongue from speaking truthfully. "Memorable."

Hawk chuckled, and it drew her eyes to him. "You look beautiful this evening." Their eyes battled across the span of the carriage. He saw her anger at being abandoned in favor of the crowd that had consumed most of his time in London. Regret was heavy in his voice when he added, "Such a gown is worth all the fittings at Madame Coutiere's the past fortnight."

"Bah!" Catharyna whispered against the wall of the carriage, with hands tight in frustration. Never had she witnessed such procrastination. She could have harvested Broeckwyck's vast fields of wheat sooner than it took London's seamstresses to finish one gown. Disguising her true feelings, she faced Meredith and replied smoothly, "I've never experienced such perfectionism."

Meredith beamed. "I am delighted you are pleased."

Hawk coughed to disguise his laughter.

Meredith continued, "Tell me your reactions to *Hamlet*?"

Catharyna didn't know where to begin. "I did not anticipate such passion in the dialogue."

Meredith laughed like a young girl, completely enthralled in the topic of her favorite play. "What of Ophelia? Do you believe she committed suicide or died by accidental drowning?"

Hawk grumbled, "Neither, boredom killed the woman."

"Boredom?" Meredith asked incredulously.

"Who could bear such an indecisive man as Hamlet?"

Catharyna's eyes narrowed. "How so?"

Hawk boasted, "I would have killed Claudius before my father's dead body turned cold. And, if not then, certainly before he touched my mother in marriage. Guilt surrounded the man."

Meredith chuckled, and looped her arms around Hawk's one arm. "But, was Gertrude protecting her son by marrying her brother-in-law? And..."

"Enough questions, Mother. You know my views well enough on Hamlet," Hawk snorted.

Catharyna whispered, "I am interested in hearing them."

Their eyes clashed in the darkness of the carriage. Hawk sensed the storm brewing in her, and it made him cautious. There was no intention to have an argument in front of his mother. "I've no interest in plays nor skill at debating their meanings."

Catharyna's face tightened, well accustomed to receiving no answers from Hawk.

Meredith looked disappointed, but did not voice it.

When they arrived at Twining Oaks moments later, Meredith bid goodnight and retired upstairs.

Hawk took Catharyna's arm to halt her from following. "There is something I must show you."

"It's late," she replied and began to head upstairs.

His hand would not release her, and soon she was being led through the parlor to the outside terrace that overlooked London.

Hawk's eyes challenged her when he said, "I thought you would enjoy the view."

She remained stiff and unyielding beside him. With disinterested eyes, she surveyed the night view of London. "Amsterdam is bigger," she mumbled.

Hawk laughed and pulled her against him. "You've never seen it to know any better." She began to protest, but he added, "New York will be one day."

Catharyna grew still. Every instinct was telling her what Hawk was sharing meant something important to him. But, *Hamlet* was fresh in her mind. The cunning of Englishmen had swindled her homeland and taken her property rights. Now, after weeks of being ignored, Hawk was spending time with her, speaking about New York. There was no doubt she was being led into the fox's den again by the clever Englishman's tongue.

And, she was determined to play along. "Our small seaport town? Why, we can barely lure any settlers to come. It will take hundreds of years to reach London's size, a thousand for Amsterdam." Disbelieving eyes roamed over his face and found determination everywhere. She could not prevent the genuine question, "Are you serious?"

"If I didn't believe it, I wouldn't have stayed seven years in a province that hated my English hide, or accepted land instead of money from the Duke." His eyes pierced hers when he asked, "Will you remain or return to Holland?"

Her throat tightened, thoughts blurred with the direction of the conversation and his hands upon her own. Her taunt of returning to Holland to marry under Dutch law was recalled.

Only now, she knew it was impossible. She could never be a traitor to her homeland. "It's my home, where I belong."

Hawk smiled and his fingers began to link with hers. "I never knew what home felt like until I stepped on Manhattan." A dark and haunted voice from deep inside him revealed, "I searched many ports, but know it is home for me."

Finally, the man was revealing aspects of himself. Catharyna jumped at it. "Why?"

"Thousands of men have left their mark here, long before me. New York beckons me to leave mine."

Catharyna's skepticism began to waver, her hands tightened on his. "What do you see to believe it is so?"

Hawk released his vision. "That it will be the greatest port in the New World, one that will affect all others."

The only man who spoke with the same passion about her homeland had been her father. That Hawk shared it with Cornelius made her traitorous heart soar. The realistic Ryna questioned pointedly, "Not Philadelphia or Boston? They are larger, many find greater opportunities there."

"They lack the lure...," his words trailed off until moments passed and he confessed, "I feel boundless, yet captured, at the same time. Only there does the earth tremble beneath my feet." His eyes pierced hers with their honesty and passion. "Tell me you feel it."

Hawk had just captured her feelings for her homeland in a few words, and it had a startling affect on her. She began to believe in the man, she had not misread him, there was an honest connection between them. He shared her passion in the land.

Her voice was deep, throat tight, when she answered breathlessly, "I do."

They smiled at each other unlike any other time in their lives. At that moment a bond was formed between them that no one would ever relate to. Catharyna knew it was his intention, and that only made her heart race faster. Things were getting serious with the ease of a breath.

"Marry me," he ordered.

Air became blocked in Catharyna's lungs. Something burned against her chest and she reached out to feel her mother's locket. Cornelius had sent Hawk to her. He had seen something inside Hawk that led him to believe an Iroquois peace treaty could be arranged by him. Her father had approved of him.

The few moments where she saw the real Hawk made her reach deep inside herself, the same way her father had. There were no thoughts or feelings of weakness beside him. Never had a man made her feel so vital and alive.

And yet, weeks of being ignored would not be any longer. She replied, "I believe in your vision for our province, such passion and words are unique by their honesty." A hand was raised to halt Hawk from getting closer. "But, you avoid all discussion of your past, ignore me for weeks in favor of the crowd that follows you, and tonight you deserted me at the first event I attended in London. Why should I consider marriage to such a man?"

The man who was rarely challenged, by man or woman, stood in silence. Tense seconds passed until Hawk scooped her into his arms, and carried her into the parlor where he dumped her on a settee.

Catharyna watched him march to the doors and lock them shut. "What are you doing?" she whispered into the darkness.

"Helping you consider it," he confessed in a cold and calculated voice.

Darkness surrounded them but sight wasn't needed to see Hawk's intentions. The sound of his boots approaching, and a chair being kicked across the room, made Catharyna reach for her knife that lay hidden under her gown.

"Don't *you* consider it," she countered and faced him eye to eye.

"Put the knife down, Ryna."

"I will, once you explain the madness that now shakes you."

Hawk stood silent, unable to answer her. His past was

all around him in London thanks to the crowds that followed him. There was no shame or guilt, just uncertainty of Catharyna's reception of it. Gerrit had cooperated by keeping her occupied at the seamstresses, but even that had been an outrageous deception. There was no longer the luxury to wait for her trust. He wanted no more part in the game.

His continued silence made Catharyna add, "I am doing my best in this foreign land of yours, but I'll not be made a fool by a gilded tongue that leads me one way and goes another. Nor shall I be victim to a crowd that shuts you out from me. Such games I will not endure."

Impatience filled Hawk's voice. "There is a mutual attraction between us. You need an heir and I seek a wife. Put the knife down, and we shall end our search."

Catharyna backed away with the knife poised to strike. "I need *nothing*," she whispered in anger.

Hawk's own anger began to rise. "You need a husband." He drew closer until the tip of her knife was touching his chest. "You'll not allow your father's blood to die with you."

Catharyna's hand trembled under the anger his words aroused in her. She struggled to know Hawk, and yet, he knew the core of her being. But, never again would she be trapped under his manipulation of her situation. It made every survival instinct surge to the surface. "You are right in that, but my husband will have one foot in the grave. A few days is all I require to gain my heir. You, *Sir William Hawkins*, are far to healthy."

Hawk reached out to grab the knife, but she slipped past him to hide in the shadows of the room. His eyes narrowed to find her and his feet approached softly until the tip of her knife grazed his neck. "Shall I fetch one of the prisoners from London Tower to oblige you?"

"Go ahead, I'll know his crimes," she snapped, amazed at his bold taunt, "and he won't plague me with lies about introducing me to London's greatest merchants, nor will he lock me up with his *mother*!"

"Tread carefully, Ryna," Hawk warned.

"Tread carefully?" Catharyna repeated in disbelief. "That is all I do, for I know nothing of your past. You speak convincingly, your words of New York..." her voice tightened with emotion, "I believe are true...but, I have no confidence in anything you say, when all I feel is you hiding your true self from me."

Hawk's hand reached out and grabbed the knife. It was thrown across the room and Catharyna was crushed against his chest. "I shouldn't have taken you to that bloody play."

His ability to wipe out all her feelings with a few words brought an instant attack. Catharyna's nails raked across his neck and face, her knee jabbed into his belly, momentarily, taking the breath from him.

She struck back, "You don't control me!" And then raced to the other side of the settee to use as a buffer between them. "I've an acceptable gown and will not be kept indoors another day. I shall meet these merchants myself, and enjoy any play I wish." She backed away when Hawk began approaching. "You'll not dictate my actions ever again."

Her squeak bounced off the walls of the room when Hawk pounced on Catharyna and they both landed on the floor. She struggled to get air into her lungs and heard a distant tearing sound. When her eyes opened, disbelief met the sight of her gown, which was now shredded in two. "For weeks I stood for fittings..." she groaned.

"*I* shall take you to meet the merchants, and *I* shall accompany you to the theater. A dress won't change that!" he swore.

"This is why I held a knife to you. I can't trust you," she said to herself more than to Hawk.

His eyes swept over the tattered remnants of undergarments, which left much of her exposed to his eye. "You've insulted me enough, by accusations, and that bloody knife!" A finger traced her lips, and his next words pierced her heart, "Do you believe I would force you to my side?"

In amazement, she asked, "You locked me in a room, ready to *convince* me. Then, you shredded my new gown. What am I to believe? That your wooing skills were honed along the Barbary Coast?"

The mention of the famous pirate-infested waters tightened Hawk's face. "You will apologize to me for that insult."

Catharyna tried to break free of his arms, but they effectively pinned her to the floor boards. "Very well, I apologize. Your wooing skills are sorely inept."

"Ryna..." he warned, before adding, "and what of insulting yourself?"

"Myself?" she whispered, dumbfounded.

"And your father," he added, "and heritage, Broeckwyck..."

Catharyna tried to buck him off and finally roared, "What game is this? I'd rather die than insult my father!"

"You would allow the blood of Cornelius to mingle with any man's to provide you an heir?"

They stared at each other in silence. The heat of shame rose to Catharyna's face, but her character rose above it. "I was angry."

"Could you allow anyone to fill your womb for an heir?"

She squirmed beneath him. "I didn't...mean...it wasn't...you were going to force me!"

Hawk's face tightened, as if it had been slapped. "Do you believe that?"

The man did not give one inch, and it made her respect him, even though it was painful to her own pride. Catharyna growled in frustration, "No."

Hawk's hands relaxed on hers, and then, once again, the unimaginable happened. His eyes lowered on her chest, spreading a wave of heat into every traitorous corner of her body. Her voice wobbled, "Stop it." But his eyes only grew bolder. A frantic pulse began at the base of her neck and made her ears beat loudly.

His lips lowered to hover over her own. "You shall yield to me, as I to you," he predicted, and kissed her softly. His hand reached inside the torn dress and rested on her stomach. "We shall become one here."

Tears formed in her eyes. Words of love would have made her run, but Hawk's words were irresistible. Her voice was tortured when she whispered, "Forgive my words, Will."

"Marry me," he replied with head bent, kissing her neck in a downward direction.

A moan escaped her lips. "I want to," she finally confessed to herself and him, and their lips met.

Hawk's finger traced the opening of the ripped gown along her chest. "I am sorry about your gown."

The scent of his skin drew her closer. There had never been a man who made everything melt away with one touch. The foreign feelings held her spellbound under his hands that made her skin reach out for more. A moan escaped her throat when their lips met.

"Promise me..." she breathed against his lips, "no more crowds."

"Marry me."

Her eyes sparkled, a smile spread. There was great pleasure in the mental jouncing she shared with Hawk. "I've not heard your agreement?"

His head lowered to her chest, warm breath grazed her exposed skin. The subtleness of the gesture was far more powerful than if he had stripped her bare. When his face rested on her belly, a powerful reminder of what he promised for them both, every wall crumbled inside her. There was no more resistance when she boldly met his possessive stare.

"I promise," Hawk swore, "no more crowds."

Catharyna's body jolted when his hands finally reached inside her dress and touched her skin.

"Will, I..." she stammered.

His head rose, and a boyish smile appeared. A voice stripped of all machinations and deceit asked, "You'll marry me?"

There was such happiness in it, and Catharyna's smile matched his. "I want to."

His finger traced her lips. "Want is good."

Catharyna groaned, "You're evil to do this to me." With every ounce of strength, she pushed him away. There was too much responsibility on her shoulders for body cravings to block out. Everything her parents had worked and died for was now under her supervision. Risks were taken every day, but never would promises or vows be sacrificed for fleshly pleasures.

"Let us end this by seeing a solicitor, then we will know if a marriage between us is possible," she added while rising from the floor on wobbly feet, that were more rubber than bone. Her hand reached out to pull away a wave of long curls in order to search for her knife. It was found in the wall and she yanked the blade free. There was no shame when she approached Hawk half naked. A leg was lifted on the settee and her gown was raised to tie the knife to her thigh once again.

Hawk watched all her actions with possessiveness. His hand reached out and grabbed her exposed thigh. There was no struggle from her when their eyes clashed. "I never wanted marriage until you," he confessed, as a hand traveled farther up her thigh daring her to stop it. "If the law makes it impossible, than God will join us without it."

Thoughts of deceit, machinations, and manipulations, which had weighed heavily on her mind, were lifted away by the relief of Hawk's words. She still had no more information on his past, but no longer cared. The future was all that mattered.

Raised in a province that mocked man's law, Catharyna replied in excitement, "God alone I fear."

His hand reached out to touch her lips. "Then we shall be one soon," he swore with a dazzling smile.

She bent to kiss him and repeated, "Soon."

Eight

Winds from the north blew fierce as snow fell from dark gray skies in large flakes, gathering speed and height. A message arrived at dawn stating the Duke's barrister was expected if the storm didn't prevent it.

Catharyna was in the library reading Margaret Cavendish's philosophical work, *Grounds of Natural Philosophy,* when Hawk entered the room.

Their eyes met when she stated, "Now I understand why Englishmen fear women and feel compelled to create laws to rein them in. Your country is brimming with intelligent English*women.*"

Hawk's brow rose over the insult and then read the title of the book in her hand. "Ah, Lady Cavendish, a kindred spirit of yours."

Catharyna found laughter in his eyes and quickly closed the book. "Don't you find it reasonable to conclude that a woman could be the intellectual equal of a man?"

"Aye, brutally so," he answered while rubbing the lump on his forehead, one of many remains of their midnight compromise.

He joined her on the settee and threw the book on the floor. Within the span of a breath, she was placed on his lap and warmly kissed. Her hands held him off and she whispered, "Must a woman disguise herself as a man for Englishmen to listen to her opinions and ideas with equal respect?"

Hawk's eyes narrowed on the vibrant woman who twisted restlessly on his lap, full of passion and energy for life, waiting for his answer. He was beginning to accept there would never be a dull moment with her. "Ha, Shakespeare haunts me once again," he whispered.

Catharyna looked confused.

"You read all the plays," Hawk added.

"Yes, but I don't see how...?"

"You're speaking about Rosaline and Portia, his female characters who dressed as men due to being limited as women."

Catharyna grinned, "I...yes."

Hawk's finger traced her lips. "What you wear will have no affect on my listening to you, Ryna. The results of your actions will always impress me more. Dress in my clothes if they please you, or none at all, which would please me, but neither matters for I shall still only see you."

Catharyna grew still and asked, "And who is that?"

"A woman who challenges everything I know."

Her arms wrapped around his neck. "You are not a typical Englishman."

The relief in her voice made Hawk smile. "Now you are beginning to see me."

There was no warning when a surge of longing escaped the tight confines of Catharyna's heart. Her eyes looked at Hawk in an entirely different way, and there was no thought to restrain her desire to trust him.

She kissed him to the sound of hair pins landing on the sofa and floor. Her hair tumbled free but Hawk's lips demanded full attention. She broke for air and whispered, "Tomorrow I shall dress in your clothes and meet the merchants."

"My mother would never forgive me, Ryna."

She pulled away and groaned, "But I can't stay shut up here waiting for a blasted grown! I've yet to learn the names of the covetous cowards who are petitioning the Duke to take Broeckwyck from me."

Hawk replied seamlessly, "Our marriage will end their attempts."

"I still wish to know them, Will. Such greed and deceit I'll not abide. To think there are men who would dare to swindle my property..."

His kiss silenced her heated words. "Trust me, no man

will take Broeckwyck from you."

Their eyes locked until Catharyna grinned. "I just want to punish one of them," her eyes brightened and she nodded, "as an example."

"There is no need," he replied, "no one will get past me to harm you."

Catharyna held her tongue. If the topic was pursued, she would insult Hawk. That lesson was effectively learned the night before, and would not be repeated.

Hawk's eyes closed as his head leaned back. "I've been behind closed doors with an architect for our manor. I never realized it would be so complicated."

The word *our* made guilt rise inside her. There was still no intention to allow him any of Broeckwyck, even though her eyes roamed over his strong face and felt it could be trusted. "You haven't spoken of this estate with me. Where is it?"

Hawk's eyes opened and a smile of accomplishment spread. "A hundred miles north of the mouth of the Hudson River on the east and west banks."

Excitement filled her voice. "That's the heart of the Hudson River. Have you named it yet?"

His face and tone were serious when speaking the Algonkin name. "*Onteora.*"

Catharyna's eyes narrowed over the translation. "Land in the sky," she whispered in confusion and confessed, "I don't understand?"

Hawk's eyes sparkled down at her. "There are two meanings, the public or personal." His eyes and voice dared, "Which would you prefer to hear?"

Certainty grew in her decision to marry Hawk. The man made simple things adventurous. A wicked grin appeared. "Personal."

At that moment, Hawk knew he had gained her trust. There would be no more fanfare or games, just the truth. "I named it after you."

Her confusion stared back at him.

His eyes sparkled when he explained, "Your friendship

has given me Onteora, my land, which I see every time I look into your sky eyes. That is the true meaning." And then he kissed her, leaving no doubt to its truth.

Catharyna's chest heaved under the power of his words. "And the other?"

The confidence of a man accustomed to getting all he desired was stamped on Hawk's face. "I tell London's greediest merchants that it is an Indian prophecy of New York's future greatness. Its destiny will have the wealth from its land sprout buildings that will span the skies higher than a human can imagine. London's rebuilding of today, after the Great Fire, is a shadow of what New York will be.'"

She was transfixed by his words and passion in the land she too loved, but replied with honesty, "There is no such prophecy."

His smile was reckless, bold and boyishly confident. "*We* know that, but it's a bloody good story!" He laughed openly and his arms tightened on Catharyna. "If we give New York a good foundation, it will happen. We need those merchants to buy into the story to make it true."

She nodded, completely in agreement with him, eager to be a part of it. There was great anticipation in her voice when asking, "When will you introduce me to these merchants you keep promising to me?"

"I'll not share you with them until we are wed." There was no argument, and their lips sealed the agreement.

A knock on the door was heard, but not acknowledged by either of them. Charles entered the room and brought with him a cold blanket that doused their passion. "Pardon the interruption. Thomas said you were expecting us."

A portly man stood beside Charles and bowed. "Sir Hawkins, it is a pleasure to see you in good health after so long a separation."

Hawk rose and brought Catharyna up with him. "Oswald, I appreciate your visit during the storm. This is Miss Catharyna van Broeck, Patrooness of Broeckwyck."

Catharyna curtsied to the barrister.

Hawk added, "We require a marital contract today." His happiness met his brother's startled gaze.

Oswald looked confused and whispered to Charles, "The Duke made no mention of this to me last eve."

Catharyna's hand reached up to fix her hair and quickly dropped it in defeat. Her long curls were in complete disarray and impossible to govern. The pins were everywhere in the room. "Please excuse me."

The men remained silent until the door closed Catharyna from their conversation. Charles drawled, "Oswald didn't travel through a storm for a *marital* contract, Will."

Oswald added, "I am here to deliver a personal message for you from the Duke of York. There is a special assignment he wishes you to handle for him immediately. You are to leave for Amsterdam tomorrow."

Hawk stared down at Oswald and laughed. "Why would I do that?"

Charles nudged the portly man aside. His face held a smile that saw the outcome of Hawk's life and knew it wasn't a happy ending. "Your ambition pushes you into corners all the time, Will. You went to his Grace asking to be named the first manor lord in his province. Well," hands spread out wide, "now you must earn it."

"I slaved seven years for him building alliances and gaining peace in the Iroquois League."

"And, you were granted more land than your sons and theirs will use in their lifetime."

Hawk's eyes narrowed on the jealousy that had drove him away at fifteen. Charles received the family business and fortune that predetermined his life in golden shackles. There was nothing Hawk could do to end the envy his freedom and adventures caused inside his eldest brother.

Oswald drew forward on shaky limbs. "I shall be happy to meet with you and Miss van Broeck to arrange a contract if this eases your mind before leaving."

Hawk began pacing the boundaries of the library. There was too much left unspoken to leave Catharyna now.

114

Charles warned, "You're a fool if you enter into a contract with her." Their eyes clashed. "Can't you see she's playing us both. You're the political wonder boy, you figure out why. I know what she wants from me, but what does she want from you?"

Hawk's face grew dark refusing to allow his brother's pessimism to destroy the first happiness he had known in years. His arrangements with Governor Lovelace were to gain Catharyna's agreement to marry him. He would be named the first manor lord, and Catharyna, a prominent Dutchwoman, would be his wife. Such a powerful marriage would finally unite the Dutch and English in the province.

There had been every intention to manipulate her into marriage, and yet, Hawk had been unable to. Instead, he had shared visions and dreams that not even Fairfax had been privileged to hear. There was a connection. He felt it. But, had she manipulated him? A crack began in his confidence, and his brother wiggled through it.

In disbelief, Charles added, "Yee gods, Will, have you fallen for her? Don't you see she plans to take all you offer? She'll never grant you Broeckwyck, and without that, such a marriage will never unite the English with the Dutch. You'll be a laughing stock if you allow her such power."

Hawk growled, "What is it she seeks from *you*?"

"The woman is *greedy*. Why settle for one brother when she can gain two prominent friends of the Duke's to assist her efforts?"

Hawk's head began to spin. He tried to remain focused on his original purpose. All his efforts the last seven years in New York did little to gain any leeway inside the tight knit Dutch community who controlled the trade and distrusted the English. He needed a Dutch wife...

And then it hit him. The ultimate mistake was made. He had fallen victim to Catharyna, who was now more desirous than everything he had striven to achieve.

Hawk's naked eyes looked at Charles in acceptance to his brutally honest words. The Dutch would forever brand him weak against Ten Broeck. But he was not a victim yet.

Catharyna reentered the room. The familiar closed look was on Hawk's face before he turned to look outside the window. His gesture made her walk toward Oswald. The tension between the two brothers was obvious.

Charles approached her with a smile that didn't reach his eyes. "Please excuse me." He bowed and left the room that was now full of his words.

Oswald smiled weakly at Catharyna and coughed loudly. Then he mumbled to Hawk's back, "Sir Hawkins?"

Catharyna's breath froze under the eyes of Hawk that held no emotion. He pointed to the chairs. "Sit." And they both obeyed, watching him pace in front of them. Minutes passed until he stopped in front of Catharyna.

"If you agree to my terms, Oswald will draw up a contract and we wed today."

Catharyna's eyes narrowed, but she nodded in agreement.

"The trade you conduct as Ten Broeck shall remain fully yours. I want no part in its profits or legal requirements. Do you agree to this."

Confusion filled Catharyna's eyes by the coldness of his voice, even though it was saying all she had hoped for. "Yes."

Hawk spoke to Oswald. "Can she maintain full control of her business after our marriage?"

Oswald stammered, "It is a highly unusual request, Sir Hawkins."

"Can she?" he barked.

"Well," he stumbled for several seconds until, "yes, but...it is not yet announced to Governor Lovelace!"

"What isn't announced?" Hawk asked in confusion.

Oswald looked uncertain, but shared the news. "Sir Hawkins, in the eyes of Dutch law, Miss van Broeck has equal economic rights in marriage. The Duke has decided to grandfather the law for the Dutchwomen in his province. If they keep their maiden name in marriage, they are given this freedom."

Catharyna beamed at the little lawyer hearing the news that she had in fact lost nothing from the English occupation of her province.

Hawk felt the ground start to shift beneath his feet. He barked, *"He did what?"*

Oswald took it personally, and became defensive. "When news reached his Grace that over a hundred Dutchwomen *fled* from his province, taking their businesses and trade, due to our English property laws," his hands spread out, "well, it was critical to grandfather their laws. *How can men build a civilized province without women?"*

Every worry that had haunted Catharyna for months disappeared. She laughed freely and said, "I like your Duke."

Hawk became dark and silent.

Catharyna made no note of it. "What of our daughters, Oswald? If they seek such, can they operate a business independent of their husband under English law?"

Oswald smiled at the woman's consideration for her unborn daughters. "Yes, with their husband's agreement, a wife could operate any business as a *feme sole* or single woman. This protects the husband from any legal ramifications against the wife's business, such as lawsuits and the like."

Catharyna repeated in astonishment, "So, English law does permit this?" With barely a pause, she asked, "What of property? Can they buy property?"

Oswald coughed uncomfortably, and then his voice grew wary when he answered, "While you and your daughters may inherit property, you have no legal right to buy property."

Catharyna's hands tightened, but her tongue was silent. The Duke had given the women in his province a portion of their rights, but not all. An inner battle began, trying to decide whether to argue. Her trade was critical to control, and that she received. But, it angered her that there was no option to invest in real estate.

Hawk stopped pacing and interrupted their private discussion. "So, Catharyna requires nothing from me to legally continue her trade when married."

Oswald nodded. "That is correct, Sir Hawkins, she needs nothing from you. Dutch law will protect her the rest of her days as long as she keeps her maiden name upon marriage to you. Now, what of your possessions, Sir?"

Oswald's words, "*She needs nothing from you...Dutch law will protect her,*" repeated over and over in Hawk's numb mind. He sat in front of Catharyna and their eyes locked. The look in his eyes made her heart tighten. "All I have will be shared with my wife and our children."

Oswald beamed and nodded. "Excellent, Sir Hawkins!"

Hawk challenged Catharyna, "What are your terms?"

The word was unspoken, yet it hung in the air. Hawk's words returned about trusting him. It was the one word he had repeated again and again, and now she knew it was building up to this moment. He had always wanted Broeckwyck. Blood pounded and thoughts raged, uncertain if she could give it. And then, anger emerged.

"I cannot give all in marriage to you," she whispered.

Hawk remained silent, with eyes that spoke loudly of her selfishness.

She rose and swore, "I cannot do this." Their eyes clashed and she added, "You can have my trade but not Broeckwyck, it shall remain in my name, protected by Dutch law."

He rose and replied, "I shall protect you and our children, *not some bloody Dutch law!* By God, I'll not be shut out and mocked by the Dutch with your control of Broeckwyck under my very nose!"

Oswald scurried out of the room in fear of the coming battle.

The implications of his words made Catharyna's heart tighten. "You view me so low?" she whispered.

"*I view you as Ten Broeck!*" he shouted, and the windows rattled under its force.

They stared at each other, knowing whatever trust had been found was now completely lost.

"There is no need for any contract," Catharyna said in a

voice dead of emotion, and began to leave the room.

"Fine, I'll marry a woman who knows how to trade fairly!" he taunted.

Anger swept all reason aside at the worst insult he could ever speak aloud to her. Catharyna's hand reached down to grab her knife, but her hands were taken into Hawk's, and held tightly. "Don't ever pull a knife on me again!" he warned.

Their eyes clashed and he whispered, "Meet me on equal terms, Ryna."

His eyes reached out to her and she met them with hope. "I shall keep my maiden name in marriage to you and control of all my properties, and you shall keep control of your properties. Our marriage will be for our children, who will inherit from both of us."

Hawk's fists clenched. "A man and woman become one in marriage. Your offer insults its sacredness, and *my character as a man*!"

Catharyna drew forward, undaunted. "Why must I place your character above my own? It's your law that prevents me from coming to you the way we *both* desire. You ask for my trust, yet your country swindled my homeland. Now, I gain back a portion of what was lost, and you ask me to hand my properties to you, all my parents perished for, when I can never buy them back under your *antiquated law*?" Her eyes blazed when she whispered, "I cannot do it."

Hawk stood in silence, a victim of the clashing of different cultures. There was no worthy argument to voice, and it increased the frustration boiling inside. Everything was just a tad out of reach, close enough to keep him panting, yet far enough to withhold the enjoyment, and savor the success. He could take no more of it and left the room and manor.

He was astride a stallion in minutes, and galloped away from Twining Oaks into the snow storm.

It was after midnight when Hawk returned against all logic. The Duke's business demanded he remain at the Red Lion Inn before leaving at dawn for Amsterdam. And yet, he couldn't leave Catharyna without saying good-bye, knowing the hard earned trust he had built with her had crumbled beneath his pride.

Riding through the snow storm had mellowed his anger at the Duke of York for sending him to Amsterdam and for agreeing to a grandfather clause, which now gave Catharyna back her control. There was every reason to believe he would be the Duke's puppet for the rest of his life, and every reason he would fail with Catharyna. Both unruly people had the ability to wreck all of his plans, and there was nothing he could do to prevent it.

The manor was in darkness when he entered. A coat of solid ice was removed from his shoulders, and the stairs were taken two at a time. Hawk paused at Catharyna's door. A hand reached up to his face feeling the scratches from their last midnight encounter, but the other hand reached for the door knob.

He entered softly, moving toward the ornate four poster bed, and pulled open the heavy drapes that enclosed it, only to find it empty. "Damn it!" he swore, believing she had left, until a blade of a knife was felt on his throat.

"What do you want?" Catharyna whispered from behind his back.

"Put the knife down."

"You entered uninvited. I've a right to protect myself."

The fire crackled and silhouetted her body against the flames to Hawk's eye. "I bear enough of your scars. Put it away."

She backed away instead and sheathed the knife. "Why are you here? To check my trunk to see if I've stolen the family silver?"

"You know why," his pride grounded out as he approached her.

She warned, "Leave me be!" But a second later he

pounced on her, and they landed on the bed. "Why do you not heed my words?" she asked under layers of pillows.

"I'm leaving at dawn for Amsterdam."

Pride and anger evaporated into the air at the news of his coming absence. Even so, she rose on elbows to warn, "I've no relatives in Amsterdam who will sway my terms to you."

His deep chuckle answered, "It's the Duke's business that sends me there." And then cradled her against him.

Catharyna whispered, "Will you be gone long?"

He heard her need of him and the coldness that had built up inside began to warm. "A fortnight."

She nodded, and then surprised them both, when she whispered, "You left before hearing my other offer."

Hawk released her and drew away to meet her eyes. "Yes?"

A blush rose on her cheeks. "If we find Dirck..."

"No."

"But, if Dirck..."

"No," Hawk repeated, and his finger silenced her lips. "I'll not scour the seven seas, wasting our future, to find your brother, who may not exist."

Pain filled Catharyna's eyes. "Dirck lives."

Hawk breathed deeply and nodded. "Very well, but we shall find our own compromise, with neither of our characters being sacrificed by our union."

"How?" she asked in complete disbelief.

His arms tightened on her. "Wait for my return, and I promise you, we shall find it then."

Catharyna's head swam with promises, lies and a desire so great that she wanted to accept all his terms and end the argument. "I will wait."

His eyes roamed over her face memorizing the contours and character lines. He kissed her lips softly and confessed, "I shall miss you."

Her eyes looked away to hide the tears quickly building. It was a battle to shut out her instincts that were begging her to keep him in London.

"Be careful," she whispered, but her voice cracked with emotion and fingers trembled.

"I'll be back soon, Ryna," Hawk whispered.

She kissed him with every fear and desire merged in a twisted and painful knot in her heart. "I shall miss you, too."

His arms tightened around her. "Wait for me."

"I will," she swore, and kissed him again.

Wrapped tightly against each other, the emotionally exhausted couple fell into a deep sleep.

Nine

Never before had days stretched to such lengths. A fortnight passed and still no word had been received from Hawk. Each time the butler walked by the parlor, Catharyna rose from the chair, believing he had returned.

Another evening arrived and she joined Meredith for dinner, listening blankly. There was no focus on the conversation of roses when her mind was full of Hawk.

"Ryna, are you feeling well?"

Catharyna's eyes tried to focus on Meredith's face, which seemed miles away. "Pardon?"

"My dear, I asked three times if you wished to take some of my rose bushes back to Broeckwyck. I fear you are unwell, your face is flushed and eyes are glazed. Perhaps you should retire for the evening?"

Catharyna rose instantly. "Yes, I do feel unusual. Please excuse me."

Meredith nodded. "Relax in bed with a good book and you'll be refreshed by morning."

Catharyna nodded and deliberately paced herself slowly out of the room. Once the door was closed, she raced upstairs only to pace about the bedchamber's four corners. Hours went by, still she paced.

Sleep arrived at three o'clock in the morning. A maid came in hours later and opened the heavy curtains surrounding the pedestal bed. "Good day, Missy, Lady Hawkins' son is downstairs impatient to see you."

Catharyna instantly rose from the pile of pillows and

relief filled her that the wait was over. He had returned, there had been no injury, desertion or death. Such thoughts would no longer torture her. There was no memory of an argument over Broeckwyck, only awareness that the decision to marry him was made.

"Hurry, I must dress," she ordered while ripping dresses out of the armoire, undergarments followed, and all fell into a growing pile.

When the maid began cleaning up the debris, she ordered, "Leave them! Please," her hands trembled with impatience, "help me dress into all these...*bloody* layers!"

The maid dropped what she was doing, and within minutes had Catharyna properly dressed. She took long strides down the stairs to the parlor. The pounding in her ears and heart was deafening as she stepped into the room.

When Charles approached her the breath left her chest. Hawk was nowhere in the room.

"Good morning, Ryna. I became fearful you were ill, my mother was quite worried." Hawk's brother approached looking handsome, confident and arrogant. His hands reached out for hers, and kissed them warmly. "I am relieved to find you in good health."

She would not allow anyone to see her hunger for news about Hawk. If that happened, all her fears would be spilled uncontrollably. For no matter how hard she tried, the sense of foreboding was all around her.

"I am fine, Charles. Rest was all I needed."

Charles noted dark circles beneath her eyes and knew the words were false. "Excellent." He escorted her deeper into the room, to the settee, where they sat down. "I had dinner with his Grace last evening."

Catharyna smiled on command, but it didn't reach her eyes. "How nice."

"I heard some confusing news."

"Confusing?"

"Yes, and it concerned your Broeckwyck."

Never had she been more alert. "Broeckwyck?"

"You shared with me Will's words that men here in London were petitioning the Duke for Broeckwyck, believing your claim as a woman would be ignored by the crown in their favor. This was the reason you joined my brother in coming to London." Charles took her hands, and their eyes met. "Is this true?"

"Yes."

Charles released a deep breath and looked away. "It is as I feared." Catharyna tugged on his hands and he met her eyes. "My brother has deceived you."

It was the last thing she had expected to hear. Confusion was in her voice and eyes. "What?"

Charles moved closer, his eyes were warm, trusting and sincere. "Will is ambitious, Ryna. It causes him to do dishonorable things. Broeckwyck never has been in jeopardy of being taken from you."

Hawk had deceived her. In that moment the dam began to be reconstructed around her heart. A familiar coldness expanded into every crevice inside her, but all of it was hidden from Charles. Instead, she ordered briskly, "Continue."

His hand reached out to stroke her cheek in comfort, but she leaned away. "When I mentioned your fears to the Duke last eve, why, he looked at me as though daft! His words were, "We just signed peace treaties with the Dutch. Am I a buffoon to have my settlers revolt against me by taking Broeckwyck from one of their own, and hand it to an Englishman?"

Catharyna's mind twirled with all the reasons why Hawk would intentionally mislead her. His gilded words that had gained her agreement to cross the Atlantic returned like a tidal wave. They now fit well with Hawk's crafty personality. Such a deed was mother's milk to the man to ensure her agreement to journey with him to London. The same method had been used to gain her agreement to introduce him to Minichque.

And then embarrassment set in, recalling how easily she had succumbed to his advances. David DeVries' talk of love had made her flee. Hawk spoke visions and dreams that had pierced through every protective instinct built since a child of five.

Shame spread in the knowledge she had been made into a fool.

All such thoughts were left unspoken. She rose from the sofa. "I shall discuss this with Will when he returns."

Charles noted the unemotional response, and knew further words were useless. "Be assured this news was difficult for me to share with you. Will is my brother and it pains me to see him treat a defenseless woman in such a way."

"I am not defenseless," she replied, and added coldly, "and I never asked you share such to the Duke on my behalf."

Charles rose from the settee and walked to the fireplace, where she stood looking back at him in fury. "My friendship led me to do this for you," he replied in a tone that made her feel unappreciative of his efforts.

She looked away from the intense scrutiny of his eyes and whispered, "I am unaccustomed to someone doing things for me." She faced him with a forced smile. "Please forgive me, Charles."

He lifted her face to meet his eyes. "I will as long as you attend my Winter Ball next week."

Catharyna mumbled, "Of course."

He saw the pain in her eyes and whispered, "I am sorry." His sincerity tore at her defenses, almost breaking through the newly constructed walls.

"I appreciate your friendship, Charles," she replied automatically, and extended a hand to him, indicating their meeting was over. His eyes held her own one last time, before kissing her hand and leaving the room.

The moment the door closed, her hand reached out blindly for the fireplace mantel and clung to it as dry sobs racked through her body. Her mind believed his words, but her heart was crying over Hawk's deceit.

She hurried to the door and shouted, "Thomas!" A few seconds later the frazzled butler came huffing into the room.

"Miss van Broeck?"

"Thomas, please send a message to Mr. Fairfax inviting him and his fiancé to dinner tonight."

"It is rather late to send an invitation out for dinner."

"Then you mustn't waste time," she advised, and swept passed him in the direction of the study, intent to find a book to occupy the time.

Thomas gazed at the Dutchwoman's departing back in bewilderment. Never had he met a woman of such make-up.

The solitude of the library allowed emotions to calm. Books were devoured. There was one on William the Conquer which held the majority of her interest. Catharyna's angry mind saw Hawk shared much in common with the Norman invader who became King of England.

A soft knock on the door made her bark, "Yes!"

Thomas entered with hands that trembled visibly to the eye. "Your dinner guests have arrived, Miss van Broeck."

A bright smile appeared. "Splendid, Thomas." There was no small talk or hesitation. She went straight to the parlor.

Meredith was found conversing with Fairfax who was seated beside a delicate blonde haired woman whose eyes were locked on him as though he were a Greek god. Beside her was a plump woman with similar features, clearly a relative in the family serving as chaperon. Emily Fielding held the appearance of a beautiful hot house flower carefully grown and protected. She would never survive in their untamed province.

Catharyna's eyes held rejection in Fairfax's choice of a wife, but remained silent in her observations. "Good evening, I'm delighted you were able to join us for dinner this evening." She stood in front of Emily waiting for the proper introduction.

Fairfax's eyes sparkled with pride. "Ryna, this is my fiancé, Emily Fielding." Emily curtsied and then leaned against Fairfax for support. "And this is her sister, Penelope."

Catharyna smiled with the knowledge why Gerrit had returned so quickly to Twining Oaks. "I am delighted to meet you both." Determined eyes pierced Emily. "There is an important matter I must speak privately on with Fairfax. Would you excuse us?"

Emily's voice was that of an angel. "Of course, Miss van Broeck. It is our pleasure to finally meet you."

Penelope smiled brightly and nodded vigorously.

"Thank you," Catharyna said, and pulled Fairfax out of Emily's hands.

Meredith looked at the departing couple and smiled brightly at her remaining guests, but deep in her eyes there was sadness.

Catharyna led him into the study and shut the door. She approached, never breaking eye contact, but was halted when he hugged her tightly. "Hawk told me of your agreement."

"That isn't..."

"I knew the moment you pulled the knife out on the sloop you were for him." He laughed and added, "Few men have such bravery."

Catharyna lost her focus under Fairfax's sincerity. She mumbled, "Hawk said many things that made me agree to come to London."

Fairfax nodded with a warm smile.

"One was the threat that men were petitioning the crown for Broeckwyck, ignoring my claim as my father's blood since I was a woman."

The man with an open face began to close.

Catharyna's voice grew cold. "I have only one question for you to answer, no more."

Fairfax nodded woodenly.

"Was that true?"

Silence filled the room for minutes. They stood staring at each other as their minds were doing all the talking. Water dampened her eyes and her heart pleaded, "Fairfax, I deserve an answer to my question."

The struggle going on inside of him was clear to her, minutes passed and still no answer. His silence said enough.

"I see." Nothing more was needed to be spoken. His eyes were full of guilt, hers distrust. She began to leave the room.

His words stopped her at the door. "Ten Broeck, it's not

that simple."

Her face held no emotion, nor did her voice. "Lies complicate simple things." Her eyes refused to look at his face. She now knew he was not her friend. "Send my regrets to Emily. I am unwell to share any meal in your presence."

Fairfax watched the door shut and knew it would take a miracle for it to ever open.

Ten

Clouds of deceit thickened, encompassing all that breathed air. Torches lit the carriage's way through the snow packed driveway of Hawk Hill, a fierce looking castle surrounded by a moat. The elaborate Winter Ball decorations of garland, holly berries, thick brocade and tapestry coverings on its cold stone walls, did little to lighten the dreary atmosphere that held no invitation of warmth or welcome to its visitors.

Obligation to Charles was not the only reason Catharyna sat beside Meredith in the carriage dressed in an elegant ruby velvet gown on their way to the ball. She had come to terms with Hawk's deceit and decided to remain at Twining Oaks. A silent arrangement had begun between his mother, who allowed a friendship to begin.

Her days had filled quickly, visiting coffee houses to discuss the philosophy of the moment. The heated discussions nurtured her mind and kept thoughts on loftier issues in life, rather than a few passionate moments in Hawk's arms. If any topic arose that involved Hawk, she was quick to douse it immediately. All the ladies knew the subject was forbidden.

Tonight she would meet Charles' friends who were traders and merchants from Lombard Street. Broeckwyck was safe and she now had the opportunity to build important contacts in London before returning home, something Hawk had promised, but never fulfilled.

The business of getting more tenant farmers to migrate to New York was uppermost in her mind. It had been her mother country's downfall, a mistake she planned not to repeat. Poverty surrounded London and its suburbs, so she planned to build upon the legend Hawk had created about her to entice the merchants to trade with Ten Broeck, which in turn would encourage people to migrate there.

Meredith held her arm tightly as they entered the ballroom. Finally, she began to be introduced to titled gentlemen, parliamentary members and prominent merchants. Every effort was made to dance with each of them.

Hours passed before Charles finally made his way through the crowd of gentlemen, to approach her for a dance. "You're popular this evening." His tone was dry.

Catharyna smiled. "I am enjoying your Winter Ball immensely."

His eyes were as cold as his words. "Ha, so this is my Winter Ball? I was beginning to suspect it was a personal business meeting arranged just for you." Catharyna laughed, but he added, "You're the only woman who has danced with stuffy Parliamentary members and greedy merchants."

Her eyes remained on the crowd when she replied, "They are entertaining company." She felt his eyes, but wouldn't meet his gaze. He shared too many characteristics of his younger brother that it was now necessary to distance herself from him as well.

He whispered into her ears, "Why not the philosophy lovers?" She moved away, and their eyes met. "Mother tells me you frequent our coffee houses and debate the meaning of life."

His teasing tone was ignored by her. "I enjoy a good debate," she replied.

Suddenly his hands tightened on her arms. "Don't ignore me, Ryna. Look at me." Their eyes clashed and he whispered, "I am not Will, I didn't deceive you."

She looked into his eyes and saw no lies, but then she never saw them in Hawk's face either. It could be a family trait.

He added, "You haven't given me a chance to show you who I am. Permit me the honor, grant me the respect."

His eyes reached out and she relented. "All right."

Charles smiled in relief, and ended their dance in order to escort her out of the ballroom.

"Where are we going?" she questioned breathlessly, as

she stretched legs to their full length to keep pace with him.

They walked through a dark corridor for several minutes until they entered the library. He reached for a candelabra and held it up toward a wall of family portraits. Faces of men and women, each dressed in different fashions spanning several centuries, met her gaze. Though one portrait stood out from the others, and she went directly to it.

Charles spoke from behind her. "That is my ancestor that started our prestigious family heritage, Sir William Hawkins, better known as Black Hawk. Will is named after him." Catharyna's eyes scanned the portrait, and her heart began to pound. The eyes that reached into her soul were staring back at her.

Charles stood beside her, and spoke softly at the picture. "He was a great seaman and adventurer."

She became engrossed in the face of the man. "Why was he called Black Hawk when he had red hair?"

A smile grew on Charles' face. "He was also the first English slave trader. That is what built our family's fortune."

Catharyna remained silent, as thoughts roamed inward, all the while keeping eyes locked on the man's face. Slave trade was serious and important business to her mother country's economy, due to western expansion and the need for labor in building new colonies. The Bible, ministers, and even philosophers in the coffee shops, saw no evil in it, and there were always eager investors for it, due to the rich profits. She wasn't certain why her father opposed the slave trade, but he had been the only patroon not to have them in the colony, whereas their relatives all had slaves due to the difficulty in getting Dutch settlers to come to New York when they were flourishing in Holland's good fortune. Cornelius had chosen indentured servants to fill their need. They worked a number of years to pay off their passage expenses, and were then given their freedom to continue on at Broeckwyck as tenant farmers, renting parcels of property.

Charles noticed that her eyes remained fixed on the portrait, and drew closer. "Do you know anything about the slave trade?"

There was no judgment on her face or eyes. "I am a trader, Charles. They are one of many goods that come in and out of our port weekly." In a province with rich natural resources, slavery was one she never traded on. There was something about bartering human beings that made her believe it was unnatural. Such personal views were kept silent.

"I meant the business of it," he replied, and smiled when she nodded no. Clouds covered his face when he explained, "Tribes warring against each other sell their prisoners, sometimes an uncle will sell a niece if she displeased him, and, more often, slave catchers choose a tribe and clean it out for themselves. It's a messy business. Over half of them die on the journey to the Americas. Of course, you know how difficult it is to get labor in the provinces, so the need is clearly there. Especially in South America, with our sugar plantations and the Carolina's tobacco crop."

Catharyna simply stared at him, unable to voice any response to the horrific description. She had never understood how the slaves were selected. It never affected her trade, so no attention had been given to it.

Charles drew closer and hissed, "I detest it, no matter the profit! But, this is my firstborn inheritance. The irony of life is that Will should have been firstborn. My adventurous brother was given the finest education in Amsterdam in order to return to London. Instead, he chose adventure on the sea, where he thrived in the business. That is, until his never ending ambition led to trouble which forced him to go to New York for the rumors to die down." His eyes watched hers, waiting to question him for details, but she remained silent.

The comment of Hawk's talent, "in the business," made her ache to know if it was slave catching. It festered deep inside, yet she refused to question him further on it. Hawk was no longer a man she sought to know. Instead, she changed the direction of the conversation by pointing to another portrait, and questioned, "Who is this?"

His voice was light and carefree. "That is someone from

the *Spoiled Early* branch of our family, spent a great deal of my inheritance, so we'll ignore him."

Catharyna laughed in relief at his teasing. He led her to a portrait of a beautiful young woman with dark hair and eyes; a dog was seated beside her in the picture. "This was my wife, Jane."

Catharyna was startled at the instant change in his voice, and found grief on his face. The mood was dark again, and she suspected this was his original purpose in going to the library. He needed to see his wife's portrait, but wanted company. Her voice held sincerity. "She was beautiful."

Charles whispered, "She was." Catharyna drew closer and put a hand on his shoulder in comfort. "She died giving birth to our son last spring; Charles died two weeks later."

His shoulders began to shake, and Catharyna comforted him in a warm embrace. The pain of death was something she understood. "I'm sorry."

His arms tightened around her and he moaned, "I miss her."

Catharyna's cold heart began to melt, his pain became her own. The familiar deep, dark ache sprang instantly to life as images of her parents and innocent baby brothers rose to the surface. Softly, she replied, "Death is part of life. We must accept it."

"I'm not that strong," he confessed, and his arms grew slack. She took a step back to break away, but his hands reached out and grabbed her again. "Ryna, don't leave me."

She wasn't sure what to do. "Your mother will begin looking for me. I wouldn't want to worry her."

His face held an inviting smile. "Just a bit longer, and then we shall return."

It wasn't an order but a request. "Of course, Charles."

Her hand was brought to his lips and kissed softly. "Mother tells me you will be returning to New York when spring arrives."

She began to pace back and forth, with eyes on the wall of portraits. "Yes."

He blocked her path, only to have her step away to view a portrait further down the hall. He followed, and turned her about to face him. His eyes beamed such warmth, she couldn't look away. "I would like to discuss a business arrangement with you."

Catharyna's hands went up. "Charles, that's kind of you, but I don't require slaves at Broeckwyck at this time."

He laughed. "No, it is a personal business arrangement." Their eyes locked. "Your agreement with Will is not decided. So, I wish to present my own." She grew uncomfortable, and looked away, but he persisted. "I need an heir and so do you. There is great responsibility on us to maintain the family line. If we marry, I would not expect you to remain in England, you can live your life at Broeckwyck and raise our children there, until they come of age for schooling. At that time they would be sent to London."

Catharyna was shaking her head and whispered, "That's very generous, Charles, but..."

He halted the words with a raised finger. "Our union would unite the Dutch to the English in the province, giving it more prestige here in London by my choosing you as wife."

"I don't think..."

"No, I don't want your answer now, all I ask is for you to consider it. You can bear your maiden name and have the power to run Broeckwyck any way you wish. I want no part of your life in New York nor do you seek one in London. We need an heir, and that is all our marriage will reap for us."

Catharyna replied, "I don't deny your arrangement would be favorable for me, but there are a number of women in your ballroom that would be better candidates as your wife, who would care for you and your children here in England."

His hands tightened on her own. "They would exhaust me after a fortnight to accompany them to balls. I've no patience for a social life."

Catharyna looked doubtful. He was the most charming man she had ever met. There were few more perfectly suited for the social life. The proposition did not ring true to her. "I'll consider it."

"Consider this as well." His kiss was soft and unexpected. It was not as unpleasant as she wished. He breathed against her lips, "We shall be good together and apart. This I promise you."

A different picture rose in her mind, being tangled in his younger brother's arms, and it pushed her out of his own embrace. She mumbled over her shoulder, "I'll consider it, Charles."

This time she didn't wait for him, but left the room in the direction of the music. Her purpose for coming to the ball had been side tracked long enough. There were a number of merchants that she still needed to be introduced to. Meredith refused to allow her to meet with them in their offices, but no one prohibited her from speaking with them at a ball. Charles' steps were heard, and her pace quickened.

Charles remained at the doorway, watching Catharyna as she was absorbed into the crowd. He became an unwilling participant in a conversation with a group of parliamentary members, thanks to Lord Shaftsbury.

"Charles, I understand your brother has dashed off on another clandestine assignment for his Grace. Rumor has it, our Black Hawk has set his sight to be the first manor lord in New York, and plans to woo the wealthy Dutchwoman into marriage, and double his fortune."

The group laughed, but each man's face and tone held a respect so deep with approval, that Charles' jaw tightened. None of his accomplishments combined, equaled one of Hawk's. His youngest brother had the ability of swimming in a sea of sharks, and have them point him in the direction of hidden treasure. Since childhood, Hawk shined against his older siblings. Richard and Edward had adored him, encouraged him to keep pace with their studies, and soon he eclipsed them. The years separating them dissolved, due to Hawk's brilliance and body which blessed him with great height, that towered over his older brothers at the age of ten. Everything came natural to him, especially the crowds that circled around. It was Hawk's grief over their brothers' death during the Black Plague that drew him to the sea. Only, Charles had never anticipated his youngest brother would become the new Black Hawk, a living legend that now festered deep in his own envious heart.

Lord Shillington joined the comradeship of the group. "Hawk told me in confidence," he winked at his friends, "this Dutchwoman was his only way to gain acceptance with two of the most powerful Mohican leaders and their father, the chief. They call her white sister, and treat her as their equal. She's been trading fur with them since a child of ten." His voice lowered before continuing, "It appears these savages take much direction from their women. I can hardly believe such is true, yet Hawk claims it is the women who pick the most powerful positions for men in the tribe, that the men marry and go to the wife's home and clan, and the women carry on most of the important bartering for the tribe, whereas the men hunt and protect it. Yet, such does explain why this Dutchwoman was accepted by the savages, far more easily than our Englishmen." His eyes sparkled. "Such fearlessness is remarkable, *she's* simply remarkable!"

Lord Shaftsbury's eyes beamed with pride. "No surprise *my* Will has landed on his feet so well in New York. I taught him how to screw a fortune from an empty purse. This Dutchwoman will make a splendid wife for him, indeed, indeed." He leaned into the group and whispered in delight, "Time is now for us to invest! Look how she dances with our tight fisted merchants, dazzling them to open trade in the province. Brilliant woman, perfect for Black Hawk. Simply perfect!"

Five pairs of eyes suddenly turned to focus exclusively on Charles for his thoughts on their discussion. He remained silent, but nodded in agreement, his face tight with a smile.

Tea gatherings had become an irresistible treat. The

sweet cakes were almost as tantalizing as the heavy conversation Lady Putnam's tea parties guaranteed. To be added to her guest list was almost as high an honor as being knighted. For the Dutchwoman from New York, it was a daily invitation that caused the hostess, and guests, several breathless moments of anxiety, in hope of her acceptance.

Catharyna entered Lady Putnam's parlor, and was immediately encircled by the philosophers of the party. Not a man was present.

She smiled at the new faces surrounding her. Each time the same questions were asked by new acquaintances. "Are there many Indian massacres with women and children?" Or, "Miss van Broeck, is it true you conduct business freely with the savages?" And the most common, "Wherever do you get your clothes?"

A familiar voice joined the discussion. "Can you really catch a fish with your hand in the Hudson River?"

Catharyna's eyes widened in surprise at the sight of Emily Fielding in the group. The pretty blonde smiled overly bright, Catharyna smelled the fear of rejection. She wanted to ignore her, but something held her back.

"Almost," she replied and the crowd laughed, "but there is no air sweeter, nor fruit trees more bountiful, than in our Valley. The Germans call it the land of milk and honey."

Emily's face relaxed, but Catharyna did not address her again. Tea was served, and she chose to be seated with Lady Putnam and her friends. "I understand women must go to University in Italy, instead of England or France. Why is that?"

Charlotte Cavendish replied, "Our wealth cannot overcome our lack of future employment, which prevents us from being given one of their precious spots here at university."

Catharyna challenged the table with an idea. "Then volunteer to assist in projects."

The ladies began speaking at once, and the debate began. Her mind sharpened on their questions, one after the other, sometimes finding a flaw in her response, only to refine it and offer up a different point of view. A smile lit up her face and eyes. Hours later, every lady rose from the table completely exhausted from questioning the choices of men, and their impact on their lives.

Catharyna was entering the carriage when Emily approached. "Miss van Broeck, would you mind if I shared your carriage? Lady Hawkins has invited us to dinner this evening and mentioned I should share your carriage after our tea this afternoon."

There was no point to be rude when the afternoon had been so enjoyable. "Of course," she replied, and they climbed in silently. Catharyna avoided eye contact. Just looking at Emily reminded her of Hawk's deceit. The evening of their introduction had deteriorated after her discussion with Fairfax. She had been rude and never joined them for dinner.

The ride went on in silence for many minutes until the sound of sobbing drew her attention. Even so, Catharyna remained silent until Emily's sobs turned into hysterics. Bewilderment temporarily froze Catharyna, but with no other choice, she sat beside the distraught woman and placed an arm around her in comfort. "Emily, whatever is the matter?"

Sniffles sounded and she hiccuped loudly. "You hate me."

Amazement filled Catharyna face. "We barely know each other, Emily. Why would you think that?"

The sobs grew more intense. "Since the evening we met, Fairfax has been in a fowl temper. It must be that I displeased you, but I cannot speak of it to him. Anytime I mention your name, he leaves the room." She turned to face Catharyna and pleaded, "Please tell me what I did?"

Catharyna smiled. "You did nothing wrong. Fairfax is angry at himself for having the devil for a best friend."

This time Emily's face grew red, not with tears, but in anger. "You can think what you like about me, but don't ever insult Sir Hawkins again. He's our greatest friend, kindest gentlemen and best of men."

Catharyna was speechless, yet wise enough to know this woman's feelings were real, and needed to be understood.

There was hope in her voice. "What makes him such a man?"

Emily looked temporarily confused, but then explained passionately, "Surely you're ribbing me? I know how to read, and I read every letter Fairfax has sent to me these past three years. Every one concerning how Hawk was working hard to make a home for us in New York, to build an estate as grand as any in England."

Catharyna leaned back in the seat with narrow eyes pinned on Emily's face, and replied coldly, "Fairfax makes him a greater man than he is."

Emily became furious and blasted back, "You must believe me, for I'm neither daft nor dumb not to *know* he never asked Fairfax for a shilling of the fortune he used to save his life! He wouldn't hear of it. Now Hawk's giving us 5,000 acres to settle and raise our family, where the air is sweet and the valley rich for growing. Do not speak so against our friend *ever* again."

The two women stared at each other in a heated silence, until Catharyna replied, "I will have no difficulty in ever speaking the name William Hawkins again." This time they turned their heads away from each other, and remained silent until the carriage halted in front of Lady Hawkins' home. Both women erupted out of it with red faces.

Meredith was in the foyer when they entered, and immediately sensed something had gone wrong with her plan. They were supposed to be laughing and enjoying each other's company. To cover the tense air, a phony smile was quickly plastered on her face. "How was afternoon tea?"

"Fine," they barked unanimously.

This was not progress. There was only one way to deal with the situation, and she knew the time was overdue to finally voice it. "In my parlor, *now.*" Both women looked at the ever gracious Meredith in amazement, but remained frozen like statues. "I said *now!*"

Within seconds Meredith was following their backs into the study, and cornered Catharyna when she demanded, "Speak now of this treachery you accuse my son of."

Catharyna refused to discuss it, and remained silent.

"Ryna, whatever you say will be kept in these walls. Share with us what is festering in you."

The frantic pounding of her heart ordered Catharyna to meet Meredith's gaze. "I cannot, it is between your son and I."

Meredith smiled at the doubt in her voice. "May I ask a favor then?" Catharyna's head rose again, this time hope filled her eyes. "May you hold off sentencing my son until he has the opportunity to defend himself? That is the law of our land here in England."

Catharyna thought hard over the request. She saw Meredith's complete faith in her son, and then looked at Emily, wiping tears away from an angry face. There was one certainty, Emily would do fine in New York, she was no hot house flower.

Catharyna also knew both of these women could not be so wrong in Hawk's character. At least she decided to hold off final judgment until he was able to explain his actions personally. "Yes, I can agree to that."

Emily rushed across the room and hugged her tightly. Seconds later Meredith was found in her other arm. Neither let go of her for a long time.

Eleven

Amsterdam

Seldom do opportunities unwrap themselves so perfectly. The Grain Market was bustling with its usual activity of ships coming in and out of port, when Hawk entered one of its many coffee houses. Women and men dressed in fine clothes, that lacked frills and ostentatious signs of wealth, littered the cobblestone streets. Their wealth, worn in subdued elegance and success, was a subtle breeze that drifted across the meandering streets of brick townhouses.

He sat at a table gazing out a window at the activity on a ship, when a tall, lean beauty interrupted internal musings.

"Would you care to join my father and I for coffee, Sir?"

Hawk glanced at the woman's father, and immediately accepted. Years of schooling in Amsterdam served him now in recognizing Henrich Craijer, a member of the prestigious Cloth Drapers Guild, which made him one of the most powerful men in the Netherlands.

"I would be delighted," he bowed, "Sir William Hawkins."

The beauty replied, "Juliet Craijer, and my father, Henrich."

Henrich rose, and smiled in greeting. "My daughter Juliet and I welcome you to Amsterdam, Sir Hawkins. What business has brought you here?"

"Some remaining items for the Duke of York with the peace treaty."

Henrich beamed.

Juliet's eyes roamed over Hawk's wide shoulders and

strong face. "Surely you jest, Sir! There's the look of the pirate in his face, yes papa?" Juliet's two dimples blossomed and her feline eyes were locked on Hawk.

Henrich laughed. "Yes."

Hawk's face became guarded. "I am no pirate."

Juliet's eyes narrowed on the rugged face that said the opposite. "What a shame, I sense it would have suited you."

Hawk appeared unmoved by the statement.

Juliet sighed, "Well, it is marvelous that the war between our countries is finally over. I do encourage you to make the opportunity to visit Staboeck on your next journey to South America. The air is filled with the sweet pungent smells of its fruit trees, and sea breezes of the cleanest air on earth."

"Unfortunately, my time will be occupied in New York."

Henrich said, "We have relatives settled there, the van Hoesen's. My cousin's widow Anna is wife to Peter van Broeck."

Hawk appeared focused on his companions at the coffee shop, but eyes wandered occasionally out the window, watching the activity aboard the ships. He took a sip of coffee and smiled at Henrich, "Yes, I know them well. Their son Gerrit and niece, Miss Catharyna van Broeck, are in London awaiting my return."

Juliet's face changed instantly, trying to remember a vague memory. She questioned softly, "Catharyna's the trader, Ten Broeck, right papa?"

Henrich smiled indulgently at her. "Yes, dear."

Juliet then turned to Hawk and added, "Yes, now I remember. I met her brother at a spring dance. We laughed over his adventures at sea and all the mischief he managed to get into. Remember, papa? He's the handsome fellow with the black curls and blue eyes?"

Hawk's eyes pinned Juliet. "Dirck van Broeck?"

Juliet noticed Hawk's new interest in her. "Yes."

Hawk straightened, and pushed the coffee cup away from hands that were now drumming on the wooden table. "He is here, in Amsterdam?"

Juliet was elated at his sudden attention on her. "No, he's a seaman somewhere in the West Indies." The closed look on Hawk's face prompted words to spring readily to her lips. "I'm surprised Helena permitted him to go back again."

Henrich looked disapproving at his only daughter. "Juliet, I told you we can't keep young adventurous men like that bunkered down by women, when demand for sea travel and its profits are so great. They are Holland's blood."

Juliet's face grew dark, but nodded meekly.

Hawk nodded to Henrich, and turned impatiently to Juliet with another question. "Does Helena live here? Catharyna would be interested in recent news of her brother."

"Of course, she's just a few streets from here in fact. Lovely townhouse next to her parents. Join us for dinner tonight, I'll introduce you. She'd enjoy meeting you and hearing about New Netherlands..." words halted and corrected herself, "New York."

"I appreciate your generosity in arranging the introduction, Miss Craijer," Hawk said with warm sincerity. Finding the man who had unknowingly caused so much of his torment with Catharyna, now became a quest. To return to London with such information on Dirck, made his eyes sparkle gazing outside the window at the clear blue sky, and he felt Catharyna's approval.

Their table was interrupted by Hugo van Crujlenburgh, the solicitor Hawk was scheduled to meet with. He rose to introduce his new guests, but was halted by Hugo, who did so himself. "Henrich, it's a pleasure to see you and your lovely daughter enjoying the morning at the Grain Market."

Henrich rose and offered assistance to his daughter to rise from the table. She smiled boldly at Hawk and extended a small card with their address in gold print. "We shall see you at seven o'clock, Sir Hawkins."

"Seven o'clock," Hawk repeated, and bowed to kiss her hand which lingered in his hand. Their eyes met, and her invitation was impossible to ignore. He nodded politely, but became eager to be done with them, to conclude the business that had brought him there. He remained standing, until father and daughter left the coffee shop, then sat down.

Hugo placed on the table the formal contracts, with the seal of the oligarchy for the Duke, and a velvet blue box, and then beamed with pride. "You'll be pleased."

Hawk opened the box, and a smile spread upon examining the sapphire ring surrounded by diamonds. "Very pleased."

Hugo grinned in confirmation. His brother was the best jeweler in Amsterdam, the Englishman would not find better quality in all of Europe. "This must be a special woman to receive such a ring."

Hawk extended a hand to the man he had conducted business with the past fortnight, and now viewed as friend. "Yes."

The day evaporated under the last few items of business required for the Duke. Against Hawk's chest lay the blue velvet box containing the ring and contracts for the Duke. At dawn he was taking the *Angel* to London. Everything was going on schedule.

Hawk arrived promptly at Henrich's home at the moment the clock chimed seven o'clock. A grin spread with the knowledge the morning had been very productive, and confidence that the evening would surpass it. Dirck was rapidly becoming far more valuable than any contract a solicitor would draw up to appease Catharyna.

A servant dressed all in black, escorted him inside Henrich Craijer's home to a formal parlor.

Juliet approached, looking beautiful in a blue satin gown, with a large white collar of the finest lace. Hawk bowed, "Good evening, Miss Craijer."

Once again, feline eyes narrowed on his face, but Juliet's smile was innocence personified. "You are prompt, my father likes promptness." An arm was extended, to be escorted into the parlor. There were no pretentious signs of wealth; the townhouse was understated simplicity.

Henrich was seated with several other gentlemen, all speaking politics. "Will, join our discussion." Hawk hesitated before doing so, with a glimpse around the room for a woman, but found only Juliet. His eyes clashed with hers in curiosity, she ignored it, and sat beside him.

The evening continued with no sign of any other woman, and Hawk's frustration began to mount. Manners insisted he remain until dinner concluded, then a private discussion with the men was demanded, which Juliet shared in. Finally, he rose, eager to leave.

Juliet escorted him to the door, but halted his departure. "I regret Helena was unwell to meet you for dinner. She asked if we might have coffee together tomorrow?"

"That's impossible, I leave at dawn on the *Angel* for London."

Juliet laughed in a rich husky tone that made him smile. "This is Amsterdam, Sir Hawkins. We've ships coming in and out of our port every day. Surely, one day more won't matter?"

He paused momentarily before agreeing. News of Dirck was critical to his plans with Catharyna. Except spring was arriving, and there was no doubt her impatience to return home would not hold her in London for long. She would take the first ship out of port with or without him. And yet, all the reasons to leave were ignored under the weight of the box in his coat pocket, that contained her ring. It would mean nothing compared to news of her brother.

"Yes, I'll join you tomorrow."

Juliet smiled. "Splendid, Sir Hawkins. We shall join you at ten o'clock."

He bowed, and quickly raced down the stairs into a waiting carriage.

Juliet watched him enter the carriage and heard the horse's hooves against the cobblestone streets until it turned the corner. Her smile turned into a laugh.

146

The sun was blocked by thick gray clouds the next morning at the Grain Market when Hawk entered the coffee house. Impatience was great to be done with the task. His eyes roamed the crowded room trying to find Juliet's face. He sat at a table with his back to the wall and eyes facing the windows and doorway. A third cup of coffee was drained when Juliet finally appeared with a burly male servant. There was no other woman.

The realization that a beautiful woman had played a foolish game with him, was bitter to swallow. Anger tightened his body as it rose from the chair. No time or words were wasted like last night. "Where is Helena?"

Juliet's slim white hand pushed him back into the chair. "Such impatience."

His face hardened. "What game do you play here?"

Her eyes appeared timid under the fierceness of his. "There is no game."

They stared at each other until Hawk stated, "There is no Helena." And then drew closer to whisper, "Do you know Dirck van Broeck or not?"

Juliet was determined not to lose her Englishman the way she lost every other handsome adventurer that passed through Amsterdam. "Yes, I know Dirck." Anger was now naked on the pearl skin face when she leaned across the table and whispered, "He spoke pretty words into my ear and left me the next day with my jewelry in his pocket!"

"I don't believe you."

Juliet became aroused that he challenged her word. Few men had such audacity to challenge the daughter of Henrich Craijer. A sensual smile spread, as did her hands on his thighs. "I've greater needs than trying to understand the mind of a thief, Will."

Hawk matched the smile and leaned closer. "Aye, you like adventure." Understanding began to unravel the mystery of

Dirck.

Her pretty features grew harsh by a cunning smile. "Your Dirck craved adventure, so I helped him get it somewhere in a sugar field."

"You sold him," he clarified.

Juliet's mind raced with excitement. There were few men that read her as easily as this man. Adventure was all around him, and desire to possess him consumed all thought. Her eyes sparkled in anticipation for him to challenge her silence.

In the cold morning light, Hawk read all the things the darkness hid in Juliet's beautiful face the night before. Her father's position, and broadminded attitude with his only child, had given her unimaginable power, and she was using it to appease selfish desires. To the man who squeezed every opportunity out of life, Juliet represented an empty waste to Hawk. Nothing was worse than power and wealth being wasted on selfish frivolities.

He rose from the chair, and bowed swiftly in farewell.

Alarmed that he was leaving like the others, made her reach out to stop him. "Stay, I've been truthful with you. Don't shame me by leaving me alone here to be mocked."

There was no expression on Hawk's face. "You shame yourself." He left her then, and walked through the crowded coffee shop, not looking back at her smoldering gaze on him. He took the first street to the docks.

"Black Hawk," someone shouted at his back.

Hawk turned to find its owner, and blackness consumed him. There he crashed unconscious, in the middle of the cobblestone street, unaware of the four men who dragged him away.

Twelve

London

Weeks flew by in the company of Emily. Catharyna had made excellent contacts during a continuous string of tea parties and balls that now had London a buzz, with New York being *the place* to settle in the American colonies.

A gloominess surrounded London after the decade of destruction it had suffered, first with the Black Plague and then the Great Fire. Death had touched everyone she had met. The rebuilding seemed endless along London's narrow streets. Catharyna's advertisements in the papers, inviting people to settle at Onteora, brought her over fifty families to interview.

Emily took her to places in London that were a trader's dream. Day after day she gathered new merchandise that began to fill Twining Oaks empty hay barn. Afternoons were spent with the architect reviewing plans for Onteora. There was no question to do it, even though it was for Hawk's benefit. Motives were left unexplored as Catharyna stood staunchly over Robert Seaman's shoulder to approve every nook and cranny in the manor. There would be no wasted space. Her constant suggestions brought irritation to the architect, but eventual acceptance came after he had a night's sleep in recognizing it was an improvement.

Although, Emily claimed it was the man's resignation in surrendering another battle.

Things were moving forward at a wonderful pace. Saturday morning found her riding through Hyde Park with Emily and her sister Penelope. Several ladies from their tea parties waved and chattered hurriedly to them as they passed by in carriages with their husbands. It was a chilly, winter morning, but signs of spring were in the air.

Emily's voice was full of excitement. "In a fortnight I'll be wed! I've waited forever for Fairfax."

Penelope's face grew red in embarrassment, and whispered, "Emmy, you mustn't admit that aloud."

Emily only gushed louder, "And I won't have to hold my tongue any more when I'm on New York soil!"

Suddenly, Emily's smile weakened upon seeing a lone rider approach them. She exchanged a silent look with her sister, and the pair simultaneously turned their horses back, and took another path in the park.

Catharyna laughed, "Well, Emmy, I wouldn't say our minister would..." The sister's departure was then noticed, and she turned to follow them down a narrow path. Her mind began to review the interviews the day before with a blacksmith and his wife. They were a charming couple, so excited to journey to New York like Emily. She selfishly wanted them at Broeckwyck, but knew the husband's skills would be required at Onteora. It was a struggle to choose after eating his wife's sweet cakes. A baker in the province was a great skill indeed.

Emily interrupted her private musings when she snapped softly, "Oh no! Do hurry Ryna before he sees us!" Soon their horses were cantering down a curvy path in the park.

Catharyna's voice was light and jovial. "Who are we fleeing from?"

Emily's face became tense as she avoided eye contact. "A persistent gentleman."

Their horses began a smooth gallop toward a private alcove with a small pond. They dismounted, led the horses to the water and sat on a bench. Catharyna surveyed the charming area and turned to find Charles Hawkins approaching them. He looked upset, but as he drew closer, his face held only a warm smile. "Good morning, ladies."

Catharyna was the only woman who rose to greet him. "Hello, Charles. It's a pleasure to see you here today. I thought my cousin Gerrit was with you? I fear his enjoyment with

London's clubs has occupied most of his time of late."

Charles dismounted, bowed to the ladies and lingered over Catharyna. "He's attending a horse race with Lord Sterling. I missed you at dinner last night. Did you enjoy Lady Putnam's party?"

She smiled and replied, "It was very stimulating company. We debated well into the evening on the equality of man."

A sensual smile spread across his handsome features. "And what was the outcome?"

She laughed freely. " Men are selfish rulers, which is why God made women to cover his blunder."

Charles grinned. "Precisely what I would have predicted a group of titled women to conclude."

They smiled at each other until Emily rose from the bench and broke their private discussion. "Please excuse me."

To Catharyna's amazement, Emily mounted her horse and took off again, heading back up the path. She was left alone with Charles and a flustered Penelope, who was clearly upset over her sister's rudeness.

Penelope's hands fluttered in her lap. "Oh dear, what is she doing now?" She was torn between which woman to stay with, her disobedient sister, or the unpredictable Miss van Broeck. It was a difficult choice.

Catharyna grabbed Penelope's hands and motioned for her to stand. "Penelope, please search for Emily before we lose her in the park. We'll remain here until you return."

With the assistance of Charles, Penelope mounted her filly and took off at an uncomfortable trot. Charles took a seat on the bench. "I have news of Will."

Life's forces suspended when her eyes swung to his face. "He is home?"

Charles shook his head. "No, he's not coming home."

Ice blue eyes pinned his face. "No?"

A cloudy haze filled his eyes. "It's difficult for me to understand my brother. He was sent to Amsterdam to handle some personal matters for the Duke, and jumped aboard a ship heading to the West Indies. My mother believes he's pursuing the possibility of a sugar plantation there, since that was his original intention before New York." He saw the bewilderment on her face, so Charles added, "The lure of the sea has captured him once again."

She rose from the bench with hands shaking, but kept them from view. She had begun to forgive his deceit, believing in his character, hoping he would have a plausible explanation. Now she didn't know where to turn. Her mind was blank of thought until a single tear fell from a treacherous eye, taking with it the memory of him. Hawk had abandoned her in pursuit of another adventure. There was nothing more to do.

She faced him with no emotion in face, eyes or heart. "Your mother must be disappointed."

Charles' eyes pierced her own, but found nothing under the intense scrutiny. "She is heart broken," he confessed and took her hand. "I know this is a difficult time for you, but my need for an heir has become even greater now. Have you considered my proposal?"

"Not yet," she replied, and brushed his hands away to mount her horse. "Please excuse me, I must catch up with my friends." She whistled a command, and the Arabian mare galloped up the path, its hooves digging deep into the frozen ground.

Charles watched the horse race away from his side, not understanding why Catharyna didn't react as he had anticipated. Time was running out, she would be leaving in a few weeks. That left one thing for him to try.

The Red Lion was full to capacity with its evening crowd. The low dark ceilings made the stale air feel heavy and suffocating to Gerrit van Hoesen, whose head was pounding. His stay in London had taken a very different direction from his original purpose.

He was to secure loans for his father to build grist mills

and a manor house for himself and his betrothed, Christina van Cortlandt, in the lowlands on Hoesenwyck. Unexpectedly, his gambling debts mounted, and all control was lost. Charles Hawkins had admitted him into private clubs, introduced him to titled friends, and there seemed to be no end to their fun or money. It was now clear he could no longer could keep pace with them.

He sat dejected in a chair, and a comely bar wench delivered him a pint of ale. Both were ignored. The one idea that continued to rise to the surface, was to climb aboard the next ship heading east, and never return. The plan was taking form in his mind, when a tap on his shoulder jerked his head up to find Charles Hawkins taking the seat beside him.

"How went the race?"

Gerrit avoided eye contact. "Not as entertaining as I had hoped." He pushed the ale away, and began drumming his fingers on the wooden table.

"So I heard."

This time Gerrit's head swung to look at his companion's face. There was joy in his tone; of this he was certain. It began to make his mind wonder why that would be.

"Any plans how to pay off your debt?"

Gerrit watched the smile on the Englishman's face, and felt the hawk-like stare corner him. He chose to remain silent as suspicions rose over Charles' intentions with him. He had reacted poorly when he first landed in London by allowing all normal caution to remain on the ship. He finally wondered if there was time to fix his recklessness.

Charles leaned forward and whispered, "Go to Catharyna. She will help you."

Gerrit's gut twisted as guilt kicked and pummeled his pride. Even so, he nodded in agreement. It was the only choice, other than debtors prison. He rose from the table, and threw a few coins on it. "Good night, Charles."

Gerrit walked the narrow streets of London, and headed for the docks. He saw a group of sailors standing around a lamp post, smoking near the vessel *Nag's Head,* and he approached

153

them. "Where ya headed?"

The buccaneer mumbled, "Jamaica."

Gerrit's eyes never wavered as he viewed the grotesque face. It had been burned on one side, so his lip was gnarled and twisted. He suspected the buccaneer was testing him, but he didn't flinch. "Need a hand?"

The group started to laugh. "We got plenty, no need for another Dutchman."

Gerrit shrugged his shoulders, and moved on. Seconds later, he turned and shouted back to the officers, "When ya sailing?"

"Dawn."

He stopped at several other ships, but they had just pulled into port. He decided it was time to seek out Catharyna. A discussion would harm no one, and if it turned bad, he'd jump aboard the *Nag's Head* and make the best of it.

An hour later he entered Twining Oak's foyer, and was told Catharyna was upstairs for the evening. He went to his room, and paced the floor over the seriousness of the situation. There was no other choice. He rose and went in search of his cousin's room.

"Catharyna, it's Gerrit."

She wrapped herself into a thick velvet robe before opening the door. "It's very late."

"I know." They stared at each other until she nodded. Gerrit entered and began to pace in front of the windows. "I'm in trouble."

She sat down, but remained silent.

"I've accrued some gaming debts."

Catharyna didn't hide her disappointment; it was strong in her voice, "Gerrit, this isn't like you to gamble. You visit the horse races on Long Island during the summer, yet you've never gambled more than a few coins on them. Why now, here in London?"

Her piercing eyes remained fixed on his movements as he turned away in disgrace and mumbled, "It's done, must we discuss why?"

"How much?"

His eyes turned away again, this time in shame. "Charles holds my debt, I am unsure where it stands."

Catharyna could not silence her amazement. "What madness is this? You choose to gamble, and then do not keep track of your losses?"

He drew away, and faced the window in dejection. His shoulders were slouched. "I lost myself in London."

Catharyna rubbed her forehead, trying to make sense of this new development. Things had gone perfect for Broeckwyck while she was in London. Yet, personally, she and Gerrit were falling apart. And her brain was too exhausted to think clearly.

She rose and took Gerrit's hands. Their eyes locked. "You are my family, and will not go to debtor's prison. Promise me you'll never gamble again, and I will repay your loan."

Relief filled Gerrit's face and eyes. "I swear it, Ryna. I'll pay you back."

Their eyes remained locked and she replied, "Yes, you will." They embraced, and suddenly, she felt an overwhelming need to release her own pain. Her shoulders shook and tears began to roll down her face.

"Ryna, please, don't cry. I'm sorry I shamed our family."

The tears continued and her throat slowly began to close with emotion. She whispered, "No, it isn't you, Gerrit. I cry at my own stupidity."

Gerrit gently dried the tears and examined her face. "No, Ryna, such cannot be true."

The respect for her in his eyes made her say dejectedly, "But it is, I trusted the wrong man."

"Hawk?" he questioned in a doubtful voice.

"Hawk."

His eyes narrowed on his cousin's shattered face and instead reflected on the Hawk he had witnessed in London who respected Catharyna and spoke openly about her to all the merchants on Lombard Street. He was a worker, didn't gamble, and was practically as tight with money as Catharyna. This wasn't the type of man to break his cousin's trust.

155

"You're mistaken."

This time hope was gone and she would not listen to any one defending Hawk. "It no longer matters, he has gone to the West Indies to scout for a sugar plantation there instead of the Hudson Valley."

Gerrit laughed for the first time in days. "What nonsense is this? Hawk would never leave all he built in New York to begin anew again. His purpose in coming here was to be given a manor grant naming him first as Lord of the Manor for his Onteora. He's no fool to walk away from that."

Catharyna listened to her cousin's words. She had never known Hawk's reason for coming to London, just her own. Feelings of selfishness surfaced again. Never had she asked the right questions to Hawk who had shared his dreams and visions to her. The survival instinct to keep him away from her heart had failed her in knowing the real man. Now it was time to get answers.

"You said Charles holds your debt?"

Gerrit nodded and shivered under the coldness lurking deep in her eyes.

"It's time we speak to Fairfax, and hear what he knows of Charles. I fear we aren't seeing his full face."

"I'll return soon," Gerrit promised. Seconds later, he greeted the evening's cold, dark and moonless night once again. It was past midnight, but that didn't slow his galloping horse down London's narrow streets. There was much to be done before dawn would arrive.

He dismounted and knocked loudly on the Fielding's door, due to the loud commotion inside. An uneasiness spread, finding the household awake at the late hour.

Gerrit entered the room and found everyone present except Fairfax. Emily was seated in the parlor with tears streaming down from puffy eyes with Penelope beside her, whispering words of comfort.

He asked the room in general, "Where is Fairfax?"

A loud shriek erupted from Emily's throat, and she began to cry in earnestness against Penelope.

Mr. Fielding pulled Gerrit aside and whispered, "He's gone, postponed their wedding."

Gerrit snapped, "When did he leave?"

"A few minutes ago, he's taking the *Nag's Head* to Jamaica at dawn."

Gerrit nodded and left the grieving household. Within the hour he was boarding the *Nag's Head* and found Fairfax on deck. There was no civilities. "What in blazes is going on?" Fairfax remained silent and Gerrit punched him in the ribs. "Don't play silent with me, I'm surrounded by crying females and we all demand answers. Are you joining up with Hawk?"

Fairfax's face softened at the mention of crying females. His departure from Emily was more painful than expected, but there was no choice. He gazed at Gerrit and made a rash decision, he had to trust someone. Fairfax wrapped an arm around Gerrit and led him into the darkness.

An hour later Gerrit raced off the deck and galloped his stallion through the streets of London, heading for Twining Oaks. This time there was a real game, and the stakes were higher than money.

Thirteen

Atlantic Ocean

Blackness consumed the small storage room, its air stale and moldy. The ritual began. The next minute started exactly as the previous one had ended. Hawk cursed his arrogance, haughtiness and pride. Self recrimination was repeated each day he remained locked, tied and gagged in his prison. He fought the binds of rope around his hands and feet, but neither budged. The cloth around his mouth was pulled taunt behind his head, causing mouth soars that were chaffed and bloody.

There had never been a time when all he could do was think, and it played a torturous game with his mind. Time ticked away at his imperfections as a man. He had accepted days ago that it wasn't Juliet, or even Dirck, that brought him to his darkened prison. The blame rested fully on his never ending ambition.

Most men would have been thrilled at receiving ten miles of the best land along the Hudson River, yet he continued to reach out for more. His ambition, and, in the deepest pit of his soul, greed, had pushed him to London for a title. He *had* to be the first manor lord in the province. If he had been a simple man, he would be building Onteora with Catharyna beside him, pregnant with their child, instead of being roped up in a storage room aboard a ship.

Frustration tore through him in the knowledge that, by failing himself, he had failed her too. There had been no words of endearment spoken, only a battle of wills and brief passion, that time would distinguish. He fought his mind to keep the picture of their future clear, but it became blurred with the knowledge that his greed had destroyed it.

Instincts had also failed him in dealing with Juliet Craijer. He'd met rich, powerful, devious women like her before, yet, sitting in the coffee shop, his arrogance had taken flight, impatient and anxious to return as savior to Catharyna with news of Dirck.

So, the ritual continued. He bashed his head against the wooden plank wall. Seconds, minutes, or hours passed, he knew not, when a bright light filled the room, and a boy's face appeared.

"Gov'nor, yu's gotta stop hurtin' yurself, or we wunt git no gold fir yee."

Hawk responded by banging his head five more times.

"Lordies, yu's in a temper t'day. I's bawt yir stew, and I's feed yu, if'in you behave."

Hawk sat up straight and looked at the boy, signaling he would cooperate. Once the gag was removed, Hawk moved his jaw around, without showing the pain it caused. Dry and stilted words were heard, due to a parched throat and chapped lips. "Release me. Gold for you."

The boy chuckled, and began feeding him. "Gov'nor, where'd yu be git'tin gold?"

Hawk chewed as quickly as his sore jaw would allow and then swallowed. "I'm Black Hawk."

The boy's eyes grew round with fear, and then he laughed as he stuffed another spoonful into Hawk's mouth. "Yu's got me Gov'nor!" Eyes opened in fear, and he shivered, "I surrender, Black Hawk!" The boy continued laughing, only seeing a broken man, roped and tied before him. He was no fool, everyone knew the privateer Black Hawk was dead, faded into the seas years ago, never to be heard from again.

Rory continued feeding his prisoner and whispered a warning, "Now hush up witcha crazy tawk on the Dragon's ship. He'll cut yur tongue out wittout blinking an eye! Don'tcha know he's ta fiercest, nastiest pirate on ta seas!" When the bowl of stew was empty, Rory rose and locked the door, without any more discussion.

Hawk leaned his head back against the wall, and closed his eyes. There was nothing more to do but think.

The rocking of the ship soon lulled his tortured mind. As sleep took hold, Hawk's dreams returned to the adventure of his life eight years ago.

1667 Port Royal, Jamaica

Word spread like fire across the island with the news Morgan was heading out again. A thousand men filled the beach, privateersmen, buccaneers and volunteers all eager for adventure and the promise of a rich bounty.

Captain William Hawkins was one of several touring the crowds to pick additional crew members. The assignment was unknown by all the captains, only their infamous leader, Sir Henry Morgan and Governor Moodyford, were aware of the location for their next venture. The privateer captains all shared a united goal: Weaken Spain's wealth for the English crown, and gather the spoils of the battle for themselves as payment. All followed Morgan, the most successful Welsh privateer on the seas, knighted by the English crown for his service.

There was no life found in the eyes of Captain Hawkins, which was one reason he had the most loyal crew in the Caribbean, where loyalty saved a man's life more than a sword. He was the youngest privateer to work for the crown, all due to his prestigious lineage to Sir William Hawkins, one of the greatest seaman for Queen Elizabeth in the sixteenth century. Beside him stood Fairfax, a ship hand who had proven his most loyal and ambitious mate.

Hawk nodded toward Fairfax, who began to walk through the crowd, picking men randomly. Those chosen were led to the ocean, and instructed to wash their faces. Soon, the men where separated into two groups. Those who washed their faces face down, and those who washed their faces with their eyes raised and alert. Fairfax continued selecting men from the crowd, and soon one line grew to two hundred feet, the other fifty feet. An hour later, Hawk raised a hand, indicating he had his crew.

Hawk approached the thirty men on the line who had kept their faces erect. "Welcome to the *Black Hawk* men. Follow me."

A grumble was heard from the crowd of men not selected. Everyone wanted to be part of the *Black Hawk's* crew. Captain Hawkins had a reputation for fearless ambition that knew no bounds, with no hesitation for yesterday or tomorrow, only the genius for knowing the moment to strike. Being on the *Black Hawk* guaranteed rich booty indeed.

A fortnight later, eight vessels, carrying four hundred and fifty adventure hungry men from a hundred different harbors, followed Sir Morgan's flagship in the direction of the horizon. They were outward bound, but only one man knew where they were headed. When they were at the coast of Costa Rica, Sir Morgan called a halt, and finally consulted his captains on their mission.

"We attack Spain's stronghold for their gold in the New World. We attack their fort of Portobelo!" Grumbles by his loyal captains were heard, so he added, "We shall prove the Spaniards' belief that their impregnable fort is a myth when we take full possession of it!"

Seven of the eight captains panicked. Cases were made to withdraw. "'Tis unthinkable, Captain! Iron Castle and Castle Gloria face each other across the narrow entrance to the harbor. Their guns will blast us before we can raise ours!"

"Indeed," added another, "if we make it into the town, it is buttressed by St. Jerome, the most heavily gunned castle in all of America."

And another, "Do you really propose we attack these formidable fortresses and the garrisons they contain, with less than five hundred men, armed with pistols and side arms?"

Each captain knew the numerous failed attempts made by other English privateers and pirates to take Portobelo. The

guns of the powerful fort had more than justified the Spaniards'
belief that their massive fort was capable of repelling attack,
either by land or by sea.

Morgan turned to his youngest captain. "What say you
Hawk?"

"It won't be easy with its landlocked harbor. But,"
youthful bravo filled his face, "their plate fleet is due to arrive
any day now, and her warehouses are stuffed with gold, silver,
jewels and pearls, and other riches waiting to return to Spain. If
we strike, the time is now with Portobelo's prizes so ripe."

Morgan smiled paternally at his young protégé. The
childless Welsh privateer viewed Hawk as a son, so great was
his courage and ambition. Hawk was living up to his ancestor's
reputation of boundless greed, and he was one of the reasons
Morgan believed they had a chance at taking Portobelo. His
other captains were not so bold.

Edward Penn blasted, "We can't attack by sea, we'll be
blasted out the water in an hour. It's impossible!"

Morgan snapped, "Yee gods, Penn! Do you take me for
a fool! Sea is not our way into the town." He turned and found
his youngest captain held a ruthless grin. "What say you,
Hawk?"

Their eyes sparkled at each other when Hawk replied,
"We attack on land."

Morgan nodded in approval, and added, "At night!"

Mumbles grew louder amongst the captains, and
Edward Penn looked at Hawk with hatred. The young captain
had swiftly ousted him from Morgan's favor and now sat at his
right hand in arrogance, placing them all into a suicide mission.
Except, he had the courage to voice his demands aloud. "We
won't proceed on this *suicide* mission unless the crew agree as
a whole."

Morgan rose instantly. "Very well." And went on deck,
calling for the ships to gather, and soon captured the crew's
attention. "We head to the City of Gold!" he shouted, and
raucous cheers bounced across each ship. Every man was eager
and ready for a rich sack. "There is gold, silver, jewels and

wealth beyond imagination. All to be yours, if we sack this city!"

The cheers grew louder as the men stomped their feet on the decks of the ship. Morgan's voice grew grim and dark. "No more will you live in want or poverty, so debt-ridden that you have to sell your clothes for food and shelter!"

The crowd grew quiet as reminders of their life of poverty hit a raw nerve. After a lengthy pause, Morgan raised his arm and shouted, "I say we strike Portobelo tonight!"

The buccaneers were led into the web of a master story spinner. All pumped up on talk of wealth, there was no thought given about the impossibility of their mission. A roar of agreement was heard across each ship, all the men clamored to be part of the booty. Cheers for Morgan began, and soon, the men were chanting his name.

Fairfax looked across the deck at Hawk, standing confident beside their infamous leader, and ignored the fear that flickered through him. If Hawk was going, so would he.

They arrived at a secluded cove at midnight, and used an Englishman, once held prisoner in St. Jerome's torture chamber and eager for revenge, to lead them to a small fort on the outskirts of town, where they sneaked upon the sentry before he could give the alarm.

At pistol point, the sentry was forced by Morgan to surrender the fort, who warned, "Surrender now or death will befall every man here due to your greed."

The audacity of his words prompted a round of shots as their reply, just as dawn broke along the horizon. The blasts woke the sleeping town, and pandemonium ignited.

The air became filled with shouts from the men, and terrified cries from women and children. Alarm bells rang in unison as the sounds of cannons exploded into the harbor.

The town's governor rushed through the town on horseback. "Citizens, gather together for defense!"

No one listened to his pleas. Saving their wealth was paramount in every mind as Morgan and his men swarmed over the town. Feverishly, every man and woman began hiding their wealth, with no clear plan. Some loaded pack animals with valuables, and turned them loose, hoping they would gallop to safety somewhere, somehow.

The governor, in failing to rally a defense for the town, and seeing Morgan and his men coming at a run, retreated to the fortress in order to join the garrison.

The privateers knew they would be able to do nothing with the town, unless the fort was first taken, so Morgan gave the order to rush it. Hawk watched in frustration as men were mowed down. When he ordered the next wave to proceed, they retreated.

He approached Morgan and shouted, "We need a new way in if victory is to come at all. The men are ready to give up. They're tired and hungry and the swarms of insects make it worse."

Morgan winked and nodded. It was a moment that would forever change Hawk when his mentor and leader ordered, "Get their clergy to storm the fort. They won't harm their priests and nuns."

The unholy idea was soon in force. Heavy scaling ladders, wide enough for four men to mount, were brought forward. Next came the priests and nuns, who were ordered to the front lines, at the head of the rabble, as it started for the fort.

The terrified priests and nuns went down on their knees and prayed for mercy. "We are people of God, and by every civilized law known to man, we abstain from war!"

Hawk looked breathlessly at Morgan for the order to release them. Instead, his leader barked, "Mercy? You speak of mercy, yet know nothing of it! What *mercy* had the Inquisition shown the thousands of innocent men and women who had died in its torture chambers? What *mercy* had the Church shown the helpless Indians here and in Peru in promoting Christian love, all while stripping them clean of their wealth? *Mercy*?" A deep rich laugh made fear rise in the priests and nuns. "There is *more mercy* here today than your Church has ever shown anyone helpless in its grasp! For I grant you the choice to open

Portobelo's coffers to us, or die if they remain shut." He roared, "Now, get under those ladders! March, *now*!"

Hawk watched as the helpless priests and nuns were jerked, shoved, and prodded by gun barrels at their backs toward the fort. Halting a short distance out of gunfire, Morgan called for an immediate surrender, while his prisoners begged the fort to hold their fire.

Time suspended for Hawk, who realized he was praying. His eyes went to Fairfax, now approaching with a dark scowl of disapproval. It was clear this was a line Fairfax had no intention of crossing. Except, Morgan held the power to have them cross it. Hawk's leadership began to weigh heavy as he waited tensely for the fort's answer.

The governor looked tortured, seeing God's holy people there at the front. He was a devout Catholic, but a loyal man to his crown. He shouted down to Morgan, "My duty is first to King and country in defending this fort!"

With no hesitation, Morgan charged a second later. "Forward, men!"

As if in a nightmare, Hawk watched as a burst of flame rose from the fort. He rushed to Morgan and barked, "Sir, the battle continues with the priests and nuns directly in its path."

Morgan's eyes were determined. "Their Governor chose their sentence, not I."

Hawk's jaw tightened until he shouted, "I'll not have their blood on my soul!" With that, he turned to Fairfax and they charged forward to release the priests and nuns who ran for freedom amidst the guns of the fort and bursts of flames erupting from it. Many clergy fell under the fire and rumble before they could make it to safety.

Hawk became trapped against the wall and barked at his men, "Move forward, now!" His crew of expert marksmen raced forward and threw him loaded pistols. Soon they won the bottom of the walls, where the cannons could not reach them, and then swarmed up the ladders and over the parapets for hand-to-hand conflict.

They fought fiendishly and pushed the Spaniards back,

pushing harder and harder. The smell of victory filled their senses, and greed their eyes, with Black Hawk leading the way. The Spaniards gave way under the brutal onslaught. Not even their valiant governor's order to hold their ground could penetrate the terror that gripped their souls.

The Spaniards threw down their guns and surrendered at the feet of Black Hawk, who leered down at them with no mercy.

Shouts of victory were heard from the privateers, who were finally able to do what they came to do. They plundered the town. At the end of two weeks, Portobelo was completely gutted of valuables when Morgan and his captains sailed away. Not so much as a teaspoon was left in the sacked city. All weapons and ammunition had been collected, and taken away, and the guns of the forts, dismantled and spiked, to render them useless.

Hawk had participated in one of the richest hauls in history for the English crown. When Morgan partitioned the booty it was to find two-hundred fifty thousand dollars in yellow pieces of eight, piles of uncoined bullion, boxes of jewels, bolts of silks, laces, linens, and numerous other valuables that would be converted into cash in Port Royal.

Morgan stood before the bedraggled crew with his captains behind him. He drew Hawk forward, placed an arm about his shoulders and shouted, "The ghost of Black Hawk stands alive before us today. England will knight his deeds at Portobelo, and our living legend will be known throughout the world as Sir William Hawkins!"

Three cheers echoed across the beach. Hawk searched out for only one man's eyes, and found Fairfax staring down into the sand. The ache that had sprouted the day of the attack began to throb, regardless of his attempts to silence it. He had achieved his goal, he would be knighted and had wealth to buy the grandest sugar plantation in the Caribbean. Life was his for the taking. The ache would be silenced, crushed if necessary.

They arrived home amidst a drunken orgy of gaiety, all but a few men remained sober. Fairfax stood in the distance on the *Black Hawk,* gazing at the horizon to the north, his face in the shadows.

Hawk approached his friend with a bright smile. "What say you, Fairfax, no drinking, cards or talk? You're a wealthy man now, it's time to live!"

Fairfax met his leader's eyes and did not hold his tongue. "Aye, live I shall. This was my last sack. I'm taking my booty and heading north."

Many buccaneers had come and gone on Hawk's crew, but Fairfax was one he viewed as friend. It never occurred that he too might leave one day. "North?" he laughed in wonderment.

"Aye, the crown just claimed New York from the Dutch. I'll be landed gentry there."

"You're serious?"

Their eyes met and Fairfax confirmed. "Aye."

Hawk's eyes narrowed and fists clenched. This was the one man who stood beside him since a junior officer. They had shared many successful adventures and Hawk wasn't ready for them to take different paths. "Don't head north. I'm purchasing a sugar plantation in Jamaica with my booty. You can do the same and be landed here."

Amazement filled Fairfax's face, hope his voice. "You are leaving privateering?"

"Some day."

Fairfax shook his head. "I'm ready to leave it."

Hawk was angry. "You abandon me now that I've made you a rich man?"

Their eyes clashed, anger in each. "I fear God more than you."

Hawk was speechless when Fairfax walked away. This man's desertion left him bewildered. He struggled to understand how any man could leave privateering when the crown handed Spanish gold to them. There was nothing evil in privateering, no law that would hang them for their deeds. Their work was to weaken the crown's enemies by stealing their wealth. Hawk took great pleasure in doing a thorough job. Overall, Fairfax's desertion was disappointing, but not painful.

Two days later when they entered Port Royal, the two men who were once close friends, ignored each other. Fairfax grinned when he saw Captain Penn's wife at the dock waiting for him. It was his last booty and last tryst with her. He didn't once consider her husband.

A fortnight passed. Hawk was seated in the Crow's Inn, gazing at the title of his sugar plantation. No matter how he willed it, Fairfax's words had continued to plague him. The fact that his only true friend in the West Indies believed their deeds were wrongful in God's eyes, festered in his soul.

The career of privateer was never chosen, but placed naturally on his shoulders. His height and auburn hair had given him the same traits as the first Sir William Hawkins, and his two older brothers' thirst for adventure soon made him restless to seek it. So, when the Black Plague took both of them in death, Hawk sought to live their dreams. It hadn't come easily to deaden a conscience to the work, but, once he achieved it, it quickly made him into a greater legend than his infamous ancestor.

Now, what plagued him, was the growing suspicion that Fairfax's words had ripped a whole in his heart that allowed his conscience to reemerge. A conscience killed many a soul in the deep shark infested seas.

His thoughts were soon interrupted by one of his crewmen, Jacob Chanler, who announced, "Captain Penn caught Fairfax."

Instantly, Hawk rose from the table, and Jacob followed a step behind. No words were necessary to know the predicament Fairfax was in. Penn was renown for his torturous punishments if any man stole from him. Being found with his wife would be death.

They found Fairfax strung up between two trees, his back bloodied from the slick leather whip held in Penn's hand.

Hawk roared, "You go too far, Penn!"

"Far? He's been cuckolding me for years! My crew's been laughing behind my back." The whip struck out across Fairfax's back. "My wife's been laughing behind my back," and again the whip struck, "and *you!*"

The men faced each other with their hatred naked in their eyes. "Today there will be no more of it!" Penn swore, and raised the whip to strike again, but Hawk caught it, and wrapped it around his hand.

"Don't touch him again."

In one graceful movement, Penn grabbed a firearm from his belt and raised it at Hawk. "Let go of the whip, Hawk, before I put a hole in your side."

There was every reason to believe Penn would do as he threatened. Pulling a trigger required no skill. Hawk turned to look at the only true friend he had known since his two brothers died. A choice needed to be made instantly. "How much for Fairfax?"

Penn blasted, "Portobelo made us wealthy men. I want *respect* now."

Hawk had no choice but to release the ghosts of his brothers and ancestor. He drew closer, toward the greed in Penn's eyes. There was no question in his voice, just an order. "How much."

Penn's eyes narrowed as he hissed, "I want more than money."

"How much!"

Penn's hatred for Hawk was insurmountable to pay. The young privateer had been at sea for seven years and ousted him as Morgan's right hand captain. Whereas he had an adulterous wife and his leader's derision for being weak in voicing objections in sacking Portobelo. "Your share of Portobelo. *And,* promise that you and Fairfax will never step foot in the West Indies again."

It was more than Hawk expected. The barrel of Penn's gun stared at his heart just as the sun broke through a patch of clouds and shined on Fairfax. Hawk didn't believe in signs from heaven, the choice was already made. But, it did make him more confident in the decision. He extended a hand to seal their agreement.

Amazement filled Penn's face. Then, realization that his personal fortune had just doubled in size, thanks to an adulterous wife. With a nod to his crewmen, two strokes of their sword cut the ties that held Fairfax, and his bloody body sank to the dusty ground.

Hawk went to get him, but Penn grabbed his arm. "Jacob can get Fairfax. You follow me, I get my booty now."

Hawk's eyes narrowed, a cold so deep that Penn took a step back. A hand reached into his vest and pulled out the deed to his sugar plantation. It was all the booty from Portobelo and more, but when he released it into Penn's hands a weight lifted off his shoulders.

Penn looked at the deed and cackled in laughter. Morgan's protégé had just given away a fortune for a ship hand's life. He bellowed loudly, "So hurls downward the great Black Hawk into the deep, bottomless pit!"

Hawk walked passed Penn, unmoved by the words, to help Jacob, who was balancing the bloody and battered Fairfax.

Fairfax gazed painfully up at him, and their eyes locked. Hawk promised, "Fear God no more, brother. We leave for New York."

Fairfax collapsed with a smile.

Fourteen

London, 1675

The earth awakened, tulips sprouted, birds chirped, squirrels scurried. Winds of spring were blowing from the four corners of the earth, slowly undermining the best of plans.

"Mr. Gerrit van Hoesen is waiting for you in the study," said the timid maid, who immediately left the room. Of late, there were many outbursts from her mistress' bedchamber, with no notice of whom, when or why they would erupt. She did not wait to encounter another, and sped down the servant's stairway.

Catharyna raced down the stairs, eager to hear the news that had delayed her departure another month while Gerrit visited Amsterdam. She closed the study doors for privacy, and went directly to him. Their eyes locked.

Gerrit confirmed, "It is true Hawk is on a ship headed to the West Indies."

She swore and asked, "Tell me how this happened. Did you meet this Juliet person Fairfax spoke of?"

Gerrit's face grew tense, but he would not hold back any information, regardless of its ill reception. "Yes, she is beautiful, unlike any woman I know."

Pure, hot jealousy stabbed at Catharyna's heart. A hand rose to continue.

"She is also devious, cunning and manipulative. If I hadn't spoken with Fairfax first, I would have fallen for her myself. There are many seaman who work for her father, and many whispered of her lovers."

Catharyna's eyes narrowed.

His eyes shifted away. "They are prizes to her."

"Prizes?"

"The men she covets are the fiercest seamen. It is a game she plays in wooing them to her."

Catharyna stared at her cousin in confusion. "But what has that to do with Hawk?"

Gerrit took her hands. "He is known as Black Hawk." He saw disbelief building in his cousin's stubborn face, and he nodded, "It is true, Ryna. Hawk stood beside Morgan and took Portobelo, one of the richest sacks a privateer has taken for any crown."

"I can't..." her head kept shaking in denial, "he spoke about being a seaman..." her hands shook Gerrit's hold free, "but never this." She began to pace as anger rose. "He never told me *this*!"

Gerrit felt the weight of guilt for not separating her from Hawk. "It is true. Now, we must pray Fairfax will be successful in finding Hawk and news of Dirck. Juliet said he is somewhere in the West Indies too."

Catharyna shouted, "Juliet lied about Dirck! It was her bait to catch Hawk." She paced like a caged animal feeling powerless. "I knew I couldn't trust him! One trip and he deceives me with Broeckwyck and another woman."

"I got the impression Juliet wasn't pleased with Hawk's reaction to her."

She stopped pacing. "What are you telling me, Gerrit?"

"That Fairfax canceled his wedding for a reason."

Her breathing and heart stopped. "You fear for Hawk?"

Gerrit approached again, and grabbed her shoulders. "She sold him."

Catharyna kicked at him and tore free, only to kick a mahogany end table across the room. "I cannot..." she gasped, "take this." Her hands shook and eyes filled with tears. "Why must I lose everyone?" Lost eyes stared at Gerrit. "What shadow hangs over me that I must lose father, mother, brothers

172

and...?" sobs shook her body. The pain building could not be controlled. "The one man I wanted."

He grabbed her tightly in comfort. "Fairfax will find him."

She pulled away again and wiped angrily at the weak tears. "Yes, I am certain," she replied with a brave face, "but I cannot live in fear waiting for it."

He whispered, "No one wants you to."

"Did you not see the greed in Hawk?" Catharyna demanded, already ousting him from her heart. "All I was to him was a valuable wife to build Onteora on."

Gerrit knew what she was doing, but would not go along. "What's wrong with that!" he shouted back. "Is not that the basic requirement in all Dutchwomen? My mother is a paragon of a wife who built Hoesenwyck with my father. And our family places far greater expectations on you to surpass that. What is wrong with Hawk expecting the same?"

Catharyna's heart tightened, realizing a desire to be loved had somehow worked its way deep inside it. Practical and frugal qualities rose to squash the weak feeling out, and a smile cracked her stiff cheeks. "Nothing."

Gerrit took her hands. "Good, I've become a weak man in London. I couldn't bear it if you grew a heart here."

Tears watered her eyes, but a deep releasing laugh broke the darkness of the mood. Gerrit was telling her to wait for Hawk, but not to love him. She shuddered, "Heaven forbid!"

They hugged each other tightly. Gerrit continued, "I have news of Charles as well."

Catharyna groaned.

"Fairfax deliberately misled him and his mother about Hawk's absence. Emily is aware, so she is all we can share it with. We cannot permit any news of this to jeopardize Hawk's life."

She nodded and whispered, "So, Charles has been truthful with me about Hawk."

"Yes, but not of himself."

Catharyna's eyes narrowed. "How so?"

173

"He is sterile."

That evening a reflection of determination in the mirror stared back at Catharyna. Anger had been controlled. It was time to provide Charles an answer to his proposal. She left the bedchamber calmly to join him, with Meredith, downstairs in conversation before dinner.

Charles rose when she entered the room. There was no tremble when she offered a hand in greeting. "Good evening, Charles."

"You look beautiful this evening, Ryna."

Catharyna ignored the praise. It was the one politeness she found in England that grated on her nerves. There was no one who was beautiful at each and every occasion. And why one should be, left her baffled.

She turned to Meredith and stated, "Please excuse us a moment. Charles and I have a business matter we must discuss in the study." She met his stare and found anticipation that tried its best to strip her thoughts bare.

Charles bowed to his mother and escorted Catharyna to the study. The last week of dinners in her company made his confidence build on the response. She had been warming up to him ever since learning Hawk was not returning to London. He closed the doors and found Catharyna at the other end of the room.

She faced him and said, "Please be assured I have given this my greatest attention." He nodded, until she confessed, "But I must decline."

The shock over her words felt like an eighteen pound sledge hammer hitting his head. Moments passed until he replied, "I see."

"I appreciate your friendship, Charles. I hope it will continue."

"Of course."

"Gerrit has informed me of his debts to you. I would like to settle them before our departure."

Charles' voice changed instantly, to cold and distant. "It is the Duke who holds those debts, not I."

She drew closer and whispered, "But Gerrit told me you held his debt...."

Charles stood ramrod straight. "He assumed such. It was his Grace who extended credit to Gerrit with Hoesenwyck as collateral."

Catharyna's eyes narrowed. "How much?"

Charles shrugged. "That is a personal matter between them. You must speak with his Grace."

Catharyna's body grew tight with anger, realizing her mistake in rejecting Charles before settling Gerrit's debts. This was his punishment to her. "I will," she stated, and turned to leave the room.

Deep masculine laughter halted her. "Your seeking him out will not provide you an audience."

She stopped, and turned about to look at him.

He added, "You'll find him in France for the season. As my wife, it would be easily arranged."

"And as your friend?"

All pretenses of friendship evaporated, like a drop of water in the arid desert. "That kind of favor is done for family." Her eyes pierced him, with every word of friendship he had uttered to her in their private discussions. Charles relented, "Would marriage to me be so unpleasant?"

"I will not marry a liar."

He looked as though she smacked him. "I am no liar."

She drew closer and whispered, "You are sterile since eleven from smallpox."

Their eyes battled and Charles demanded, "Jane carried my baby, I am not sterile."

She too stood ramrod straight, unrelenting and unforgiving. Minutes ticked by until Catharyna could bear it no longer. "Charles, I want to remain your friend."

Anger was stripped away and desire blossomed out; it's

magnitude overwhelmed her. He reached out for her hand. "I want nothing more."

"Then be honest with me."

He heard the conviction and knew she would not relent. She had found out his dark secret. Denying it wouldn't erase it, especially since she believed it. "It is true my Jane was an adulterous wife, but our babe was *mine*. I stood by her even when she welcomed death, believing it was payment for her sin. She pleaded for my forgiveness and I gave it to her."

His throat grew tight, with emotion and eyes wet with unshed tears. "Our child came too soon. I was with him every second he breathed; there was nothing more I wanted than for him to live. But, I wasn't good enough, strong enough, fearless enough to make that true." His eyes were naked with pain in their depths. "It's true, I had small pox has a child, but I will not believe I will never be given the blessing of a son. No doctor has said it, so I pray it is not so. If that makes me a liar, so be it, I am a liar."

Truth shown in his eyes. There was no pride or pretense. Charles the man stood before her in complete honesty. The weight of her words and their impact on him made her feel cruel and evil. She drew closer and extended a hand in friendship. "Please forgive me, Charles. I had no right to judge you, and will not again."

His eyes began to clear and acceptance lit them. "Nor will you marry me."

She gazed at him for a very long time before answering. "No, I will not marry you, but I would be sorry if I lost your friendship."

A deep breath was released from his chest. "You have my friendship." A smile hovered over his lips. "And as such, I will accompany you to the Duke. He will be lenient about Gerrit with me beside you." They smiled at each other, and a true relationship was born.

Fifteen

Winds of opportunity were blowing, elusive, unpredictable, constant, and utterly impossible to determine their direction. The morning had not begun well. Gerrit was overseeing the trunks being loaded aboard the *Elizabeth,* when Emily Fielding erupted, unannounced, into Catharyna's cabin.

"I'm going with you."

Catharyna swore, "No, you are not. I'll not be responsible for you."

"My parents and all of London know that I will return to New York with you. 'Tis time you accept it."

The two woman glared at each other. Eventually, Catharyna answered, "I am not going directly to New York. We leave first for France to meet with the Duke. And, Charles is accompanying us."

Emily's face grew tight, frustrated she would be traveling with a man she so detested. Seconds passed, and her hands were thrown into the air. "Very well! It matters not how we get there as long as we get there."

Catharyna grabbed the stubborn woman by the shoulders and warned, "You must face the reality that there is no guarantee Fairfax will return to New York. I suggest you wait with your family here until he writes you."

Emily's eyes glowed with anger. "Fairfax *will* return to New York, just as he swore to me he would. I will be *there* to welcome him *home*. That is where my family is now."

Catharyna nodded. It was no use to challenge Emily's stubbornness. "I see you are determined."

"I am."

"Very well, you are welcome to join us."

Emily jumped on Catharyna in joy, causing her to fall into a copper tub in the corner of the cabin. A wave of black curls cascaded down to the floor as hair pins went eschew, landing on the floor. Emily giggled in delight, whereas Catharyna mumbled in Dutch, "The English will kill me yet."

Two days later they landed on French soil. The benefit of having Lord Charles Hawkins in their traveling party was quickly evident. No problem or nuisance was too little for his attention to ensure Catharyna had a pleasant and safe trip. When the Livery offered Gerrit a squeaky carriage with four old swayed back horses to take them to the Loire Valley, Charles immediately had it replaced with the finest carriage and four dapple gray Arabians the Livery kept for its noblemen. The next day Gerrit was turned away from a crowded Inn. Yet, moments later, Charles was escorting them inside to a table next to the fireplace. After a delectable meal, they were shown to the Inn's finest sleeping quarters.

Emily's eyes no longer held hatred in them as she looked at Charles, but they did contain distrust.

They were informed that the Duke was staying at the Chateau de la Guillonniere. Charles was seated beside Catharyna in the coach when he briefed her on their plans. "You will not be permitted to see his Grace immediately. Be patient, for I cannot predict when he will request your presence."

Gerrit and Catharyna sat beside each other. They exchanged a look and she replied solemnly, "I understand."

"During my business with his Grace, I will prepare him about your purpose in seeing him, so it might encourage him to seek you out faster. However, I make no promises."

"I understand."

Gerrit added, "Thank you, Charles."

Charles nodded and smiled at Catharyna.

Emily was silent, observing their conversation. The

purpose in their visiting the Duke was a mystery to her. However, there was something happening so subtly before her eyes, that it demanded full attention. She didn't understand why it had begun, but there was a growing dependency in Catharyna for Charles to handle matters for her. Each day Emily witnessed the strong Dutchwoman rely on him for the most mundane tasks, items that were well within Catharyna's sphere of ability. Furthermore, Gerrit seemed to encourage it. While she didn't voice the observations, she was alert to them.

So, when Charles announced they were invited guests at the Chateau, due to their patronage with him, Emily's teeth grounded against each other. The man was too smooth, too perfect, and far too charming to be real. Although, even her breath was held upon entering the Chateau which contained an opulence never before imagined.

Catharyna stared in horror at the wealth that screamed before her eyes. Waste was everywhere, but it was the most beautiful showcase for it she had ever seen.

A servant dressed in ivory and blue silk welcomed them. As a guide, he moved them forward into the magnificent rising foyer, pointing to important portraits and sculptures along the way to their suites, up a suspended curved staircase.

Emily and Catharyna were given a large suite decorated in pink and cream, with luscious brocades that adorned the walls and windows.

Emily's eyes glowed. In awe, she whispered, "I feel like a princess."

Catharyna smiled, but remained silent on the way to the window to view the lawns and sloping mountains. Her heart tightened over the landscape that resembled Broeckwyck. Loneliness plagued her daily, even with the knowledge that London had proven an excellent business trip. She had established relationships with several of London's most respected merchants and signed on fifty families as tenant farmers for Onteora. Though none of it took away the pain of Hawk's continued absence, which weighed more and more on her mind each day.

Emily interrupted her private thoughts with a touch on the shoulder. "Which gown should I wear for dinner?"

Catharyna pointed to one dress without seeing it, and looked back out the window.

Emily refused to be ignored. "Please tell me what is wrong, Ryna."

A weak smile answered, only to turn back and stare outside the window again.

Emily persisted, "I feel you are pulling away from me! Am I so terrible a nuisance to you?"

Catharyna shook her head.

"Then what is holding your tongue?" Catharyna's shoulders were grabbed, and Emily glared into her vacant eyes. "Release your demons, Ryna!" she ordered, and swore, "I am your friend and swear to be silent."

The volcano erupted. Catharyna drew a deep breath and everything was shared. "I worry how to approach the Duke, that if I displease him, he'll throw Gerrit in debtor's prison! I worry if he might decide to take Broeckwyck from me. I worry my brother is dead." She glared at Emily's stunned face. "I worry how Broeckwyck is fairing without me, and...I fear..." her throat grew tight but confessed, "I fear for Hawk."

Emily hugged her and whispered, "I know, Ryna, I know. We must pray each minute of every day."

Frustration radiated out of Catharyna, and she pushed away to pace the room. "Yes, yes, yes! I'll pray till my voice and knees give out, but that won't answer my questions *now*. That won't tell me where Hawk is and...." she paused and growled loudly, "if I should *wait* for him!" Angry tears began to slide down stiff cheeks. She faced Emily with the power of it. "He told me to wait for him and I agreed. I had expected a fortnight, I never anticipated such...uncertainty." She whispered in defeat, "I've begun to question if I should marry Charles."

They stared at each other for several tense seconds. Emily replied, "You do not need Charles to accomplish this. You will meet the Duke and get what you need from him."

Uncertainty was heard in Catharyna's voice. "And how

will I accomplish that?"

"The same way you captured Hawk."

A brow arched high on her forehead and she questioned, "Really?"

Emily squeezed her hands. "There was never a word spoken of marriage by Hawk until you. The man is boundless. Yet, somehow, you captured him." Then, she leaned closer and whispered, "Could you truly give yourself to his brother when your heart is his?"

Catharyna whispered, "I've no heart."

"I believe you do."

Her anger replied, "I've no luxury for frivolous words or emotion. Truly, if love exists, it flew by so quickly I missed it."

Emily persisted, "Do you want Hawk?"

A haunted voice replied, "Yes."

Emily smiled brightly at her. "Then you have no choice but to wait for him. Hawk will return to you and then you will see your heart."

They stared at each other for a long time before Catharyna would release Emily's hands.

West Indies

Hawk closed his eyes against the sudden flash of light in the storage room prison. The boy was back again with his daily meal of stew. The soars around his mouth now oozed with blood when the gag was removed. Eating had became a double edged sword, he knew it was critical, yet the pain was unbearable. Shreds of pain tore through his body when his mouth opened to eat the tasteless meal.

Rory looked over his prisoner's deteriorating form, and concern grew, seeing the beast of a man shrink before his eyes. He knew the Dragon's booty was in jeopardy if measures weren't taken quickly. "Yir not keepin yir bulk Gov'nor. 'Tis o'l that bangin ya duwin takin o'l yir strength from ya body."

The time was now for Hawk to be listened to. If he remained locked up a moment longer his mind would be lost. He croaked, "Let me see Dragon."

This time Rory nodded a head in agreement. The short lad assisted him to stand, but his size was too much for him to carry, and Hawk buckled over and crashed against the wall for support. "Gov'nor, ya's gotta help me."

Hawk's eyes narrowed and pinned the boy to the floor boards. Pain engulfed his entire body from being in the same position for two months. He growled through gritted teeth, "I'll try my best."

Rory slapped him on the back. "Fone, fallow me, Gov'nor."

Hawk's steps grew stronger the closer he came to the warm Caribbean breezes. Deep breaths of the fresh salty air began to recharge his body, mind and soul. Intelligent eyes now scanned the deck and latched on a muscular black man, staring at him as though he were a ghost.

Jacob Chanler's eyes turned to his new captain in confusion. Dragon had never told the crew Black Hawk was aboard. Jacob's eyes turned to his old leader and silently questioned him. Hawk's eyes commanded silence, and Jacob obediently turned around and took up a whittling stick again. Their exchange went unnoticed.

Hawk watched as Rory approached the captain, Terrance O'Malley, who was now the infamous Dragon. His red hair blazed like flames under the Caribbean sun, and a constant snarl twisted his lips. He was not the height of Hawk, but his shoulders were as wide as two normal men, and his muscular legs as thick as a tree truck. Many buccaneers witnessed Dragon's one fist squeeze life's breath from a man.

Hawk concentrated on breathing, and gathered his strength. His eyes witnessed the heated exchange between Dragon and the cabin boy, who was soon thrown across the deck.

Dragon approached him with fists clenched in anger.

182

"So, we meet again Black Hawk."

Hawk's eyes were hooded. "Dragon."

The crew began to surround them as word spread through the ship of their prisoner. Hawk eyed several familiar faces, who all stared back at him as though seeing a ghost.

The men began to ask questions at once, but Dragon silenced them with one swish of a sword. "Silence!"

Dragon's eyes roamed the crew, and then fixed eyes on Hawk. "Yes, we have Black Hawk as prisoner thanks to a beautiful and scorned lady." He chuckled loudly into Hawk's face, "The scorn of a woman hath no bounds! She has succeeded whereas we failed in sacking you."

Hawk faced Dragon with no fear. "I have no desire to privateer again; I am no threat to you."

A deep raucous laugh erupted from Dragon as he pointed to the bounded man. "*You* were *never* a threat to *me!*"

Hawk remained unmoved. "How much gold for my freedom?"

The crew began to whisper to each other, knowing the worth of Black Hawk to his enemies. Dragon would ask a fortune, and get it.

"Morgan still speaks of your abandonment of him. He viewed you as a son. He will pay me whatever I ask."

Hawk nodded. The childless Morgan would do as Dragon claimed. Although, if Morgan bought his freedom, Hawk would be expected to remain in the West Indies for the rest of his life. The darkened prison had provided ample time to plan his move once given the opportunity. And now, Dragon was ignorantly handing it to him.

"My enemy will give you more."

Dragon's eyes were full of greed. "You speak of Penn?"

"Aye."

Dragon drew closer. "How much?"

"Eighty gold coins."

"Even his hatred is too stingy to pay that price for you."

Hawk wooed, "If you untie me, I'll tell you how."

Their eyes clashed, Hawk's with a confidence that drew

Dragon closer. The man's courage was unlike any man Dragon knew, and it was too potent to resist.

The facts were undeniable. Black Hawk's sacks were the most successful Morgan had ever participated in. Without Black Hawk, Portobelo would never have worked.

Seconds passed until he barked, "Untie him!"

Sixteen

France

A gilded tongue was never needed more. Things were not progressing as Charles had expected. He stood in silence as the Duke voiced deep displeasure with his younger brother.

"Charles, I'll not grant Will ten miles of land in my province when he's so susceptible to where the wind blows. He's a privateer at heart and now it beckons him again. You nor I can change his adventurer's spirit."

Charles was torn. The Duke's words rang true. He didn't understand why his brother had left unexpectedly for a sugar plantation in the West Indies, after stating his intentions to return to New York as a manor lord, and build a life there. He was unprepared to handle the argument.

So with no other choice, Charles made the decision to have faith in Hawk. "Your Grace, I have never lied to you, nor would I now on my brother's behalf."

The Duke nodded.

"However, I must remind you of Will's loyalty to the crown, as first a privateer, and now, the most influential Englishman in your province. Men follow my brother, and it is this leadership you need for your province to grow and prosper."

The Duke's reply bellowed across the room. "I've no misgivings in your brother's loyalty, only his ability to stay put!

Now that he's negotiated the Iroquois peace treaty, I fear there's no challenge there to hold him. I need him to grow roots *there*, not go off to another adventure."

Charles countered, "Then give him the honor of being the first manor lord of your province. He seeks this recognition from you. I assure you, it will keep him landed."

"I am uncertain anything can keep Will landed."

Charles brightened. "Please hold your final judgment of Will, until you meet with the Dutchwoman."

Amusement was found in the Duke's voice. "What has this Dutchwoman to do with Will and my province?"

"You must meet her to understand."

The Duke ordered impatiently, "Very well then Charles, send her in!"

Charles bowed, and left the study. His feet quickened up the long flight of stairs to Catharyna's suite, and found it empty. He spun around and raced back downstairs to the salon, and found her there with Emily and Gerrit. She was reading a biography on Alexander the Great.

"Ryna, come," he gushed, and then paused to catch his breath. "His Grace is ready to meet with you."

Their eyes locked. This was what she had waited weeks to do, and it was now upon her. There was no uncertainty or self doubt when she rose from the settee. An exchanged look at Gerrit and Emily renewed the purpose of what held her in France. A bright smile spread in confidence as she left the room. Steps were measured to maintain the stiff composure. The challenge began to unfold as she drew closer to the study. A slight tremble raced across her hand when the door was opened by a servant.

Charles looked deeply into her eyes with faith. He raised an arm, and escorted her inside the room. They approached the Duke together. He was seated at the back of the room in a large high back chair, reviewing morning mail and the several contracts which were piled on the desk.

Charles led Catharyna forward, and bowed gracefully. "Your Grace, it is my pleasure to introduce Miss Catharyna van

Broeck of Broeckwyck, from your province of New York."

Catharyna curtsied, and lowered her head in respect. "Your Grace, it is my honor."

The Duke ordered, "Rise, I've kept you waiting a fortnight, tell me what you seek."

"I come to settle a debt my family owes you."

His head rose to scrutinize her. A quick survey noted piercing blue eyes and black ringlets that complimented handsome facial features. Not a beauty, but a spirited one from the tone of her voice. No fear was found in her eyes, and her English was fluent for a Dutchwoman. He questioned her in French. "What debt?"

Catharyna responded in such, just as fluently. "My cousin Gerrit van Hoesen's loan on Hoesenwyck."

The Duke rose and unrolled a map on the desk. Catharyna pointed to the land grant her uncle held. He questioned her in German this time. "This property is near Albany, yet you are from Broeckwyck. How am I to settle this with you?"

"I have a proposal to pay the amount, your Grace."

His eyes narrowed when he sat back down. He now chose Spanish and questioned, "Your cousin Gerrit arranged a loan against his father's estate, gambled it away and has sent you to deal with it? This is not a strong man, Miss van Broeck. Why do you meddle in business that is not your own?"

Catharyna replied in Spanish, "He is more than family, your Grace. We are few in your province. It cannot afford to let any turn away to other shores that promise wealth and riches."

She just voiced his greatest weakness. The fact that he agreed to a grandfather clause for Dutchwomen proved to Catharyna the Duke was desperate to civilize his colony.

The Duke leaned forward and whispered in Swedish, "And how do you propose I keep them there?"

"To avoid the mistakes my mother country made."

He noted her eyes sparkled with passion on the topic, and his ears heard that her Swedish was better than his own. The Duke's hand summoned to continue, disguising his

187

eagerness in her next words and which dialect to be spoken. It was Russian.

"Make it a true settlement, not a trading station."

He bellowed in English, "Lovelace is doing that! He's cleaning the town up, extending the roads. Your oligarchy invested but a few coins around an ineffective fort."

Catharyna spoke in English, no longer sensing her language skills were being tested. She continued undeterred in a persuasive voice, one that had made Ten Broeck the best trader in the province. "That is a beginning, but more investment is needed there if you wish to fill it with settlers. And settlers are the only way to make profits and protect it for the crown."

"Continue," he mumbled.

"My countrymen's loyalty is to profit first, as are all the adventurers and frontiersmen who occupy your province. In order to gain their loyalty, and unite the Dutch who hold the wealth, to the English who seek it, you must open trade that promises more profit to them. And to lure settlers, a visible sign of the crown's investment in the province."

"Why should I do that?"

"Because they will aid your efforts to protect it from France. Don't be misled, the French will copy your success by trying to squeeze us out and back across the Atlantic. The crown now owns the eastern coastline, but the French are at its back door."

His eyes narrowed. "What type of investment do you speak of?"

The frugal woman answered, "Not a sizable investment, your Grace, but a *visible* one, for settlers to see the crown's presence. Such a sign would build their confidence that the province is ripe for building their own future there. Your advertising in the papers to lure settlers there will remain fruitless unless you do this."

His eyes began to glow with the energy of her enthusiasm. The Duke reassessed her, no longer seeing a handsome woman, but an advisor. No complications, just the facts. He reviewed her words and found them all too true. The crown had been publishing ads in the papers to encourage settlement in the province, yet only twenty families had settled there in the last year. Money was in London to rebuild after the Great Fire, and Spanish gold was in the West Indies, which lured the young adventurous souls into privateering and, many, piracy. Able bodied men had too many opportunities due to England expanding Her reach around the world. It seemed impossible to get settlers in his province.

His face was now serious, and ears, alert when he asked, "What do you suggest?"

"Build a working farm in the province and name it Duke's Farm."

"A farm?" he bellowed.

"Yes, a farm that the papers would write about before and after each banquet of yours that caters it. Your province will be known as the land of milk and honey that grows food worthy of royalty." She paused when seeing the Duke's face break out into a smile. "All advertisements for settlers would stop, another potent sign that something special indeed is across the Atlantic in New York. Settlers would rush to own such fertile and blessed land."

His eyes sparkled. "Ha, I do see advantages to this. And it would not tax me greatly to achieve," he added with a nod. "Where do you suggest?"

A slight tremble raced across her hand as it went to the map on his desk. She had given it extensive thought, and it was the plan she would voice aloud. A finger pointed to the 10,000 acre parcel her uncle owned a hundred miles south of Albany, which was Gerrit's inheritance, and the land that had introduced her to Hawk.

"My uncle, Peter van Broeck, is the largest Dutch landowner in your province. He will pay off his son's debt in exchange for this parcel. I suggest this is where Duke's Farm be built. It is in the heart of the Hudson Valley."

She waited breathlessly as the Duke was silent in thoughtful contemplation.

He drew closer. "This idea has merit, but I don't like

the location."

"This location is rich rolling meadows and fruit trees. There is great wealth to gain from this land."

"No." His fingers began roaming over the map and landed on the island of Manhattan to be placed at the heart of Broeckwyck. "This is your land, is it not?" His shrewd eyes now glanced at her.

"Yes," Catharyna replied, in the knowledge the Duke was testing her loyalty.

"Your cousin Gerrit's debt would be paid in exchange for this." And his finger circled the east side of Manhattan where a small portion of Broeckwyck's wheat fields resided, but not the manor or grist mill, nor the bulk of the land north of Manhattan. The Duke now grinned and said in excitement, "Yes, this is the location most visible as settlers come into the harbor to see Duke's Farm." His voice now held a dreamy quality as the mental picture grew in form and color in his mind.

Catharyna knew to take the trade. "This is an excellent location as it also flows along the East River and into the Harbor."

"Yes, it is perfect! It is decided, I will take this parcel."

Catharyna's heart was tearing apart, but she smiled brightly. "Thank you, your Grace."

The Duke's eyes sparkled, and he began to ramble quickly, "Now we must discuss the layout, plans and such things. This must be a glorious site for the settlers entering my province, but it must be profitable, absolutely profitable. Come, let's begin."

Catharyna pulled up a chair and sat down.

The silent figure in the back emerged, and Charles interrupted the two who had their heads bent over the desk. "Your Grace, after considering Miss van Broeck's words, would it not be prudent to name the first manor lord to coincide with the building of Duke's Farm? If you choose the landowner most respected in the province to honor with this title, it will also be to your benefit."

The Duke belched, "My thoughts are on Duke's Farm."

He then handed a stack of papers to Catharyna. "Look through these requests and give me your recommendation for the first manor grant."

Her eyes met Charles and he nodded to accept the order. The Duke had just handed her the power to select his first and most favored, therefore, most powerful manor lord in his province. Amazement momentarily froze all her actions. For years her father had been amused by her ideas and suggestions. The knowledge the King's brother had just handed her the largest political decision to make in his province, made her eyes sparkle in excitement.

It was a serious decision, and she took it as such. "I will review these tonight and provide my recommendation tomorrow."

The Duke never raised his head from the table. "Duke's Farm must have the best horses, sheep, goats, pigs, as a start. Stone craftsman will be the devil to settle there. What do you suggest we do to obtain them?"

Charles looked in wonderment as the Duke listened to Catharyna, and agreed to most of her suggestions. He no longer existed in the room, but refused to leave it so he could witness her successful tactics with the Duke. He took many notes.

Port Royal, Jamaica

The auction was moving slower than a snail in the high noon sun. Fairfax remained still in the shadow of the crowd, disguised in similar dress as the other buccaneers. His hallmark handsome face was covered by a full beard. Dirt was rubbed on the portions of his face that were naked. His eyes were kept downcast, but captured all in their gaze.

In front of the crowd stood Captain Penn, dressed in the finest silk, while his long shaggy beard hid rotten teeth. Beside him was Dragon.

Fairfax drew forward to eavesdrop on their

conversation. "He's coming out next," Dragon said with a snarl.

"I don't believe it. Black Hawk would never be stupid enough to fall into a woman's lair."

A deep chuckled rolled in Dragon's chest. "You've never seen my Miss Juliet," he boasted, and the men around them joined in. "She's got more curves than the Jamaican coast line. Told me Hawk insulted her, and I promised to take some skin off of him so he'd never forget it. I thought you'd want him. Maybe you could put him to work at your plantation?"

The thick hair on Penn's face hid his smile, but not the sparkle in his green eyes. The thought of having Black Hawk as his slave made his bruised pride soar. To crush him in the heel each and every morning for the rest of his days was a dream come true.

"How much?" he asked in haste.

Dragon looked at Penn with eyes dead of emotion. "Make an offer now, or I send him out for the crowd to bid on. I've no quarrel with Black Hawk, I only want my gold."

Penn stammered quickly, "Five gold pieces."

Dragon ignored the offer. "Our Lieutenant Governor Morgan might want him back under the deck again. He'll be willing to give me what I seek."

"Twenty."

Dragon's eyes blazed into Penn. "Eighty."

Penn choked, "That's a bloody fortune!"

Dragon remained silent.

Penn's eyes darted around the crowd to see if anyone had that kind of gold. Suspicion then entered his eyes as they roamed over Dragon's face. The pirate had mentioned Morgan's name. His old captain was no longer a privateer for the crown, but Lieutenant Governor of Jamaica. There was every reason to believe someone in the crowd represented Morgan's interest in the auction, nor was there any doubt Morgan would pay eighty gold pieces for Black Hawk. All knew Morgan would give anything to have him back, and Penn would not allow that to happen.

"Eighty it is."

Dragon's eyes glowed. "Your hatred runs deep."

Penn ignored the words and snapped, "Bring my slave to Fortuna tonight. I want him working the fields at dawn."

Dragon nodded and turned back to the auction. The moment Penn's carriage left town, Fairfax crept up behind Jacob Chanler and whispered, "Ready?"

"Aye."

Fairfax whispered a few words into his ear, and then backed away from the crowd, to disappear into the thick foliage.

Hours passed until day turned into night. There, in the shadows at Fortuna, stood a silent and prepared Fairfax who watched Hawk be delivered to the sugar plantation he had once owned, returning now as a slave to it. Guilt fueled Fairfax's every move.

The mansion was large in scale with wide wood clap board painted a soft yellow. The first and second floors had a verandah that wrapped around the front to the back. Full length windows rose from the floor to the ceiling and opened as doors to allow the sea breeze in every room.

The plantation proved as profitable as Hawk had anticipated, and had made Penn a wealthy man. Beyond the mansion were huts, scattered for the forty or more slaves that operated it, and the overseer's house.

Penn approached to greet his new slave with a treacherous laugh. He belched into Hawk's face, "You didn't heed my warning!" And began to pace around his prize, only the veil of hatred saw a shell of a man, nothing like the vibrant living legend who had left in the midst years ago. "I'll not pay eighty pieces for *this*."

Dragon hissed, "Eighty or I speak to Morgan."

Penn's face screwed up like a sour lemon. "*Don't* speak to Morgan, here's your eighty pieces. Go bite it!" And he thrust the heavy bag of gold at Dragon, who did exactly that. The next second, blasts of gun fire were echoing through the plantation. Men swarmed from each corner, north, south, east, west, as slaves began pouring out of their huts in hysterical bewilderment.

Fairfax's blade sliced through Hawk's ropes. Once again, Black Hawk was leading the group of buccaneers he had led in the Portobelo sack. The murmurs of the men rose higher and higher in the air until it merged as one omen. "Black Hawk returns for Fortuna!"

They roamed over the plantation, stripping Penn of his wealth and land as he stood in bewilderment, witnessing his men, not protect or resist the assault, but were a party in it. There was no battle from Penn, who was now tied and gagged.

An hour later, the eyes looking at Penn, were not William Hawkins', but Black Hawk's, known by all for having no life or hope in them. Beside him stood Dragon.

Penn took several steps back until he was against a palm tree. The words were expected, but hearing them spoken aloud sent a chill up Penn's spin.

Hawk ordered, "Yield Fortuna for your life."

Penn refused.

In one fluid movement, Hawk's sword was staring straight into Penn's face. He hissed, "Yield!"

Penn's appearance was stubborn on the outside but fear raced through veins as organs trembled. "Never!"

Their eyes locked for several tense seconds until Penn surrendered, and closed his eyes, waiting for the blade to strike him down.

Hawk looked at the man who had stripped him of his fortune, and vowed he would never walk away from it again. There was no turning back this time, Hawk cut through Penn's bindings. "Then we fight for it." An empty hand was held up, and a sword was immediately thrown into it by Fairfax. Hawk thrust the handle into Penn's chest. His eyes were narrow slits, his words fatal. "To the death."

The buccaneers roared with pleasure, Dragon glowed with anticipation, and soon, the two men were encircled by a bloodthirsty crowd. There was no escape for either man now, only one would walk away.

Penn's eyes sparkled as he twirled away. His sword

crashed down to splice Hawk's back, but it was blocked in time. Penn's every move was anticipated by Hawk, who appeared amused by the battle. It was clear his two months of being tied and gagged did not sap his strength, compared to Penn's life of comfort the past eight years. Gone was the sinew body with muscles and lean taunt limbs that Penn once possessed.

The first five minutes were the only sign of Penn's past performance as a razor sharp swordsman. He had lost his edge, and the knowledge was now shown in his eyes. Hope was gone as images of death took its place.

Penn stumbled, and was soon face down in the dusty ground. Hawk stood above him. A warm Caribbean breeze blew his loose hair away from a now tan face that was rough, jagged and unrelenting, and a body taut with muscles ready to strike. There was no sign of fat or forgiveness in Black Hawk, the days spent in his darkened prison had taken it from his hide and mind.

The buccaneers looked at the man before them. His great height soared above them, and they began to chant for their returned leader. Before his own eyes, Hawk saw the legend of Black Hawk come alive as their voices grew louder. The energy of the crowd fed him. He felt limitless.

Impatiently, he kicked Penn to rise from the ground, but the man remained with his face in the dirt. Hawk's sword began cutting off Penn's vest and shirt until his back was bare. "Rise!"

Penn refused, remaining on the ground as his only protection.

Hawk warned, "I'll not attack your back."

There was no movement or change in Penn's position. Fury filled Hawk that his victory would be darkened by Penn's cowardice. It was but a moment, and then his sword began to descend when another blocked its path.

"Enough!" Sir Henry Morgan shouted, and his sword clashed with Hawk's an inch from Penn's back.

Hawk looked at his leader, and immediately bowed in respect. Their eyes locked and Morgan bellowed, "Lay down your sword. Fortuna's fate will be decided by me!" Then he eyed the crowd and ordered, "Leave now with your portions, stay a moment later and I take them all!"

The buccaneers immediately dispersed in fear of repercussion with the hot tempered Morgan, Dragon included. Morgan approached his protégé, and a confident smile emerged on his face. "I knew you would come back."

"Winds of opportunity blew me back."

Morgan slapped him on the shoulder in comradeship and chuckled, "You guided them here." He winked at Hawk and then approached Penn, who was now shaking the dirt off his body. "You best hope the men left some Madeira in your study, or this discussion will go bad for you. Come, both of you, follow me."

Hawk and Penn eyed each other but they followed their old leader inside the mansion that was ransacked. Furniture was tossed everywhere, flour, sugar and other foods were on the floor, and there was not a plate or piece of silverware left. Morgan entered the study and opened the desk drawer to see Penn's private stock of Madeira. A smile spread on Penn's face, but Morgan remained aloof and lifted an arm chair and sat himself down. Hawk and Penn did likewise.

Morgan's eyes sparkled in anticipation of the enjoyment ahead. "Gentlemen, I've given this much thought." He searched for a glass to fill the Madeira into, but didn't find any. He drank it straight for the bottle, and then offered it to Hawk, who accepted, but didn't offer it to Penn.

Morgan chuckled and continued, "Hawk, what are your plans for Fortuna?"

"To reclaim it."

"Will you settle here?"

Hawk's eyes clashed with Morgan. This had been the one flaw in his plan to recapture Fortuna, but he would not back down now. Morgan would want him to remain here, the Duke wanted him in New York. The contest for which battled in his mind until Catharyna appeared. "The Duke of York has granted me a land patent in New York. He demands my presence there."

"Why should Fortuna go into the hands of an absentee landlord?"

Hawk knew Morgan didn't doubt Fortuna's health under his distant management. His mentor was asking what he would gain. "I'll increase imports from the colonies with flour, furs, precious woods, and you would garner the duties on such."

"And how would you accomplish this? Are you also a trader in New York?"

There were only a few men who knew of Morgan's fidelity to his wife, his loyalty to her was complete. While he had no formal contract with Catharyna, there was certainty she would be his with or without the law. A grin spread across Hawk's face. "My betrothed is the best trader in the province. The Mohicans call her white sister. There is nothing she cannot obtain if it exists."

Morgan's eyes sparkled. "You choose wisely, Hawk." Then he turned to Penn. "What do you offer?"

Penn blasted, "This is my plantation, he's no rights to it. I hold the deed, and I'll not barter him for it back!"

Morgan's face became dark as it leaned into Penn's. "You swindled it from Hawk and tonight he swindled it back. You no longer have any hold on Fortuna. You stand on equal ground, so heed me well, Penn. Build your case now if you ever will have Fortuna again."

Penn grew quiet as his mind raced to do what Morgan ordered, but nothing emerged. He knew nothing about the sugar business. His manager, who had been hand picked by Hawk, ran Fortuna. Hawk knew that and so did Morgan. His wife was no trader, but had run a brothel in Santiago before their marriage, and even those talents were no longer provided to him.

Penn felt himself getting squeezed into a corner that was quickly consuming every thought, breath and pulse.

After a minute of silence passed, Morgan resumed dryly. "Penn, your case is weak, but you have served me well these years, and for that I will reward you." Life emerged in Penn's eyes and suspicion clouded Hawk's. "I will send you to London, accompanied by my letter, to be recognized for your bravery and courage as a privateer for the crown. There you will remain and serve as my eyes and ears, sending me important information."

Penn's face was mixed. "Sir Morgan, it is a high honor you give me, but London..."

Morgan took over where Penn had left off. "Will welcome you home as a hero." His eyes locked on Penn's and were filled with the silent order to accept immediately. "This is an overdue honor for you, Penn."

Penn had no desire to return to cloudy and damp England. He enjoyed the warm Caribbean breeze and island women. With no choice, he replied, "I accept this honor."

"Very wise, Penn." He extended a hand. "You shall be my guest until you depart for London. You are excused."

Penn nodded and left the room which had once been his study, and closed the door of the mansion which had once been his home until Black Hawk blew back into town. There was no anger or resentment in Penn. It was the life of a privateer to know when to abandon a failed venture.

Inside the study the atmosphere changed upon Penn's departure. Morgan smiled with proud eyes. "Well done, Hawk, well done."

Hawk grinned, and drained the bottle of Madeira. Things had worked out far better than he had anticipated in his dark prison.

Morgan swore, "Fortuna belongs to you, of this there is no dispute."

Hawk's eyes gleamed in triumph. The thought of reclaiming Fortuna entered his mind the moment Dragon's cabin boy released him from the storage room, and fresh ocean air filled his lungs. The wind had beckoned and enticed him back to the sugar plantation which had never left his thoughts. Seven winters in New York had kept the fire burning inside of him to reclaim it one day, and that day was today.

Morgan asked, "How did you get Dragon to assist

you?"

Hawk's eyes roamed over Morgan's tall frame, which was still as lean as remembered, except now he had a slight pouch. "You trained me well, captain." The two men smiled at each other, knowing the power of persuasion. It was a gift. Some men drew crowds to follow them, while most could not get a soul. Both men knew each shared it.

Morgan's eyes noted the restlessness in his protégé, and knew it would pull him away once again. He became blunt. "You deserted me."

There was a trace of regret in Hawk's response. "The crown's support was shifting away from us."

"They still need privateers!" Morgan blasted.

Their eyes met, and Hawk confessed, "It was time to abandon my shadow."

Morgan's parental abilities emerged. "Haven't you learned by now the shadow you chase is your own? You are Black Hawk for your abilities, not your ancestor's legend." Hawk's face remained uncertain. It made Morgan weaken when he added, "The crown knighted us for our service, but yes, your choice was prudent." Deep laughter rumbled in his chest. "Now I protect the riches we stripped from the Spaniards'." Hawk finally relaxed and joined in the laughter. Morgan's chest grew with pride at hearing the admiration for him in it. "How goes New York?"

Catharyna rose before his eyes. "Adventurous."

Morgan rolled tobacco in paper, twisted the ends and lit it. He breathed deeply and exhaled. "When do you sail back?"

"I have one other matter that must be settled before I depart."

Hope brightened Morgan's eyes. "Aye, one last venture? Ah ha! You have land, but no gold coin!"

Hawk grinned. "I need to find a Dirck van Broeck. He's been missing five years and..."

Morgan began to laugh, his deep baritone voice bounced off the mahogany paneled walls of the study. "Speak to Golden Eagle, he'll know where to find him."

"So he lives?"

"Speak to Golden Eagle."

"Where is he?"

"Anywhere and everywhere the sea beckons. Its pull is fierce on that one."

Hawk nodded and opened a case of rum. They talked of past adventures until dawn. Portobelo occupied most of their discussion, with laughter and arrogance filling the room.

Seventeen

France

There was much to do before returning home. The next morning Catharyna joined the Duke for breakfast in his private room, with Charles beside her. The pile of requests from the largest landowners in New York seeking to be a manor lord were in her arms. They would all receive it, but the sequence and time was the decision now in her hands.

"Good morning, Ryna." The Duke beamed at her and nodded at Charles, who bowed respectively to him. "An idea occurred to me in the middle of my sleep that Duke's Farm will produce the flour for the royal family."

Catharyna's eyes glowed hearing the idea she voiced to him the evening before. Her father had always warned her to pace her ideas, that most people could not keep up with them. This was the result of voicing them at once to the Duke. She had overwhelmed him last night and now they were being absorbed and taken by him.

"Brilliant idea, your Grace."

A smile split his face. "Yes, it is excellent, simply excellent." He nodded to a servant and a chair was quickly pulled out next to his. "Sit, I'm interested in your recommendations for Lord of the Manor."

"I suggest you choose the first manor lord. All other

201

requests henceforth should be handled by the Governor of your province. This will place greater honor on the bearer to receive the position first."

"Yes, I agree."

"The majority of the requests are from Dutchmen I am related to, seeking the position they held previously as Patroons with Holland. All would serve you faithfully, if given the honor, primarily due to the great profit they will reap from it."

His eyes warmed over the remark about her countrymen's greed, completely captivated by her. "Continue."

"They are all ambitious, but one has a heart that loves the land greater." She pulled out several pieces of paper, and spoke aloud potential candidates. "John Archer, Samuel Willes, Stephanus van Twiller, and my Uncle are able men, but none possess the courage or leadership to unite the province at all costs. Therefore, I recommend this honor be given to Sir William Hawkins."

The Duke's head was shaking in disapproval. "No, we must choose another."

Catharyna persisted, "But your Grace, no other man has done more for your province."

"Yes, Will is more leader than all of them, but that leads him into adventures *away* from New York. It's no good! His ancestor's blood is too potent in him. Such a man is boundless by a privateer spirit elusive as the wind, never resting anywhere for long. Sack after sack is all Will's soul seeks. Once the challenge is gone, so is he. Choose another!" Catharyna gazed stupidly at the Duke, incapable of speech.

Charles spoke up. "Your Grace, I disagree. He will return to New York to build his *family* there."

The Duke snapped, "Charles, we spoke of this yesterday. Unless there is a way to keep Will in New York..." his words trailed off by the wounded doe expression on Catharyna's face. The Duke's eyes met Charles, who nodded. They exchanged a long silent look.

Charles swore, "Will's heart is in New York. He will return, your Grace."

After a lengthy pause, the Duke finally agreed. "I see that now." He turned to Catharyna and beamed. "Yes, I agree with your recommendation. I shall grant Will the manor status first."

In a dreamy haze, Catharyna heard the words. There was no pleasure in the Duke's approval of her choice. Every accomplishment in England and France returned like a tidal wave of her efforts, in securing tenant farmers, trading contracts, and now manor status for Onteora. For the first time the face of Hawk was stripped away and with it came the long hand of Black Hawk, who had squeezed everything out of her an ocean away.

Jamaica

The flight of a seagull flying low over the horizon marked the day of a new dawn. Hawk rose from the mahogany four poster bed and looked out at the blue green seas that beckoned. Paradise surrounded the senses, yet his mind was far away in Onteora, Catharyna, New York, Catharyna, the feel of his feet on Manhattan, Catharyna, the trees lining the Broad Way, Catharyna, Catharyna, Catharyna. His eyes stared up into the cloudless sky above, unable to look away, for, as long as he did, her presence was beside him.

Their last battle over Broeckwyck returned. And then the game began where greed and mind convinced him that Catharyna would demand he not return home without news of Dirck and Fortuna's deed in his breast pocket. She would understand his delay to put the plantation in order. A smile spread in the belief the thrifty businesswoman would insist upon it.

Fairfax entered the room without knocking. "The *Queen Elizabeth* is sailing to Charleston in two days. I've booked us passage. We can take a ship to New York from there."

"No."

"Hawk, your plan to reclaim Fortuna cost us a month in

recruiting men. We agreed to return to New York when it was accomplished."

"Not yet."

Fairfax's fingers plowed through wavy hair and battled to restrain the heated words threatening to erupt at the new delay. "Why?"

Never in their association had Fairfax ever questioned Hawk's orders. It was the first time, and both men were surprised by it. Their eyes locked, but Hawk did provide an explanation. "Fortuna needs my attention and I'll not return without news of Dirck."

"Dirck's dead!" Fairfax replied, knowing Fortuna could take two months to restore, if not longer. Searching for Dirck would be a fool's quest.

"I agree but need proof."

Fairfax's hands shook with impatience. "I received a letter from Emily that she is with Ryna. They are traveling together to New York."

Hawk beamed. "Good."

"I sent a reply a fortnight ago that we would be meeting them in time for the fall harvest."

"Why?"

Fairfax became angry. "You reclaimed Fortuna, there is nothing more keeping us here."

"I decide when I go, not you," Hawk snapped, but knew it was time to allow Fairfax to live his own life. His abduction had caused Fairfax to postpone his wedding in order to follow him to the West Indies, only to realize he had rescued himself. "Go."

"Not without you."

"Go," Hawk ordered, and left the room.

Fairfax's eyes narrowed in frustration. The seas of opportunity were too potent to keep Hawk in the Caribbean without him. Fairfax knew if opportunity arose, as it surely would, Black Hawk would consume his friend's soul for good, and New York would never be seen again. There was no way he would leave without Hawk.

Hands and teeth clenched, but he followed Hawk downstairs. Neither spoke another word about the *Queen Elizabeth.*

Weeks passed in a blur for Hawk and Fairfax who worked getting Fortuna back in shape. Hawk dictated daily notes to Stewart Wiltcomb, the best sugar manager in the West Indies, who accomplished them in quick order. Fortuna was not damaged irreparably from the raid, and was quickly returning to normal.

It was a Saturday morning when they were having breakfast on the verandah, overlooking the west sugar fields, when a new development emerged. Stewart was on Hawk's left, Fairfax his right.

There was great accomplishment in Hawk's eyes that roamed over the fields and the blue green sea that lay east of the estate. "Everything is in order."

Stewart beamed at his boss. Hawk was a man he respected. Stewart's ideas were not only listened to, but he was given the tools and money to accomplish them. There was one more that burned inside to be spoken aloud. Finally, the time had come for it to be released. "There is one thing, Sir."

"What?"

Stewart swallowed loudly under the heated stare of Fairfax. It was a look that threatened him to hold his tongue. There was no secret the man was impatient to return to New York and his betrothed who was waiting for him.

Stewart took a deep breath and ignored Fairfax, eyes were focused on his employer. "Sir, you would reap far greater profits if you shipped your own sugar instead of having Billingsford make the profit himself."

"Get me the ledger," Hawk ordered.

Stewart had it beside his leg anticipating the request. It was instantly handed to Hawk. Stewart ignored Fairfax's glare that was now simmering. "Bloody thief! Billingsford makes as much profit as I do just for transporting it."

Excitement began to pound in Hawk's body as he contemplated ways to build a shipping fleet. There was one that rose to the surface, one that Fairfax anticipated instantly. "Don't consider it."

Hawk rose. "Let's see Morgan."

Stewart was grinning broadly and followed the illustrious leader, Black Hawk, eagerly, enthusiastically, hoping Morgan had been alerted to a potential Spanish attack to a British holding in the West Indies.

Fairfax was a step behind Hawk and grew angrier with each passing second. This was exactly why he had remained. Deep inside fear questioned if his friendship with Hawk was stronger than Black Hawk's pull on his soul.

"What about Dirck? We haven't done anything about finding him yet?"

"Jacob's handling it for me."

Hawk quickly mounted a black stallion. Stewart bowed respectively and took several paces back to avoid being trampled under the hooves of the spirited horse.

Fairfax mounted and grumbled loudly, "Hawk, think of the risks." Black Hawk's eyes pinned Fairfax and all the fight left his body. There was no emotion, just ambition to claim more for himself. Fairfax nodded obediently to his leader and followed silently on their way to the pink mansion on the hill.

Morgan was entertaining on the verandah and welcomed them immediately into the party of friends, all from England. "Ladies and Gentlemen, may I present Sir William Hawkins, known as Black Hawk in the seven seas."

They clustered around Hawk, leaving Fairfax in the background. Comments of "bravery, courage, greatness" were all Fairfax heard over his own grumbling. At Hawk's signal, he followed inside the mansion to the study.

Morgan's eyes were twinkling with anticipation. "You seek me out, Hawk?"

"Yes. I've come to offer my service as privateer."

Morgan laughed and then got down to business. "I just

got wind of Spanish plans to attack the island. As acting governor of Jamaica, Vice-Admiral, Commandant of the Port Royal Regiment, Judge of the Admiralty Court and Justice of the Peace, I offer you a letter of marque making you a legal privateer if you attack the Spanish vessels first and share any spoils with me."

"I accept."

The Saturday afternoon sun had reached its zenith when Jacob Chanler entered the Nag's Head Tavern. He sat in the middle of the room, drinking a Kill Devil, and listened to conversations as he had done for weeks in pubs all over the island. Hours passed, and ten drinks later, Jacob rose with the information that Golden Eagle had pulled into port at dawn.

A narrow path was taken to Nellie's Bordello, who catered to the fiercest pirates of the seas, when a loud cry was heard and then a shout. Jacob entered cautiously and found three Spanish girls clinging to each other crying. Everyone's eyes pointed to a burly rough and tough buccaneer who lay sprawled over a young girl who, no more than twelve, with a knife pointed against her slim throat.

Jacob cursed softly and approached the randy man, but a buxom blonde haired woman brushed by him. "Butch, Golden Eagle is upstairs waiting for me and I swear I'll go fetch him to straighten you out once and for all."

Butch's response was a lecherous leer at the scantily clad Nellie, who was wearing only a corset and pantaloons. His lips puckered at her until a shot rang in the air. Instantly, he released the small Spanish girl and stood up.

"What say you Butch?"

Butch began to take small steps backward as Golden Eagle descended from upstairs. The pirate had cold eyes that pierced one to the floor boards. His wavy hair was darker than midnight and fell past wide shoulders, which only added to the aura of his ruthlessness. "Don't leave Butch, we must speak."

Butch didn't wait but turned to run out of the bordello. He got as far as the door when a loud explosion was heard, and a second later, he crashed to the floor. "You shot my leg, you cold-blooded Dutchman!"

"Better a leg than a hand. Now git before I shoot the other one!"

Butch raised himself awkwardly and left the bordello cursing loudly to all that came in his path.

The bordello was crowded due to Golden Eagle and his crew's return fresh from Santiago. They carried with them a rich booty and were eager to enjoy the spoils with Nellie's girls.

Jacob had only seen Golden Eagle once, but never spoke to him. After witnessing the man's anger at having his time with Nellie interrupted, Jacob turned to leave the bordello.

The voice spoke again, but this time at his back. "You're a new face."

Jacob turned and stared into Golden Eagle's eyes. He nodded at the pirate who now approached him. "I don't like new faces." He leaned closer and hissed, "They smell like a *rat*."

The crew laughed and grew excited that a fight was on the horizon. The black man was tall and well muscled, but Golden Eagle was insatiable when it came to winning. His handgun was now pointed at Jacob's forehead. "Are you a black rat?"

Jacob's dark eyes rose to meet the dead stare of Golden Eagle, and succeeded without wavering. He whispered, "Morgan led me to you for information on a Dirck van Broeck."

"Upstairs, now!" Golden Eagle ordered.

Jacob obeyed and grew tense after entering the room and hearing the door lock pulled into place. The pirate approached him with skepticism. "Who seeks information on Broeck?"

"His sister Catharyna of Broeckwyck in the province of New York."

Golden Eagle smiled. "She is well?"

Jacob relaxed, and white teeth flashed briefly. "Yes, sir, I am told she is well."

As quick as a snake, Golden Eagle's hand reached out and started tightening around Jacob's throat. He hissed, "You don't know her?"

Jacob nodded no and the hand tightened.

"Who sent you here?"

Jacob croaked, "Black Hawk." The grip on his throat relaxed.

"I have heard great stories of his courage."

"He is betrothed to Miss van Broeck."

Once again Jacob's throat was being squeezed by large merciless hands. Golden Eye growled, "Ryna to marry a privateer? I think *not*! Do you seek to die, mad man?"

Jacob stammered, "No, 'tis truth I speak! Her trade name is Ten Broeck."

Finally, Golden Eye withdrew his hand and Jacob knelt down and worked to get deep breaths of air into his lungs.

"Where is this Black Hawk?"

Jacob rose and held out his hand in warning. "Fortuna, he reclaimed it from Penn."

Golden Eagle's eyes became cloudy. Black Hawk's ambition was greater than his, there was no wish to meet the man, only to step into the middle of his web. "Tell him Dirck no longer lives."

Jacob persisted, "But Morgan said..."

"He died a slave in a sugar field. Black Hawk should tell his sister to grieve no more. Dirck is at peace now."

Jacob nodded and left the room with the knowledge his journey for finding Dirck was over.

Eighteen

France

Summer breezes drifted a medley of fragrances, making the air vibrant with life. It was time to journey home. The ships were loaded with provisions so vast that they would be returning to New York with five vessels. Three were loaded with one specific item and labeled accordingly, *Cows*, *Pigs*, and *Sheep*; while the other two were for seed, farming equipment, a saw mill driven by wind power, three families that would be servants to Duke's Farm and fifty tenant farmers for Onteora.

At dawn Catharyna would board the ship that would finally take her home. She would return at the end of August, the beginning of the harvest season. Almost a full year had passed since she was lured to London by Hawk.

An amazing amount of accomplishments had been realized and it pleased her that Hawk had no involvement in any of them. She had come to forgive his deceit in getting her to London, but not his silence of Black Hawk. There had been successes, but no peace. She drove herself from dawn till dusk in the hope the darkness of night would grant rest from the loneliness that continued to ache. Many things had become unclear since Hawk entered her life, but loneliness would not hold her in its black grip.

Time had come to bid farewell to the Duke. She entered his study by herself, no longer requiring a special invitation. He was seated alone as was his custom.

"Your Grace, I came to bid you good-bye. We depart at dawn."

His hands rose, a silent order for her to accept them, and she did so warmly. "You have proven your loyalty to me, Ryna."

She smiled. Never had she worked so feverishly to get everything achieved in time to leave. It would have taken a normal person six months to recruit and gather the supplies that she was ordered to do, yet she had met her own timetable. She was physically, mentally and emotionally exhausted. There would be no fear crossing the Atlantic this time, just much needed rest.

The Duke extended a thick piece of parchment to take, and she did with a quizzical look. He whispered, "Read it."

It was from Governor Lovelace addressed to the Duke. At first glance, she became breathless at the sight of her own name, but then anger soon overwhelmed both body and mind that made her hands tremble. It was a warning to his Grace about a Dutchwoman trader with a gilded tongue that spoke over five languages and whose hatred of the crown continued to divide his province.

Her eyes narrowed over the description of a brilliant strategy set in place by Sir William Hawkins to woo the woman into marriage to unite the English into the Dutch wealth, and end the enmity. The letter concluded with supreme assurance of Sir Hawkins' success, since he is at heart a ruthless privateer always getting what he seeks.

She folded the letter neatly in place before handing it back to the Duke. "Interesting."

The Duke's eyes looked at her with understanding, but his voice held the spirit that roused the dead to fight on a battlefield. "You have proven your loyalty to me and now I share mine with you."

Catharyna raised startled eyes to his face, but a hand silenced her. "You gave me 1,000 acres of Broeckwyck to pay off your cousin's debt, then coordinated all the necessary plans for Duke's Farm, including hiring ten families to serve there. And, you taught me Algonkin, a language I have been most eager to learn. You are a most loyal subject to the crown, and you will be rewarded as such."

Another piece of parchment was extended to her. Their eyes locked when he saw her reticence to reach for it. His face warmed under a smile. "This will be more to your liking."

She smiled weakly before accepting it. The Duke's impatience was so great, he began speaking of its contents instead. "I have decided to use the west region of Manhattan for Duke's Farm instead of Broeckwyck land. This is a far better message to send to my Dutch landholders that the crown is investing a long future in the province along with them. Broeckwyck will remain intact upon your marriage." A smile began to spread across Catharyna's face when he said, "Your cousin's debt will be paid with 400 beaver skins, which he can send me *himself* within a year. And, my personal gift for your loyalty and friendship to me, is a black Arabian mare who is due to foal next spring. She was sired by my prize stallion. It is my hope this line will grow strong in the province. I know you will treasure this gift as greatly as I enjoy giving it to you."

Humbleness filled her voice. "You are too generous, your Grace."

He laughed. "Yes, it is quiet rare for me to be such," and then his eyes narrowed on her, "but I expect great things from you, Ryna. This will remind you of that."

Her voice was solemn. "I am deeply honored, your Grace."

The Duke gathered her hands and their eyes met. "I allowed you to read Lovelace's letter to show you the motives Will had in taking you to England." He then confessed, "I want you to wed him, Ryna. His tactics may seem evil to you, but his ambition is what builds kingdoms, and with you beside him, it will come to be." Her face tightened, so he added, "This is what I want, but I will not judge you harshly if you choose another."

Catharyna's eyes held hope, but her voice was cold.

"Will himself will make that decision."

They stared at each other until she curtsied and he waved a hand that she could depart.

Dawn arrived ready to take Catharyna away from France, England and all of Europe, wishing never to return again. The political games and amusements of the people had almost sapped her strength. It seemed ludicrous to waste energy on such things when so much was waiting to be done in New York. The mental list inside expanded by the minute as tasks were noted on projects for Duke's Farm, Onteora, and Broeckwyck. Her mind was completely engrossed in the topics occupying it, that she wasn't aware Charles had been speaking to her for several minutes.

"Catharyna, this is good-bye," he repeated. After the third attempt, her eyes registered on his face and a smile appeared.

"Forgive me, my thoughts were occupied."

His face tightened. "Your thoughts and body have been occupied ever since you met the Duke. Now you leave me for good. I ask for a moment of your time so we can say our good-byes with no distractions."

"Of course."

Hungry eyes roamed over her face and regret grew until it was no longer hidden. "Might I change your mind?"

There was regret in her voice. "I wish you could."

An accepting smile spread. "You have been loyal and true to my family. Mother will be pleased to hear Will has indeed been given the manor status he so coveted."

Catharyna fought the anger that began to rise over Hawk's deceit and succeeded. "That was due to you, Charles. You are a loyal brother to Hawk."

His face darkened. "I wasn't for a long time." And then he confessed, "Your friendship allowed me to see him finally as brother instead of foe. I thank you for that, Ryna."

"I did no such thing."

Charles brushed a wayward curl away from her forehead, and lifted her chin to gaze into the challenging eyes. "Your loyalty is absolute. You were wooed by the best cavaliers London offers, and yet you wait for Will."

She thought of the dandies who had plagued her while in London, and huffed in disgust. "That's not true."

Charles looked sad. "I am not strong enough to hold you an inch in front of me whereas Will holds you effortlessly oceans away." She began to protest, but was silenced. "You wait for the right man. It is the way it should be."

"There is no conclusion in the matter between your brother and me."

Charles touched her cheek and grinned. The tenderness in the gesture tightened Catharyna's heart, and they hugged tightly. "I will miss you, Charles."

"You have my friendship, Ryna."

They stared at each other for an timeless moment and then drew apart. He watched her climb aboard the vessel and stand beside Emily and Gerrit. They waved down at him and then she turned in the direction of a couple who were questioning her. Charles watched as Catharyna soon became engrossed and never looked back at him again.

Port Royale

There was every reason to leave. Hawk seethed as Fairfax continued to ignore him. They had their first argument, and neither were giving in. Fairfax wanted to abandon the mission to leave at dawn for New York and Emily, Hawk wanted to remain to make one last sack.

"When is enough for you, Hawk?"

"After this sack."

"No, Morgan has you now and won't let go."

"No one claims me."

"In New York no one does."

"The Duke holds my throat there, it's no different than Morgan's grip on it here," Hawk snapped with glowing eyes. All the deeds he had accomplished in New York were never enough. Even after the Iroquois Peace Treaty, he had to journey to London, and then Amsterdam, for proper recognition that was still not received. The tasks would never be complete because the crown knew he wanted New York and they would squeeze everything out of him before they gave it to him. The anger radiating out of Hawk made Fairfax take a step back. "I won't be held by either of them! This last sack will make sure of it."

Fairfax looked dubious, but the determination surrounding Hawk was too powerful for him to resist. "I follow you this last time, then I leave."

Hawk grinned and for the first time shared his strategy with Fairfax before setting sail. "We're going to use pinnaces for the attack to sneak up on the Spanish merchant ships. We'll get control of the ship even before the crew's aware they're under attack. You and Jacob will man a single-masted sloop, to be hidden in the bay and inlets. You'll support us with two dozen or so cannons on deck. I'll lead the crew with the hand-to-hand combat."

Fairfax had watched the past two months as Hawk listened and followed the ideas of Fortuna's manager, and his confidence emerged to finally share his own. Hawk was treating him as an equal for the first time and he would speak openly. "We could pull this off without a single shot being heard."

Hawk laughed in derision at the foolhardy idea.

Fairfax persisted, "Black Hawk is a living legend in the Spanish Main. The fear of your name would issue a surrender. Morgan crushed Panama that way, and they know you were his right hand at Portobelo. It will work."

Hawk's eyes narrowed and began to think over the idea seriously. The order confirmed its acceptance, "Instruct the crew to raise the fervor of my return. We'll prepare for the attack as planned, but we'll test your theory first." They looked at each other as equals, no longer leader to loyal soldier. The time was overdue.

The plan was set, crew gathered, yet one last item needed to be complete. No time was wasted.

People and carriages moved out of Hawk's heaving stallion's way toward Nellie's brothel. The door of the brothel opened the moment Hawk dismounted. He entered impatiently and felt overwhelmed by the blood red walls covered in Spanish velvet and the heavily draped windows in gold brocade. The air was thick with perfume, sweat and rum. Men were groping harlots on chairs, stools and in corners.

The sound of Hawk's boots under the wood plank floor caught the attention of one buccaneer who then alerted the crowd of Black Hawk's presence. A large arm chair was immediately emptied by the buccaneer who carried his wench to a corner.

Hawk sat down and announced, "I seek Golden Eagle."

A voluptuous red headed woman approached and sat on his lap. His face turned away from the sickening perfume that failed to mask her dirty body. Her hands loosened the ties on his raw silk shirt to reach inside, and her lips began a path downward. Hawk rose and she dropped to the floor.

"*Now!*" he ordered but no longer waited. Impatiently, he took to the staircase taking three steps at a time. At the landing, he began pacing down a narrow corridor that was lined with closed doors. Each were kicked opened, one by one examined in order to find his prey, until a woman approached.

"Stop, I say! Golden Eagle is here, follow me."

Hawk obeyed the curvaceous woman and his eyes surveyed her scantily dressed body until they stopped at the end of the corridor. She opened the locked door, leaned against it, and intentionally thrust her breasts up to his view and looked hungrily at him.

Hawk's eyes narrowed on her bosom and moved closer to find a clean and appealing scent. A rakish smile spread and met the buxom blonde's that took her breath away.

Nellie's smile froze when Golden Eagle pulled her roughly away from Hawk. "You seek me, not Nellie."

The woman was immediately forgotten when Hawk kicked the door open and entered the room. Nellie was caste out into the hallway and the men faced each other.

"You share your sister's features."

"I have no sister."

Hawk ignored the false words. "Your father died last spring."

Golden Eagle remained silent.

"Broeckwyck is your inheritance. It waits for you."

The words drew no response.

Hawk warned, "I need no agreement from you to bring you home."

Stubbornness grew. "The seas are my home."

"Ryna needs you."

Golden Eagle began to fade and Dirck surfaced. "She needs no man! Holy thunder, my father trained Ryna better than me!" he laughed and inspected Hawk with a brother's eye. "So, aye, I am Dirck, but you are not betrothed to Ryna."

Hawk grinned. "It is my intention and it is hers to make my quest hell until I succeed."

Dirck began to like the tall Englishman. His defenses lowered. "Does she know you are Black Hawk?"

Now Hawk was silent.

Dirck's face grew serious. He inadvertently shared the reason that kept him away from the shores of New York. "It is never and always with Ryna. If your deeds are judged harshly, it will be so."

The men stared at each other and Hawk swore, "It is God alone we pay our deeds to, all others be damned."

Images of a naive man dashing off to adventure blocked the guilt from Dirck's eyes. Two years of slavery on a sugar plantation had thickened his skin, and when escape was available, there was nothing he didn't do to protect his freedom again. "Yes," Dirck swore and extended a hand to Hawk. "I will return home with you."

Hawk grinned. "*After* one last sack. Come."

All remnants of doubt disappeared from Dirck's face being replaced with the excitement of adventure. He grinned back and swore, "Always." And walked a step behind Black Hawk out of the room.

Weeks passed in drudgery at sea. There were no calling cards or appointments, only opportunity if it sailed your way. A month past until they found worthy prey. In the horizon sat three Spanish merchant ships, heavily laden with goods en route home to their mother country.

Preparations began for the sack. Dirck, Fairfax and Jacob each captained a one sail sloop, for speed and cannon power if necessary, while Hawk led thirty pinnaces. The small boats contained no more than sixteen men each. All lay hidden in the lush foliage of the inlet and crept silently toward the Spaniards with the luck of the moonless night as their shield.

Like mice, the men scurried up the ropes onto the decks of the ships in silence. Their preparation and cunning had gained them surprise as the ship's lookouts were searching for large warships. Each man knew their mission.

Within minutes, they secured the ammunition room and had locked the majority of the crew below in the hull. Hawk's signal of a lit torch alerted all the pinnaces and the men were positioned on deck. A second later, his crew began to chant softly, eerily into the deep darkness of night, "Black Hawk returns."

The whispers ensued a shrill of fear in the merciless dark. The Spaniards fled in no predicated pattern as pandemonium and confusion engulfed all three ships. When each captain was taken and disarmed, the crews on deck surrendered the few firearms they had assembled. Black Hawk's presence made their cannons and firearms useless under the Spaniards' deadened limbs that were full of fear as Fairfax predicted.

The only shots that were fired were in victory.

Before dawn rose on the horizon, they abandoned the Spanish crew on the island of Hispaniola. The single-masted sloops drew forward, and the remaining buccaneers boarded the ships.

Fairfax, Dirck and Jacob approached Hawk, who was glowing in triumph at the ease of their sack. The four men laughed in exhilaration as the crew began opening the food and wine cellars to gorge themselves on roasted pig, chicken and barrels of rum.

Hawk brought Fairfax's hand high in the air and shouted, "Cheers to Fairfax who won us our booty with nary a shot!"

The men cheered and raucous laughter soon echoed across the glittering sea. Fairfax's eyes held no guilt in the attack as the merriment and rousing of the men filled his self-esteem.

Hawk leaned closer and whispered, "You won yourself a merchant vessel, brother." They grinned at each other and he added pointedly, "All while weakening our enemy. The crown will praise our efforts here tonight."

Each man's mind was full of the opportunities the vessels now held open to them. Hawk voiced some of them. "We'll take Fortuna's sugar crop to the Carolinas and Philadelphia and trade some for cotton and tobacco for New England." He reached out and hugged Fairfax as a burst of adrenaline raced through him over the future before them. Their eyes locked, both sparkling with excitement, and Hawk swore, "*Now* we go home."

Dirck laughed and added, "After you settle with Morgan." Both men leered at him, but he simply laughed louder. "And me."

Hawk's eyes narrowed and his hand reached out toward Dirck, who took a step back, only to feel his hair being tousled.

Laughter followed, but Dirck growled. Hawk treated him like a brother already and the Dutchman wanted none of it.

Jacob was not so reticent, and joined in their merriment. His loyalty was absolute to Hawk. Only this time he would get the agreement to be taken with them. He knew little about New York, but it would be his home if that was where Hawk led him. The intentions were spoken aloud. "I go home with you too."

Hawk grabbed Jacob's shoulder and swore, "I'll not leave you behind again. You stood beside me at Portobelo and in reclaiming Fortuna. You are a loyal friend."

Jacob's eyes glowed at his leader. Never did he forget the day Black Hawk came and sacked the Spanish city where he was held as slave. "You freed me from slavery, I follow you the rest of my days."

Hawk recalled his own dark prison and how Jacob had helped him out of it. "And you freed me. In New York you will no longer follow me, but build a life of your own." Their hands met to seal the agreement.

A week later they approached Port Royale at day break. As the three merchant ships rolled gracefully into the harbor, with masts billowing gloriously against the deep blue sky backdrop, the alert was made Black Hawk had arrived victoriously.

The crew raced ashore to spend their booty in the island's brothels and taverns. All were eager to brag about Black Hawk's ability to wrestle three ships without a battle. No mention was made of Fairfax's name, or honor in the success of the sack.

Hawk moved past the crowd to the pink mansion on the hill to settle matters with Morgan. He handed the acting Governor a written account of the Spaniards' fiendish threat against Jamaica, which had been no threat at all.

Morgan beamed and patted his back. "Well done, Hawk. We will soon bankrupt Spain with attacks such as these. The crown will no longer feel any threat from them."

Hawk looked at the higher meaning of his attacks on the Spanish the same way Morgan did. Any other way would make them the devious and greedy pirates that sprang from the bottom of the earth, cutthroats with no morals or code.

He nodded in agreement, and saw a twinkle of envy in Morgan's eye. His old leader missed the adventure. He searched for the hunger in himself, but it wasn't answering back. He had garnered two merchant ships from the sack, Fairfax the other, his mission was accomplished. The hunger for New York now beckoned and impatience filled him to be headed in its direction. Morgan accepted his share in the booty which amounted to 200 gold coins, the rest was split with the crew. Hawk wanted no coin, only the ships and their shipment of the finest Madeira.

His work was now complete in Port Royale. Regret filled his eyes when looking at Morgan. "I leave privateering for good this time."

A raucous laugh was released from Morgan's chest, and his eyes sparkled with anticipation. "It isn't the warm Caribbean breezes that lure you, it's the brand on your soul, Black Hawk."

Hawk's smile was measured, unsure what his words implied, so he remained silent. Morgan's eyes held the look of a venture in the unchartered future, and it too was ignored. It was his mentor's words that were ominous, laden with truth, that would prove impossible to forget. "Son, heed my words, for I know you as I know myself. Your appetite remains strong. You may become landed gentry and turn your back on your privateer days, but never forget all our best sacks were on land."

A chill of foreboding flitted through Hawk, but he dismissed it. Morgan was the greatest strategist he had ever met. If some of that rubbed off on his soul it would be all the better to have it.

Hawk chose to ignore the words. "I leave in a fortnight, I will meet with you when the shipping contracts are complete."

Morgan's raucous laughter boomed against the walls. "So begins your next venture as landed gentry and shipping merchant."

They smiled at each other and shook hands.

Nineteen

New York

The harbor beckoned them forward. Long Island's coastline came into view and shouts of jubilation rang out across all five vessels. The ship's crew scurried on deck to race up and down ropes that soared into the sky in preparation for arrival.

Catharyna approached the railing and closed her eyes as hungry lungs filled with New York air. The feelings were savored which slowly wrapped around mind and body. Imagination soon visualized Broeckwyck before her.

Jamie Harrison broke her privacy. "'Tis true, the air is sweeter here." He was the Duke's manager for Duke's Farm, and was accompanied by his brother, a doctor.

Catharyna's eyes sparkled with anticipation in the overdue homecoming. "The air is sweet, but it is our harbor that will make this province the greatest port in America one day."

Her voice contained such passion that it captured Jamie's interest. "Why is that?"

"When the Algonkins first arrived and stood at the banks of the Hudson River and saw the down current stop, then be overcome by the rush of upstreaming tides, they named it 'the water that flows two ways.' This harbor is destined to take in and let out continuous prosperity."

Jamie leaned closer and whispered, "Tell me more of the Algonkins."

There was no hesitation to speak of her province's past, one Minichque had related in-depth during their youth. "They had spread out along the shores, organizing small tribes, painting and engraving rocks and trees with their tribal insignia, in order to stake out their exclusive hunting rights in certain areas. At the river's mouth was the land of the Raritans, north of them lay the wooden shores that belonged to the Hackensacks, the Tappans and the Haverstraws. They were joined in the Lenape alliance of the Unami, the Turtle. Above them was another union called the Minsi, or Wolf, whose river tribes were the Waranawankongs, the Catskills and the Wawarsings. Across the Hudson from the Lenape, were the Manhattans and Wappingers, and to the north live the strongest of all the tribes, the Mohicans, who took their name from the old prophecy - 'people of the water that flows two ways.'"

Jamie's eyes roamed over the strength of Catharyna's features, and replied in awe, "Is there no fear inside of you with the savages?"

Her father's words were automatically repeated. "I fear a hateful mind, not a different face."

"I believe you would love anything about New York."

The English name no longer bothered her. She had journeyed a long way since her father's death. "It is my home."

Jamie took her hand. "And now it is mine." They smiled at each other and he added boldly, "I am eager for this new adventure. It holds much promise for me." His eyes lingered on her full red lips, and watched them spread into a smile.

Catharyna felt herself getting drawn in to Jamie's warm personality each day. He was a handsome man, much like Captain DeVries, yet it didn't intimidate or make her feel undesirable. Quite the contrary, his eyes reflected a very desirable woman each time they fell upon her. The fact that he was a genius with accounting added much to his charm. For years, the accounting books of many cousins fell upon Catharyna's shoulders. Jamie's skills would be put to use and grant her time for other work.

Dr. Simon Harrison interrupted them. "Excuse me, Jamie, but wherever did you place my bag? Mrs. Benton has an upset stomach and my pills are in it."

Catharyna turned away to hide the rising laughter. No two brothers were more opposite in appearance. Jamie was handsome with light brown hair, littered with golden streaks and had a tall lean body, whereas Simon possessed mousy brown hair that was quickly thinning and was several inches shorter than Catharyna. Simon's mind was known to be scattered at times, but what he did possess was a heart of gold. There was no person too old, young, little, tall, rich or poor that he would not treat in the same gentle and honorable manner. Catharyna had accomplished much in Europe, but securing Simon as a doctor in the province was one of the highest items on the list.

"You'll find it where it always is, our cabin."

Simon's eyes squinted and fingers scratched his head in thoughtful reflection. A moment later a smile appeared. "Yes, it is in the cabin." A soft white hand reached out to touch Catharyna. "My excitement at seeing my new home addled my brain a bit. 'Tis the most beautiful view, just as you described." He winked and then hurried to the stairs to go below.

Jamie looked concerned at his brother's retreating back. He leaned closer to Catharyna and conspired, "Will this land of savages welcome my soft hearted brother?"

"Definitely."

His voice grew husky. "And what of me?"

Merriment sparkled in her eyes. "If you work hard..."

"Yes, but not alone."

She finished, "Many maidens will welcome you here."

"I seek only one."

She laughed aloud at the new boldness that left little doubt for whom he sought. Hawk's desertion of her, his privateering and the shadows that surrounded him, all faded under Jamie's warmth. This was a man who would stick by her, and it made her draw closer to him. And, of course, his accounting skills were attractive, too.

Emily interrupted excitedly, "Ryna, is that Manhattan?"

"Yes." An arm pointed at a speck in the distance. "Over there is Turtle Bay which begins Broeckwyck's lands. Our patroonship is north of Manhattan, as far as your eyes can see." She left Jamie's side and wrapped an arm around Emily. "You will be happy here, Emmy."

"I will when Fairfax and Hawk arrive home."

Catharyna refused to be baited, and remained silent. It was an argument they had during the two month voyage home. There was nothing the men could do wrong in Emily's loyalty to them. A voice full of skepticism replied, "Don't wait to enjoy your life, live it now like they are. My children will have babies before I see Hawk again."

"Ryna, you don't understand..."

Catharyna's eyes turned deadly cold and a hand rose to halt Emily's words. "Let's not discuss this again, Emmy. You refuse to see who they are, I do. If you continue to try to change my thinking, it will only serve to destroy our friendship."

"But Hawk..."

"Will receive my warmest welcome if he is waiting in the harbor for us." Their eyes clashed until Emily nodded in acceptance. It was at that moment when pandemonium broke out on the ships. News spread like fire that they were restricted from entering New York Harbor.

Emily grabbed Catharyna's arm. "What is it?"

Fear broke through the dam of emotions, there was no restraining it from Catharyna's eyes which looked down at Emily. There was only one reason for the harbor to be closed off. "Smallpox."

She didn't wait for a discussion, but ran in the direction of the Captain for answers, and eavesdropped on his heated discussion with the First Lieutenant. "Nutten, Bedloes and Bucking Islands are housing the infected, we are not permitted to enter the harbor. We're ordered to dock here, or go to another port."

Captain Baynard was a burly man, aged and weathered by the seas. He learned early the wisdom of leaving ports where the plague festered. "We leave for Boston."

Catharyna interrupted by countering his order. "We remain here, Captain. The Duke's provisions are aboard for New York, not Boston."

Fear unfurled and wrapped itself around her heart, squeezing it tightly in lungs which barely breathed. All her efforts with the Duke would be for naught if they left for Boston. It was already the favorite port to the English, and she would lose all Onteora's tenant farmers on board to it. They would indenture themselves to Bostonian's who would pay their passage to her. All the skills critical to building Duke's Farm and Onteora would be lost to Boston, who would eagerly welcome all into Her harbor.

Catharyna's mind raced for logic in the life and death situation the plague had just thrust them into. Things had gone too smoothly in Europe, it had misled her to believe all would go easy for a change. The cynic within chastised herself that life was never easy, only a fool saw it as such.

Captain Baynard's white whiskers hid the bright red flush consuming the angry face at the woman's audacity in challenging his command. "Miss van Broeck, I am Captain here and will be obeyed as such!" He instructed his first lieutenant again, "We leave for Boston."

And again, Catharyna intervened. "Captain Baynard, I ask for but a moment to review the situation here before making your final decision."

He nodded angrily to continue.

"May we ask the Governor to send us more information concerning the scope of the plague? Which areas are affected, the health of the town itself, if we might be of assistance before we leave?"

His face warmed to the idea, and signaled to his First Lieutenant. "Send a message on my behalf to the Governor as Miss van Broeck described." His eyes rested on her when he warned, "We shall give him one day to reply."

She nodded in agreement and watched him walk away with head bent down and hands tightly clasped behind a stiff back.

The weight of her promise to the Duke began to crush her. Water dampened her eyes, but years of training refused to give them release. Instead, she looked in the direction of Broeckwyck, praying to find the answer and strength to see this through. Hours passed until the weight of promises felt like cold iron that shackled her down to the floor boards of the ship.

The sound of anchored ships rocking against the choppy current in the Harbor enhanced the sense that time was moving nowhere. As each ship stood still, the passengers grew restless, but none more than the Duke's employees and Onteora's tenant farmers. One burly voice rose among the group as their leader, the blacksmith Philip Morrison. At first, he began discussing thoughts with a few men, but soon it grew to include over fifty. The following morning, the crowd's complaints had jelled.

Philip Morrison bellowed, "New York is cursed, God is not in this province. I say we leave for Boston!"

The crowd's fervor grew more passionate as each minute passed. In the span of a day, all were now determined to heed the blacksmith's advice and settle in Boston.

"Is this not the new world of unlimited opportunities? Why must we risk all in New York when other coastlines offer greater wealth?"

His words reached Catharyna, who remained silent. Not a word would be uttered until information came from the Governor. There had never been a moment where she prayed so diligently. Her bible was crushed between hands, only to be reopened to scriptures read repeatedly for comfort, wisdom and answers.

The sun reached its zenith when the Governor's secretary, Rudolph Berryman, arrived on a one mast sloop. The Captain did not permit him to board the ship, but bellowed down to him. "What news do you bring us?"

Rudolph was a short, thin man who had poor eye sight. "The plague is contained at Nutten, Bedloes and Bucking Islands. It began on Long Island three months ago when a girl of two and ten had a blister on her palm. A fortnight later there were forty cases, all were immediately sent to Nutten Island. The Indian village of Sapokanican was hit hardest. Over half their number have died thus far, the others are suffering greatly on Bedloes and Bucking Islands."

Captain Baynard shouted back, "Where is your Governor now?"

"He remains in town at his home."

The Captain began speaking with his First Lieutenant, deliberately keeping Catharyna out of their discussion. The Governor being in town was a good sign the plague was not as severe as they had believed yesterday.

Catharyna took advantage of their private discussion by questioning the Governor's secretary herself. "Mr. Berryman, this is Catharyna van Broeck of Broeckwyck. How goes things there?"

Rudolph straightened and bowed to her, prompting a weak smile to appear on Catharyna's face at his manners under such circumstances.

"Broeckwyck had no outbreak, but most of the families have fled to the country due to fear of the plague spreading. There is no one harvesting the fields, your cousin Rolfe is managing with the dairy barns, but that is all. He is hopeful families will begin to return now that the plague has reached its peak."

The Captain nudged Catharyna aside and took over. "Does the Governor seek our help?"

Rudolph beamed. "Captain Baynard, the Governor believes we have quartered off the plague with no new cases in the past fortnight. We have rounded the bend and believe it safe to open the harbor to your ships."

His voice grew bold. "But the Governor will not make this choice for you, Captain. It is why he kept the harbor closed

228

until you were advised of the situation. He requests you consider this closely. The news of your five ships entering our harbor would send the message the plague has passed. People will return and we will have time to harvest before the first frost comes and takes it from us."

The Captain nodded and turned blazing eyes on Catharyna for putting him in the situation. He remained silent for several minutes. The sound of ships creaking under their anchor binds, which kept them from soaring out into the deep ocean, and the passengers rising complaints to depart for Boston, tormented the Captain.

"I cannot make such a decision with so many lives aboard. This will be presented to the passengers and my crew to decide. It will be agreement from all whether we remain, or leave for Boston."

Rudolph nodded. "I understand, Captain."

"You will know our answer by the direction of our sails."

"Yes, Captain Baynard." Rudolph bowed and was soon turning back toward Manhattan.

The Captain signaled the crew to gather their passengers together on deck. Within a short span, over one hundred people crowded the decks of three of the five ships. He stood on a platform overlooking the people, the First Lieutenant was on his right, Catharyna his left. "We have a decision before us that needs each of your agreement on the course we take."

The crowd nodded, having heard the rumors of the meeting's purpose. Catharyna saw the closed faces and eyes, and knew their minds were set.

Once again, Philip Morrison, the blacksmith, bellowed loudly, "New York is cursed, God is not in this province. We choose Boston!" The crowd all cheered in one united shout of agreement.

The Captain whispered something quickly to his First Lieutenant and boomed, "Silence!"

The crowd grew quiet, but whispers were still heard as they spread throughout the group.

"There is new information I received that no longer makes it absolute we leave this harbor."

The crowd roared, "Boston! Boston! Boston!"

"Silence!" The Captain's voice now held anger. "I will not turn away in fear from a harbor that possesses no threat!" The crowd now grew deadly silent. "The facts are these. The Governor remains in town, no new outbreaks have occurred in the past fortnight, and those infected are quarantined on three islands. My vote is to remain here as planned."

Two tears fell unheeded when Catharyna met the Captain's gaze, which was full of determination to stick to his word. She nodded at him, but remained silent. No words were necessary.

Philip Morrison's voice rose above the crowd. "We won't have any part of this cursed province. Miss van Broeck misled all of us with stories of milk and honey, fish jumping into our palms from the mighty Hudson River, and a land bountiful with fruits and grains. Such lies led us to the province of death and plague! We choose Boston!"

Nothing had prepared Catharyna for the hostile words, or when the Captain's hand tapped her shoulder. The turmoil of the situation made her blink at him, wondering what more could be said to make the nightmare complete.

"You must address their fears, Miss van Broeck, not I," the Captain instructed, and then he and his officers, all in unison, stepped back and lowered their heads.

Catharyna stood alone with an angry crowd that believed her a liar. Eyes closed and mind raced inward, flashing back to moments with her father, Hawk, and the Duke, until each man's dreams and visions for the province entwined. She locked on Onteora's meaning Hawk had conjured up, which had held London's merchants tightly in its grip. And then, a restlessness began in the deepest region of her soul, and spread like a forest fire growing in force. Conviction rose that the land in the sky would not be a made up ploy. Deceit would not lure innocents to Manhattan, but the opportunity to rise.

Determined eyes opened to face the angry crowd. "The

plague knows no bounds. Leave here today and you may be certain to face it again in Boston, or wherever your fear leads you this moment onward."

Whispers spread and a few heads were seen, nodding in agreement. Philip Morrison's voice rose above the crowd again. "God is not here!" There was no roar of agreement, but many heads nodded.

Catharyna drew closer and countered, "God is not destruction! He did not put the plague here just as he did not bring the Black Plague or Great Fire to England."

The wives began to whisper into their husband's ears, and shame began to fill some faces.

"This province *does* have more opportunity than one could reap in a lifetime, but it needs every one of us to bring it to fruition." She drew forward and boldly met the eyes of the doubters. "Each of you must decide the role you wish to have in its future. Do you seek to be part of building it into the land of your dreams, or play a hand in its destruction?"

When Philip Morrison began to protest, she raised a hand to silence him and shouted, "This is no lie!"

The crowd exploded with questions, but one rose to the surface higher than the others. The baker's wife, Molly Seward, stepped forward and asked boldly, "You love this land to view it so, but why should we?"

The crowd grew silent, and all turned to look at Catharyna. The weight of each person's life settled heavily on her shoulders, and yet clear blue eyes sparkled in brilliance at the crowd that held them spellbound. "Because of all the places you could have chosen to settle, Molly, this land directed you to Her shores." The commanding voice reached inside every man and woman who gazed in wonder at her. "I tell you this truthfully, opportunity is here and surrounds those with the courage to seek it. That you are here proves you have been honored with both. But you must have faith in this land to allow it to rise under the sweat of your labors." A confident smile spread. "Doubt no longer, for it shall take you higher than you ever imagined. And then you shall love it, as I, and be proud it is your home."

Molly swiped at the tears that spilled down wet cheeks, and drew forward to stand beside Catharyna. Proudly, she replied, "Aye, this is my home!"

Gerrit and Emily approached next, then Dr. Harrison, and moments later the blacksmith forged forward and nodded his head. "Aye, this is my home, too, Miss van Broeck. May God bless us all to rise up in the skies!"

A sigh of relief and laughter rolled throughout the crowd that a decision to remain had been accepted, and the Captain drew forward. The crowd was silenced when he bellowed loudly, "Proceed into port, men!"

Cheers emerged across each of the five ships as the crew raced to raise anchor. Passengers began final preparations to arrive on their homeland for the first time. Gerrit managed to work his way through the crowd to Catharyna and grabbed her hands. They exchanged a look of loyalty in each other that needed no words.

Gerrit's head rose proudly and stood beside his cousin whose love of the land had wrought a miracle. The future ahead was unchartered, risky, and uncertain. Everyone knew that would never change.

Twenty

Squirrels were off scurrying for egg corns, bears ate hungrily, and geese flew southbound in preparation of winter. The weight of responsibility grew heavier, unyielding, and blindly suffocating. There had been no peace or rest the moment their feet touched Broeckwyck's soil a fortnight ago.

The time of day mattered not, there was always something to do. When dawn broke Catharyna would be out in the fields harvesting or overseeing the grinding at the mills. In the evenings, it was work on ledgers and preparing instructions for the workmen in the buildings at Onteora.

No one accomplished more than Catharyna, who worked like two men and thought like ten. Continuous focus was on the fall calendar, which was quickly fading away. The knowledge that the first frost would be fast upon them, drove Catharyna feverishly to get Broeckwyck's harvest complete with only a tenth of the help. Everything needed to be done and each second that passed settled like dust follicles on her shoulders and mind. There just weren't enough hands to accomplish all that was required.

Slowly people began returning from the country as news spread about the five vessels that had entered their port. Each day new vessels arrived, and the town was slowly being restored to normal activity.

Emily's eyes followed the razor thin form of Catharyna,

who was at the head of the group, dictating assignments for the day. Tears sprouted at the sight of another family returning to Broeckwyck. The tenant farmers ran to Catharyna and were soon beside her in the fields.

Emily approached Catharyna and halted the sickle in her hand. "Ryna, give that to me. You need to handle some paper work today."

Determined eyes chilled her to the ground. "The harvest is not complete. Jamie's handling the paperwork."

Emily was equally determined and whispered into Catharyna's ear, "He should be here, not you breaking your back. Look at your hands, Ryna! They are covered in rags because of your blisters! Please, I beg you, rest today. I promise to work twice as hard."

There was no hesitation or change in her focus. "Grab a sickle or return to the manor."

Emily took a step back before the sickle sliced into her thighs. Never had she witnessed such determination in a human. There was no rest for Catharyna. She wouldn't permit it. With no other choice, Emily took a sickle and worked beside her in the warm autumn sun.

A fortnight later the first frost appeared, and the Fall Festival began at Broeckwyck. The work was complete and the new settlers were rewarded with the best festival they had ever witnessed. The knowledge that it was their energy that made it possible made it far sweeter than the sweet cakes the baker and his wife brought. The month of working side by side each other from sunrise to sunset had united them all into a family.

Catharyna walked through the crowd with a smile that transformed her sunken cheeks into the once energetic woman she had been. All eyes turned to her in respect. The blacksmith bowed each time they passed, his loyalty to her complete. Wives curtsied and children handed her trinkets of wild flowers, apples or hickory nuts.

A tap on the shoulder drew Catharyna's attention to a petite woman who looked up at her with haunted eyes. They stared at each other for a timeless moment and tears spilled unchecked. "Maria!" It was all Catharyna could say before grabbing her cousin tightly, neither wanted to let the other go. "Come, let's speak in private."

They held hands on the way to the wind mill and stood at the widow's peek overlooking the harbor, now graced with an abundance of sloops and merchant ships. "Oh, Maria, this is such a wonderful surprise. How I have missed you!"

Maria's head hung low until a low whimper rose to the surface. The tears flowed naturally, as they were want to do of late. "I missed you, too."

Catharyna raised Maria's face and saw dark shadows. "What is it? What has happened at Furwyck?"

Maria's head nodded back and forth in a crazy tempo until she cried brokenly. "The plague reached us! Johannes ...dead....race on Long Island...my babe! So young...too weak...innocent...gone."

Within seconds, tears streamed down both faces that gazed in pain at each other. Catharyna's voice cracked with emotion. "This...this one must not bear." Her heart had grown cold to the death around her, yet one innocent life had turned it back into liquid fire.

Maria whispered, "I don't know what to do now. I can't return to Furwyck, it's too painful."

"Stay with me and I will care for you."

"Nay, you've too much here, I ..."

Catharyna warned, "I couldn't bear your absence. Not now when you are so grieved. We shall manage Furwyck here."

There was no argument. For once, the two women sat in utter silence and watched the stars over head. Catharyna's thoughts returned to the man who haunted every minute of her day. Her traitorous heart wondered where Hawk was and if they were looking into the same midnight sky.

Charles Town, South Carolina

Hawk had never wanted to be rid of Fairfax more in his life. There was no peace due to the man's complaints that never ceased. "Another delay? What now? Emmy's waiting, I've given my word, we're already too late. Bloody hell, don't anchor or I'll shoot!"

The moment the ships anchored, Hawk took long strides on the dock to gain as much distance from Fairfax as possible. He went straight in the direction of the merchant exchange building to trade some sugar for rice, tobacco and cotton.

Jacob Chanler walked beside Fairfax, who was cursing loudly at the new delay. Jacob had reached his own limit with the love lorn man. A hand reached out and grabbed Fairfax by the throat. "Listen, and listen good, friend. We're finished hearing all your belly aching about missing your woman. We all miss our women!" And then he threw him against a tree and strode away.

Fairfax dusted off his pants and dove at Jacob's back. Within moments they were surrounded by their crew and onlookers who were all placing bets on who would win. The bets were in Jacob's favor, especially after he lifted Fairfax with one arm and tossed him easily across the town square.

A loud splash was heard when Fairfax landed in a trough of dirty water. The crowd applauded and swarmed closer to the two men. A grin spread across Jacob's face as he extended a hand to Fairfax, but it was angrily slapped away. Instead, Fairfax's swift move pulled him face down into the water.

They were soon sprawled on the cobblestone streets, rolling around or knocking each other down. Finally, Dirck broke up the fight by hauling Fairfax up by his ears and putting a knife to his throat. "Give now or luscious Emily won't enjoy your scarred face!"

Fairfax's eyes clashed with the dead cold eyes of Dirck. At last Fairfax spit out, "Give!" And then shrugged his body angrily out of Dirck's grasp. He stomped into a tavern with Jacob and Dirck a step behind. They sat at a table together. There was no mention of the fight.

A petite brunette approached with doe eyes that fluttered at Fairfax. In a world of his own, he ordered drinks unaware of the beauty's attention on him. Dirck's eyes followed the barmaid's movements, her resemblance to Maria too bittersweet to ignore. Memories of a naive time in his life flashed briefly. He lived for the moment now, not the past, yet eyes continued to linger.

Jacob flexed his hands and chuckled. "This soil brings out the devil in me."

Dirck looked at Fairfax, who gazed at the wall far away from them and countered, "Are you certain it isn't a love lorn sea man?"

Jacob's smile vanished. His voice grew deep, eyes full of sadness. "My family is here."

Fairfax raised his head finally. "Slaves?"

"Aye."

Dirck's voice turned colder as the words grew. "Whose here? Your father, mother, brother?"

"My wife and two sons."

Anger coursed through Dirck who stood up under its impact. "Let's go get 'em." There was no hesitation. He left the tavern and went straight in the direction of the livery. Jacob and Fairfax ran to catch up.

Fairfax grabbed him and whispered, "Whoa there, Dirck. We can't just go and grab three slaves." He leaned in closer and spoke into his ears alone, "What the hell is wrong with you?"

Dirck's eyes glowed, and a smile more treacherous than any Fairfax had seen on the seas, was aimed directly at him. "Afraid?"

"I'm not bloody crazy!"

"Follow me and all will go well."

Jacob stood beside Dirck with a smile that split across his face, and they continued forward to rent horses for the journey. Fairfax grumbled but followed.

They road for two hours by horse until they came upon Fox Hill. It was a rice plantation that had almost one hundred slaves operating it. From afar they watched the fields that were littered with slaves working, head down, back bent and baskets slung over shoulders in the midday sun.

Dirck whispered to Jacob, "This is along the coast, we can anchor there and grab the whole lot of them on our way home."

Fairfax's eyes rolled in disgust while sitting in the swamp listening to Dirck and Jacob plan a sack on Fox Hill. It became clear that Dirck had been named Golden Eagle for a reason, and shared the same appetite as Hawk.

At that moment, Fairfax knew there was a fundamental problem with his choice in friends. In anger he swore never to get involved in any more of their activities. If necessary, he'd get new friends.

Dirck left them to enter the fields and question some of the slaves. He grew bolder, moving closer to the mansion and slave quarters.

Fairfax groaned while instincts had him load both pistols. "Holy thunder!" he hissed to Jacob who grinned in delight, "the man's possessed," he swore while automatically getting into position to cover him.

Long, agonizing moments passed until Dirck returned breathless. His eyes sparkled with adventure when he patted Jacob on the shoulder. "Aye, your wife and sons are in the house closest to the slave master."

Jacob's voice trembled with emotion. "Esther, is she well? My boys?"

The questions tore through Fairfax and dissolved all his complaints. There was no question Jacob would return to New York with his family. The question yet to be determined was whether the other slaves would be as fortunate. That would be for Hawk to answer. Even so, he drew closer to Dirck and listened to the plan.

Broeckwyck

Leaves blew across rolling pastures emptied of their fruits and grains. Broeckwyck was asleep when Catharyna rose silently from the bed, careful not to awaken Maria. She dressed quickly and entered the kitchen.

Alice greeted her while stoking the fire. "Missy, sit and I'll get you some hot tea. I'm fixing a grand meal for Maria and you to chat and relax today."

Impatience racked Catharyna's body with the list of items that needed to be completed. She paced back and forth in the kitchen ignoring the growls from an empty stomach. A hand reached for some crullers. "Tell Maria I will return for an early dinner."

She was out of the manor before Alice had the chance to stop her. Harvest was over. Now was time to focus on Duke's Farm and Onteora. The stable was entered for a quick inspection on the gift from the Duke.

"Good day, Bella," Catharyna whispered against the Black Arabian mare's soft muzzle.

The stable boy, Timothy, sprang out of the tack room that served as his sleeping quarters. His hair was tousled but a wide crooked grin spilled across his face. "Morn, Ten Broeck."

"How is she settling in?"

"Fein, fein. She's a real beauty."

"Winter approaches, I want blankets on her, plenty of fresh air and exercise during the day."

"Aye."

With one last pat on Bella's neck, she left the stable and

headed to the East River to board a one mast sloop to sail into the harbor. The road that led to town was really a cumbersome old Indian path. All traveled by the river for the fastest route to town.

There was no sign of activity in the early hour of morning when she arrived at the Governor's Mansion. The steps were taken two at a time, and she knocked on the door for entrance. No response was received. After another loud knock, she entered and went to work.

Much was accomplished by the time Governor Lovelace arrived. He stared at the strange woman who was seated in his office and apparently busy at work. "Madam, what are you doing in *my office?*"

Catharyna's eyes briefly scanned him, and then went back to the papers on the desk. "Working on Duke's Farm."

A smile spread across Lovelace's face, and drew forward for proper introductions. "Ten Broeck, it is a pleasure to finally make your acquaintance. May I introduce myself, I am..."

Ice cold eyes halted his words. "You need not waste time on frivolities with me, Lovelace. I know who you are, Sir, including the malicious letter you sent to the Duke to transpire against me."

Disbelief flickered across his face and held the politically correct tongue silent.

"I am not the Duke's enemy, but friend. Whether that holds true with you remains uncertain." She rose and approached him. "I have given my word to the Duke to assist you in uniting this province. His bouwerie will require support from you."

"Of course, I shall be delighted to assist you with Duke's Farm."

A feline smile spread across Catharyna's face. "Good, I'll need an office here until further notice." She raised a hand to halt his words. "Also the three warehouses that once belonged to the West India Company need to be emptied. The Duke's provisions must be stored there until spring."

Lovelace began to turn red with anger. He personally rented the space to merchants and made a handsome profit by it. He suspected the shrewd Dutchwoman knew it.

Catharyna raised a brow waiting for his agreement.

It was given grudgingly. "Of course."

"Good. Since my attention will be focused at Duke's Farm, I'll need your help to procure additional workmen to build structures at Onteora by January."

"January!" he shouted, now suspecting the woman was mad. "Three months cannot possibly...it's an impossibility!"

"Your roads are nearly complete."

"Aye," he agreed in a whisper, not understanding.

"I need twenty of your best skilled men. They will each be given a year's supply of flour and corn meal to assist my crew in building a lodge and barn by January. Stone work will be handled in the spring."

Lovelace simply stared at her, ill prepared to face such determination in the morning hours.

His silence made her add, "More hands are welcome if you can accomplish it." She turned back to the desk and pulled out the tax journal. Her delicate fingers flipped through the pages while her tone was even more flippant. "I came across this." Judgmental eyes rose to pierce Lovelace. "I must say I'm greatly disappointed in the changes you've made during my absence."

Anger punctured his enormous vanity. Never had he endured such treatment by a man, much less a woman. His teeth began to grind. "What changes?"

"You've closed down a third of the taverns in town."

He smiled arrogantly. The woman was not the genius the Duke believed her to be. He would take enjoyment in putting her back in place. "I am the Governor here, Miss van Broeck, and must govern according to the laws. The more taverns, the more crime."

She laughed openly at him. "Lovelace, this is not New England," and visibly shuddered. "We Dutch are broadminded and learned long ago the more taverns the *more tax*." Doubtful

241

eyes narrowed on him. "Do you fear your ability to protect the town?"

He stood in bewilderment in how she used his own words against him. "No!"

A genuine smile appeared. "Good. I need not remind you building a province requires money, Lovelace. If sailors coming into our port want to squander their coin away on drink, let them."

He simply stared at her. Such thinking froze his tongue. "Now, where is that office?"

He looked blankly at her.

A black brow rose when she repeated, "An office?"

"Ha, yes, an office," he stammered still reeling from the tax lecture, "Rudolf shall get you settled shortly."

Catharyna grinned seeing the familiar face of bewilderment. Even so, she decided to rein in the frustration with Hawk which had made her attack the Governor so harshly. "You've done an excellent job containing the plague. It could have been far worse had not your measures been taken. Such leadership compels me to forgive your libelous letter to the Duke about me."

He blinked twice and then a smile spread. Every word she had spoken earlier was erased from thought. There was truth in her voice and the recognition that she approved of his leadership, was savored.

He bowed graciously.

Catharyna added, "We're on the same side now, Lovelace. We have a great job before us, but together we'll get it done."

Lovelace's eyes narrowed, finally seeing an opportunity to rein in the Dutch. "Does that include the smuggling?"

Their eyes met.

Lovelace drew closer. "Tax from taverns is but small compared to the import and export tax we lose to your Dutch seamen who continue to disrespect our law."

Catharyna's shrewd eyes smiled at him. Ever since the English arrived in 1664, the Dutch had been smuggling goods to Amsterdam, boldly ignoring the law to trade only with England. None felt any guilt since the English had stolen their province, especially Ten Broeck.

Lovelace drew closer and added, "Having you obey our law will make many follow."

She laughed. "I am but a woman."

"You are Ten Broeck."

Their eyes battled while faces appeared civil and warm. She had given her word to the Duke, and would keep it. Convincing DeVries, who led the smugglers, would be harder than having the new tenant farmers enter a province in plague. There was no avoiding the handsome Dutchman now.

Catharyna extended a hand. "You have my word."

Lovelace accepted it with a brilliant smile. "And I give you mine to protect our province and make it prosperous." He bowed one last time and left in a rush. Orders were soon heard echoing in the hallway. "Rudolf, give Ten Broeck your office and get those warehouses cleared immediately! We need workmen sent to Onteora and I must see the tax collector post haste!"

Catharyna hummed, returning to the plan of Duke's Farm. Days passed like hours as the details began to fall into place.

Lovelace indeed proved a worthy partner. Two days later, a crowd of carpenters arrived at the mansion waiting for Catharyna's instructions before heading north to Onteora. The news of flour and corn meal as payment brought out men who had retired for the winter. Now all were eager to work in the cold.

After the selection of twenty-five men, she left the Governor's mansion and headed to the Blue Dove. There was hope Captain DeVries was out on a run to the Carolinas and the task could be pushed off another month.

It was not the first time she entered the tavern. Much trade was handled there with new ships arriving into port. The faces of the men instantly told her DeVries was there. One of his ship hands bounded up the stairs and Catharyna's face

243

tightened, knowing where and what the handsome sea captain was doing. She took a seat and ordered a Kill Devil to the raised brow of a buxom wench.

By the time it arrived, so did DeVries. His blonde hair was loose and clothes hastily thrown over a muscular frame. Though it was his sea green eyes, chiseled features and bright smile that brought her own out of hiding.

"I wasn't expecting you," he confessed. His eyes roamed over the woman he desired and grew concerned over the gaunt and thin shell that contained the spirit he so admired.

He whispered, "We returned from Amsterdam two days ago, I've some merchandise for your consideration."

She grinned. "Which wharf?"

DeVries laughed, ""Such impatience!" And then a drink order was shouted, "A Bride's Tears, Sally!" His hands gestured Catharyna to a corner table where they sat alone. "I heard the port had been closed due to plague. How goes things at Broeckwyck?"

"None were affected. We were able to save the harvest."

"Good," he nodded as hands closed over her own. "If you have need of help, I am here now." Concerned eyes narrowed on her, and he chided, "You are too thin."

"I am fine," she whispered, and their eyes met. "I've come to ask something of you."

DeVries straightened by the business tone in her voice. Their work relationship was the only area he had found success with her. "Aye?"

"There is no one who hates our English rule more than me."

He laughed boyishly. Such hatred had brought them together. "Aye!"

A voice of earnestness said, "I have come to believe it is time to accept it."

Their eyes locked.

"What are you telling me, Ryna," he whispered in warning.

"It is time we obey their law."

DeVries released her hands. "I heard Hawk has gained manor status for the property he swindled from the Mohicans, which is larger than Scotland."

Catharyna tightened for the anticipated battle. "I've no knowledge of its vastness or how he acquired the land."

"And that Onteora's manor status was announced at Broeckwyck's festival."

"Yes, but..."

"You chose him," DeVries stated.

"This has nothing to do with whom I marry, " Catharyna warned.

A deep sarcastic laugh rumbled. "Then why are you in bed with the English suddenly, Ryna? The very men you despised and mocked the past ten years when their ships pulled into our harbor and *swindled* it from us?"

Heat rose to her cheeks and blood pounded in her ears and chest. "It is not my doing the English are here." Her hands clenched. "We were abandoned by our mother country for sugar, DeVries! I would give all I own if it were otherwise, but it is what it is, and we must accept it now if we are to prosper."

He leaned across the table and snapped, "Have I not made certain you prospered under English rule? When Dirck abandoned you, who handled your smuggle trade?"

Catharyna said tightly, "Yes, but I never knew marriage was the payment."

A dark laugh warned, "Don't twist my words, Ryna!" He rose and began to pace. A finger pointed at her. "You'll not gain my agreement again with such tactics."

Innocence looked back at him. "Fine, I'll simply nod and remain silent while you are strung up by a rope."

Their eyes battled. DeVries swore, "I'll not do this for then Hawk wins all!"

"Hawk has nothing to do with this!"

"Then who does?"

Catharyna squirmed in the chair. "You!"

"You ask this for me?" he asked in a dubious voice, and eyes narrowed. "How so?"

"You lead the smugglers, they will follow you." He laughed and she added, "I shall make certain you are rewarded," she paused to stress, "handsomely for doing such."

His anger pushed chairs out of the way to pace back and forth. Veins bulged from his neck and a hand was pointed at Catharyna. "You're a fighter, Ryna! I cannot believe you ask this of me."

She approached him in fury. "We shall fight in other ways to keep our place in this province, far more powerful ways. This I swear to you, DeVries."

Their eyes met until he growled, "I shall consider it."

Catharyna drew closer and touched his face. "I trust that you will."

His hands covered her own and eyes bore through her. "You know I cannot say no to you."

Knowing eyes roamed over his face and then turned to a red haired tavern wench, who was staring at them with jealous eyes. "Nor to others."

DeVries turned to see whom she meant and frowned. "I am but a man."

"No," she whispered, "you are a leader of men."

His eyes gleamed with the pleasure of hearing the conviction in her voice when speaking the words. "I shall need much to convince my men. How will you accomplish such?"

Catharyna grinned. "If the English want our friendship, they will find it as costly as our smuggle trade."

They both laughed.

Twenty-one

Fox Hill, South Carolina

A month later the *Ten Broeck, Meredith* and *Golden Eagle* were stocked with tobacco, rice and cotton. Fairfax had sold his vessel in exchange for tobacco. Money was needed more than a ship to build his manor and outbuildings.

The three ships headed north but kept close to the coast line. The cost of the venture was every coin Jacob had made from his last two sacks. It was agreed he'd pay for the horses, wagons, and carriages to retrieve his family. The rest would be covered by Hawk and Dirck. The slaves courageous enough to risk the opportunity, would be given passage to New York, and work seven years as indentured servants at Onteora or Broeckwyck to pay off their expenses for clothes and shelter.

The one flaw in their plan was the ignorance in knowing the number who would flee. It would be known at midnight when Dirck, Jacob and twenty buccaneers returned with no opportunity to fail.

Hawk walked along the beach, staring at the slice of moon in the midnight sky. The weather was perfect, yet something was wrong. They should have been here by now. He continued pacing, and then signaled to Fairfax aboard the *Ten Broeck* he was going inland to search deeper into the marsh. A knife was poised in hand, passing three snakes, all harmless thus

247

far. It was then he felt the ground begin to shake as horses and wagons drew near.

In disbelief, Hawk saw over seventy slaves crammed into the wagons. His long legs lengthened to a full run to meet the wagons at the shoreline, and began helping the men, women, and children aboard the row boats that would take them to the ships.

Thirty slaves were safely aboard when the shots began. Then the dogs came. Dirck ran directly into the path of the slave catchers and Hawk growled at his stupidity, now unable to do anything but follow him. Chaos was all around. Slaves began crying and some were pushed out of the boats in fear and fright, unable to swim, only to drown.

Fairfax dove into the water and grabbed two small children, who now clung tightly to his neck, and brought them to the *Ten Broeck*. "Climb on these ropes and *don't look down!*" The boys nodded and scooted up to safety. He climbed on the boat returning to shore only to dive into the frigid water to pull out another two, this time girls. He made three more trips.

Jacob watched from afar as his wife and sons safely reached the deck of the *Ten Broeck,* and knew peace for the first time in many years. Then he followed Dirck loyally with a determination never known before.

Dogs began attacking, one reached for Dirck's throat and Jacob slit its throat in short order. Both went head first into the onslaught of slave catchers.

Hawk arrived and grabbed Dirck by the arm and began pulling him back toward the shore. "Back, *now!* We take no more."

Their eyes clashed and Hawk stared into the eyes of a man possessed. Dirck continued going forward, but Hawk had enough. There was no intention of losing Dirck on the mission. The man would return home alive, gagged and bound if necessary. The butt end of Hawk's pistol knocked Dirck out cold and seconds later he was slung up over a shoulder.

Hawk ordered Jacob, "Back, now!"

Jacob nodded, and covered Hawk's back as they raced

to shore. Only the slave hunters approached at a faster pace, and bullets were everywhere. One bullet hit Jacob, two hit Hawk; neither man stopped as they raced toward the boats.

The moment they left shore, cannon fire from *Golden Eagle* erupted on the beach, halting the slave catchers. Their gun fire stopped and the slaves that remained in the water and along the shore, were gathered together to be returned to Fox Hill. Cries and pleas for rescue were ignored. Their opportunity had passed.

The three vessels headed into the deep ocean and were soon swallowed up into the shadows and darkness. Word spread Hawk and Jacob were hit.

The ship's doctor was a toothless buccaneer who held the title because he used rum to douse all wounds and knew how to use a knife to amputate limbs with a bullet wound. Tools were taken out and readied to begin work on the Captain.

Hawk bit the cork of the rum bottle off and poured the brown liquid over his right calf muscle and left arm that oozed with blood. Dirck sat in the corner of the cabin emptying a bottle of Hawk's finest brandy, never once offering to help stop the blood flow. It was Jacob's wife who came to his aid.

Esther was a woman with proud facial features, and a voice that spoke flawless English. Her humming soothed Hawk while ripping strips of linen and tying them tightly around his arm and calf to slow the bleeding.

Jacob entered the cabin with a warm smile and white cotton shirt, covered in his own blood. Esther welcomed him with a close inspection to his stomach, and then smiled. "You, my bold buccaneer, will be fine. The bullet grazed your side."

Jacob crushed her against him and whispered, "Nothing could have pierced my skin tonight."

They hugged each other tightly, and then Esther pushed gently away. "Your Captain needs serious attention." She turned to Dirck and stated, "I need boiled water, more linens, the sharpest knife on board and lots of alcohol."

Dirck ignored the words. Leisurely, he raised the brandy bottle and drank.

Jacob nodded, and left the cabin to gather the supplies. Esther raised a brow at Hawk who was slowly losing consciousness from the loss of blood. The last thing remembered was soft, soothing music that drifted him into a deep sleep.

Two days later, Hawk woke to a throbbing hot fire in his shoulder and leg. Eyes closed shut under the pain.

"Feeling better?" a voice, which sounded like Fairfax, asked.

"Only if hell is an improvement."

"You're damn lucky Esther is aboard. You'd be walking around on a peg leg and holding one arm."

Hawk whispered, "How many?"

Fairfax knew the cryptic question. It was the first time Hawk had taken a bullet, two at that, yet all he cared about was the success of their mission. "We have fifty-six aboard. Two were shot, but they'll live."

"How many drowned?"

Fairfax's face grew dark. "Don't know."

"Damn."

They sat in silence until Esther entered with soup. She sat beside Hawk on the bed and fed him slowly. The dryness in his throat began to open and slowly eyes followed. A warm smile greeted him.

"My thanks Captain Hawk for rescuing us."

Hawk tried to rise again, only the pain was too intense in his shoulder. He bit down to handle it and grounded out, "Sure."

Esther turned to Fairfax. "Help Captain Hawk rise, and take those hot towels to clean the wounds. Be very thorough."

Fairfax followed the instructions. When he lifted the bloodied linens away from the wounds, there was amazement over the precision of her work. Doubt filled his voice. "Did you get the bullets out?"

She looked insulted, but returned with a cooper cup and handed it to him. He saw the two bullets there. "Well done, Mrs. Chanler."

"It's my honor to care for the Captain."

Hawk cursed over the hot linens pressed against the wounds, but remained still. Fairfax whispered, "You're bloody lucky."

"Lucky? I got shot, you didn't."

"It's a sign to slow down."

A deep laugh burned in his belly. "Hell, no."

"Ha, so you're not going to wed Ten Broeck."

"Hell, yes."

Fairfax's brow rose when seeing Esther cover her ears and glare at Hawk.

Hawk clarified, "Ryna won't slow me down."

"She won't permit these..." Fairfax's eyes felt the heat of Esther's glance and finished, "adventures."

"I'll handle her."

Disapproval was now naked on Esther's face, which made Hawk's eyes narrow in speculation over what was wrong with his words this time.

Fairfax grinned over his fearless leader's restraint in front of Jacob's wife. The opportunity was too good to ignore, and chose to deliberately bait Hawk. "You can't begin a marriage with no boundaries."

Hawk growled, "You can live by the reins, but not me."

To both men's amazement, Esther began to laugh. She looked at them as though naive boys lost in the woods. "You've no knowledge of women," and added pointedly at Hawk, "either of you!"

Fairfax was insulted.

Hawk thought about the complex personality of Catharyna and said rhetorically, "Who does?"

These men rescued her family. Esther felt obliged to educate them since they were woefully lacking in it. "I do, and will share it if you are interested to listen."

Hawk groaned, but saw Fairfax's interest, so nodded.

"Women love adventure just as much, if not more than men. It's just that our adventure is far riskier and has no boundaries."

Hawk laughed, and even Fairfax looked doubtful.

Esther drew closer and grinned. "Woman have the courage to risk the adventure of love," her eyes pinned Hawk, "whereas men use adventure to run away from it."

"That's ridiculous," Hawk countered, "men marry for practical reasons, nothing more."

Esther nodded. "Yes, for you it is."

Fairfax laughed.

Hawk growled, "I run from *nothing*."

"You are courageous, Captain Hawk."

Hawk's eyes narrowed. The words were fine, but her voice said the opposite. "Fairfax loves, and it leaves him crippled," he snapped.

Fairfax began to protest, but Esther's words silenced him. "He's been given the one thing that matters to his happiness and seeks to protect it. What do you protect, Captain?"

There was no hesitation. "My freedom!"

"And you build walls to shut everything else out," she added.

"Love is a frivolity," Hawk grumbled, and closed his eyes and mind to her words. Both body and mind were weak, and his strength was waning.

Fairfax whispered, "If love is difficult for men, what is difficult for a woman?"

"To respect a man. Their love hinges on it."

Fairfax looked at his best friend with sad eyes. He whispered to Esther, "Ten Broeck is a mountain lion, very unforgiving."

Hawk appeared asleep, but was heard mumbling, "I don't mind scratches."

Twenty-two

The sound of slumber echoed from a sky of snow flakes, heralding winter's arrival at Broeckwyck. There was nothing to be done until spring. The town had bounced back from the plague, as did Broeckwyck. The new tenant farmers continued to send small presents of thanks to Catharyna, and Governor Lovelace sent invitations to every winter party. Progress was also found at Onteora, where the carpenters were finished with the frames of a barn and lodge that now housed many of Duke's Farm's animals. Everyone was happy; except the three women at Broeckwyck.

Emily peered out the window pane for the hundredth time that morning. Maria snapped, "Nothing has changed since you last looked, Emmy. Come and join us for breakfast. It's rare that Ryna is with us."

She joined them at the table, and her eyes widened at the feast prepared by Alice. There was little talking to be done. This was Catharyna's first breakfast with them since Maria's arrival, and the amount of food she consumed left Emily speechless.

Maria had no such problem. "Why did you send my brothers to Albany? We need Rolfe and Gerrit here during winter."

Catharyna shook her head in disagreement. "They deserve to be rid of me and Broeckwyck. Some fun in Albany with their friends is overdue. Besides, Gerrit's wedding will be upon us none too long. He should spend time with his fiancé."

Maria's eyes narrowed. "Yes, all can rest but you."

"I'm not running about today."

Emily snorted, "Bah! One day, you'll be out and about tomorrow."

Maria smiled at her new friend. They disagreed on many topics, but agreed about Catharyna and their worry over her disintegrating health.

"There's nothing more for me to do for the next two months. I'll be fattened up and rested in time for spring."

Both women eyed her face and body suspiciously.

Catharyna added, "I've nothing planned for today," a smile of excitement spread, "other than ice skating with you both."

Emily rose instantly and gathered their skates. She stopped to peek out the window before returning to the table.

Maria whispered, "Will she ever stop waiting for Fairfax?"

Catharyna's eyes were sad. "No."

"How long has he been away?"

"A year."

Maria shook her head. "I too waited years for Dirck, until my father pushed me into marriage only to lose both husband and babe." Tears gathered in grief swollen eyes. "Now I wish I had been strong enough to wait."

Catharyna hugged her. "You had no choice. If you had, it would have been thus."

"No," Maria countered, "you made a trade for your freedom while I was meek, which led me to wed your intended."

"Bleecker was never my...," Catharyna stopped the words, realizing their inappropriateness and pain for Maria. Eager to change the subject, she ordered, "We must hurry, the sled is waiting for us."

They were soon bundled in thick layers of wool clothes. A blast of cold air hit their faces upon meeting the outdoors, and a sleigh greeted them. Blankets were quickly piled on top of their huddled bodies.

Maria put an extra blanket around Catharyna's

shoulders, which she fought. "You've grown far too thin. A strong breeze will blow you across the Hudson!"

Their eyes clashed until Catharyna relented. "Very well, I shall allow you to coddle me today."

"Very well, but you need not tread carefully with me, Ryna. I'll not break," Maria swore.

Their eyes met and Catharyna saw the pain of loss deep in Maria's eyes. There was one way to take it away, temporarily. "That I have known since you were five and threw mud in my face because of the bucket of water I threw over Dirck's head for refusing to do morning chores."

Emily laughed and snuggled closer. "You didn't, Maria!"

The widow soon giggled like the young woman she was.

Catharyna continued, "Oh, it's true. You've no idea the evil that lurks within the small body of my meek cousin, Emmy." Her eyes latched onto Maria's. "I still don't understand how you managed to get all those frogs in my bed. I tortured Dirck for weeks until he confessed it was you."

Tears of laughter were now found in Maria's eyes, and Catharyna grinned. "And I'll never forget the pitch fork I sat on in my best Sunday dress, which put holes in the most embarrassing place."

Emily now had tears of laughter on her face. "Oh, Maria! Wherever did you get the courage to do such to Ryna?"

Maria's eyes sparkled with childhood memories. "Because she loved me like her baby sister. I believed it was my job to get her to stop working all the time. She never had any fun."

Catharyna groaned. "A pitch fork in my bottom is fun?" Maria began to laugh again. "I couldn't walk straight for a week!"

The journey was lively with childhood memories that warmed the winter air. The sleigh, pulled by four horses, took the ladies west, across the island toward the Hudson River. Catharyna was thoroughly relaxed. It was her favorite time of year, and sharing it with her two best friends was the rarest of treats.

Emily groaned at the sight of Jamie Harrison and Dr. Harrison, who welcomed them at the foot of the carriage.

Jamie escorted Catharyna from the sleigh. "Good day, Ryna. Mrs. Bleecker, Miss Fielding."

Emily leaned over and whispered into Maria's ear, "He's so bold, using her nickname!"

Maria's eyes ordered Emily to be silent. She obeyed, but suspicious eyes narrowed on Jamie's hand, now holding Catharyna's arm as they walked toward the frozen river. Emily's eyes followed the pair throughout the day. Innocent skating and friendly conversation were heard, with much laughter and giggles, from Catharyna and the handsome estate manager. Efforts increased to eavesdrop and interrupt, or beg, to skate privately with Catharyna. And when Emily accomplished it, the result was chiding her friend.

"Ryna, you mustn't spend so much time with Mr. Harrison. People will talk."

Catharyna laughed. "I thought you couldn't wait to get to New York where it didn't matter what people said."

Emily frowned. "I don't care if people talk, but not when I hear he's such a coward."

"Coward?"

"All know he remained locked away in the Governor's mansion when we arrived here, afraid to expose himself to the plague."

"We mustn't judge. That is a real fear, Emmy."

Emily's teeth bit down in frustration, trying to find another flaw in the man. It was no easy task. He was handsome, charming, well mannered and treated Catharyna with respect.

All too soon Maria and Jamie interrupted them. Within seconds Emily was holding Maria's arm and braced herself for another tirade. "Why must you take the few crumbs of happiness Catharyna is given?"

Emily gasped, "I do no such thing!"

"Your friend Hawk has shown his true face to my cousin

and it's his deceit that separates them. You yourself wait for Fairfax, who said they would be here before harvest time. Yet, it is nearly February and he lingers. Ryna has decided to move forward with her life and you must accept that decision."

"It is an impossibility for me."

Their eyes locked and Maria warned, "Then you will destroy your friendship with her." Stubbornness was stamped on Emily's face, and Maria could take no more. Years of waiting for Dirck made her speak boldly. "How can you be so devoted to Fairfax? You know not what he does in the West Indies? Why, I've heard tales of piracy, debauchery, harlots, ..."

Emily's hand silenced Maria. "Speak no more!" There was no tolerance to hear her own fears spoken aloud. "You have my agreement."

The women continued skating in silence. The change in Emily was immediately apparent. Each time they passed Catharyna with Jamie, she smiled.

They remained well into the afternoon, enjoying the bonfire and roasting chestnuts. Hot tea was offered by Simon to Maria with a shaky hand. She smiled warmly at him, but remained silent. There was no desire for any man in her life.

Catharyna had no such hesitation with Jamie. The day was pure enjoyment and no thought of Hawk disrupted it. There was a sense of relief that the hurdle of Hawk had been crossed.

The Harrison brothers escorted the three women home, astride their horses, who trotted beside the sled. Exhaustion claimed Catharyna, who slept on the journey home. Body and spirit rebelled under the workload carried the past months on emergency resources, which were now gone. Never had she been so weak or empty of energy.

When they arrived at the manor, Catharyna almost stumbled out of the carriage, had Jamie not been there to catch her. They all made light of her clumsiness.

"Please join us for dinner."

Jamie looked startled at the unexpected invitation from Emily, but quickly recovered. "It would be our honor." He extended an arm, and she gracefully accepted the escort inside the manor.

Maria and Catharyna followed on Simon's arm. The doctor was clearly flustered at having a woman on each side of him.

Emily proved a charming hostess throughout dinner and its conclusion, going so far as to walk their guests outside, and watch them safely depart Broeckwyck grounds. When she entered the manor, she was rewarded with a sparkling smile from Catharyna.

"Thank you, Emmy."

Emily sought out Maria's gaze and found approval there too. "It was my pleasure." She hugged Catharyna and whispered, "You are my dearest friend. I do want your happiness."

"I know you do."

Emily saw water dampen Catharyna's eyes, and hugged her impulsively again. It was a rare sign of emotion from the strong Dutchwoman, and Maria appeared even more emotional. Her two Dutch friends were stone castles that couldn't be plowed down by the strongest team of oxen, yet, tonight they made her wonder if they were just as delicate as she in life's frailties. She kissed them goodnight, and retired for the evening.

The two cousins rose and entered their bedchamber, arm and arm. It was Maria who said, "She loves you."

"Yes, but it is her loyalty that makes me humble."

Maria chuckled. "I've never seen such devotion!"

Catharyna sat on the bed and gazed at the floor boards for answers. "What does she see in Hawk that I am missing? Am I wrong to judge him with written proof without hearing his defense?"

"Your judgment is fine. If he is the man she speaks so highly of, he will prove it to you."

Their eyes met, and Catharyna's held sadness. "And yet, I wait for him."

"No, I see none..."

A hand halted the words. "Daylight deceives me into

believing otherwise, but at night it is all I know. I cannot break free of it."

Maria's voice was haunted. "This I tell you is truth. My husband's touch never took Dirck from my heart." A tear fell down her cheek, and it was angrily wiped it away. "I miss him even now."

"I'm sorry, Maria. Let us not speak of this."

"No!" Maria ordered. "We are Dutchwomen, are we not?" she challenged. "Yes, we are brave enough to love but is our choice wise?"

"I know not," Catharyna whispered in surrender. They took each other's hands. "I only know I am through deceiving myself. I am not done with Hawk."

"Then we shall pray he returns soon." Maria placed the candle in the window sill and climbed into bed beside her cousin. They both had a restless sleep.

Golden rays of sun light peeked through the window, kissing Catharyna's face awake. There was nothing to do, yet she rose and dressed hurriedly by habit. The brisk, cold air tasted of anticipation. It was always that way when something was about to happen.

She began doing simple tasks to occupy idle hands. The fire needed stoking, she added more logs, and then she went to the window pane and gazed out. A smile appeared at the sight of Minichque and brother Sokoki astride their white stallions, headed toward the manor. Both were dressed heavily in animal skins, and were accompanied by ten tribe members and Governor Lovelace, who rode beside them.

She rushed outdoors to greet them, forgetting about covering herself from the cold. The two brothers dismounted, and Minichque took a fur robe and covered her with it. They bowed to each other and she ushered them inside the manor.

Minichque announced, "Ten Broeck, we go hunting."

Sokoki laughed and added, "We spoke of your prowess with bow and arrow to your Governor, but he is...unbelieving...as you say."

Lovelace smiled, now well accustomed to the two Indian's humor. He ignored it and bowed gallantly. "Ten Broeck, we insist you join us."

"Of course," she answered en route to the bedchamber and found Maria seated on the bed with a frown. "I'm going hunting with Lovelace and Minichque!" Seconds later she slammed the door, missing Maria fall back into the feather bed, groan loudly and throw an arm over her face.

Catharyna chatted happily with Minichque as they headed toward the stable. "There's a great English custom I'll share with you when we return. They serve tea with sweet cakes *before* dinner."

Minichque confessed, "Albany baker arrested for selling our tribes sweet cakes, we banned from sugar."

Sokoki whispered, "Will your Governor allow us to eat the sweet cakes?"

Catharyna remained silent, letting her eyes assure them it would be no problem. The brothers laughed lightheartedly. They went to the falconer and Catharyna whistled softly to her hawk, Golden Eagle. Within a short time, she was fully prepared with bow and arrows, galloping at the head of the hunting party, with Golden Eagle latched onto her shoulder. The hawk was black with eyes that turned gold when prey was in sight. Dirck had trained it to attack and protect at Catharyna's command. It was the last gift Dirck had given her.

Jamie Harrison appeared just as the hunting party was departing the gate of Broeckwyck. When he saw Catharyna surrounded by savages, regardless that they were supposedly friendly, he argued to also join the hunt in the belief she had need of his protection. Minutes later the party departed with another member added to it.

They road for hours through the north end of Broeckwyck's forests, filled with deer, fox, rabbit and turkey. A herd of deer were chased into an open field by Sokoki.

Catharyna took aim at a buck and her arrow pierced it in the chest. Minichque circled round to quickly finish the kill. Lovelace drew his first arrow and found success in a twelve point buck, and grinned like a boy. Four warriors took the bucks and tied them to pack horses.

The party proceeded onward. A fat turkey waddled by and Sokoki's knife flew into the air and pinned it to the ground. He leaned down from astride his horse to grab it at a gallop, and threw it to the warrior handling the pack horse.

Sokoki raised a hand to signal the hunt was over. "We have our food, now we find fun." Immediately, two warriors left in the direction of Broeckwyck with the pack horses.

Sokoki instructed, "Gather here when sun sinks to this line of trees. Largest fox wins prize." He held out a knife with a pearl handle. It was a valuable trinket, but for the hunting party it was the thrill of winning that led them forward.

They began to spread out in search of their new prey. Jamie stayed close to Catharyna, who was beside Minichque. They galloped at a frantic pace, almost undoing Jamie's desire to remain for the hunt. There was no let up until the destination was reached, and then all grew silent.

Golden Eagle flew off Catharyna's shoulder and began circling around the glen, sloping downward to fly straight up into the sky only to drop back down again.

Jamie opened his mouth, but Catharyna's cold stare instantly shut it. She exchanged a glance with Minichque, and suddenly her horse reared upward and bolted in the direction of Golden Eagle. Minichque was a step behind, but Jamie chose to remain. He was exhausted, cold and starved from the hours spent astride a horse on a frigid day. If the details of a hunt had been shared at the beginning, he would have prepared better. In boredom he watched Minichque and Catharyna dart from each end of the clearing to the other.

Jamie straightened in the saddle and decided boredom was just that. It was time to best them all by finding a fox himself. He entered the forest and approached a rocky cliff, looking into its crevices for a long tail. There was a cave about twenty feet above him, but he wasn't that eager to find a fox to crawl up and search it. Instead, he threw rocks at it to see if any fox could be flushed out.

All too soon his weak efforts melted determination like a snow flake. There he sat, slumped in the saddle, completely bored with the hunt. Thoughts drifted away from the forest, returning instead to the ice skating party shared with Catharyna yesterday. Confidence grew over the gradual warming she had shown to him the past weeks. It was true she worked more than he liked, yet she made time to speak to him, and it was always with the warmest of manners. Their attraction to each other was real. To possess a woman of such unique spirit made his cold body warm. The discomfort of the hunt would be endured. Anything could be endured for a woman such as Catharyna. Evening would provide another opportunity to sit beside her and see her eyes sparkle with such life that took his breath away.

A growl caught his attention. His eyes swung to its source and met the stare of a young male bear awoken from hibernation. Both stared at each other not knowing what to do. Fear coursed through Jamie, freezing him in the saddle.

He began to pray.

Catharyna followed Golden Eagle as he flew into a hole and, this time, she and Minichque smiled in anticipation of their prize. The hawk's piercing cry was all they needed. They dismounted and each covered the hole. Golden Eagle flew out and a second later the fox appeared. It didn't have a chance to run back inside as Minichque's arrow pierced his heart straight through. His hand reached in to pull out their prize, and they smiled at each other.

"Cunning fox." Minichque said.

Catharyna replied, "Ha, but we think just like him."
They exchanged smiles of comradeship. Golden Eagle's piercing cry interrupted the moment of victory. It was then that

Catharyna noticed Jamie was not with them. She was astride in seconds, as agitation grew, and followed the direction of Golden Eagle, who began circling over one spot. The eagle's cries continued to grow louder.

Knowledge that Minichque was a step behind made her more bold than usual to approach the young male bear a few yards away from Jamie, who was frozen in the saddle. Her eyes met Jamie's, ordering him to be still and silent, instead he became hysterical.

"Kill it!" he ordered.

The bear no longer remained idle, but began to move quickly toward the man who had awakened his slumber. Catharyna didn't think, as instincts took over, and moved forward in between the bear and Jamie's horse.

She offered an arm to Jamie to leap onto her horse, but, instead, he pulled her off, tossing her to the ground and at the feet of the bear. She rose instantly and slapped Jamie's horse away and watched it gallop out of the forest.

A steady, expert hand reached into the quiver for an arrow. Catharyna aimed it at the bear's heart and pulled with every ounce of strength to hit its target. It shot straight through the heart, but the bear did not falter, he moved forward, angry at the attack on him.

Her hands rose to imitate the pierce of an eagle's cry, a signal to Golden Eagle for help. Minichque raised his bow and one arrow, then another, pierced the bear's chest. Still it moved forward at Catharyna, who was moving backwards while simultaneously withdrawing another arrow and another into the bear.

Lovelace and Sokoki approached from the south and east bearing down on the bear's back. Sokoki's knife sailed through the air and found success in the bear's neck. Golden Eagle swept down to protect Catharyna from the bear's large claw that rose to grab her. The distraction went astray as the bear swiped her, while turning to see what had attacked his back.

Catharyna sailed through the air and was thrown against

an oak tree. Like a crumpled rag doll she lay unconscious beside the bear, who also collapsed into the snow that now turned red with their mingled blood.

Golden Eagle's piercing shrill echoed throughout the forest. Minichque was first to reach Catharyna and found her heart beating weakly. Lovelace's hand surveyed her head which had a wide gash in its side. Both men's eyes locked in fear, when his hand pulled away soaked in blood. Minichque grabbed her protectively against him and began an ancient chant. Sokoki pulled his brother away to wrap her in fur blankets, and waited for Minichque to mount a horse. The unconscious body of Catharyna was handed to Minichque, who gently cradled her atop the great stallion, and immediately galloped back to Broeckwyck.

Golden Eagle soared high in the sky with a voice that shrieked hauntingly over the horse and rider. The hawk's cries knew no rest as they followed its mistress back to the manor.

Sokoki remained to oversee the warriors who gathered the bear and went to find the white face coward who had caused Ten Broeck's fall. With fists clenched, he found Jamie shaking in the saddle, alone in the middle of the field.

The bear had frightened Jamie, but the savage approaching him with bloody hands and painted face terrified him. He kicked the horse and it took off in the opposite direction of Sokoki. The attempt was weak. Sokoki caught up and, all too soon, Jamie was grabbed by the neck from his horse's back.

He was led back in shame to Broeckwyck, tied and gagged.

Twenty-three

Nothing can prevent the inevitable. Three merchant ships asked for entrance into New York harbor, and were given admittance.

Hawk breathed the cold sea air and eyes narrowed to find Broeckwyck in the distance. Unconsciously, a shoulder was rubbed, trying to take with it the uncertainty of his homecoming welcome. The shrill of an eagle's cry was heard, and he smiled up at the sky in welcome. It was a good sign.

Everyone was eager to renew and begin their life, but there was work to be done. Finding shelter for fifty plus people and their crew in the dead of winter would be no easy task in a small sea town.

He was joined by Fairfax, Dirck and Jacob walking through the narrow, newly cobblestone, streets. "Let's visit Samuel Cohen to see what type of accommodations he can offer us," Hawk ordered.

Something was different, and impossible to ignore. The deeper into town they walked, Hawk began receiving bright smiles and nods of respect from merchants, traders and burly frontiersman, who paused to greet him. Women of all ages and stations smiled deep in their eyes at him. Gone was the distant cold stares he had received for seven long years, solely due to his English heritage.

His head shook out the cob webs, believing exhaustion played tricks with it. The town hardly noticed his presence before, unless he demanded it, yet, now a simple walk to the Jewish merchant's building had the town treat him as royalty.

The reason was made clear the moment they entered Cohen's General Mercantile building.

"Lord of Onteora, welcome home!"

Hawk's eyes narrowed, lips remained silent.

"We've been awaiting your arrival since harvest time. The Governor announced Onteora's manor grant status at Broeckwyck's fall festival. 'Twas a grand occasion, my lord. 'Tis a shame your business kept you away. Was it a success?"

Hawk straightened and mumbled, "Yes, I..." He exchanged a silent glance at his friends. The realization that the manor grant, so coveted, was obtained, made him beam. "It was very successful, Samuel. I have need of storage and housing accommodations for fifty new tenant farmers for Broeckwyck and Onteora. What can you pro..."

"My lord, t'would be my honor to handle those arrangements. In fact, I know quite clearly Ten Broeck has arranged for two structures to be built at Onteora for your arrival. Of course, with the Hudson iced over, we'll use an ice boat to ship everything north. It will be easily accomplished."

Hawk felt in a dream. "Structures at Onteora?"

"Yes, a barn and lodge. It should be enough space to meet your needs for now, even though they are housing some of the Duke's animals."

"The Duke's?"

"Whoa, my lord, 'tis not an evil done to you! When Ten Broeck returned from England with five vessels loaded with sheep, pigs, cows, a saw mill, seed, and..." his hands rose in the air, and a deep chuckled added, "well, we simply couldn't fit them all at Duke's Farm immediately. The Governor believed it would meet with your approval to house them there since she had returned with masons and carpenters and had them begin at Onteora instead of Duke's Farm. Your structures were complete and laying empty a month ago, and ..." His shoulders shrugged at the foregone conclusion.

Hawk's head shook in bewilderment, now convinced a lack of sleep had addled his brain. Dirck pushed forward, feigned an insulted look, and declared, "*Lord* of Onteora, have you a problem with my sister's management of your manor property?"

Samuel Cohen's eyes grew large with excitement. He scurried around the counter and bowed instantly at Dirck. "Tis a pleasure to see you in good health, Patroon of Broeckwyck. How happy your homecoming will make your sister!"

Dirck's face warmed by the man's sincerity. "Aye, I welcome coming home."

The merchant beamed. "You'll be amazed at Broeckwyck's growth. Your sister is such a wonder, such a wonder!"

Dirck's eyes smiled at the short man. "I know."

Fairfax interrupted, impatient to see Emily. "Hawk, all things are in order here."

Hawk looked at Fairfax, and blinked to test the reality of the discussion. "Yes, ha, I...we're done." He led the men outside into the streets, and once again heard the piercing cry of a eagle, only this time there was an urgency to it.

Dirck's arms halted them and he stood still, looking into the sky. He blew into cupped hands and the sound of an eagle's cry vibrated out of them. A black hawk circled over their group and slowly landed on Dirck's shoulder. It shrieked loudly into his face. Another whistle command was heard and the hawk was back in flight, circling above.

Dirck said, "We must go to Broeckwyck immediately." He met Hawk's stare. "Something is wrong." The men turned toward the dock and began to board a sleek sloop.

Hawk halted Jacob. "I need you to work with Simon on accommodations for tonight. I'm at Broeckwyck if needed."

Dirck sailed north up the East River with nary a word from Fairfax, who was finally headed in the direction he longed to be for months, whereas Hawk held back in the shadows. The air was unable to fill his lungs. Weeks recuperating in bed made him lightheaded. He cursed the unaccustomed weakness, breathed deeply and tightened his resolve to gain strength back. He would handle the homecoming, however it would be.

When they reached the gates of Broeckwyck it was to

find Indians surrounding the manor. Golden Eagle circled over head and Dirck moved directly to Sokoki, who was pacing outside.

"Sokoki, it is Dirck."

Sokoki's eyes widened and bowed at his old friend. "It has been many moons since we met."

"Where is my sister?"

Sokoki's face turned sad. "There was an accident, a bear..."

Hawk heard nothing more under a thunderous pounding of his blood that blocked out all sound. The door to the manor was kicked open and hawk eyes roamed the kitchen, filled with men and women, but did not find its prey.

He passed Emily, who gazed up in wonderment when he walked silently by, and kicked open the door to Catharyna's bed chamber. It was then the ice grew inside, hardening each step taken to approach the still white form lying in the center of the bed.

A pain ripped through Hawk's chest, its swiftness so powerful that it brought him to his knees. His large warm hand reached out to take her own, and found it cold and frail.

Hawk then noticed a man standing by the bed. "She lives, yes?"

Simon Harrison looked at the fallen giant with a broken heart. The man's love for Catharyna was clear in his eyes. "She fights," a tear slid down Simon's face, "but there is naught we can do but pray."

Hawk's heart roared inside a numb shell, and arms reached out to cradle Catharyna against him.

Maria pummeled his back. "Release her! She is...too frail," she sobbed.

But Hawk refused. "Ryna, fight!" he ordered. "You must fight."

Maria signaled to Simon to leave the room. She remained silent in the corner and watched Hawk's attempts to awaken Catharyna. Hugging, touching, cradling, praying, cursing and threats were made, all to no avail. Nothing worked to rouse Catharyna back to them.

Maria turned at the foot steps of another intruder, and faced the ghost of her past. "Dirck?"

He nodded. "How is she?"

Their eyes locked and sobs filled Maria in happiness and fear. They embraced and he whispered, "Ryna won't leave on my homecoming."

A sob shook Maria. "She's so weak, I fear..."

"She's too stubborn to leave us just yet," he swore, and pulled away to go to his sister, but Maria halted him. "Hawk is with her."

The sight of Hawk praying over his sister halted Dirck's steps. Seeing the fearless privateer on bent knee was unsettling, but it was the intimacy between them that kept him rooted to the floor. For the first time he believed the Englishman cared for his sister.

Hawk shouted, "Leave us!"

But the cold words did the opposite. Dirck went to the other side of the bed and knelt down beside his sister. A hand reached out to touch her forehead and found it cold. "Holy thunder, Ryna, why must you take so many risks?" He stroked her hair and peered down into her face. "It's Dirck, I'm home!" When his words brought no reaction, he slapped her face. "Wake up, I say!"

A hand reached out like a snake and grabbed his arm. Hawk's eyes and words said, "Don't slap her again."

Their eyes clashed and Dirck whispered, "She's all I have."

Hawk's face trembled with emotion. Never had he envied a man more than Dirck. "She's all I want," he confessed, unaware the words were spoken aloud. They stared at each other until Hawk whispered, "Leave us."

Dirck nodded and bent to kiss her lips. Their coldness brought a dampness to his eyes. He rose and left the room, not stopping until he stood beside Sokoki, who handed him some tobacco to share.

"Who did this?"

Sokoki's eyes narrowed. "Come."

They entered the stable and Dirck saw Minichque standing guard over a white man who was tied and gagged. Eyes full of fear gazed up at him, pleading for help. Dirck's knife cut through the gag around his mouth. "Plead your case."

Jamie Harrison trembled before the two fierce Indians and man with eyes glowing down at him. His throat was tight with fear, the words came out painfully. "Bear...frozen... couldn't get away...pulled Ryna down...she ordered me away...I ran."

Dirck looked at Minichque who nodded agreement. He began to pace. The white man's cowardice was written on his face, yet how could a man be faulted for following his sister's order? Many men followed her orders, she demanded obedience. Dirck looked at Sokoki and Minichque knowing they would demand the man's blood if his sister died. He too wanted the man's blood, yet doubt lingered.

"You will spend your time shackled as my sister fights for her life. Your judgment will come when her own is decided."

Jamie fought to swallow. Fear consumed his eyes, which witnessed the fierce faces breathing down on him, eager for his death. The knowledge that his days were limited became the cruelest of tortures.

Hours later Maria entered the silent bedchamber with food for Hawk, but he ignored it. "You must be strong for Ryna now," she chided.

Their eyes clashed but Hawk began to eat. Minutes passed slowly until another hour was gone. He snapped irritably, "Bloody thunder! She's still cold!"

"Then warm her," Maria snapped back.

Exhaustion consumed a weak body, crazed mind, and tortured heart. When he collapsed into bed beside Catharyna a sense of peace entered the room. He gathered her cold body against his warm one and seconds later was deep asleep.

Maria pulled off Hawk's boots and covered him with a blanket. She felt Catharyna's forehead and found it still cold. Fear made her throat tighten, wondering what the morning would bring. With one last prayer, she left the room.

Days passed in the same pattern. The only sign of change was the crowd around Broeckwyck grew. Governor Lovelace arrived and camped outside with the Mohicans who all stood in readiness for any sign of hope. They feasted in Ten Broeck's honor on the rewards of their hunt and her legend grew as the fearless white woman who stood before a bear with bow and arrow.

The tenant farmers delivered hot meals and Catharyna's favorite sweet cakes as each day passed. Traders came with gifts of wooden crates filled with precious fruits and spices from the West Indies and Orient. They too lingered with the Mohicans and Governor for news. Gifts began to fill Broeckwyck's storage attic above the kitchen, demanding Alice to make room in the cold cellar.

Satins, silks and linens were presented in a finely carved wooden chest from Captain DeVries with a special note nailed on its top for Catharyna's eyes alone to read. Dirck had it delivered to her bedchamber and Hawk scowled at it. For the first time in days, he left the room to vent frustration and anger due to the unaccustomed idleness. Astride a spirited stallion, the hours passed for Hawk. He returned to Broeckwyck that was aglow with excitement that vibrated among the crowd. Maria was found crying, but a smile lit her face.

"Her body has lost its coldness," Maria wept.

The weight of fear lifted and a boyish smile spread. Hawk entered Catharyna's room finding little different other than the temperature of her skin. His hand felt blood pounding strongly in her veins. So little had never made him so happy. "Why does she still sleep?"

Maria replied, "It is good, she has known no rest since her father's passing. Soon nothing will keep her thus. Unless..."

Hawk's eyes narrowed on Maria, his heart thumped loudly. "Unless what?"

271

Maria avoided the cold stare. "Dirck is home, Ryna no longer needs to wed. All has changed."

"*Nothing* has changed."

Their eyes locked until Hawk stormed out of the room once again. This time frustration had reached its zenith. He passed Fairfax and Emily whose besotted faces recalled their wedding vows spoken just yesterday. Everything drove him straight to the wind mill and up to its widow's walk. Except everything reminded him of Catharyna. Without her beside him, there was no beauty in the nature surrounding him.

He walked for hours emptying a mind that sought peace. Evidence surrounded him that Catharyna had come to trust him. The work at Onteora, the tenant farmers she brought over, and the manor grant she secured for him. It humbled him, and at the same time, fed the guilt that continued to mount. The certainty that reclaiming Fortuna would please her began to wane. Black Hawk's deeds began to haunt him.

It was midnight when he returned to the manor and climbed into bed beside Catharyna. He gathered her against him and went into a deep sleep.

Time was meaningless for Catharyna, who finally stirred. A moan escaped when eyes fluttered open only to shut down under the pain that encompassed her head. The coldness that had once been was warm under a solid wall that imprisoned her. She attempted to lift it away and became engulfed against a warm chest that beat strongly against her fingers. A familiar scent drew her closer and hands drifted upward. They felt muscles and spanned their width. A sharp cry was then heard above the ringing in her head.

"Ouch!" Hawk said and sat up in bed by a sudden pain that gripped his arm wound. He rubbed the soreness away and looked in wonderment at Catharyna's fingers that were moving over his chest. The wayward fingers were grabbed, and felt warm in his hand. "Ryna?"

"Mmm."

Hawk bent down and touched her nose. "Look at me."

She grimaced. "Hurts."

"Please."

Catharyna grew still on the bed. In disbelief, she whispered, "Hawk?" Pain exploded in her head, but excitement made her eyes open. His hair was loose and his face now had a mustache and goatee. But it was Hawk.

He gathered her against him and laughed deeply.

Her eyes closed, tears of pain and disbelief poured from them. "Hurts."

Hawk wiped them away. "Your head took a hard blow from a tree. It's soon to be christened the hardest oak in the province, thicker than Ten Broeck's head."

"Funny," but a smile was on her face, feeling his lips on her.

"I feared for you."

"Mmm."

"I prayed."

"Doubtful."

"On my knees!"

"Miracle."

"Aye, my Ryna has returned. You're still saucy."

"Has Black Hawk..."

Hawk held his breath.

"Or Lord of Onteora?"

His voice grew deep. "Just Will."

"We've yet to meet."

"We've shared a bed before."

A smile spread across her lean cheeks. "Briefly."

His lips began to graze hers. "There is an English custom I've yet to share with you."

A giggle rose from her chest and Hawk's heart soared. "Midnight tea?"

"Tea?" he growled in derision.

Her eyes opened painfully to see Hawk's face when she admitted, "Not tea?"

273

"Definitely not."

Her body curled against him. "So tired..."

Hawk gathered her against him and warned, "Oh, no! You've slept for days."

"You left...too long."

"I've been beside you for days."

"A year."

"Impossible."

"You are!"

"You're changing the subject," Hawk warned.

"About time."

"About this custom that definitely isn't tea...."

"A hot bath?"

His voice was husky in her ear. "Much better."

Her arms wrapped around him. "So tired..."

He lifted her face and finally surrendered. "You win," and kissed her in welcome softly, only to deepen it till they clung to each other.

She confessed, "I waited."

His voice was deep with emotion. "Was there a choice?"

"Many," the pause was tangible in the room, "but all you."

His eyes glowed down at her, pleased by the words, and hands stroked her hair, releasing some of the tension from her head. Sleep overcame her. Moments later he fell victim to the same peaceful slumber.

Doubt found no breath in the room.

Twenty-four

Deep penetrating roots rumbled impatiently for spring to rouse them to life, though nature's calendar would be obeyed. The fear of man held no sway.

Maria entered the room and found her cousin entwined against Hawk. It appeared nothing had changed, so she readied the room for morning, as was habit. The wooden shutters were opened, the smoldering embers were stoked and logs were added to the fireplace. Before long the room was roaring with warmth and life once again.

A croak from the bed drew Maria's attention. A pale arm peeked out of the blankets to block the sun's rays. "Light, hurts."

Maria rushed to the bed. "Ryna?"

"Mmm. Light hurts."

Maria rushed to close the shutters and returned to her cousin to stroke her face lovingly. "Ryna, you have returned to us?"

"Head hurts." A light stroke was felt across her forehead, a smile spread. "Better."

Maria's lips touched Ryna's face with soft kisses. Wet tears fell and were wiped gently away. "I have missed you, dear cousin."

A growl startled them and then the bed came to life when Hawk sat up taking Catharyna with him. Her mind twirled and body ached. "Ouch!"

A devastating smile spread across his face that kept Maria's eyes there momentarily, until they dropped to see his naked chest. She quickly turned around. "This is not proper,

Hawk. I told you the terms for sharing Ryna's bed!"

His smile grew wider. "Speak to your cousin," was ordered, while he disentangled himself from Catharyna to swing legs to the floor. The search for his shirt found blood shot eyes staring back at him.

Catharyna's words were spoken so softly that he strained to hear them. "You leave me so easily?"

With no hesitation, he returned to the bed and found a considerably warmer stare due to the choice.

Maria watched her cousin come alive before her eyes now that Hawk was home. Tears brimmed, being witness to the end of her cousin's wait. There was every reason to remain in the room, yet she couldn't bear it a moment longer.

"Excuse me," she said and left the couple to share the news of Ryna's returned health. It drew cheers from the crowd who had remained. They all began to request immediate entrance, but Maria held them off. "She has only just awoke, allow her some time. You may see her this afternoon."

Dirck brushed her aside and entered the manor. Minichque, Sokoki and the Governor were a step behind. He opened the door without warning and found his half dressed sister kissing Hawk. The men continued forward.

"We've waited long enough."

Catharyna's eyes grew wide in disbelief, first looking at her brother, then at Hawk. "You brought home Dirck?"

Dirck answered for himself. "'Tis I, the wayward brother returning home at last." The words were light, but the voice was thick with emotion at the sight of his frail sister who stared in awe at him.

"How?"

Shoulders shrugged. "Hawk convinced me it was time." The men all chuckled but Dirck's rose above them all.

Catharyna held out weak arms. "I never doubted your return."

Dirck hugged her tightly and they kissed. "I missed you, Ryna."

"Not enough," she whispered. Their eyes locked and he

looked away first.

Her hands were held out as a signal to her friends standing respectfully in the doorway. "Come, come, I have slept a lifetime away."

Hawk took a blanket and pulled it tightly across Catharyna's chest. "It's cold," was mumbled.

Minichque bowed before her with a gift extended. "You caught the fox."

Sokoki added, "Prize yours, knife with pearl handle."

Catharyna grinned. "What of my friend, the bear?"

Governor Lovelace quipped, "His hide is drying out for you to step on the length of your days."

"Nicely done, Lovelace."

He bowed graciously.

Catharyna's eyes darted around the room. A worried brow rose when looking at Minichque and Sokoki. "And Jamie, where is he?"

It was Dirck who answered. "He's tied up in knots over you, but it now appears he'll live." The men joined in Dirck's private joke.

Catharyna warned, "He did as was told, Dirck. This was my fault."

The men remained silent, but none agreed with her. Minichque couldn't still his tongue any longer. "White face coward, should die!" he vowed and spit on the ground. "Hawk return to you, you return to us."

Sokoki nodded.

"I'll deal with him," Hawk ordered. All the men nodded with eyes sparkling in anticipation of the coward's fate.

Catharyna was about to protest but Fairfax interrupted by entering the room in a flourish. All tension was gone from his face, which held a smile of pure masculine virility. Emily was beside him.

Fairfax kissed her hand. "Our sleeping huntress awakens."

Emily kissed her forehead. "Welcome back, Ryna, we've missed you."

Catharyna frowned at the ring on her friend's hand. "I missed the wedding?"

Emily's eyes looked away and Fairfax replied, "Aye, I could wait no more Ten Broeck."

The men made lewd comments, Emily blushed, and Fairfax never looked happier. The laughter began to pound painfully in Catharyna's head. A moan escaped and she leaned against Hawk who scowled at the growing crowd in the room.

"Enough, all of you, leave us! Ryna needs rest. You may visit her later."

Catharyna held out hands to Minichque and Sokoki who made their good-byes, and fell down into the pillows when everyone left. She turned weakly to Hawk, who was now fully dressed, and frowned. "You leave me, too?"

His fingers raced to fasten boots and jacket. "Yes, I must see to Onteora now."

She bolted upright in anger. "You stayed with me these many days, I awaken and you leave?"

His eyes avoided her while he gathered scattered possessions. "I'll return in a fortnight when you're stronger."

Her eyes narrowed so the pain was not as intense, and finally gazed at him in full light. His hair was loose and mustache and goatee neatly trimmed. "You look the pirate."

He froze.

She spoke the question he was running from. "Tell me what happened to you?"

"Later."

"Now."

Their eyes clashed, but he relented. "You were told I was abducted."

"I know about Juliet."

He cringed by the no-nonsense tone in her voice. "She misled me with information on Dirck. I landed on a pirate ship and struck a deal to win my freedom. It worked and here I am."

"There is more."

"Nothing important."

"It is to me."

"Trust me."

"I want to."

"Then do so."

"Help me."

He looked at her in bewilderment. His mother had followed his father blindly, yet Catharyna demanded everything. "You ask too much of me."

"You can give this."

She would not relent. And to his amazement, it drew more words than normally would be exposed. "I know not this man I have become in my quest for you, but with certainty I know there is no more to give you."

Catharyna's eyes closed over the crush of pain and waning energy. She whispered, "There is such greatness in you, Will." He began massaging her head to ease the pain, and a smile appeared. "I shall show it to you."

Hawk leaned down and kissed her parted lips. There was no response as she drifted off to sleep.

With nothing to occupy her time other than gaining back her body's strength, Catharyna's investigation on Black Hawk began. It was meticulous, subtle, and relentless.

Each night Catharyna stretched out beside Maria in bed with a mind reviewing and dissecting facts, stories, and cover-ups, all aimed at protecting Hawk. An evening with Dirck provided the missing details.

Seated in a dark corner, she awoke to sounds of Dirck entering the room with the only light coming from the fireplace. He slouched low in their father's favorite chair with a bottle of rum half finished in his hand.

"How did the trade go?" she asked.

He searched the darkened corner where his sister's voice came from. "Very well, Sokoki is pleased."

It was the first time they spoke without someone present with them. The silence grew uncomfortable until

Catharyna took a chair opposite him in front of the fireplace. "Tell me about the sea."

He laughed. "It's impossible."

"Did you seek it out or did it enslave you?"

Their eyes clashed.

"You sought it out?" she persisted.

His face closed up. Silence was all that answered her.

Catharyna grabbed his hand tightly. "I ask not to judge, but to understand." Their eyes continued to battle. "We are alone now, Dirck. I need you in my life."

His voice was emotional. "You have changed, Ryna."

She laughed darkly. "Life leaves us no choice."

"What you ask is not about me, but Hawk, true?"

"Both."

He nodded. "Black Hawk's deeds are his own to tell. I shall tell you the life of Golden Eagle."

"My hawk?"

"No, it is my privateer and pirate name."

Catharyna nodded, while hands grabbed the arms of the chair to absorb the shock of his words.

The rum bottle twirled in Dirck's hands, and then lifted for a quick gulp. "It's a different world than you will ever know, and it soon swallowed me up. At sea there are laws, but not the type to rein in a man like me. The power blocks out all thought, and the greed drives you forward, until your soul is lost in exchange for men to follow you into hell and back."

"You were successful?"

"After I escaped from slavery." Their eyes remained locked. "I left here full of envy, my father preferring a daughter to a son. It made me careless."

"Dirck, it was my fault, I demanded so much of father's time after mother and the babies..." Tears gathered and she looked away.

His hand touched her cheek. "I could have loved Broeckwyck the way father wanted, but the sea pulled me more."

She whispered, "Slavery?"

"Aye, two years of work under the heat of the Caribbean sun and sugar fields. It was there that I came to reconcile with father under the bonds of my chains." He paused to drink more rum. "I managed to escape with the help of a few jaded buccaneers, joined them on a sack, found I was successful at it, and ..." shoulders shrugged, "my fearlessness soon made me their leader. I forgot Broeckwyck, father, you..." he guzzled more rum, "Maria...everything."

The shocking news of slavery made her reach out for the rum. It was swallowed too quickly, causing a path of fire down her throat. A string of coughs followed.

Dirck grinned. "You still can't out drink me."

"I can try!"

Dirck's voice grew hoarse. "I never want you to stop." His hand reached out and she took it. "I feared losing you, Ryna. You take too many risks."

"We share the same blood."

He looked sad. "If mother hadn't died so young, you would know how to be a woman."

"I know enough."

His voice grew cold. "Then where are the babes filling up the manor?" Amazement in his words now bounced across the room. "What in blazes is wrong with DeVries for not bedding you by now? Holy thunder! That man's a bunch of hot air. When I think of all the boasts..." His fingers raked through his hair. "Didn't anyone think of your happiness while I was away? How could father allow you to become an old spinster!"

"I'm two years younger than you. Besides, your return has ended my need of marriage."

"Ha, now I see why you had Hawk fetch me home. To get out of it all together."

"Broeckwyck is now yours."

"Half."

"No, I wish Broeckwyck to be in tack for you." Their eyes met and her hand tightened on his. "I now understand English law and their customs. So, we shall play their game, brother."

Dirck smiled. "I'm listening."

"Broeckwyck will not be broken up by us and our descendants to weaken all memory of what father built. I shall have Lovelace name you the first Dutchman to be given manor status."

"Before Uncle Peter?" Dirck chuckled.

Catharyna grinned. "You shall stand beside Hawk as the most powerful Dutch manor lord. This honors all father accomplished by having you recognized as such."

"But this is not our custom, Ryna. Father wanted you to have half."

"I shall have my half," she swore. "There are other things you are unaware of that will make it so. Your son and his will be mighty Dutchmen because of this." Her voice held cold, relentless, determination. "Time will not erase the Dutch presence in this province."

Dirck swallowed more rum, realizing it was the first time in many years that the thought of children entered his mind. Catharyna had his future all planned while tomorrow was a blur to him. "And what of Hawk? He's no DeVries, they'll be babes and a marriage whether you seek it or not. You do not wish to give your children Broeckwyck land that father built for both of us?"

"One day our descendent will marry yours," Catharyna replied in an excited voice, and then laughed. "Think of what a marriage that will be!"

Dirck shook his head in defeat. "Very well, speak to Lovelace."

Her eyes narrowed and she said coldly, "I will once you prove to stay landed."

Dirck turned the tables on her. "That's fair, but you control too much. Holy thunder, you've already planned our grandchildren's marriage!"

She blushed under the truth of the words.

"Heed me well, Ryna. Tread wearily with Hawk. You've caught him, but he'll fly if you rein him in."

"Perhaps," she whispered.

Dirck's eyes narrowed on her too innocent expression. It was a brutal one that he knew far too well. "Don't test him when there is no need," he warned.

Catharyna grinned. "You like him."

They both stared into the flames of the fire, each thinking different thoughts. Dirck drank deeply on the rum bottle and announced, "Aye, I like Hawk, but what did you see in Harrison?"

"He's great with bookkeeping."

"Ha, I understand." They both laughed. "How'd Hawk deal with him?"

"Married him off to Matilda Wilhelm."

Dirck's laughter shook the walls. "Yee gods, that's worse than death! Married, or was he sold?"

"Both," she confessed and chuckled. Her eyes narrowed on her brother's empty rum bottle. Words had begun to slur. The time had come to hear the truth. "Tell me how you met Hawk." Relaxed and unguarded, Dirck's words tumbled freely. Her suspicions crystallized into facts, but grew complicated by a rescue of slaves.

Catharyna left the room when he fell asleep. Nothing about Hawk was typical. It was why she had waited for him, yet the burden of what Black Hawk had done weighed heavily on her. Something was needed to take it away.

Twenty-five

Time had run its course when Hawk entered Broeckwyck for the first time in a fortnight. He departed the sloop impatiently with arms loaded with packages. Crewmen followed at a slower gate with crates and wooden chests that all made their way inside the manor.

Alice rushed to get Catharyna, who just entered the kitchen through the back door, hastily storing a bow and empty quiver.

"The Lord of Onteora is here with presents for you," Alice announced, and a look of horror crossed her face at the sight of Catharyna. "What are you doing dressed as such?"

She merely shrugged on the way to the bedchamber. "Tell him I'll be a moment."

"And where might Maria be? I haven't seen her all day," Alice inquired.

"Out and about," was heard before the door slammed shut.

Breathlessly, Catharyna began shedding the male attire, casting it haphazardly on the floor, and raced into the layers of female undergarments.

She was tightening the stays of her corset when Hawk entered the room unannounced. Hunger was in his eyes as they took in her half dressed body and the new roundness in it. Weight had been gained and her skin was flushed with a healthy glow.

"You look..." a worldly grin spread, "ready to end our wait."

Their eyes met and she smiled. "You're early."

Hawk did not conceal his intentions nor was time wasted. Catharyna was crushed against him in a kiss that made thought disintegrate. The stays just tightened were quickly undone by expert fingers. "I wanted to surprise you."

Her heart pounded at the boyish excitement in his voice. Doubt rose over her actions that morning under the softening in Hawk's eyes. The decision was made to silence her tongue.

After another breathless kiss, he swore, "No more games, no more waiting."

"I wish it as well."

His eyes sparkled. "No contracts?"

"No."

Hawk's eyes narrowed knowing Ten Broeck could not have faded from Catharyna's heart, who, at its core, was a trader. "What do you seek from me for our marriage?"

She swallowed painfully and said, "No traces of Black Hawk in the life we build together." Every desire she had come to accept asked, "Can you give that to me, Will?"

He looked down into the eyes that matched the color of Onteora's sky. The happiness in holding a vibrant Catharyna again made Black Hawk and the West Indies fade away. The past two weeks away from her had been the most trying days in his life. Even his darkened prison aboard ship had been pleasurable compared to keeping his distance from Catharyna to allow her to heal.

"Yes, if you swear everything to me." His eyes roamed over her face before he explained, "I want your heart, mind, and soul for the rest of my days."

Catharyna was unprepared for what he was demanding. There had been moments of wishful thinking of being weak to love him. Now, Hawk was demanding it from her. But, what surprised her most was the lack of hesitation in her response. "I swear everything to you, Will."

They stared at each other knowing they had crossed a

precipice neither had ever imaged could be traversed. There was no halting the emotions that came with it.

Hawk threw her on the bed. "Now I'll take everything."

"It's daylight," she laughed, but rose on knees with arms out to him and crashed back into the mattress when he dove on her. "What of Alice?"

"I sent her to fetch the minister on a very old horse."

Catharyna pushed him away as if a bucket of cold water fell from the ceiling. "Then you best rise, for he is just a short walk from here, and none are more diligent than Alice to seek him out."

Hawk scowled when she left the bed. "God alone you fear," he taunted.

"I'll not be chastised again by him," she swore, and fastened her gown. "Alice said you brought gifts, but I never thanked you for Dirck yet."

"Later," he whispered and brought her back on his lap, "I'm not through with this gift yet."

When their eyes met, emotions swept over her. Ignorance had blinded the depth of desire she possessed for him. Now a new awareness was found in her eyes when meeting his naked gaze. "Will we ever be?"

Hawk was startled by the question. His eyes narrowed as a finger traced her lips. "This is new territory for us, and we're both too greedy to be satisfied in one lifetime exploring it."

The words of DeVries and other men were recalled with flowery, romantic words of love. Such words had been ineffective to span the depth inside to reach her heart, and yet the words of Hawk pierced it every time. Water gathered in her eyes. "I missed you."

He teased, "There wasn't time for you to miss me with all you accomplished."

Her hands rose to gently hold his face. "You took two bullets because of my brother."

"I expected worse having already fallen victim to you."

"Victim?" she whispered.

"Victim," Hawk repeated. "He was our marital contract and the only way you would relinquish Broeckwyck to marry me. I am no fool, Ryna. I've always known your family's patroonship would never touch my hand."

"Dirck is the eldest son, Broeckwyck belongs to him. It is English custom to do so, is it not?"

"Yes, but not your own."

Their eyes met and Catharyna whispered, "Your customs are now mine."

His hand caressed her skin that rose instantly to the touch. "That is good, for there are many..." he paused over the rising blush on her cheeks, "I've yet to introduce you to." A victorious grin spread on Hawk's face. Catharyna was his. Their mutual desire for each other he had expected, but never peace. For the first time no restlessness gripped him.

Her face grew serious. "I trust you."

"Ha! Another gift."

She kissed him and whispered, "I trust you for giving up Black Hawk."

"*He* never left," was growled when he pounced on her again. She stared up at him in trepidation. "Did you not give up all traces of Black Hawk to me?"

Hawk shrugged and got out of bed. "Your gifts are waiting. Dress and meet me in the parlor unless you wish to shock the minister."

Her cold words stopped him from leaving. "You swore it."

He reached out and pulled her against him. "Ryna, Black Hawk is me. The things I've done as privateer are over. That is what I gave you."

A sigh of relief was heard. "I'm sorry," she said.

"Dress! I'm anxious to give you your *other* gifts," he ordered with a wink and lecherous grin before closing the door.

She obeyed with no concern her actions that morning would harm their future. The parlor was crowded with wooden chests and crates when she entered, yet her eyes only saw Hawk in front of the fireplace. Everything was ignored in favor of him.

She leaned against him and offered, "Let's go to the wind mill."

He accepted the invitation of her lips, but no more. "Later." Her wayward hands were held and their eyes met. "Here we remain until the minister arrives. Now, start opening your gifts."

She relented and sat obediently in the chair beside the fireplace. His eyes sparkled down at her with the first gift. "Your enjoyment of the plays in London should have you enjoy this too." It was a book that contained several of Shakespeare's works. The pages were edged with gold along its binding. It was a precious gift.

"It's lovely," she whispered, looking at the pages written in Spanish. Her heart tightened, it was placed on an end table.

A carved chest was brought forward with its key. Silks, satins, velvets, brocades, and linens, all in shades of blue, greeted her eyes when the lid was opened. This time her heart began to pound. "This is too much."

He kneeled down and took her hand that began to tremble. "This is a taste of all the ports I stopped at on my way home to you." His hand then swung out from behind and withdrew a dress and hat. "When we docked in Charles Town, I saw a woman in a gown of this cloth. She directed me to the merchant who sold it." The cloth was held up to her face and a grin spread. "The same shade as your eyes," he confirmed. "The dress and hat were made in Philadelphia by the best French seamstress in town." He held it up against her body and the length was exact.

"How did you accomplish such when I stood for weeks in London until they could?"

The game played in London with her would never be shared. His shoulders shrugged. "I want you to wear it when we exchange vows tonight. Fairfax and Emily will be joining us here shortly."

Her fingers touched the fabric and the stitching was viewed with a merchant's eye. "It's beautiful, Will."

The hat was placed on her head. "No bird's nests are permitted on your head again."

"You burned my hats, remember?" Her hand rose in warning, "Not that there was *ever* anything wrong with them."

"Agree with me if you seek to be a dutiful wife," he warned.

"I'll take the risk," she confessed and kissed him.

"I want you to give DeVries' gift to another, you've no need for his silks any more."

A smile spread across her face at the jealousy in his tone. "I did weeks ago to Maria, who's enjoying them."

The confession drew a kiss from him and one of his own. "There was a special gift I had made for you in Amsterdam but it was stolen. It was...."

"What is this?" A wooden crate filled with hairy brown rocks was of unusual interest and examined closely.

He took a knife and slammed it down hard into the thick shell to slice it open. Creamy white fluid poured out of it. The other half was raised to her lips to taste.

"It's delicious!" she said, and watched Hawk in excitement, when he carved out some of the fruit's flesh. "What is this called?"

He laughed over her enthusiasm. "A coconut."

"Co-co-nut? Why have I never tasted these before? No trader brought such to me."

"They never opened them to find out the treasure inside."

For no apparent reason, water dampened her eyes. The gifts fell to the floor when she rose impulsively to kiss Hawk. "I love coconuts," she croaked through a wobbly voice.

He gently cradled her. "I hoped you would," a hand reached out to grab the book, "though this was the gift I thought you would enjoy."

Catharyna's voice became guarded. "Why is it written in Spanish?"

Their eyes locked until Hawk turned away. "What matter is it? You read Spanish."

"Did you purchase this book?"

Then pandemonium broke loose. Jacob Chanler erupted

inside the room breathless, a hand was on his chest fighting for breath.

Hawk immediately became alert. "What's wrong?"

"Ships...exploded....harbor...couldn't stop the explosions....all three down."

Hawk's amazement turned into fury. "Holy thunder! What lunacy is this?"

"Don't know...all was still...flaming arrows...and... they exploded!" He breathed deeply. "They're gone, your two and the *Golden Eagle* are gone."

At that moment Alice entered the manor with the minister. Both watched in silence from the hallway, unable to enter the room that was now charged with energy.

Shreds of ice began coursing through Hawk's body when his eyes narrowed on Catharyna. There was no emotion on her face or body that sat in a chair unfazed by the news. Her half dressed body and surprise of his early arrival were then recalled.

His eyes held her to the chair and demanded complete attention. The ice blue eyes that had bewitched his mind from their first meeting now rose in judgment at him.

Catharyna raised the leather bound book of Shakespeare's plays and tossed it into the fire. "I'll have no plunder in my home."

Jacob's eyes rounded in amazement, Alice began to tremble and the minister took a step back toward the front door. Hawk's fierce scowl silently ordered them all out of the manor.

Catharyna's throat tightened so quickly it was impossible to swallow. Hawk's anger was directed at her in a controlled and calculated fashion. If he had thrown things at her it would have been a relief.

"You torched my ships." It was a statement.

Her voice remained unemotional and in full control. "What direction were those *Spanish* merchant ships pointed in when you *attacked* them?"

"Not a shot was fired."

"They were headed to Spain, *not* a British settlement.

They posed no threat to your English crown!"

Ice now turned into molten fire inside Hawk as anger consumed him. His hands trembled underneath its power. And then, Dirck's words were recalled of Catharyna's judgment. "You know not whom you judge."

Her voice was clear, unrestrained and merciless. "I judge Black Hawk!"

His eyes turned dead, no emotions stirred. "You swore no games and knowingly began the one that ends us."

Fear seized her heart. "This is no game! Black Hawk will have no say or part in whatever we accomplish together for our family and theirs."

Hawk's cold eyes chilled her. *"No one controls my actions."*

Catharyna rose and swore, *"And I'll not share a life with you built on two ships you plundered under the order of greed!"*

But there was no awareness of her words on Hawk's rigid face that was miles away from the room. Instead, his mind reflected upon his mistake. The path chosen with the heart had led him astray. It would never be broached again.

Darkness descended amid the bright afternoon rays of the sun. Its coat clung to him, familiar, tailored, flawless to size. It was no good running from whom he was, Morgan told him that. There would no longer be a need to search within for answers, instincts would be his guide as they always brought success.

A sinister smile hovered over stiff lips when he bowed swiftly. "Then I shall find another who will."

Catharyna raced to the door to stop him. "Will, let me explain," she pleaded.

"We are finished," he swore. There was no hesitation. Long strides took him out of the manor. Direction was uncertain as was his future. It was the way he knew how to live.

Twenty-six

Broeckwyck's tentacles reached everywhere. It was impossible to outrun it even though Hawk tried. The first stop was to witness the destruction of the vessels. The crowd opened as he stepped onto the pier that once harbored the *Ten Broeck, Meredith* and *Golden Eagle*. Wreckage floated everywhere. People were using large branches to grab whatever pieces were of value. There weren't many.

Fairfax drew up beside him. "Unbelievable."

Hawk's eyes pierced his best friend, seeking a sign of guilt in the plot. "I know who ordered it, but who did it?"

Fairfax grew tense. The way Hawk looked made it clear things would get a lot worse before they got better. "I don't know."

"I want them. Anyone involved, bring them to me."

Cohen the merchant rushed over. "Lord of Onteora, such a catastrophe!" A smile of confidence spread on the merchant's face. "It is goodness insurance shall cover most of the loss."

Hawk's eyes narrowed at the merchant in warning to move quickly away from his presence, which was exactly what Cohen did.

Fairfax grumbled rhetorically, "Who puts insurance on booty?" And then whispered to Hawk, "Who ordered it?"

Their eyes clashed and now Hawk said rhetorically, "Who would torch only Dirck's and my ships?"

"Ryna?" Fairfax whispered in astonishment.

"I'm finished with her," Hawk swore and added the order, "don't speak of her again."

Fairfax nodded in understanding. Loyalty was absolute

to Hawk. Sad eyes watched his friend walk away in frustration.

Hawk left the wreckage, but it remained deep in his mind along the way to the Governor's mansion. Lovelace rose the moment Hawk entered the office uninvited. "What the blazes happened to your ships?"

There was no emotion in Hawk's eyes or voice. "Ryna torched them."

"Ten Broeck did *what*?" When Hawk remained silent, Lovelace sat back down and began mumbling excuses. "Perhaps the blow to the head addled her thinking? Her illness still lingers. I will send Dr. Harrison out immediately."

A hand rose to halt the action. "Her mind is sharper than mine. Speak no more of her in my presence."

Lovelace hid the disappointment at the sudden turn of events. It had been a wonderful surprise to witness Catharyna's heated embrace with Hawk, knowing the Duke's desire for their marriage. Everything had been moving along splendidly.

He chose to plead her case one more time. "I am doubtful it was Ten Broeck. There is no thriftier person, she would never waste three fine vessels just for fire works..." Words faded, shoulders shrugged and hands were held out in silent appeal.

Hawk ignored them all. "I need your help."

"Of course!"

"Seven out of ten people will believe anything, I need you to convince the other three. Issue any statement in the papers that will silence the tongues."

"An absent-minded crew member lit his tobacco near gunpowder is plausible, one that might even be truthful," Lovelace offered in hope. Hawk's eyes narrowed, but the Governor persisted. "You just don't walk away from a woman like Ten Broeck. You will go far with her beside you."

"So far I lost two vessels that would have made me a fortune. I made promises to Morgan to increase trade to Jamaica with them, and now Fortuna is in jeopardy. If I remain with her, is debtor's prison next?"

Lovelace laughed and then straightened at seeing

Hawk's dark scowl. "Let's not forget what she did for you during your *extended* absence. Secured Onteora's manor grant, had structures built there, garnered fifty tenant farmers, commissioned..."

"Enough, I need not hear the accomplishments, I know them all."

Lovelace met angry eyes. "*If* she did this act that you accuse her of, what reason could there be?"

"She has judged Black Hawk's deeds and seeks to rid all of them from my life."

Lovelace grew tense. Things were far worse than anticipated. "Ryna judges work you did for the crown?"

"Yes."

"Tis an outlandish impossibility! Why, she should view you as hero!" He then began to nod vigorously. "Tis what I suspected, her head has been addled from the accident. Give it time to heal, she will return to you."

Hawk remained silent.

Lovelace spoke bluntly. "Time is now for you to marry. You have an obligation as Lord of Onteora. Forgive her and it will go well for you." He stood still waiting for the reply. Without Catharyna, all knew Hawk would fly from the province. There were few, if any, ways to contain him. Lovelace had no desire to feel the Duke's wrath, even an ocean away.

"My plans remain unchanged. There are many Dutchwomen. I will begin discussions." He rose to leave. "I will require accommodations here until Onteora is completed."

Lovelace nodded and crumbled into a chair when Hawk left the office. Disappointment was great at the sudden turn of events. And then an idea crossed his mind. There wasn't a conversation in the Governor's mansion that didn't carry Ten Broeck's name. An arrogant smile blossomed. Never was Lovelace more in control of the Lord of Onteora than now.

Silence greeted Hawk when entering the Blue Dove.

The ridged face grew fierce under the speculative glances from the frontiersmen and barmaids, who held their breath waiting for the anticipated wrath to be unleashed. The look of the man said more than any words that could be spoken. Someone's neck was being sought.

Hawk's fists tightened when his eyes narrowed on their prey. David DeVries was found in a corner with a voluptuous wench. Just as he rose from the chair, a knife sailed through the air and pinned his jacket to the wall.

"What the devil?"

Cold, calculated, steps brought Hawk to him. DeVries pulled the knife from the wall and faced Hawk eye to eye. He would not be shown weak in front of friends. The knife was handed back to its owner. "I assume this got away from you."

Hawk's face tightened. "It hit its mark."

Now anger turned DeVries' face red. "What business do you seek with me, Hawk?"

"You know."

"I've no business with you."

Hawk's dead eyes made DeVries take a step back. His voice was emotionless. "You saw an opening and took it."

"I took nothing."

The energy radiating from Hawk in the tavern was magnetic and pulled all toward him. The crowd was silent as they waited in excitement for the destined fight.

Hawk's chest pounded with a pain so tight that it demanded relief. Instead, every emotion was pushed down and turned into a growl at DeVries. "You sought my place!"

"It was mine first!" DeVries shouted.

Words dissolved when Hawk's fist slammed into DeVries' face and sent him hard against the wall. The crowd drew back in fear at the sight of their leader crumpled on the floor only to be pulled up by the neck and dangled in the air to meet the threatening face of Hawk.

"Speak your guilt!"

DeVries swore, "I did nothing."

Hawk slammed him against the wall. "Speak it!"

The room became cloudy to DeVries. Blood began to drip from his forehead. "I did nothing."

Frustration made Hawk drop him to the ground. The man was guiltless in torching the ships, but not in coveting Catharyna. Fury raged and unknown emotions demanded release. With no hesitation, Hawk grabbed the hand of a spirited brunette, who had been eyeing him during the fight, and headed upstairs with a full bottle of rum. No other thought entered his mind about DeVries again.

A stuffy room greeted him. Uninterested eyes watched the barmaid move to the bed and disrobe. There was no passion, only a cold, growing ache. Memories of the afternoon blurred his vision. All attempts were made to rid the mind of Catharyna's innocence and vow to give everything. They were forgotten temporarily when the woman joined him on the bed.

The room began to close in around him. It was one of many reenactments, only with a different face and body. Coldness began to consume the rage. His hands reached out to the soft body, only to feel the emptiness spread.

"Leave," he ordered, and blindly reached for the bottle of rum.

"But...we haven't..." she stammered by the coldness that looked back at her, "begun."

"Leave."

Minutes passed like days. He rose to gaze out the window pane to the harbor below and saw a few remnants of his vessels floating. Nostrils breathed deeply the stale air that had lingering traces of the barmaid's heavy perfume. The tavern's raucous shouts were heard. This was the life he knew. As the sun peeked above the horizon to begin a new day; pain pierced his heart, rendering it in two.

The Governor's announcement of the incident stopped the wagging tongues. Fairfax's boots pounded on the cobblestone streets, trying to find a crumb of evidence to appease Hawk. Everyone was talking, but no one was speaking to him. After a week of questioning every ship hand, tavern wench and harlot, he had come up empty. One thing was clear. The Dutch were shutting them out again. Once Hawk walked away from Catharyna, all doors of friendship were shut tight. Not even his title opened any mouths. With nowhere else to turn, Fairfax went to Broeckwyck.

Fairfax found Catharyna inside the wind mill. "Morning."

She nodded with haunted eyes. "What business brings you, Fairfax?"

"Can we speak privately?"

Her body tightened for the expected pain of bad news. "Follow me." She led him outside and stood overlooking Turtle Bay.

"I am here for Hawk."

Her face turned away. "What is it you seek?"

"The truth."

She heard of Fairfax's investigation. "My hand alone torched the ships."

"It's more than that," he confessed, and stopped her from leaving. "Please, Ryna, he needs your help."

She stood frozen.

Fairfax drew closer to plead the case. "I've known Hawk for ten years, yet never this man. He's different..."

"This is his choice. There is nothing more I can give him."

"Yes, there is."

The torment over her actions was written in tortured eyes. "This is not what I wanted, but what *had* to be done!"

Fairfax gathered her against him in comfort. "I understand."

Their eyes locked. "You do?" she whispered.

"Aye, you had the courage to do what I should have done in Port Royale."

Water began to dampen her eyes. Catharyna whispered, "I lost Will."

Fairfax nodded in sadness. "Yes."

Hearing him confirm it made the failure all the more bitter. She broke away from his arms, desperate to be free of all memory of the destruction her hands had done. "What brings you here?"

"He's getting ready to bolt, but this time I won't chase him. Emily is pregnant."

Catharyna's heart froze. "Where?"

Fairfax's eyes said more than his words. "He'll return to the West Indies and never surface here again."

She stood in silence for many minutes until the tide of pride surrendered. "What would keep him here?"

Fairfax was ill prepared to witness the naked emotion on Catharyna's face. It was a side of her unknown; a woman in love. The original purpose in meeting her began to be a painful burden. "He must marry a Dutchwoman."

"He'll not have me."

"No, not you, Ryna." Their eyes clashed. "There are many who will unite him to the Dutch."

Catharyna turned away to hide the pain of his words. The knowledge that her actions had prompted this made it all the more bitter to accept. The dam holding her emotions threatened to erupt, but they were held back, fighting until there was nothing left inside. As the sea breeze renewed her spirit, Maria's face rose above all else. There was no greater gift left to give Hawk, but Maria. It would accomplish all the Duke hoped for the province. There was but the growing ache in her heart that made it seem impossible to endure.

She turned to face Fairfax with none of the thoughts visible that were now racing through her mind. "I will speak with my relatives."

Fairfax hugged her. "Thank you, Ryna."

She watched him leave and could only wonder if Emily would be so generous in giving Fairfax to another. The thought didn't linger long. She went to the manor to write her uncle and relatives, and then went to the stable.

"Timothy, I need you to deliver these messages

immediately."

"Aye, I'll not dally," he replied, trying to meet her gaze.

Catharyna avoided the stable boy's sympathetic face. "Return their responses to the Lord of Onteora at the Governor's mansion." She handed him a coin. "God speed."

"Peace be with you, Ten Broeck," Timothy whispered, and then dashed off.

The core of her being stiffened in readiness to prove she was a fighter. Everyone had been treating her gently, as though she would break because Hawk walked out on her. There was no glory in having a man who had no other choice. All would see Hawk would be given many. If he left, life would not end.

Twenty-seven

Dark clouds began to disperse and sun light flitted through randomly. Hawk sauntered arrogantly into the Red Lion Inn for a meeting with Stephanus van Twiller. It was one of several recently requested. There was now no mystery for the sudden invitations from fifteen of the largest Dutch landowners in the province. They all sought the same thing from him. Each were offering a daughter for a marriage contract. Arrogance assured it was the news of his estrangement from Catharyna that had sparked the private meetings.

Stephanus was standing at the back of the room. Beside him stood a blonde haired woman, no more than eighteen, with crooked teeth, round blue eyes and a wraithlike figure. Introductions were a swift bow and light kiss on the girl's skeleton-like, white hand.

Stephanus beamed. "Lord of Onteora, thank you for joining us. I made arrangements for you and Christina to be taken to Long Island where our stables house my prize stallions. Sir Gallahad has won thirty-six races, you'll find him worth the trip."

Hawk's smile didn't reach the eyes. Ears listened with half interest when van Twiller spoke of his estate, family lineage and daughter's accomplishments. It soon blurred with similar meetings of very accomplished, wealthy and equally dull women. Claudia Van Wyck had poor eye sight, pretty Annetje Loockerman trembled at his glance and wailed in fright when he kissed her hand. Angelica Winkoop's heavy girth split the tavern's chair in two, while Gitty Jansen looked like a boy, and the beautiful Johanna Van Alen had the mind of a babe.

Hawk looked deep into Christina's round eyes for a sign of intelligence. She met the dark stare with no fear; an impish smile appeared. He returned the smile, determined to keep an open mind before passing final judgment. Moments later a feather-like hand ran up his thigh, instincts grabbed it instantly. When Christina's eyes met his, this time they were filled with lust. The fact that she was not a virgin made no difference. It was the lack of interest in the invitation that was disappointing. All hope in a match was doused. A hasty excuse was made after lunch.

It was mid-afternoon at the Governor's mansion when he was advised of another party to prepare for that evening. Hands tightened having to endure polite conversation with men speaking Ten Broeck's name and Lovelace's fuel in it.

The north wing was entered with a frown upon seeing the door to his suite ajar. At its entrance was an envelope. Impatient hands grabbed it at the sight of the van Broeck family crest. His heart began to thump as it was ripped open. Peter van Broeck's bold strokes asked to meet privately at the Governor's ball that evening for a special discussion.

The purpose was intentionally left absent, though it was impossible to prevent speculation. He ordered a bath and began to prepare. A jaunty tune tumbled from happy lips, laughter was occasionally heard. Catharyna was coming to apologize and admit guilt. All such comments of Black Hawk would never again be spoken by her. There would be no quarter given on *that*.

Evening arrived when he entered the ballroom with a confident smile. The guests were mixed as usual. He spoke politely, appeared interested, yet eyes roamed the room seeking one face, waiting for it to appear.

Peter van Broeck entered with his wife and children. Catharyna was not with them. His face tightened as they approached. "Good evening, Peter, Mrs. van Broeck, Mrs. Bleecker, Gerrit and Rolfe."

Anna beamed at him. "Lord of Onteora, my niece speaks very highly of your plans for a grand estate. We are all eager to view its completion."

His heart pounded. "You must visit soon."

Anna's arm wrapped around Maria. "Yes, we would

love to visit, wouldn't we, Maria?"

Maria's eyes looked painfully at Hawk. "Yes, of course."

Hawk finally understood the woman Peter was going to offer tonight. The animal within began to pace, frustration grew to fever pitch, the glass of Madeira in his hand was drained instantly. He bowed, "Excuse me, ladies."

Maria looked torn in being entangled in a situation controlled by her stepfather. Desperate to fix the situation, she followed Hawk outside. They both avoided eye contact and instead, chose to stare at the river.

"This is awkward," Maria whispered.

Hawk kept silent.

"Please listen to me."

His eyes finally surveyed the woman, not Catharyna's cousin. She was pretty, with a kind gaze. Her strength came from a giving heart and it softened his face. "I'm listening."

"My father is determined to make this match between us. There is no reasoning on this with him."

Suddenly, Hawk began to see advantages in it. This woman would never question his actions or seek to right them with her own judgment. "You object?"

Maria snapped, "Of course, you belong with Ryna!"

"She ended us."

Maria huffed softly, knowing it was an impossible subject to discuss. "I married once for an alliance, I'll not do so again."

Hawk's face appeared to be carved in granite. There was no human tenderness in his voice. "What else is there? Dirck won't linger here long, the sea beckons him." He saw water fill her eyes and added, "What of children?"

She whispered, "I want them."

"So do I."

Her eyes roamed over the jagged, rough, cold lines of his face. Ice chilled her blood over its determination.

Hawk ordered, "Think about it."

It was impossible for Maria to focus on one correct

answer. There were so many people to consider. Voices mingled what was once clear and just. It became impossible to do anything but nod and return to the drawing room.

Hawk remained outside and began to roll some tobacco, deep in thought. A light appeared before him. "Need a spark?"

Hawk bent, drew deeply on the tobacco, and exhaled. "Gerrit."

"I understand you are interested in a marriage contract with my sister."

Hawk paused to decide whether to accept the decision to proceed with it. A nod of confirmation then stated it aloud.

Gerrit whispered, "Damnation! That must have been one hell of a journey down in the West Indies to change your mind from Catharyna to Maria."

"That has nothing to do with this."

Gerrit's laugh was sarcastic. "It's got everything to do with it."

A dark scowl hung over Hawk's face, but he remained silent.

"Ryna sent me to Amsterdam when you were abducted. I found this." A blue velvet pouch was handed to Hawk. "Your brother bought it back for you. It's his wedding present and blessing for you. Of course, we both thought it would be on Ryna's hand."

Hawk opened the bag and the sapphire ring fell out, it sparkled under the full moonlight. His original plans returned like a tidal wave, crashing down on his bruised pride. "Gerrit..," was whispered while struggling for the right words. There were none.

Gerrit slapped him on the back. "I swallowed my pride a year ago when my gaming debts got out of control. Ryna straightened me out, never said a word to my father."

Hawk's voice was ice. "She has no remorse for torching my ships."

Their eyes clashed. Gerrit's voice held pride. "She torched Black Hawk's and Golden Eagle's booty."

Hawk's fists tightened, and eyes pierced Gerrit whom

303

remained eye to eye with him, refusing to cower. Instead, he added, "Tonight you stand here seeking my sister's hand in marriage, all because Catharyna took steps to prevent the first manor lord of this province and your Onteora, to be built on piracy."

They stood facing each other with fists clenched, nostrils flaring. Hawk grounded out, "I've never been a pirate."

Gerrit whispered, "There is a thin line between privateer and pirate."

"You go too far!"

Gerrit laughed. "You fault Ryna for taking your ships, yet you took them from the Spaniards." Their eyes met and he added, "Is not that the law on the seas?"

Hawk's eyes narrowed, but he remained silent.

Gerrit's disapproval grazed Hawk's features. "You still don't know Ryna. I fear my cousin chose the wrong brother." With that, he walked away.

Hawk watched the tall Dutchman walk into the midst, intentionally leaving the mansion. The anger passed but Gerrit's word were too deep for him to ignore or explore in a crowded ballroom. They were set aside as he entered the mansion, confident that they would haunt his sleep for nights to come.

The dinner party was an unpalatable experience with Maria stiff beside him. All attempts at conversation were stilted, their lack of attraction to each other was painful to bear. Though it had been the attraction to Catharyna that was his downfall. Determination grew as the choice in Maria began to crystallize.

When Peter tapped his shoulder, he followed to a private room. "I understand you are seeking a Dutch wife."

"Yes."

Excitement became unleashed in Peter's voice. "My daughter brings in a marriage Furwyck, family ties to my estate and support from our extended family in the area. Maria is the wealthiest woman in the province, intelligent, well respected, dutiful and mild. There is wisdom in joining her to the province's first manor lord. Lovelace agrees this is an excellent arrangement."

Hawk's voice sounded strained. "And Maria as well?"

"She follows my wishes."

Hawk's head began to spin. Ryna's harsh judgment, Fairfax's blind loyalty, Gerrit's brutal honesty, Emily's disappointment and Maria's submissive eyes. They all burned deep inside while Peter smiled brightly waiting for an answer. He would be crazy to walk away from this proposal, yet uncertainty remained whether he could live as man and wife with Catharyna's cousin. If he rejected it, there was one course left, one that his feet were positioned and readied for. The West Indies lured him, Fortuna was his original destination if Fairfax hadn't changed that plan.

The air left the room. "You honor me with your proposal, Peter."

Peter beamed and nodded.

"However, there is unfinished business that prevents me from accepting this. Please give me a few days to take care of it."

Peter looked pleased. He knew many of his relatives and friends had made appointments to meet with Hawk and assumed they were the unfinished business. He slapped Hawk impulsively on the back. "Of course, I understand."

Their hands shook on it.

Peter pressed, "When shall we conclude this?"

Hawk mumbled, "Saturday, at the Spring Ball."

"Excellent, all will be present. Yes, I must go tell Anna, she'll be pleased, very pleased." He entered the ballroom and informed his wife, who glowed, whereas Maria looked stricken.

She did not utter a word, but kept a head down and mouth shut. There was no choice. Maria felt the familiar sensation of suffocation.

Twenty-eight

Unfinished remnants of the past stirred, seeking peace. Frolicking and drink did little to avoid the resolution that was near at hand.

Broeckwyck lay in darkness when Dirck entered the manor. His boots pounded loudly on the wooden planks. "Maria!"

Catharyna awakened and raced into the kitchen. Angry eyes met his drunken stare. "Dirck, it's ungodly late, hush up and go to bed."

Dirck stumbled and then approached her awkwardly, grabbing hold of the table for support. Bewilderment and anger filled his voice. "Gerrit told me what you did!"

"Hush, I say! You'll awaken the servants."

His voice grew louder. "First you blew up my ship, and now you give my Maria to Hawk, to the man you wanted! You've no heart, no soul! How can you sleep? How can you do this to your own brother?"

The shell tightened around Catharyna who stared lifelessly at blood shot eyes that peered down in anger at her. "It was my ship that sent you from our shores for *your* own adventure. What happened to the smuggling trade you promised me?"

He blinked, but eyes remained unfocused.

"My needs were abandoned for your own!" Catharyna snapped. "*I* had to deal with DeVries since my own brother deserted me. *I* had to grovel at English merchants' feet and shake hands with the braggarts while you set off for adventure."

Nostrils flared and eyes blazed, except Catharyna wasn't finished. "What did you think I would do when finding my ship gone and a French ship, which you clearly sacked, bearing your *pirate* name in our harbor?"

Dirck's eyes of guilt looked away.

She didn't allow it and met his eyes again. "I'll not permit my blood to have a trace of pirate in him!" Determined hands grabbed his shoulders. "You are my brother, I give all I possess to you Dirck, but I'll not allow anything to tarnish the van Broeck name!"

Their eyes spoke to each other in a storm of emotions, until Dirck nodded ever so slightly.

Catharyna's voice grew soft as did her hold on him. "It was you who left Maria years ago, Dirck, not I. And now that you have finally returned, what have you done to prove yourself to her?"

More guilt met her gaze.

"I know guilt has made you shun her, but if Maria weds Hawk you must accept it will be your fault, not mine."

Dirck stumbled, fighting to explain. "I...didn't...the time...not right."

"Fight for her now, show your love for her."

"Not sure...Maria...*expects much!*"

Catharyna released him in frustration and turned back toward the bed chamber. He followed her inside and whispered, "Maria?"

"She isn't here. Her parents took her this morning to remain at the Governor's mansion."

Dirck's feet gave out, sending him to topple down in a drunken slumber. Catharyna swore softly and pulled him across the floor into the bed. She stared at his face, so similar to her own, for hours praying and cursing, only to pray harder.

Hours later she woke him. "Dirck, it's high morning, time to rise and fight!"

He fumbled awkwardly out of bed, grabbing at the waist for a sword. In bewilderment, he looked down at his sister, and a wave of black curls fell down.

Catharyna groaned. "The fight is for *Maria*, Dirck."

He squinted painfully and croaked, "Aye, Maria." There was no warning when he collapsed back down into the bed.

Catharyna's patience was gone. "Rise, Dirck, or else I get a bucket of water."

A muffled, "I'll gag you for a month if you try that again," was vaguely heard.

"Then rise, brother, *now!*"

He rose, but grumbled angrily. "This is why I stayed away from you. All you do is *nag, nag, nag*." The grumbles continued all through the bath Alice gave him. Food was stuffed down his throat in an ungodly fashion by Catharyna, and he was dressed haphazardly, only to slap Alice's hand of assistance away. "I can handle my britches alone!"

Alice's face turned purple in embarrassment, and ran from the room. Sobs were heard from the kitchen and Catharyna became furious. "*That* is enough, Dirck! None of us will do your fighting. If you don't want Maria, go back to bed, laze about all afternoon, then go drinking in town. Maria is better off without you."

"That's a terrible thing to say to your brother!"

"When you start acting like Dirck, I'll treat you as such."

Cold eyes battled in silence for endless minutes. It was Dirck who relented. "Fine, I'll go speak to Uncle Peter and clear up this mess."

Catharyna warned, "It's not that easy."

"Why the hell not?"

"Don't use that fowl tongue at me!" she warned, while looking over her shoulder.

In the light of day, Dirck found his voice. "Holy thunder, your tongue is worse than any buccaneer I've stood beside!"

Catharyna's face tightened. Ever so softly, she confessed, "Aye, but I'll not have Alice send the minister here again to lecture me on it."

Dirck laughed loudly and stated, "Ha! She best fetch ten to control it."

Catharyna's eyes grew cold with warning. "Do you wish my help or not?"

"This is help?" Dirck asked in amazement.

She ignored the bait. Impatience was found in her voice. "Uncle Peter will view Hawk's offer higher than your own for Maria."

"That's nonsense, Broeckwyck is a splendid match. He'll come round to me."

"You've no manor grant yet. Titles impress Uncle Peter."

A lecherous smile spread across his face. "I've got more titles than Hawk, they just aren't spoken in public."

"Don't you *dare* speak such things to Uncle Peter, you'll ruin everything."

He peered closely at her, finally seeing the desperation in her eyes. "So, you *want* me to win Maria now?"

"Of course."

He scratched his head and laughed. "I'll never understand you, Ryna."

"Let's hope not."

They both laughed.

Minutes ticked by in sluggish agony. Maria began tearing at her cuticles as nerves became stretched and twisted. Dirck had finally come, even now he was speaking to her stepfather. It was an impossible dream, one she believed would never be real. Nothing worked out for her, it all fluttered around for a few precious moments only to blow away for good.

Eyes closed tight in prayer that Dirck would remain this time. The tension was so great, she couldn't bear it any longer. Down the wide corridor she ran in the direction of her father's suite. The frantic pounding of her heart blocked out all sound, everything she sought in life was behind the thick oak door. Even though logic warned it was a foolhardy attempt, she remained at attention and listened.

The surprise was sudden, an explosion couldn't have been more startling. One second her ear was pressed to the door, the next she had landed on the floor at Dirck's feet. Her eyes rose and saw anger that halted any words that would have been spoken.

Dirck's eyes cleared and his hand reached down in assistance, which she accepted. "Maria."

Her palms became sweaty, but she smiled brilliantly. "Good day, Dirck. You've come to visit?"

He turned and looked at Peter. "No, I am *not* welcome here."

Peter drew forward. "That is not true, Dirck. You are my brother's son, you are always welcome."

"Aye? But you'll not grant me Maria's hand."

Horror filled Maria's eyes, who looked at her stepfather. "This cannot be true, father. Please, say you accept Dirck! He is my choice."

Suddenly she was pulled against a wall of stone and kissed passionately. The room and Peter's face faded as Maria clung to Dirck. They were pulled apart seconds later. "Don't touch her again, Dirck! She will be in contract with the Lord of Onteora this Saturday. If you had come sooner, it would be different."

Dirck ignored Peter and smiled at Maria. "Come with me now, Maria. We need only ourselves." He grabbed her hand, but found resistance. The meek and mild woman stood frozen to the floor boards. Tears ran down her cheeks.

"I cannot."

Dirck and Peter exchanged glances, one desperate, the other victorious. Except, Dirck would not back down so easily. He looked at Peter and threatened, "Then I'll speak to Aunt Anna."

"No!"

Dirck didn't wait, but raced down the corridor and the stairs. He found his Aunt in the parlor having afternoon tea, and quickly accepted her extended hands in a warm greeting and sat down. "Aunt Anna, I have been the prodigal son for too long."

Her face beamed at him. "It's your father's adventure that flows strong in your blood, son."

Dirck's eyes narrowed on Peter who was now approaching. "I've come to ask for Maria's hand in marriage. It's what we both desire. As her mother, I plead with you to halt any contract between Hawk and recognize my own that you agreed to with my father."

Anna's eyes narrowed, but emotion was still found in them. She saw her husband's frown and frantic silent signals, which doomed Dirck's request, and faced her nephew with understanding. "You waited a long time to return to my daughter."

"I was wrong."

"Why should we trust you so again?"

"Here is where I shall stay the rest of my days as the Lord of Broeckwyck, building a family with Maria."

She said doubtfully, "Yes, but will you be happy here?"

Anna's eyes pierced his soul, but the answer was spoken honestly. "With Maria, yes."

She nodded and remained silent. Peter sat down at the table and whispered hurriedly into an ear, but she raised a hand in silence. Anna saw Maria approach in silence and stand behind Dirck's chair. Her daughter's wishes were shouting at her.

Anna spoke bluntly. "Dirck, my daughter loves you, but you have brought her great sadness. I know not what to do with you."

Dirck's eyes sparkled and his smile was even more brilliant. "Give me the opportunity to show you, Aunt Anna. That is all I ask."

"And how are you to do that before Saturday evening?"

"I'll do what my father failed to do years ago. I will donate land and resources to build the grandest church in Manhattan." His eyes sparkled when Anna drew forward. Confidence began to pulse inside his veins again, and it reached out to take Maria's hand. "It will also contain an orphanage to care for those that lost parents in the plague."

Anna's voice masked the growing excitement. "You say you wanted to do this before you left us? Why is that, Dirck?"

True anger flashed across his face. "For my mother and

brothers. This I know would please her and honor what she had wanted to contribute to the province, if death had not claimed her so young."

Water dampened Anna's eyes, and a hand rested on Dirck's and Maria's. "This would, Dirck, and it is honorable for you to do such." A tear was wiped away. "Are you prepared to remain and build this fine church and orphanage?"

"Yes, with Maria beside me."

Anna gave Dirck's hand to Maria. "Then we shall not delay."

Dirck bent forward and kissed Anna's cheek. Peter bellowed, "Anna, we must speak in private! Nothing is settled."

Anna rose to face a furious husband. "You are right, there is much we must speak of in private. For one, how much we will contribute for a church in Albany? It's high time we led that effort. We've much work to do, much work indeed. Come, Peter!"

Peter swallowed any further words to keep up with Anna, who dragged him inside the mansion to begin their new project.

Maria gazed up in wonderment at Dirck. "I feared to believe but...."

Dirck crushed her against him and smiled. "But what?"

"Nothing," she replied, and stood on toes to meet his lips.

Eyes of guilt looked down at the love shining up at him. Dirck confessed, "There is much I have done that..."

A finger silenced the words. "We are together at last. That is all the matters to me."

Dirck wouldn't permit it though. "Ryna torched my ship, but that cannot atone for what I owe you." Tears gathered and she turned away to shield them. "I squandered our youth for my adventure, but I swear the rest of my days to you, Maria."

A giggle was heard and Dirck's eyes narrowed at the back of Maria's head, which refused to meet his eyes. A warning rose inside his mind, but it was shook free to rid it of such suspicion. Instead, he captured the face of the woman who had never left his heart, and prayed for the first time in many years for it to take the memory of a dead husband and a baby from her thoughts.

Maria ended the kiss by pulling away to wipe at the tears that rolled down her cheeks. "I fear I cannot keep this from you, Dirck."

He stiffened to bear the news. "Aye."

Her voice wobbled with a mixture of emotions that played havoc in the mind and heart. "It was I who torched your ship."

Dirck stood as a statue, frozen in denial. "Ryna did."

"No, I did," Maria persisted, "and I told her to torch Hawk's."

"You did *what*?"

"Yes, it was all my plan." His look of disbelief made her punch his chest. "You shunned me after years of waiting for you with a ship anchored in our harbor, threatening at any moment to take you away? There was never a doubt I would permit that to happen again!"

Dirck continued to shake his head in denial. "This is my sister's doing for our deeds. It's her judgment."

Maria laughed and drew away from Dirck's arms to stare at him with a boldness that had never existed before. "That was her reason, but not what sparked the idea."

"So, I am to believe you led Ryna to destroy Hawk's property and their relationship?"

Maria's eyes now held guilt. Her voice trembled softly, "I know it was selfish, but when I saw Hawk's devotion to her I knew it could overcome such a deed." She saw the doubt on his face and added, "If he cannot, he isn't the man for Ryna!"

Dirck cursed softly, but gathered her into his arms. "Maria, you've become fearless in my absence."

"I've become fearless due to your absence," she corrected. Their eyes met as equals for the first time and guilt of Dirck's past melted away under the power of Maria's determination for their future.

A lecherous grin spread across his face. "I shall savor your manipulation of Ryna for the rest of my days."

Maria chided, "Don't say such, I love Ryna more than you at times."

He shuddered visibly. "She's worse than any pirate on the seas with her iron fist of judgment."

"You love her completely."

Their eyes smiled at each other with years of childhood memories. "Aye, I love her, but you I shall love completely."

"And you'll be kept landed to prove it."

Dirck's brow rose in warning. "Now you're sounding *too* much like Ryna. Holy thunder, a sister is bad enough, but a wife with a tongue such as that? I swear to separate you from her if such continues."

She looked doubtful and kissed him, ending the discussion.

Twenty-nine

Spring ushered in at the Governor's mansion with the grandest ball of the year. Every prominent land baron, merchant, trader, sea captain and government official was there. It was the event in which to be seen and to make a name. Though there were two people who did not require either.

Catharyna entered the ballroom with Dirck and Maria. There was no plan or purpose in her presence. It was required, so she had come. The fact that she wore the blue silk dress that Hawk had given her had been Dirck's doing.

"That bastard tried to take my Maria," he swore.

"That bastard awoke you to Maria," Catharyna countered. "Now return my gowns."

"This gown is more than suitable." And then he slammed the door and the discussion.

As she stood in the ballroom seeing all eyes on her, Catharyna felt eerily exposed. It did not sit well to be wearing the gown Hawk had given when the feelings that had prompted it were gone. However, the trader, Ten Broeck, soon found that worry a luxury. A crowd of men descended and left no other thought in her mind on it.

Music began and dance after dance she was seen with a different man on the dance floor. It was the distraction of Hawk that tested her sanity. All attempts were made to avoid eye or body contact.

Several of her cousins surrounded him, and many other women who had traveled a great distance to attend the ball. Few were unpleasant to look upon, and one was strikingly beautiful. Their names were unknown to Catharyna, but the look in their eyes and sway of their bodies said all one needed to know.

David DeVries interrupted her internal musings. "You are beautiful this evening, Ryna."

"Hello, David."

He smiled at hearing his name. A new approachable gaze met his, no longer were barriers blocking him out. "Would you care to dance?"

She couldn't bear another circle around the floor. "I'd rather not."

His arm was offered. "Come, let's get some fresh air."

The offer was accepted and they left the ballroom for the balcony. A deep breath of the sweet spring air greeted them, until a bruise on his face caught her interest. Her hand reached out to examine it and his face turned to kiss her fingers instead.

DeVries whispered, "It's nothing."

"It's a fine bruise." A brow rose. "A quarrel at the Blue Dove?"

"Aye," he whispered, not wanting to discuss the beating Hawk had given him.

They leaned against the balcony railing and stared up at the stars. DeVries asked, "Remember the day we met?" They both chuckled. "I felt a fool when you rescued me. I, a world traveler seeing Hong Kong, maroon my ship in the East River to be pulled out by a mere girl. It was brutal to live that down."

"It was a fine ship."

"Aye." A hand reached out to draw her closer to his side.

Catharyna's voice was full of reflection. "I stood in awe watching her glide by with sails billowing against the breeze..."

David finished, "And then I hit the sand bar and crashed." The sound of her laughter made his heart soar. The change in Catharyna was drastic. There was no pushing away or avoidance of his touch. It was how they dealt in business and now it finally was transferring over to personal.

The success made him continue. "It was an honest mistake, being new to the area." Their eyes met for the first time. "Now we are old friends."

"Yes," she smiled.

"Yes," he repeated and drew her closer, "Dirck is here, Broeckwyck no longer needs you, there's nothing standing between us now."

Catharyna turned to stare at the river as the words made no impression in the coldness that surrounded her heart. The pain of losing Hawk had scarred her into a cynical woman. Frivolity and romance had been sacrificed to reach the destination.

"I am not the woman you knew."

"I see that," he said, with hope in his eyes. "Perhaps now you will let me win your heart?"

Her eyes met his confidence. "It's foolishness to try, for it is too treacherous to know."

DeVries gathered her against him. "Let me try." And then he kissed her with a passion that reached down to the roots of the trees and made them sway in the breeze. "I'll not let go of you again, Ryna."

She broke away with hands that trembled at her side. Thoughts of Hawk consumed everything. It felt impossible to allow another man the intimacy they shared.

"I must return."

DeVries grabbed hold of her. "Not this time, Ryna. We settle this now."

Their eyes clashed, yet she remained. "I'll not be coerced into marriage."

DeVries looked insulted. "That wasn't my intention."

A cold laugh erupted from her. "Your handsome face takes you far with the ladies, but not with me."

Now he was confused. "I am your friend, Ryna, how do you speak so to me?"

The pain of Hawk's desertion was released on DeVries. "Marriage is a covenant I'll not enter into lightly. I trust your friendship, not your fidelity."

Pain filled DeVries' eyes over the harsh words. He didn't disguise it from her. "It was I who brought all the traders that made you the greatest in this port. And, I stopped the smuggling, at great derision from my men! Don't judge me for dallying with wenches when all know I wait for you these years."

Her eyes pierced him. "Ending the smuggling saved your neck by a rope. What was your purpose in sending the traders to me?"

His face looked thunderous. "I care not if I swing by a rope! Nothing would have stopped me from taunting the English, yet it was what you wanted, so I gave it to you. Both the smuggling *and* the traders."

His anger made no impact to Catharyna, whose eyes narrowed, envisioning their future together. He would step back and give all she desired the rest of their days. She would enjoy his handsomeness and charm, but there would be no visions or inspiration that would create excitement in building a life together. And she knew that wasn't his fault.

"Please forgive me, David. You have been and remain a true friend to me."

He relaxed and a smile spread. "I treasure our friendship."

Catharyna held his hands tightly. "Then I ask you to leave it as such for now."

He remained silent until a loud breath of air was released. "Hawk will wed another in that ballroom tonight and still never leave your heart! It's English greed that takes all in his reach, and my heart that suffers under it."

Catharyna looked helplessly at him, there were no words of denial. "Give me time to let him go."

DeVries looked torn. "I can, but I don't think he will."

"He left me."

"I'm not so certain," he whispered, while rubbing the brow that held a large lump.

Catharyna did not hear the words in her excitement of seeing Gerrit arrive with his fiancé Christina. "Come, we must welcome my cousin."

Hawk watched from afar when Catharyna reentered the ballroom with DeVries on her arm. The sound of her laughter rose above all others. One after one, men approached her and a crowd soon gathered, blocking his view.

Peace had never been farther from Hawk. Stubbornness shrugged the feeling off. He shared words with the Governor and several Dutch landowners who now smiled openly at him. There had been no whisper of Catharyna's involvement in the torching of his ships. That his pride had survived it went unnoticed under the fierce scowl on Hawk's face and eyes, which remained on his prey.

A tug on his coat sleeve brought his attention to Jane Van Kyrt. There had been nothing found wanting in the beauty from Albany who had traveled to the ball just to make his acquaintance.

"Tell me about Onteora," Jane said, and placed her hand on his arm.

He looked down into the pretty face that had tempted him two winters ago. Tonight he saw only the softness of her beauty instead of the strength in Catharyna's. "It is just being built. Ryn...," he said, and stopped with the realization of the words almost spoken aloud. "Excuse me a moment," he mumbled, and bowed but his eyes remained fixed on Catharyna, noting the exact moment DeVries left the ballroom.

Neither had yet acknowledged the other's presence at the ball. Hawk could take no more of the game and approached while she was speaking to Gerrit. When he joined the intimate group, the Governor approached Catharyna for a dance and she quickly accepted. Hawk's eyes blazed but she continued to ignore him, and walked by.

Gerrit smiled. "Hawk, this is my fiancé, Christina van Cortlandt."

Hawk viewed the pretty brunette with a brief glance. The necessity of being polite was wearing thin on an already impatient personality. "My pleasure, Miss van Cortlandt."

"Thank you for bringing Dirck home to us," Christina said.

Hawk bowed.

"And for helping Ryna settle our claim with Minichque." Hawk looked momentarily confused. "That was never in question."

Christina looked at Gerrit and smiled, even though Hawk had no knowledge of what warranted it.

Gerrit changed the subject. "I apologize for the other night. I am glad I was wrong."

A brow rose on Hawk's face, now thoroughly confused by the couple.

Gerrit added, "About Maria."

Hawk grinned. "Yes, I chose not to proceed with the marriage."

Gerrit and Christina laughed, but something made Hawk suspect it was directed at him, instead of with him. "You mock me, Gerrit?" he growled.

Gerrit wiped the dampness of laughter away. "No, you are naive." Christina jabbed him in the ribs only to hear him add, "No one can compete."

Hawk drew closer and whispered, "Compete?"

"Ryna was trained by the best."

Christina now frowned darkly at Gerrit and pulled on his arm. "We must speak with my mother, *Gerrit.*"

"*Gerrit* will join you shortly," Hawk ordered, and left Christina in fear when he pulled Gerrit into a corner. "Continue."

There was no hesitation. "Dirck needed to be jolted and Ryna used you to do it."

Hawk's scowl grew dark.

"I didn't see it either until it was all tied up. Nicely, too." Gerrit grew serious. "Uncle Cornelius played everyone, there was no one like him until Ryna." His eyes then locked on Hawk. "It was my uncle who led you to Ryna, was it not?"

Hawk recalled Cornelius' instructions to visit Catharyna at his death and give her the locket. He mumbled, "Yes."

Gerrit nodded with a grin. "Forgive her and find peace."

"I cannot."

Gerrit sighed, "I'd hoped...oh, well." He looked into the crowded ballroom and watched Catharyna dance with the Governor. "You should know, Christina and I gave Ryna the

10,000 acre parcel that brought you together. It is our thanks for saving me from debtor's prison in London."

"Why so generous a parcel?"

Gerrit looked appalled. "She bartered with the Duke on my behalf and saved my betrothal with Christina due to it."

"Is that why the men are sniffing after her all evening?" Hawk snapped, only seeing the value of the land and Ten Broeck's trading business had once again made Catharyna a wealthy woman. Now he understood why she gave her brother sole ownership of Broeckwyck. She was building her own fortune. And yet, no matter how hard he tried, no anger could diminish the pride he felt for her in such an achievement. He had told her man's laws could be navigated to suit one's purposes, and she had found a crack in the English law that just granted her 10,000 acres. A woman could not buy real estate, but she could receive it as an inheritance or gift.

His possessive eyes followed her every turn on the dance floor in another man's arms. Each second that passed brought with it the memory of their afternoon, her vow to him and his peace. Madness was slowly consuming his mind.

Gerrit saw the haunted face of Hawk and patted his shoulder. "Forgive her, Hawk," he whispered one last time before walking away to retrieve Christina.

Except Hawk couldn't. He also refused to be held in a province by Catharyna's dead father and be put off by her any longer. He found her surrounded, and strongly suspected at this point, guarded, by Dirck and Fairfax. Their visible support made his hands tighten. Everyone had taken her side. It now became a quest.

"Good evening," Hawk said and bowed.

Fairfax nodded and Emily said, "It's a grand ball, is it not, Hawk?"

"Yes," but his eyes were on Catharyna's, who refused to meet them.

Maria pointed to the group of women waiting for Hawk. "I see you've met the rest of our family."

The smile didn't reach his eyes at her taunt. "Yes, your

cousin sent me the wealth of your family lineage to select as wife." And then he bowed directly at Catharyna.

"I did no such thing," Catharyna whispered.

"Their names and attributes are brutally clear," Hawk added.

A blush rose and she warned, "You need not elaborate."

"But I insist," he said with a brilliant smile, and their eyes clashed. "There's four eyes Claudia, sharp tooth Annetje, portly Angelica, manly Gitty, and the beautiful, but oblivious, Johanna."

Emily stifled her laughter under Fairfax's frown, whereas Maria smothered giggles against Dirck's chest, who held her protectively away from Hawk.

Catharyna whispered, "You're impossible," and turned to leave, but Hawk prevented it.

Fairfax instantly appeared beside her and changed the heated subject. "Jacob's been looking for you. There's a problem with the drainage at Onteora's south field."

Hawk snapped, "Another problem?"

"Ha, you heard about the broken axle on the plow?"

"No."

"There's also been a fire in the smokehouse."

"Of course."

"One of the plow horses is lame."

"I knew about that."

"They found a ledge while digging the foundation for Onteora. I told them to move the location fifty feet northwest."

Hawk's fist pounded in the air. "Blast it out! I want the manor on that spot."

"It will take longer."

Hawk look pointedly at Catharyna and said, "Everything takes longer here."

Fairfax grew concerned at the sound of his friend's voice, and left the group to speak privately with him. "What's up?"

Hawk was ready to bolt. "We need to go to Fortuna." Fairfax remained unmoved, so he added, "With no ships, I need to meet Morgan to assure him all is well. Besides, Emily will be happy there."

"She loves it here."

Hawk's face grew dark.

"And so do I." Fairfax's voice was cold.

Hawk became blunt. "Things aren't working out as expected." The knowledge Catharyna's dead father was holding him in a province to wed his daughter, and that he almost succumbed to it, fueled his anger.

Fairfax's face began to grow red in anger. "Everything and more has fallen into your lap. You somehow gained Ryna's trust and rejected it. Then, you bounce back to be offered the most beautiful women in the province. And now, you insult each of them because your damn pride won't forgive Ryna."

"I told you not to speak her name!"

Fairfax scowled, "Ryna no longer concerns you," their eyes clashed, "and I will not follow you this time," Fairfax swore and stormed off to return to Emily, without looking back.

Amazement filled Hawk's face. Never had Fairfax walked out on him. In life threatening situations his friend had always followed loyally. The gravity of falling from Fairfax's grace doused him like a bucket of cold water. He grumbled to himself, "It's the bloody title that strangles me here."

And then his eyes pinned Catharyna, who was dancing with Gerrit. Fists tightened and he stormed onto the dance floor, though none of the anger was shown. His finger tapped Gerrit's shoulder to interrupt. "May I?"

Gerrit beamed. "Of course, Hawk." And quickly handed Catharyna to him.

She avoided eye contact until Hawk whispered, "We need to talk."

For the first time in a month, their eyes met. This time Catharyna's held hope, not judgment. "Let's," she whispered and could not control the smile that spread.

Blindly, she followed him, passing family and friends who beamed at them, only to whisper hurriedly into someone's ear at the reconciliation they believed they had just witnessed.

They entered a dark corridor, and he led her up a flight of stairs. When a door opened to a bedchamber, that too was entered in blind trust. The flickering light from the fireplace lit their surroundings, but the sound of a lock being pulled into position on the door aroused her suspicions.

"Why are we here?"

Hawk turned away from the door and the look in his eyes made her take a step back. Never had she feared him, but now it filled her being. Wary eyes watched him approach and a hand went to grab her knife. "Don't," she warned, but Hawk was already on her and the knife was flung across the room.

"You swore everything to me," he reminded her with dead eyes.

"You ended us."

His hands began undressing her. "Vows last forever."

Catharyna was crushed against him and asked in confusion, "You forgive me?"

He laughed.

Memories of a similar situation made her remain limp. "Release me."

"Are you a liar as well as a thief?"

"I'm neither!"

The gown swished to the floor and she was tossed on the bed only in undergarments,. "You shall give me what you promised," he swore and cornered her on the bed. "This is your game, not mine."

She fought him off with finger nails that dug into his back and face. Her hands were quickly taken by him. "Forcing is no game, Will," she whispered in a voice naked with pain.

Hawk looked down at her finally and saw where his anger had led him. A voice softer than his own repeated, "You swore this to me."

Tears gathered in her eyes. "You will wed another and still take me this way?"

Hawk only saw what he wanted. "You swore it!"

Catharyna lay limp beneath him. "I can't..."

A pounding on the door halted her words when it

crashed to the floor. Dirck entered with two pistols aimed, and Fairfax beside him. "Leave her be!"

Hawk rose and refused to look at his friend, who had now sided with Catharyna. "I take only what she swore to give."

Fairfax stepped forward to block Catharyna from Hawk and said, "You took enough."

The men's eyes clashed but neither budged. Catharyna dressed quickly, and soon stood between Fairfax and Dirck.

Dirck warned, "If you seek my sister, it will be with the honor she deserves."

Hawk looked at Catharyna with regret. "I tried, but it wasn't enough." And then he walked out of the room and the mansion.

Thirty

Time was moving in the wrong direction. Fingers drummed repeatedly on a wooden table. Hawk's eyes were mere slits in a face now taunt with frustration.

Nothing had gone as he had wanted at the Spring Ball. Gerrit's words had fed his frustration, which led to the unexpected. The look in Catharyna's eyes at his actions could not be erased, nor Fairfax's desertion of him. Walking away from her had also taken his best friend.

The irony of the situation didn't improve his mood. The manor grant he had worked the past seven years for was a hollow victory without either of them at his side. Everyone smiled, bowed and curtsied respectfully to him. The Dutch opened their doors of business now with a warm smile.

How it had gone astray was brutally clear. The two people closest to him had done this. And both refused to give. For two weeks he had waited, and neither came forward. That Fairfax had taken Catharyna's side after torching his ships was incomprehensible to Hawk.

Now there was no other choice. Patience was spent. The reasons not to speak to Catharyna were gone. An urgency began to grip him and build. As the sun began to rescind into the horizon, he was aboard a sloop in the direction of Broeckwyck. It had been over a month since making the journey, and each step brought things back into focus.

Gerrit's words played over and over in his mind. In them he tried to find a measure of understanding for what Catharyna had done, but still could not forgive it. Desperation to be rid of the darkness that consumed him was the one thing that led him to Broeckwyck.

The journey was made under the dimming light of a slice of moon. Three strong knocks on the manor door brought Alice to answer it. She pointed wordlessly in the direction of the stable, not uttering a greeting. Hawk anticipated the cold reception, and tossed it aside on the way toward the stable. His steps were hurried, but they couldn't keep pace with the pounding of his heart which continued to grow.

Catharyna's words were muffled until he drew closer. "Are you certain?...careful, David!...will it hurt?" Hawk's fists clenched, approaching the far end of the stable. The door was shut, but Catharyna's words rang clear. "That's right, just like that. Don't stop."

Instincts overruled logic. Hawk kicked open the door, startling all its inhabitants. He blinked several times at the scene he intruded upon. Dr. Simon Harrison was beside Catharyna and both were kneeling over a mare in full labor. DeVries was on the other side massaging the round belly of the horse with the stable boy at his side. All four of them gazed at Hawk expectantly while he looked at them stupidly.

It was Simon who settled the dilemma. "Hawk, would you ask Alice for more hot water and blankets. It will be another long night I'm afraid."

Hawk nodded and left. DeVries' face darkened and he grumbled, "What the devil is he doing here?"

Catharyna yawned and remained silent. Simon looked relieved and said, "Ryna, whatever brings him here is goodness. I must be off, two days of waiting for this foal has left my other patients in dire need of me."

Catharyna's eyes turned fearful. "But you mustn't leave, I can't do this without you."

DeVries pleaded, "Ryna, it's gone too long, we've done everything."

Simon nodded, tears filled his eyes. "I fear it's time we give her peace."

Hawk reentered the stall and remained silent now, understanding the situation.

Catharyna wrestled out of DeVries' arms and rose. "There's no question here, Simon. You must remain however long it takes. We can't let her die! This is the Duke's gift to this province, the foal *must* be delivered."

Simon turned to Hawk and silently pleaded with him. Hawk bent to view the mare, her breathing was labored, but weak. He rose and studied Simon's hands, the stable boy's and then Ryna's, even though DeVries blocked him from doing so, he was nudged aside. He compared her hands to the stable boy and then went to Simon. He said matter-of-fact, "We'll save the foal."

DeVries asked sarcastically, "How do you propose we take over where nature fails?"

Hawk replied, "We'll pull it out."

Simon's eyes widened and nodded at Catharyna, who did likewise. DeVries noticed the group's quick agreement and silenced any more protests.

Hawk ordered, "Simon, you and DeVries massage her belly, I'll assist Ryna."

DeVries argued, "No, I'll assist Ryna."

Hawk nodded and stepped aside. "As you will."

DeVries walked over to Ryna and pulled her beside him. He hadn't a clue what Hawk meant by assisting, but remained confident while searching for answers in Simon's blank gaze. Catharyna looked at both men and waited for instructions. Hawk raised a brow at DeVries who suddenly decided to step aside.

They switched places and Hawk instructed Catharyna to sit down and he sat directly behind her. He explained, "We must work as one. Your hands are small enough to reach inside. My strength will pull the foal out."

Catharyna nodded and immediately plunged her hands inside the mare. She reached deeper until she felt the sack. "I feel it."

Simon whispered, "Gentle now, Ryna. You don't want to tear it. Get a good grip on the foal's neck and hold steady for Hawk. Aye?"

"Aye." She reached deeper until her elbows were inside. She whispered brokenly, "I can't do it, I'm not long enough."

Hawk leaned on top of her, his arms held hers tightly, to guide and support. "Relax, use my strength."

She closed her eyes to the angry face of DeVries and focused on the foal's position. She was braced against Hawk, whose strength seemed to flow into her. Simon's words of instruction guided her onward, placing her hands confidently on the foal. She said excitedly, "Okay, I'm ready."

Hawk's boots were dug into the straw and dirt, and then he began to pull. Simon shouted, "Push her belly, DeVries." As a team they worked. When the mare's breathing grew to a whimper, Simon shouted, "Hurry, we're losing her."

Hawk gritted and grunted as muscular arms bulged under the task that demanded all their strength. Catharyna cried, "I can't..."

Hawk barked back, "Do it!"

Her eyes closed under the pain of the foal pulling inward and Hawk pulling them outward. It felt as though she were ripping in half. "Will, help...," she whispered.

Hawk obeyed and slowly Catharyna's elbow came out. The stable boy began to jump in excitement. Simon coached, "Easy now, Ryna."

Hawk was wrapped around Catharyna's body as his arms became her muscles. The foal's hooves soon sprouted out, and then the muzzle and legs appeared. Simon cleared the membranes from the foal's nose and then Hawk pulled the foal out little by little. One final pull brought the foal completely into the world.

They collapsed against the stall wall and gazed in wonder at their accomplishment.

Simon laughed joyously. "Ryna, the mare, look! She fights to live! We saved them both!" All eyes turned to see the mare's head rising to view her newborn son. Seconds later, she broke open the protective sac and began licking him clean.

The stable boy began to dance the Irish jig around the stall and DeVries' temper snapped. "Boy, get Ryna some hot water to clean herself with!"

Timothy sang an Irish ditty and laughed, oblivious to the order. Impatiently, DeVries left the stall to fetch the water himself, missing the bucket behind his back. In a daze, Timothy handed the bucket to the stunned couple who lay crumpled in each other's arms gazing stupidly at the foal and mare. Hawk cleaned Catharyna's and his hands, while watching the first movements of the foal. Catharyna leaned against his chest, her head held snugly beneath his chin.

Simon rose and stated sleepily, "I must be off, Ryna. Bella looks fine, as does the foal. I'll visit on Sunday at Gerrit's wedding."

She yawned unladylike. "Thank you, Simon."

Simon bumped into DeVries on his way out of the stall. "Time to go, Captain."

DeVries' eyes latched on Hawk's arms that were still wrapped around Catharyna. "I'm not leaving."

Hawk disentangled himself and rose. "I'll take you back, Simon."

DeVries began to stammer. He was exhausted and had no strength to keep up with the energetic Ryna. It had been two days since he slept. "Well...no, I'll take him back. Come, we'll leave together."

A smile spread across Hawk's face. "I've business to conclude with Catharyna first."

DeVries' tone was suspicious. "Details to finalize before announcing your betrothment?"

"Yes."

His eyes narrowed on Hawk in distrust. DeVries wasn't fooled by the cool face of disinterest, it was a countenance he had lost many coins to at cards. He decided to be direct. "There is no more Ryna can give you. Leave her be."

Hawk replied, "That is her choice to make."

The two men stared at each other until DeVries bent a

head and whispered, "It is, so I must accept what she chooses." And then he walked toward the East River to board his sloop.

Hawk stood in confusion watching the Dutchman depart Broeckwyck. Such broadmindedness with women baffled Hawk. DeVries' gallant move to step aside for Catharyna's choice never entered his mind. Her choice had always been irrelevant to his desires.

It made him pause to consider the original purpose that brought him to Broeckwyck.

Thirty-one

The air was still, the earth silent. Hawk entered the stable with purposeful strides and found Catharyna on the floor, waiting for the foal to take its first steps. Images of the beauties that passed through his life were recalled quickly in Hawk's mind, and faded at the sight of Catharyna in disarray. Hair was tousled with straw and knots, dress torn and littered with mud, and other undesirable things clung to it. A woman had never been more desirable to him.

Her face rose and their eyes locked. "I thought you left."

It was a moment like Portobelo, one that would change his life. Hawk fought to control the unknown emotions that tried to storm his ridged defenses. Weeks of separation from her made him reply, "It isn't easy to walk away from you."

She approached him with eyes and words that dared, "Then don't."

The pain of her betrayal returned in a wave of anger. "You bloody well made it impossible not to!" Disbelief consumed his question, "Why did you torch my ships? To chastise me in front of the province, or was it to *control* me?"

Catharyna did not cower. "I torched Black Hawk's ships not yours."

His jaw clenched tightly. "I *am* Black Hawk."

Catharyna persisted, "You are Sir William Hawkins, Lord of Onteora in the province of New York. You are the man who used my friendship with Minichque to bring peace to the Iroquois League and this province, and who just gave life to my mare and foal. Black Hawk plunders and you build. I beg you, let's be rid of him."

Confusion filled Hawk's face at the turn of the conversation. It was a clever response, one not anticipated. He felt naked under her all-knowing gaze and searched for words, only none rose to the surface. He grasped vainly for the anger that had once filled him. In desperation, he countered, "You cannot change me, Ryna."

"There is no need to, Will."

He stood mesmerized when her eyes rose and shared every thought, desire and dream for him to see. They all revolved around him into areas never imagined.

"What do you want, Ryna?"

"You."

Frustration, desire, and a dark faceless ache all merged into a growing pain in his chest. The room grew airless and his patience exploded. "How can I accept that when you dangle *Maria* for me to wed and torched my ships ..." his trembling hand then pointed at her, "without first discussing your thoughts to me before taking such action?"

Fatigue marked Catharyna's face. There had been no rest the past two days her mare went into labor. Her eyes closed, in an effort to find the energy required to answer the questions Hawk had finally managed to ask. In a silent plea for strength, she straightened to face him, knowing their future depended on it.

"I was wrong not to discuss it first with you. I'm sorry for that."

"Ha, you're sorry for that but *not* torching them!"

She didn't relent. "You would never have given them up."

"Everything I did was under the authority of the crown!"

Their eyes clashed when she swore, "Damn the crown's authority, you *stole* those ships. They were no threat to *any*

British holding. You reached out and took what you wanted under a privateer's commission. And I did what I did because I was raised to right the wrongs for people I love."

They stared at each other with nostrils flaring. Catharyna watched his jaw clench but no words came forth. Emotions surged, she no longer could stop the words from being spoken. "And *don't* taunt me about Maria. It's exactly how you wished it to be. She's the richest woman in the province and the woman Black Hawk would choose to wed."

Hawk's voice was thunderous when his true thoughts were finally released. "Then don't taunt me with riddles in being Will, Sir Hawkins, Lord of Onteora but *never* Black Hawk!" He leered down and blasted, "I don't bloody care what people call me! The only way I live my life is by grabbing it by the throat and squeezing every drop out of it. Put any name to that and I'll answer by it."

He stood ridged for several seconds until he confessed, "Aye, it's true, everything is another sack to me. No boundaries, no guilt. Easy makes me anxious to take all I want!" His hand trembled as it raked through his hair. "And you did just that, you opened this province for me to reach out and take *very* easy." The brutal assault did not end even when her eyes grew damp. "But...then..." his hands were thrown in the air, "you torched my ships!"

Silence entered the stall momentarily until his boot kicked the wall in frustration. "And I *don't* want to forgive you for taking them from me."

Catharyna's face was red with rage. "Then don't!"

He growled, *"It's not that simple!"*

He began pacing the small confines of the stall, no closer to finding an answer. His frustration faced her when they stared at each other for an ageless moment. It was then the truth he had been searching for finally rose to the surface. He looked at the bedraggled woman and found nothing remarkable in her appearance, yet his soul demanded her unlike anything he'd coveted before. Onteora was nothing without her. He drew forward with a face black with emotion.

Catharyna took several steps back until coming against the wood plank wall of the stall.

He whispered, "I cannot fight this any longer." And then a voice deep with longing, pierced her soul. "I must forgive you."

They stared at each other in amazement. Catharyna whispered, "You forgive me?"

"I must," he paused trying to absorb what he was about to confess, "because...this land...doesn't tremble beneath my feet unless you're beside me," acceptance now filled his tone, "only then does it become the home for my restless spirit."

Catharyna stood speechless at the powerful confession, and then captive when she was gathered against him for a kiss that was just as unique as the words. She felt him draw out her soul and entwine it tightly within his own.

She gazed up at him and swore, "You asked for my trust when we first met, and now I ask for yours."

His face tightened, but he nodded slowly.

Water dampened Catharyna's eyes, witnessing the struggle inside him to trust her. "There is nothing I would take from you if I didn't have the ability to give it back."

He warned, "Never discuss the ships again."

She ignored it. "I made a trade with Dirck for my portion in Broeckwyck land. Four ships are being built for us in time for this year's harvest, to take to the West Indies for trade."

"Ships?" he whispered in confusion.

Her arms tightened around him and she laughed. "Yes, merchant ships built for the man who wants to leave his *own* mark on this province."

His face softened, realizing she had listened to him so long ago in London when sharing his visions and dreams. A grin spread. "That is all you received from Dirck? Four ships and the harvest?"

The pride in his eyes belied the words and fed Catharyna's spirit. "I was a *bit* greedy, but I am my father's daughter. I kept some of the Manhattan coastline property for us, investments in Amsterdam, the West Indies, a partnership in..."

Hawk was no longer amazed by her. His lips silenced her. "I'll not doubt you again," he swore.

Catharyna's eyes and voice held faith when she swore, "I give my life to make your dreams live, Will."

"I know that, Ryna," he whispered, and added in awe, "I *am* lucky."

The relief in the sudden change of emotion in the stall made her laugh. "And why is that?"

"Why need I sail the world when God has given it to me every time I gaze into your eyes?" Their eyes smiled and Hawk's arms tightened on her. "I'm sorry for leaving you."

Catharyna whispered, "You never left me."

"We wed at dawn."

"Yes."

A brow rose and he warned, "No games!"

"I like games," she laughed.

Hawk's eyes narrowed and a grin spread. "Very well, we can right each other when wrong, but let's agree to discuss *first* any that involves destruction of property."

"Always."

"You're being far too agreeable. What do you want?"

She swore, "Not another thing."

"I don't believe..."

Hawk was silenced by Catharyna's kiss. His hands reached into her hair and clutched straw instead, so he began to shake the long tresses vigorously to be rid of it.

"It's hopeless, I'm a mess," Catharyna said, laughing against his chest. And then, she whispered bravely, "There is something I *wish*."

"Wish?"

"Take me to Fortuna!"

He laughed, "Oh, no! You think me mad to allow you within 100 miles of Fortuna, located on the pirate infested island of Jamaica?"

Her hand waved in the air, erasing his fears away.

Excitement vibrated in Catharyna's voice, eyes and body. "Yes! We shall travel the triangle trade together." She began to sway back and forth in his arms as energy and ideas rolled through her. "Just think of the goods we can trade in the West Indies if I am on the ship! From there, we go to London..."

Hawk silenced her words with another kiss, but Gerrit's words were in his ears, and Fairfax in his mind. All had sided with Catharyna over the destruction of his ships due to this. Everyone had seen what his battered pride had clouded out. He ended the kiss as abruptly as it had begun to inspect her face, seeing only strength and the independence which somehow captured his own restlessness.

He said in an ominous voice, "I want you to trade as a *feme sole* under your Ten Broeck trader name, but in all else, you shall bear my name in our marriage."

She swallowed loudly.

"I'll not have my name cloud out your achievements as Ten Broeck, or English law shadow your legacy for our daughters to remember. But, you shall be known as Lady of Onteora and bear my name Hawkins, as will our children. We shall be one in our marriage, Ryna."

Catharyna knew he was asking her to choose him over man's law, to decline the protection of the grandfather clause, and trust him. She took a cleansing breath to release the solitary loneliness of trying to control her life, and became filled with certainty and trust in the character of William Hawkins.

And there was no greater way to demonstrate the unity of their marriage than by standing tall before Dutch society and swearing all to him before God.

She met his gaze and said firmly, "Yes, I wish it too." And then an exhausted laugh was heard against Hawk's chest when Catharyna collapsed against it. "This is why my father sent you to me."

Hawk cradled her tightly against him. "Perhaps."

"It is, for he knew your privateer heart," a yawn escaped Catharyna before adding, "breaks open coconuts."

"Ha, so *now* my privateering has become useful."

"Perhaps," she mimicked, as her head snuggled deeper against him.

Hawk scooped her up, allowing her long legs to dangle in the air. "What happened to never and always?"

Her head snuggled against his neck. "Perhaps is more fun."

He chuckled and lead them out of the stable to the point overlooking Turtle Bay. Hawk's knees buckled to lower them to the ground at a small perch that overlooked New York harbor. Catharyna snuggled closer against his chest and was soon asleep. The sea breeze whisked long strands of hair away from her face, which was trusting and defenseless in his arms. Peace descended over Hawk, who never felt more powerful.

In that moment, he felt the earth wrap silken roots about his soul and pull it forever into its core. Arrogance faded away, replaced by the wisdom that no man's mark could ever compete against the spirit of the land that tamed him, and Catharyna. The future unfolded, clear and bright before Hawk, who watched the sky turn purple, and then pink, as dawn broke across the horizon. Nothing was missed about the moment yesterday turned into tomorrow, the day that would finally grant him what he had been searching for his entire life.